Benet Brandreth is a highly-regarded Intellectual Property barrister, rhetoric coach and authority on Shakespeare, working regularly with the Royal Shakespeare Company, the Donmar and others on Shakespeare's use of language. He has also written and performed for radio and the stage – his one-man show, 'The Brandreth Papers', was a five-star reviewed sell-out at the Edinburgh Festival and on its London transfer. He is qualified as an instructor in the Filipino Martial Arts and as a stage combat choreographer. He lives in London with his wife and two sons and is exhausted from all his efforts at becoming a Renaissance Man.

The Spy of Venice

Benet Brandreth

twenty7

First published in the UK in 2016 by Twenty7 Books

This paperback edition published in 2017 by

Twenty7 Books
4th Floor, Victoria House, Bloomsbury Square, London, WC1B 4DA
Owned by Bonnier Books
Sveavägen 56, Stockholm, Sweden

A CIP catalogue record for this book is available from
the British Library.

Hardback ISBN: 978-1-78577-037-1
Ebook ISBN: 978-1-78577-035-7
Paperback ISBN: 978-1-78577-036-4

1 3 5 7 9 10 8 6 4 2

Typeset by IDSUK (Data Connection) Ltd
Printed and bound in Great Britain by Clays Ltd, Elcograf S.p.A.

Twenty7 Books is an imprint of Bonnier Books UK
www.bonnierbooks.co.uk

For Kosha

Those lines that I before have writ do lie,
Even those that said I could not love you dearer

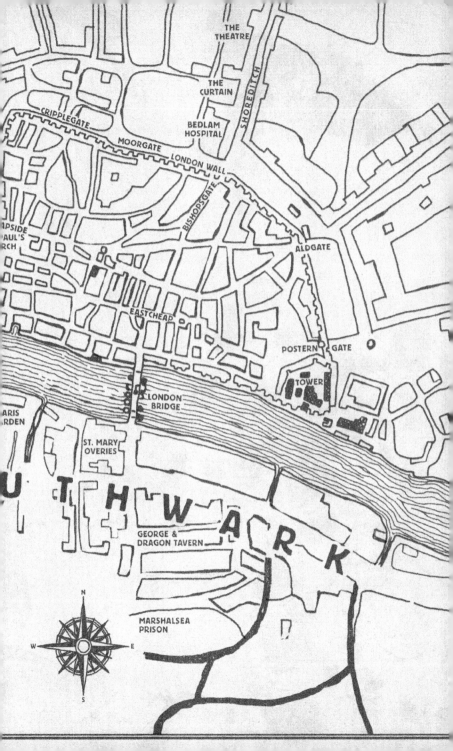

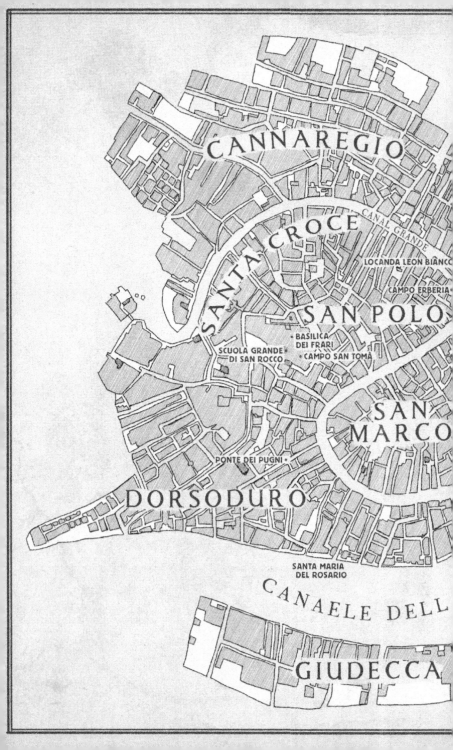

CASTELLO

PIAZZA
SAN
MARCO

SAINT MARK'S
· BASILICA

· PALAZZO DUCALE

· PIAZZETTA DI SAN MARCO

GIUDECCA

VENICE
1585

Dramatis Personae

Stratford

John Shakespeare	Alderman of Stratford. Father to William.
William Shakespeare	A shrewd-faced lad who might have made something of himself in the glove trade were it not that his mind wandered.
Mary Shakespeare née Arden	Wife of John and mother of William. A woman of whom it is said that had she been Hercules' wife she would have done six of labours and saved him so much sweat.
Anne Shakespeare née Hathaway	William's wife and mother to his children.
Sir Thomas Lucy	Justice of the Peace and MP for Warwickshire. A robust defender of Her Majesty and of the Church of England.
Matthew Hunt	Steward to Sir Thomas Lucy. A man as gross in manners as in appearance.
Alice Hunt	Daughter of Matthew Hunt. A fire waiting only the right fanning to flare.

London

Sir Henry Carr	Ambassador to the Serene Republic of Venice.
Henry Carey, Baron Hunsdon	Patron of players, the Queen's cousin, some say half-brother.
John Towne	A usurer, hot in temper and deed.
John Hemminges	Actor. Is like the mountain that first announces itself by a sudden avalanche.

Nicholas Oldcastle	Actor. Is there space enough within his tun of flesh to fit all the meat and sack and still have room for such good humour?
Ben Nightingale	Actor and writer. If talent were water, he'd not fill a thimble.
Adam Watkins	Sir Henry Carr's man. His nose is broken. Do not ask him how it came so.
Fallow	Sir Henry Carr's steward. Such efficiency as his is bought at the price of grey hair and a short temper.
Christopher Hall	Sir Henry Carr's secretary. Young ambition, eager for advancement.
Arthur from Norwich	A lad for the ladies' parts.
Robert Greene	Playwright, poet, rogue, rascal and keeper of grudges.
Constanza Briaga	Daughter of a musician at court.
Ben Connor	A carter. Sour in disposition and demeanour.

Venice

Isabella Lisarro	Courtesan of Venice. If beauty had a name, it would be Lisarro's. Double-gifted for, to her jewelled appearance, she adds the lustre of a brilliant mind. Double-cursed then to be surrounded by men who value these things not for themselves but only as adornments to their own raiment.
Maria	Isabella Lisarro's maid and mother to Angelo.
Vittoria Accoramboni	Duchess of Bracciano. Widow of the Pope's nephew and married to her first husband's murderer. When the Devil comes he does not show himself with cloven hoof but in the guise of an angel. The better to trap the unwary.

Antonio	Captain of the Duchess of Bracciano's guard. Hair as steely grey as his regard, eyes as hard as his grip.
Salarino	Landlord of the House of the White Lion.
Jacopo Comin or Robusto, known as Tintoretto or Il Furioso	Painter and lover of women and all things that have in them light and energy.
Francesco Tiepolo	A bravo of the town. Gorgeous as a peacock and just as loud.
Lucio Dandolo	A young nobleman of Venice. As prideful as the lion and as fierce.
Marco Venier	Patron of arts, beauty and wit.
Faustina	One of Marco Venier's circle. A tongue as long and sharp as a blade.
Andrea	Another of Marco Venier's circle. Just because he is round in appearance does not mean he has no sharp edges.
Iseppo da Nicosia	Merchant of Cyprus. His words mint coin.
Pasquale Cicogna	Candidate for Doge. One must hope him equal to the dignity of the office.

Others

Pope Sixtus V	The former Cardinal Montalto. In three things is he abundant: coin, spies and ambition.
Giovanni Prospero	Count of Genoa. The poisoned dagger in the Pope's hand.
Borachio	Servant to Prospero and villain of low mien.
Salerio and Solanio	Associates of Borachio. Friendship, loyalty and honour are virtues too costly for their purse.

Scenes

A Note to the Reader

I have used the Gregorian Calendar throughout for consistency and to ease the understanding of the modern reader. I have sought to avoid anachronism in words and grammar, but have not tried to match all the usage of 1585. *Thee* and *thou* ring false and mannered to modern ears. I have taken advantage of our ignorance of certain events to fill them with my own imagination, but strived to keep with the historical record in all other things.

This is not a work of history, but it could have been this way …

Prologue

Venice, August 1585

Piece out our imperfections with your thoughts;
Into a thousand parts divide on man,
And make imaginary puissance;
Think when we talk of horses, that you see them
Printing their proud hoofs i' the receiving earth;
For 'tis your thoughts that now must deck our kings,
Carry them here and there; jumping o'er times,
Turning the accomplishment of many years
Into an hour-glass: for the which supply,
Admit me Chorus to this history;
Who prologue-like your humble patience pray,
Gently to hear, kindly to judge, our play.

What news on the Rialto?

It is an ill-omened day that begins with a killing.

Dawn in Rialto.

The rising sun unpicks steep shadows in the narrow alleyways between the canals. It is quiet, save for the gentle knocking of boats as they bob against their moorings – and the sound of a man running.

William hurtles along San Giovanni and over the narrow bridge towards Ponte Olio. He is breathing hard. Exhaustion and the terrors of the night have drawn tight lines around his dark eyes. Wise eyes, that make him appear older than his twenty-one years. William looks about for escape. He can feel, to his fury, his shoe coming loose. Ahead is a small square, quiet at this early hour.

He darts into the shadow of the arches beside the little bridge. He presses up against the dark stone of one of the columns, struggling to control his breathing. The clattering of running feet can be heard approaching from the north. One man still pursuing after all these hours, he thinks. Then, the skittering of nails on stone, the sound of the dog's claws. His mouth dries. He worms his foot deeper into his shoe. His eye falls upon a broken oar propped up against a wall. He reaches out and clutches it in front of him.

The running feet slow. The dog can be heard panting and straining. There is no hiding from the dog even if he wanted to do so. He looks up at the tip of the broken oar, held before him in both hands like the cross in a procession.

The dog rounds the corner; a heavy thunderbolt of dark flesh, red maw and teeth. William strikes. All his strength is focused on the tip of the broken oar as it crushes the dog's back. The mastiff tumbles, mewling, dying. Its death-throes knock the oar from William's hand. William stares at the ruin he has wrought. The dog's master turns the corner, takes in the sight, and pulls back his cloak to bring a heavy flintlock pistol to bear. There is a grim squealing of metal on stone as the flint strikes. Its shriek is echoed inside William, he hears his efforts coming to nothing, reducing to a bloody death beneath an arch in Venice.

Then nothing.

No retort.

The man looks at the misfiring pistol. William looks at his arms, flung out in front of him as if to catch the bullet. The two look up at each other and grin. The armed man recovers first. He lifts the gun above his head as a club but William is already upon him.

There is a moment when William's face and his assailant's are only inches apart. William can smell the strong tang of garlick and sweat. The gun comes down on William's back but there is no power in it. All the man's strength has flowed out of him with the blood that gushes from the hole where William has put his dagger.

The squealing of the dying dog continues as the man collapses to the ground, mouth gaping for air like a fish. William picks up the oar and brings merciful silence to the dog. As he casts away the bloody stave he throws a final glance at its carcass. The man he ignores. Anger has driven mercy from him.

The square is still silent and empty as William scurries back through it and into the alley beyond.

Cows and goats he had butchered before. His morning's work adds a dog and a man to his tally. He thinks that his friend Oldcastle would approve of the experience he was gaining.

'Treasure it all, my boy,' Oldcastle would say with glass raised. 'For it will cost you to acquire it.'

It is indeed a bad world, Oldcastle, thinks William, as he races towards Cannaregio. Were I some Puritan weaver, I would sing psalms for it.

The Campo San Bartolomeo is not empty. Early morning has begun to bring out those making their way to work. In balconies around the square women lay out linen for the first of the morning's rays to catch. William slows to a walk. He does not want attention. He needs to catch his breath. The whoreson shoe is still slipping at his heel. Glancing back he sees two men enter the square a hundred yards behind him. Cloaks drawn tightly around them despite the beginning of the morning's heat. Their eyes are intent on William as he weaves through the gathering crowds. Paces quicken.

He pushes through a throng intent on their morning's shopping. William's head flicks back and forth like a bird's. Where are his pursuers? Head down, cloak gathered about him to disguise his bloodstained front, he tries to shrink within the crowd. He has no thought other than reaching the other side of the Canal Grande. If he can lose himself in the crowd outside San Giacomo di Rialto, then he can double back along the western bank of the canal and from there make it back to Salarino and to Oldcastle.

If only he can calm himself, he thinks, he can plan. He is momentarily distracted by the idea. It is not, he reflects, every day that one turns killer. To be calm is to be unnatural. He pushes towards the side of the canal where *traghetti*, the little canal boats, wait for custom. He raises his arm to signal to one and is drawn by the sight of his hand, smeared red from the morning's work.

He almost walks into her.

He is still half-looking behind him and then, there she is. Isabella, standing before him. She looks as tired as he feels. He frowns to see her there. Her presence unexpected, her person exposed to the threats that follow him. He opens his mouth to warn her of the gathering dangers.

William only half sees the glimmer of the metal as it whips towards him. He feels the stiletto blade slide through his cloak and clothes and the hot shot of pain. He looks down at the thin hand that holds the blade and then up at Isabella's face. He is surprised by the fury he sees in the tight lines of her jaw and the teeth clenched between the beautiful lips. Why? Why is she angry with him when he is the one betrayed?

Stumbling back he catches his foot on the raised stonework by the canal's edge. He trips and staggers hard against a wooden railing. With a crack, sharp in the morning air, it gives way.

Then he is falling into the Canal Grande below.

Before the waters cover him, there is only time to wonder how things came to such a pass.

—

Act One

Stratford-upon-Avon,
Warwickshire, March 1585

My youth hath faulty wandered

William didn't know what he wanted from life, save that it wasn't this.

He twirled an apple across the countertop as he stared at the empty street, dark beneath grim, grey clouds. Fitful rain pattered against the window of the glove shop. It was just before midday. The apple spun haphazardly between his hands, as it had done for near half an hour. In front of him sat the open ledger with its neat rows of sums in William's small, swift handwriting.

'Is the new leather ready?' William's mother, Mary, called.

'Cut and sorted,' William replied without looking away from the window.

Mary willed the weather to break before her son's patience did. The long quiet of a Warwickshire winter did not suit William's temper. It brought him out in mischief. So she feared it had already and she would task him with it.

'The lace prepared?' she asked.

'Already sewn on.'

'Both pairs?' Mary could not keep the note of surprise from her voice. Her son had skilful hands but this was fast work indeed. William simply nodded without turning.

Mary contemplated her son. He was twenty years old. Already married and with three children to show for it. He did not lack for ability. The Lord knew, the boy's mind was swift enough. Too swift; it was never in one place long enough.

'The accounts?'

'Done.'

The spinning of the apple paused momentarily. William turned the ledger so his mother might read it but did not trouble to look away from the bleak view beyond the window.

'The Apsley brothers are charging too much for dye,' said William. 'Try Mathew Deller. I heard rumour he had bought at a good price.'

Mary did not ask how William had come by this intelligence. William showed no particular interest in matters of business, yet he was a more reliable source of information than the town crier. Mary had a suspicion that in the days of the old Catholic rite one could have gone to confession only to find William emerging, telling you not to trouble yourself. He had confessed all your sins for you already.

'William,' Mary said.

William stopped the apple's spin. He turned to look at his mother over his shoulder. If he felt any trepidation at the stern note in her voice he did not show it, only curiosity.

'Look you at this,' his mother said, 'this, which I found within a package of gloves ready to be sent out. What means this?'

> *The gift is small, the will is all*
> *Alexander Aspinall*

His mother eyed him over the top of the note.

'Master Aspinall intends the gloves as a gift for his mistress,' William said. 'He asked if I could think of suitable words to accompany the gift.' William was unable to keep a prideful face from his mother.

'You have seen Master Aspinall's mistress, I suppose?' she asked.

'Yes,' William answered, 'and she is worth a better gift than a pair of gloves – even ours.'

'No doubt that is why you find it wise to refer to yourself in the note?'

'What? I do not –'

'I am not a fool, William,' she replied. ' "The Will is all"? You think I do not understand the reference? You think Master Aspinall will not?'

Mary crumpled the note in his hand and tossed it on the counter. 'Was this wise, William?'

'Not wise but well enough.' William straightened from his slouch to face his mother. 'Who knows what opportunity may come?'

A little grin broke into a broader smile. Quick hands smoothed the crumpled note.

'Besides, Mother, you are more astute than Master Aspinall. If I have judged him rightly he will be too concerned with how the gift is received by the lady to absorb the subtleties of the rhyme.'

His mother leaned back against the wall. Her eyes did not leave William for a hard minute. Perhaps the boy was right. Mary had thought before that her son was a shrewd judge of character, even if he could not control his own.

'The rhyme is clever,' she said. 'I wonder only if it will be your cleverness or your desires that land you first in trouble. Perhaps both will combine? It is a fault in the clever to think too little of the rest of mankind. To value their thoughts and desires but not those of others. You may have seen Aspinall's character clearly, but have you understood your own? Is your self-regard so great?'

William gave no answer but, sensing no further chiding followed, rested himself once more against the counter. The small smile was still in place, kept there by the thought of the Thursday past. His careful pursuit of Alexander Aspinall's mistress had come to conquest in a barn that – oh serendipity – sheltered them from an entirely predictable rain storm. It had been but a brief diversion. Achieved, melancholy had draped over him again.

William thought his mother wrong to call him selfish. He understood duty. The duty to his father to help in the family business. The duty to Anne, his wife of three years and mother of his three children. Duty was boredom and constraint and sat upon him heavier than the firmament on Atlas' shoulders. Would that duty would drive him from Stratford and into the arms of opportunity. Scarce twenty winters and already his whole life set before him in endless repetition of overcast days such as this one.

The bell set over the door of the shop tinkled as it opened. In crept Matthew Holmes, the tanner's apprentice, his face crinkled with excitement.

'Do you hear?' he cried. 'The players are come!'

William straightened. Here was news.

'Their cart's just pulled into the King's Hall courtyard,' continued Holmes, 'a grand company. Grand.'

William's fingers drummed. The prospect of the fair at the week's end had been but a mild delight. He had feared it would be all prize ewes and haggling over the price of leather. Only the rumour of the players' visit had given him hope.

The first time William had seen a play he had been seven. Sitting cross-legged at his father's feet, rapt. The flow of the words, the gaudy costumes, the dancing at the end, transported him. His father taken him after the performance to meet the actors. He had been shocked by the boom of their voices. Even without their costumes they seemed larger than ordinary men; more expansive.

As he grew older he found the plays diverting and the players themselves more so. To hear their stories of travel across the country and sometimes across the Channel to France and beyond was to attend a second play with characters more remarkable and events more miraculous than the first.

'Mother –?'

Mary Shakespeare did not trouble to look up. 'Go,' she said.

As well try to hold back the tide as keep her son to the shop when the players were in town.

'Keep a sober head, boy,' she called as an afterthought, but looked up to see she spoke only to a startled Matthew Holmes.

William was only to be seen through the window, performing a small and unexpected dance.

The suburbs of his good pleasure

William could not visit the players' company dressed in shop clothes. The very idea of a sideways glance from one of the actors, his pitying eye observing the stained and slightly frayed housecoat, caused William to shudder. He would have to go home, to Anne, and change. Resolution made, he set his course.

A few doors away from the shop, reached by a back path, was the house on Henley Street that William shared with his father, mother, brothers and sisters and his own wife and children. He let himself in. Anne was in the front room with the babies. The squalling of one of the twins struck William's ears as he entered. Round Anne's feet ran another child, Susanna, his firstborn. She was yelling at full lung and wielded a stuffed rabbit like an axe. At the centre of this storm Anne smiled calmly. William was always struck with admiration by the contrast between his own reaction to the chaos produced by the children and the measured ease of his wife's response.

His daughter caught sight of him and ran over to hug his leg.

'Apple,' she squeaked, her eyes turned up to him.

William still held the uneaten apple from the glove shop.

'You want some, lambkin? Wait while your father cuts it,' he said.

William walked to the kitchen dresser and took out a knife.

'Watch,' he ordered Susanna.

He took the apple in his right hand, palm down, and rested the knife carefully on the back of the hand. Then, raising the index finger of his left hand in the air to indicate that the attentive two-year-old audience should prepare for amazement, he flicked his right hand up. Knife and apple flew up into the air. The heavier knife fell first and William caught it by the handle, point up, to spear the apple that followed. After a moment's pause for Susanna to admire the apple spitted on the knife like a head upon a stake, William spun and proceeded to cut the fruit into slices.

'Lord, William,' his wife scolded, 'must you play with knives around Susanna?'

'Perfectly safe, chick,' he said.

'So you say, yet even the most skilled may stumble once in a while.'

William, squatting at Susanna's height, made a slice of apple disappear in his hand and then found it behind his daughter's ear. Susanna squealed with delight. Anne glowered at her husband's bent head. He craned his neck to look at her and flashed a wolfish smile. Her glower lessened and was replaced by a shaking of the head.

His grin continuing, she smiled back.

'The players' company is in town,' William announced.

Anne's smile broadened. 'Ah, there is explanation for your good humour.'

'My good humour is born of your company, chick,' William protested.

Anne snorted.

'There will be a play at the fair,' he said.

'You know I've never cared for the plays,' Anne replied.

William's shoulders slumped.

'Don't pout, Will,' Anne answered his pose.

William pushed himself up from his crouch before Susanna. He kissed Anne and walked to the bedroom they shared. Not for the first time he asked himself how his life might have been had he not been seduced by Anne or if their dalliance had not resulted in a child. It was what it was. He thought of how calm he had found her at their first meeting. So serene even as he whirled about her, a young man full of activity, displaying it to the older woman he wished to seduce. 'Sit still,' she'd said and he had. Now Anne and he, by virtue of that afternoon of stillness in the quiet field, found themselves partners when each, in temperament and interest, had little in common with the other. The old saying was true: hanging and wiving both go by destiny. They were two wandering planets whose spheres crossed, struck sparks, and by their meeting were pulled from their paths to new aspects.

'You will not mind that I go?' he called.

His voice was muffled as he searched in the chest at the end of the bed for a clean shirt.

'I shall be glad of the quiet,' Anne called back. 'That the children should rush about my feet I'll endure, but must I have you pacing like a caged wolf?'

William's face poked round the bedroom door. 'Wolf, eh?'

'Will you be drunk again?' Anne asked, ignoring his smile.

'Again?' William's face changed to a look of injured innocence as he buttoned his shirt. 'I am never drunk, Wife. Though I grant I am prone to periods of great wit followed by deep sleep.'

'Mind you don't wake the children on your return,' Anne chided. 'Bad enough that I must endure your snoring, but that you set the babes to mewling too.'

'I shall be as silent as Lavinia,' William replied.

'Who is she?' demanded Anne.

'A Roman gentlewoman,' said William. 'She had her tongue cut out.'

William mimed the process to delighted, horrified shrieks from his daughter, before disappearing out the door with a parting wave.

'God, William,' said Anne. 'Such things you say.'

A tun of man

'A jug of wine,' William called.

The King's Hall on Rother Street was a large coaching inn in the north of Stratford, where the players were lodged. New company is best welcomed when it bears gifts, William knew, so he had paused to call for drink from Susanne, the owner's daughter and principal ornament of the inn, before he went to find the players.

The rear of the inn opened onto the stable yard, where five men, a patchwork of sizes, ages and activity, were gathered by a long, roofed cart.

On the roof of the cart balanced a square-set man of about thirty-five. He threw sacks down to another below. He had a look of strength about him. He turned and threw with a powerful grace. He paused for a moment as William emerged from the back door and cast his eyes across the newcomer before returning to his task.

A squat, pot-bellied fellow stood below, trying to catch the thrown sacks. He struggled with their weight.

'Have a care, Hemminges,' he cried up to the figure on the cart's roof. Hemminges made no sign of having heard. The rain of sacks continued.

At the front of the cart a man, face red and pocked, struggled with a horse in its traces, cursing as he did so.

'Damn beast,' he said.

'Careful with him,' called Hemminges from above, 'he's worth more than you are, Ben Nightingale.'

Nightingale spat.

Off to the side, observing this activity, sat a youth with pale eyes and hands crossed demurely at his lap. The slender young man seemed oblivious to the struggle of man and horse beside him.

Above it all, sat upon the driver's bench of the cart, was a vast man; full as round at the chest as a barrel of ale, with crimson cheeks sinking into a bushy white beard, like a sun setting over a snowfield. At William's entrance this figure's beard parted to reveal a broad smile of yellow teeth. A voice resonant as any William had heard emerged.

'*Aha*, an ambassador of welcome.'

The great man unfurled himself from his seat, revealing a height to match his prodigious girth, and clambered slowly down to the ground. He advanced on William, a heavily ringed hand held before him like a lance. William found his right hand firmly grasped and his left relieved of the jug of wine. He was guided to a small set of cups nearby, into which the wine was splashed, the vast smile holding him all the while.

'Your health, sir, and gracious thanks for this generous welcome,' said the great man.

'The pleasure is mine,' William replied. He watched as the fat man held the cup to his mouth in a long swallow.

'William Shakespeare,' he proffered to fill the silence while the drinking continued. The fat man wore a brightly coloured doublet of yellow wool, much faded and stained across the bib. His face was dominated by a nose that had been generously given by nature and then much enlarged and reddened by drink's careful nurture. Grey eyes twinkled with mischief across the rim of the cup, which, now emptied, was lowered.

'Oldcastle, sir,' the man introduced himself. 'Nicholas Oldcastle. Actor and manager of our little company. The preparation for a show is thirsty work.' He gestured towards the wine as he poured another cup. 'For this relief, much thanks.'

William turned at Hemminges' approach. A calloused hand took William's in a grip hard as a gauntlet.

'John Hemminges. Also of the company.'

Ignoring William for a moment, Hemminges tried to catch Oldcastle's eye. 'Our first performance is in two hours. A wordy piece.'

He looked pointedly at the cup in Oldcastle's hand.

'A piece I have performed many times,' replied Oldcastle, patting the air as if commanding a dog to sit, but William noticed he set the cup down.

'You appear young to be a member of so august a body as Stratford Town Council,' Oldcastle continued to William.

'And I am not yet so,' said William. 'I am merely a great admirer of plays. What is this part that you have performed many times before?'

'Mercy, Lord. Don't get him started,' Nightingale said.

The pocked fellow who had been wrestling with the horse had given up the fight and come to join the company, specifically the wine. Not waiting to be invited he reached forward to grab a cup.

'We've only two hours till we perform,' he said, 'and still all to do. Have Oldcastle start on his stories and he'll still be talking at the point he nudges your elbow and tells you, "You'll like this bit. This is where I come on."'

Nightingale began to convulse with laughter at his own joke.

'It is the role of Pyramus in the tragic story of their love that I have played many times,' Oldcastle said.

'So many times his nose and cheeks are now as stained as the mulberry bush,' quipped Nightingale.

William must have stared a little long at Oldcastle. The idea of this portly giant ever playing the young lover Pyramus was hard to picture, let alone at this advanced age and girth.

'You must be a very great actor,' William managed to offer.

This brought a grin to Hemminges' face.

'He's not playing Pyramus tonight,' he said, 'those days are long gone.'

Oldcastle's cheeks puffed out in indignation.

'Great though those days were,' Hemminges finished. 'Anyhow, William, do you bring some message from the council?'

'No, no, only the welcoming gift of the wine,' answered William, 'and the curiosity of the small town bumpkin keen to hear tales from the wider world from those that have travelled it.'

Hemminges looked about him. 'I regret we've little time for gossip now, sir. Too much to be done before the show begins.'

'Perhaps after?' asked William.

'Of course, of course,' said Oldcastle. Recognising the promise of more free wine, he was less desirous than Hemminges to see William off.

Hemminges had already turned to Nightingale, who was busily pouring further wine into his cup. 'Why is the horse not yet stabled, Ben?' he asked, grasping the man's arm and causing the wine to slop over the cup's rim.

'Curse you, Hemminges. That hurts.'

Hemminges ignored his whining. 'The horse, Ben, and we need to get the backcloth to the market square and set.'

'When I have finished my drink. Bloody nag has the devil in him anyways.'

'Now, Ben.'

Hemminges gave a shove that sent Nightingale stumbling and the rest of the wine spilling. Anger flashed over Nightingale's face. He took a step in Hemminges' direction. Hemminges turned to face him. Seeing the broad set of the shoulders and the calm face staring at him, Nightingale thought better of his anger and turned back to the horse, muttering to himself.

'Such a company, Nick,' Hemminges said to Oldcastle and spat into the dust of the yard.

'On the money we pay, dear John, we are lucky to have so fine as him,' said Oldcastle. 'Besides, his kind are no trouble to you.'

Realising that William was still observing this old argument, Hemminges abandoned whatever he had been about to say. He nodded at William and turned back to the cart without a further word.

Oldcastle's big sail of a smile once again unfurled. 'Wearily I must wend my way back to my work.'

He held his arm straight out before him indicating the cart. A gesture that, outside of a person giving directions, William had only ever seen players use.

'For the wine, again, much thanks,' he said. 'I shall look to see you after our performance. A man of your sophistication will no doubt have as much to offer in the way of news as we.'

Oldcastle bowed low to indicate that the audience was at an end. He held out the emptied jug of wine to William. Slightly bemused by the course of the short conversation and the speed with which the entire jug of wine had been consumed, William found himself bowing in response. He took the stoup from Oldcastle and turned back to the inn.

As he closed the inn door behind him, William caught sight of Oldcastle. The old man reached for the cup he had set aside earlier, cast a glance at Hemminges' back and threw the remains down his throat.

The Yeoman of the Wardrobe

William anticipated double pleasures that evening.

The first would be in the performance of *Pyramus and Thisbe*. A play that he had not seen before, though he knew its source, Ovid's poem, from his schooldays. Two lovers in adjoining houses, their love forbidden, the tragic elopement ending with Pyramus committing suicide in the belief that Thisbe is already dead and her then doing so on discovering his dead body. Good stuff.

As a grammar school exercise in rhetoric he had been made to compose a speech that would sway Thisbe's father to let the lovers be joined. William had argued that Thisbe's father allow the marriage, so that her inevitable future betrayals would fall like punishments on her new husband Pyramus, the original betrayer. He had received praise for the form and language in which his speech was couched; condemnation for the argument. William suspected that Ovid would have appreciated the poetic justice.

The second pleasure would come after the play, the revels with the players. Oldcastle seemed entertainment in himself. William was not certain of the others, though there was bound to be amusement in the obvious tensions in their company. The horse-wrangler, Nightingale, was a troublesome creature not long for that fellowship if William was any judge. In Hemminges he saw an iron will; in Oldcastle, a constant whetstone to that will. For William had found on past occasions that seeing the players in their revels on the first night, and then prophesying how their humours and their fellowship would find reflection when they played their parts the following night, was fascination. By luck or judgment, William found he was not often wrong in his predictions.

Two pleasures then, and the better for it. William had found double pleasures were not their sum but pleasure multiplied. A sadness then that, as he had also observed on past occasion, an expected pleasure dashed was double sorrow.

William had returned to the glove shop from his visit to the players and it was from there that he and his father set out for the play. March is still a dark month in England; winter not yet broken, spring not yet here. As William and his father closed on the market square their fellowship increased as they were joined by others in twos and threes, gathering from various directions for the performance.

At the centre of the market square sat a stone cross on an elevated dais. It was here that the crier would stand on market day. A small rostrum had been built across one side of the dais. A wooden framework rose above it. Strung across the back was a painted cloth showing the white columned portico of a temple with the peaks of seven hills visible across the landscape behind: Rome.

There was loud prattle across the square. All Stratford was in attendance. The first performance of any play was free. The 'Mayor's Play' was put on for the councillors of Stratford, that they might judge whether the players were worthy of their licence.

William and his father made their way in front of the stage. William watched his father grasp the hands of friends and rivals alike and exchange small nothings and gentle jibes as he passed. The market brought many for their rare visit to town and a special entertainment like the play brought more seldom seen strangers still. The play was business as much as entertainment for his father.

'Jesu, Father,' said William, 'here comes Hunt.'

The whispered warning was hardly needed. Matthew Hunt, two-hundredweight of fur-clad man, advanced like a barge and parted the crowd before him as a wave, his arrival heralded by his brass chain of office clanking about his fat neck. Matthew Hunt, steward to Sir Thomas Lucy, the local Member of Parliament and Stratford's most prominent landowner, was the unlooked-for bone in the fish, the unexpected pit in the stewed apricots, the taste of gristle as one swallowed the last bite of pie.

'Master Shakespeare.'

Hunt greeted William's father in a voice like the deflating of a bladder.

'Master Hunt,' John Shakespeare replied.

'I trust the play will be suitable,' Hunt said.

It surprised William that Hunt, barely the same height as he and his father, should be able to tilt his nose far enough back as to be able to look down upon them both. The fat of his neck, William thought, should surely obstruct such movement. That air of superiority was as unmovable as it was unjustified, born of Hunt's status in Sir Thomas Lucy's household. Sir Thomas was not a man to be trifled with, particularly in these days. Lucy stood hard with the Protestants. William's own family, particularly his mother's family – the Ardens – had uncomfortable papist connections. It was a fact that made Sir Thomas Lucy watchful of them, something he had not troubled to disguise.

'I trust you are well, Master Hunt.' John Shakespeare paused to see if such common courtesy would be reciprocated; curious more than hopeful. 'You will find in tonight's entertainments nothing that offends and much that amuses.'

'I should hope so,' said Hunt. 'My master, Sir Thomas, is not glad to hear of this frippery in town. He himself is in London, but, of course, as his steward I stand here for him.'

Hunt's chest, already prodigious in girth, expanded yet further as he puffed himself up.

'You surprise me, Master Hunt,' John answered, 'for I had understood that Sir Thomas was aware of this market day's entertainments and took no issue with them. In any event, I assure you that they are entertainment of the purest virtue.'

'Would that your assurances were sufficient, Master Shakespeare. Yet were we not also assured that your son, William here, would not trespass again upon my master's land?'

'And neither did I,' William said.

Hunt turned with calculated slowness to take in the hot-faced son before returning his gaze to the father. 'The morals of the town are my master's charge,' he intoned.

John Shakespeare raised an eyebrow. Hunt ignored his questioning look.

'A charge he takes with great seriousness,' he continued. 'As do I, as his representative. Not the least because I have brought my wife and daughter with me.'

Hunt endeavoured to deliver a stern look, but was undermined by the glistening of sweat upon his brow. To William's great frustration John merely nodded and bowed before walking away. William hurried after.

'You leave that fat tumble of flesh unanswered, Father?' he said.

'If you want the organ to stop making noise, stop feeding it air, William,' his father replied. 'What do I care for the posturing of one like Hunt? I am assured by the players that the performance will be entirely respectful of the sensibilities of the town. Hunt can have no cause for offence. Besides, whatever Hunt may be, his master, Sir Thomas, is not a man to be lightly dealt with, and your escapade on his lands has done our position no good.'

An embarrassed scowl crossed William's face. He had poached one bird and was yet to hear an end of it.

'Come, William.' His father interrupted the young man's thoughts. 'Our seats are here.'

Four wide wooden steps had been built directly opposite the stage. On them were benches and chairs taken from the town hall for the benefit of the aldermen and their guests and various of the town dignitaries. Two near the right-hand side of the front row had been reserved for John Shakespeare and his son.

A fair-sized crowd was gathering in the space before the stage. Though it was afternoon, torches had been lit before the stage and at the sides. The hubbub was building at the expectation of the entertainment's start. The cries of hawkers of ale and food rose above the crowd.

William did his best to glare at Hunt as the fat man stumped up the wooden steps to the chairs set aside for him, his equally fat wife and his daughter. Hunt was oblivious, too wrapped up in his dignity to observe the common man. There was a noisy shuffling as the seats were rearranged to make space for Hunt. A man whose death, thought William, would free a county from famine and, boiled down, make candles for a year's light. William took note that the daughter was not yet run to fat. She was, indeed, a surprise in the fairness of her appearance. Even from the darkest mines, he mused, can come a diamond.

Those on the benches stood as the mayor entered and took his place at the centre. That arrival marked the moment for the play to start. John Shakespeare nodded to a fellow stationed by his feet. He rose and disappeared behind the side of the stage. His disappearance prompted a corresponding apparition on the stage, the giant figure of Oldcastle, dressed as Father Time.

Cakes and ale

A hush fell upon the crowd as Oldcastle began to speak.

William sat, rapt. It was not the dialogue that took him – he thought it mannered – but he knew enough to recognise a master at work. Oldcastle's voice leaped and dived as he spoke, bringing light and shade to the lines. He held the crowd at a hush. The only noise that competed with him was the crackle of the torches.

Until, that was, there was the scraping of a shifting chair behind him and the audible whisper of Hunt's voice declaring his concern at the pagan references to Father Time. William bit his tongue.

The play moved on.

Pyramus declared his love for the beauteous Thisbe. Hunt coughed his concern for the lustful thoughts of youth. Thisbe shared her desire for the noble Pyramus. Hunt muttered of how Thisbe's father had spared the rod and spoiled the child. The lovers planned their elopement. Hunt spoke loudly of the dangers of conspiracy. At the place of their assignation, Pyramus came upon the wild lion, maw bloody with what he feared was the remains of his slaughtered love. Pyramus killed himself in despair. His death rattle was accompanied by a loud harrumphing at the sin of suicide.

Those on the benches stiffened with each statement of discontent from Hunt, the moments between serving only to stretch out the tension in anticipation of the next interruption. Yet none, not even the mayor, dared challenge Hunt.

The groundlings, those stood before the stage, seemed unaware. Far enough from Hunt to hear only the players, they remained, for the most part, swept up in the tragedy before them. Oldcastle's stern performance as Thisbe's father held them tight. The slender boy William had seen earlier was transformed into a lithe young woman, distraught at her love denied and moving in her pleading. Hemminges, a powerful presence as Pyramus' father, growled his anger at lost honour. All to the good.

Then Pyramus had come to the stage. William winced. Nightingale, his hands sawing at the air as if trying to pull down the talent that he desperately needed, paced back and forth like a man with the itch. His voice had all the subtlety of a stallholder crying his wares on market day. As for the lion – the pot-bellied fellow coughing out a piteous mewl, lips choking on Thisbe's white veil as he did so – the less said about him the better. Yet even these grim performances and a script that continued to grate on William's ear could not break the effect of the play entirely. The players finished with a dance to the applause of the groundlings and the relief of the great and good of Stratford.

Hunt rose and marched down the steps towards John and William.

'It was much as I feared, Master Shakespeare, despite your promises. Licentiousness held up as admirable. Two houses with children lacking respect for their elders. Suicides.'

'It was just a play,' replied John Shakespeare.

'All plays are lessons for the weak of mind,' said Hunt. 'I liked it not.'

'Then you like not Ovid, Master Hunt, which they teach the children in the school,' John said.

'I thank the Lord I have had little dealing with Ovid,' Hunt said. 'The Bible is all my reading. The play was not sound, I say. Worse than that, Master Shakespeare, it was not even good. That ghastly old man with the beard. His voice rising and falling like a bird's squawking. *Faugh!* At least with the fellow playing Pyramus you could hear him speak.' He turned abruptly to William. 'What?'

The start of Hunt's speech William had met with wide-eyed incredulity but by the end he was in howls of laughter.

'I'll not be mocked,' said Hunt.

'William,' his father hissed.

'Your pardon, Master Hunt.' William struggled to gain his composure. 'It is just that I had not thought to find in you such knowledge of the arts.'

William burst into laughter again.

'I'll not be mocked.' Hunt's voice was low. He turned to William's father. 'I shall make full report of tonight, Master Shakespeare. I see that not only in the play are there households where children lack respect for their elders.'

Hunt pointed at William and glared as he turned away; a gesture of such mummer's artifice that William was shocked from his chortling into silence.

Spending your wit in the praise of mine

William and his father watched Hunt walk away.

'Father ...'

John did not glance round at his son. He simply held up a stiff, quivering finger. William threw his head back and looked up at the sky. After a long moment John let his arm drop. Without saying a word to his son, John Shakespeare crossed to the mayor and began to engage him in conversation.

William seethed. His anger travelled in many directions. At Hunt, the pompous windbag who nearly ruined his pleasure in the play, who stood in judgment over his father and himself, as if armed with divine understanding. At his father, who, supine in his silence, did not take Hunt to task for his overbearing manner. At himself, for having so unguardedly revealed his contempt for the fat fool, and thereby made an enemy.

William shook his head and turned towards the stage. People still milled about the space before it in knots of two or three. Most had dispersed to the stalls that now, reopened, served food and drink again. The buzz of conversation was accompanied by the sound of horn and lute from travelling players.

William found Oldcastle by the side of the stage wiping his face clean with a rag.

'Fine work, Master Oldcastle,' said William.

'*Aha!* The herald of the town, Master Shakespeare,' said Oldcastle. 'You enjoyed it?'

Oldcastle's face glistened with sweat and he gazed eagerly on William, waiting for praise.

'You, sir, were magnificent,' proffered William.

'Naturally, naturally you should say so. Yet I am not immune to the pleasure of a compliment, even when social graces demand that it be given.' Oldcastle let out an odd rumbling noise. 'You see, I purr.'

He leaned in to William and whispered, 'The crowd, I felt, a little flat. What thought you?'

William found himself whispering in reply, 'Perhaps a little.'

Oldcastle nodded. 'They did not wish to upstage our lion, I suspect.'

He turned his face and raised an eyebrow in the direction of the portly fellow now padding about behind the curtain of the stage still draped in the moth-eaten lion skin.

'Would that they had rather matched the heights young Pyramus reached,' William responded.

William's and Oldcastle's eyes locked.

'Yes.' Oldcastle dragged the word out. 'A nuanced performance.' He raised his other eyebrow.

'As full of hidden meaning as a Jesuit's argument,' said William.

'And just as welcome,' said Oldcastle, a fat smile splitting his beard.

'Fortunate for us that Master Nightingale should also write our pieces,' said Oldcastle, 'so many talents.'

'The Bible has a parable about those with talents ...' William began.

'Aye – best buried, sayeth the Lord,' Oldcastle finished.

'I recall it differently,' William said.

'You are, no doubt, more the scholar than I,' said Oldcastle.

He scrubbed his face one more time. Emerging from the rag, he declared, 'Our work is done. Now time for pleasure.'

'The Bible also has a parable about that,' William said.

'Enough, Shakespeare. My throat is quite parched by the dryness of all this wit. To the tavern.'

Vows made in wine

The King's Hall sounded to the loud laughter of happy people. William sat in a circle with the players' company passing a jug of wine while they sang catches like tinkers. Hemminges sat on a stool leaning against the back wall and picked at a lute. The young lad, who William now knew to be Arthur from Norwich, sang along beautifully but quietly, his voice quite drowned out by the hubbub around him. Glanville, as William had discovered the portly lion was called, mumbled along drunkenly.

The laughter, wine and pleasant company were not having the effect on his humour that William hoped. The cold pang in his stomach had become a knot of tension. A battle of wits with Oldcastle where each sought to outmatch the other in pointed parable and proverb proved but fleeting distraction. His thoughts returned to Hunt, to his father and from there to thoughts of duty. The pleasures of the present moment served only to raise thoughts of contrast with the chains of daily life.

'More wine?' He asked the group generally and, not waiting for the expected grunts of approval, rose and wandered to the bar.

The discordant words at the play were still to be resolved. He would have to make peace with his father. He would have to wait out Hunt's revenge. William knew Hunt too well to fool himself the matter would be let pass. Hunt would not let a rogue like William stand and laugh at him unanswered. Not knowing where the blow would come, or against whom, was a torment. He hoped to find in wine inspiration towards a solution, though he was some way into that plan and, as yet, without success. The whirligig of his thoughts was interrupted by a new arrival in the King's Hall, Hunt and his wife and daughter.

William and his party were sat in the back of the inn, where they were served on rough wooden benches with sawdust on the floor. The King's Hall, however, catered to more than just roister-doisters. The great inn had, at the front, a room where those of a more refined nature might enjoy the pleasures of the alehouse. Fresh reeds covered the floor and carved oak benches were plumped with cushions. With the town full of visitors on this special market day, the King's Hall bedrooms were crammed with those who had too far to travel to return home that night. The elegant front room hummed with the chatter of wealthy farmers and their wives, and it was into this room that Hunt and his family now came.

William ducked back into the shadow of the bar. Hunt strode towards the stairs that led to the rooms on the first floor, then stopped short, as if coming to the end of an invisible tether. He turned back to see his portly wife, cross-armed and red-faced, staring at him. He hastened to her side, provoking a short conversation involving much finger-jabbing on each side. It ended with Hunt visibly deflating and making his way upstairs, alone. Hunt's wife, head held aloft in victory, set sail for a small table in the corner with daughter in tow. She settled herself down, snapped her fingers for the barmaid's attention and, having ordered, began to talk at her daughter with nearly as much finger-jabbing as had accompanied her speech to her husband. William's gaze fell on Hunt's daughter. A plan began to form in his head.

My thoughts are ripe in mischief

William had not heard the argument between Hunt and his wife. He could guess at it. Hunt had planned to leave town as soon as the play had ended; to signal his rejection of Stratford and its denizens, the Sodom of Warwickshire. A plan that had wrecked itself on the rocks of his wife and daughter's desire to enjoy the pleasures and opportunities of market day. No doubt Hunt had made his irritation at being forced to traipse about after the two women quite clear. It appeared Hunt's wife intended drink would dilute the unpleasantness of that memory.

William waited till Hunt's wife was the better for two glasses of sweet wine of canary in swift succession. Then he beckoned Susanne, the barmaid, over.

'Doll, would you take a stoup of wine to the lady there and her daughter, with my good wishes.'

William gestured at the table where Hunt's wife and daughter were sitting, the girl in bored silence while the woman talked on heedless.

Susanne pursed her lips. 'What mischief is this that you're about, William Shakespeare?'

'May a gentleman not make a gesture to a lady without it being questioned?'

'A *gentleman* might,' she responded, but took his money nonetheless.

When Susanne reached their table she placed the stoup of wine upon it and gestured back at William. The two women watched as William made an elaborate bow in their direction. Hunt's wife made a feeble gesture of refusal to which William responded, as if it were a summons, by going over to where they sat.

'Forgive me, mistress,' he said as Susanne returned to the bar with a shake of her head. 'I fear that I am in part responsible for your husband's distemper. I foolishly questioned his knowledge of Ovid this afternoon and did not acknowledge my error as readily as I should. I would hope you receive this wine as a small gesture showing my contrition.'

William unleashed his finest smile in the direction of Hunt's wife and allowed it to pad over to the daughter.

'So you're the unmannerly rascal he was railing at this evening,' Mistress Hunt said.

The wine was already beginning to take its toll. There was a slight slur to her speech and her eye struggled to focus on William's.

'I fear so,' said William.

He managed to look contrite and wolfish at the same time. It was a combination he had had occasion to master. He was rewarded with a smile from the girl.

'Well, I thank you for your kindness,' said Mistress Hunt. 'As to forgiveness, that is for my husband to say, but,' she drew the stoup of wine towards herself, 'I shall tell him of your gesture.'

William bowed graciously to both and retreated to the shadows of the back bar and waited. Sure enough it was not long before all the drink converted itself into a need for the privy. Hunt's wife rose and wove her way outside. At once William padded back over to the table.

'Your good mother has gone to bed?'

The girl looked about her. She was not used to the conversation of strange men with handsome features and cunning eyes.

'Forgive me,' William continued. 'I did not mean to fright you. It was only that I meant to ask if your father would attend the fair tomorrow also. So that I might make apology to him in person.'

'I do not know. I think my father plans to leave. My mother speaks of staying for the market.' The girl blushed in her confusion and embarrassment.

William thought the colour suited her complexion well. Here was a flower kept too long from the light. Let her but see the sun and she'd spring forth a rare blossom. William felt the rush to dare all come upon him in heady combination with the wine he had himself consumed in strong measure. He switched his tone to sincere desire and leaned towards her.

'I pray he does. If only that I might admire his daughter once again.'

Her bright eyes opened wide.

'Sir ... you go too far ...' she said, leaning in herself.

'To the ends of the Earth, I think,' said William, 'to *ultima Thule* and beyond if it meant I might see you again.'

Too much? William wondered. Surely so, but one cannot think over-much on wooing or all seems ridiculous.

'Say that you'll come to the play tomorrow,' he said, 'and I promise you'll hear words that speak the true extent of my heart's desire.'

From the corner of his eye William saw Mistress Hunt open the door and lean unsteadily on the frame at the threshold.

'Tell me your name,' he urged the girl.

'Alice,' she said.

William repeated her name in solemn tones and spun and left.

Alice squawked as her mother slumped into the seat beside her. She looked up to see if her mother had been witness to William's love-making, but Mistress Hunt was having considerable difficulty seeing even her own nose.

For certain, neither woman saw William strolling back to the group in the rear of the King's Hall. Nor the impish grin upon his lips. Nor did they hear him lean into Oldcastle and whisper in his ear, 'Master Oldcastle, I have a favour to ask ...'

A critic, nay, a night-watch constable

The following morning Anne saw William walk out of the door of the house on Henley Street with relief. He had been more than ordinarily restless that morning, rising even before the children while it was still dark. By the time Anne rose herself he was making ready to depart. He kissed his wife, grabbed the papers that represented his morning's labour from the kitchen table, danced out the door and strode towards the glove shop.

Despite the lateness of his going to bed and the earliness of his rising William was full of industry. Much labour had been done in the shop by the time his father entered and was confronted by a beaming William.

'You're gay this morning, William,' said his father.

'I am,' he replied.

The father stood at the threshold while his son stood behind the counter smiling at him. Eventually the older man shook his head and strode in to join the younger.

Neither man made comment on the events of the night before. Several times John, having spent much of the previous evening rehearsing angry words in his mind, opened his mouth to chide his son. On each occasion the sight of his son's eager good mood and energy stayed his breath.

At noon William begged his father's indulgence to depart. Such had been his industry the day's work was done. His father granted his release with relief. William made his way to the King's Hall for food and the furtherance of his plan.

Oldcastle had to be shaken awake.

'Dear God, why mock poor fellows thus?' he said. 'It cannot be dawn already.'

'Up, Master Oldcastle. It's past noon,' said William.

A groan emerged from beneath the nest of blankets.

'There is work to be done,' said William as he booted the bed.

'Fie on you,' Oldcastle responded.

The fat man rolled onto his side and pulled a blanket over his head. William whipped it away. Oldcastle sat up with a growl. William thrust a beer into his hand. The sound of drinking muffled that of Oldcastle's outrage. It took William a further half-hour to cajole Oldcastle and the other actors to the yard and show them his morning's work.

'Arrant nonsense,' Nightingale yawned in response.

Oldcastle, looking the brighter for a cold sausage and some hot eggs courtesy of William's purse, mumbled through a full mouth, 'I like it.'

Glanville, the portly player of the lion, had nodded back to sleep. The youth, Arthur, simply shrugged. William waited for the deciding vote.

'It's well written. Short enough too.' Hemminges tapped his lips. 'We'll do it instead of *Murcello*.'

'Hold now,' Nightingale interjected, 'I worked hard writing *Murcello* and took great pains to con it.'

'Would that quality in writing were simply a consequence of labour,' said Hemminges over his shoulder.

'No, it's a consequence of thought,' said Nightingale. 'Consideration, revision, craft. Look at these hatchings.' He gestured at William's paper.

The short scene that William had worked on early that morning was spread out before Hemminges.

'Barely a word crossed out,' said Nightingale. 'It's just the uncrafted outpourings of a rank novice.'

'And yet still better than yours,' said Hemminges.

Nightingale's mouth hung open. He gasped for breath. Oldcastle snorted and waggled his hand at him.

'Lord, Ben, is there no safety when players turn critics too?'

'I'll not be usurped. I write the pieces for this company.'

Nightingale leaned forward to sweep William's scribblings to the floor but found his wrist caught by Hemminges in a painful grip.

'Don't,' Hemminges said.

Nightingale snatched his hand back. 'I'll have no part of it.'

He spat on the yard floor, then looked round for support from Arthur; finding none, he stamped back to his room.

Hemminges looked over at William.

'There are five parts here and only four of us,' Hemminges said.

'I'll do it,' said William. 'I wrote it, after all.'

'You act?'

'Only at school. If you've a better choice, I'd take it,' William said.

'Fine.' Hemminges nodded. 'We'll take half an hour to learn the piece and then walk it through.'

Hemminges looked at William. He chewed at his fingertip.

'Remind me why we're doing this again?' he asked.

'For love,' said William.

'For love,' Oldcastle echoed through a full mouth, clasping his hands over his heart.

'Well,' said Hemminges, 'best do a good job then.'

The play's the thing

The town had tested the players' quality the day before and found it worthy. Though this time they must pay for the pleasure from their own pockets, a good crowd had built up around the little stage. Hemminges and Glanville weaved between the people collecting coins. From behind the curtain William scanned the audience. He found Hunt and his wife and daughter perched upon the same seats as the previous day. Hunt was sitting with arms crossed, gazing at the sky. His wife, looking a little green, was slumped upon the seat beside him. Next to her Alice Hunt was sitting, eager and alert upon her chair like a hunting dog waiting the first flight of birds. William smiled.

'I'd have thought the anticipation of your first step upon the stage would fright you.'

William turned at Arthur's whisper. The lad was right. This was to be his first step onto a stage as a player. He wondered at his own lack of fear.

'Perhaps it should,' said William, 'but no. I find my thoughts have already gone beyond the playing of the piece to the applause after.'

'A brave conjecture,' said Arthur.

Before William could reply he saw Oldcastle stride upon the stage and a hush fall across the crowd. The play had begun.

Three stories of love Oldcastle promised the good people of Stratford, and a lesson in every one. William knew the form. Each story to build upon the last; a message of ever greater perfection of love. The last scene a rendering of the parable of the Good Samaritan to show God's love for man.

William had read Nightingale's draft of the three stories briefly while waiting for the players to rehearse. It was execrable. It had been no wonder that Hemminges had seized on William's proffered drama as an alternative to the first of Nightingale's three stories. Even the finest players could not overcome the stilted nature of Nightingale's writing. William wondered briefly if that had been the point. Was the tedium of the writing supposed to undermine the message of the piece? He dismissed the thought from his mind. Such subtlety was beyond Nightingale and it was impossible to believe that Oldcastle would hobble himself with such bad writing for a trick but one in five hundred watchers might note.

In truth he cared not either way. All his mind was bent upon the first story, his draft, the net in which he would snare his partridge. His composure began to fade and trepidation build as the moment he crossed into the light drew nigh. He heard Oldcastle's words die away. Hemminges marched upon the stage in the guise of King Mark of Cornwall.

> Go now and bring to me, Tristan, my sword
> The closest companion of my heart's thought.
> There's none I trust so much as I do him.
> He stands as close to me in love as does
> The sea, the sky. One ends, the other begins.

William took a breath and crossed the shadow of the curtain onto the stage. He felt more than heard the scrape of chair on floor as his father saw him for the first time. He saw Alice Hunt sit up. Hemminges turned expectantly towards him. William looked out across the craned necks of the crowd before him. He opened his mouth to speak – and his mind went completely blank.

He had not foreseen the effect crossing the line would have. The same light struck the ground before and after the curtain. The same rough wooden planking stretched from wing to stage. Yet in that single step much changed. A hundred eyes fixed upon him. He was no longer simply the open-mouthed spectator; he was part of the action, the author of it.

The silence stretched. William's brain tumbled about. There was a muttering from the groundlings. He saw Hemminges' eyes roll and Oldcastle's narrow, urging him on. He could not remember a single word he had written.

He heard a small snort from the seats. William looked up. Hunt's expression of grumpy boredom had changed to a smirk of amusement. As the smallest weight can tip the balance of the scales, so that tiny noise made all the difference. William's mind cleared, the crisis passed. He stepped forward and spoke.

William had chosen his theme with care. The tragic story of Tristan and Iseult was perfect for his purpose. The unhappy queen and the loyal knight who loves her. The lovers who know that they do wrong but are powerless to resist their attraction. The foolish King Mark, oblivious to the treachery in his own house. William had taken some liberties with the story. In his version King Mark was not the noble figure of legend but a cuckold corpulent from surfeit of meat and drink. A hypocrite glutton who confined the beauteous Iseult to his castle for fear that she would find the wonders of the world too tempting. William had the King come upon the lovers intertwined and slay Tristan with a poisoned sword.

As William lay dying in Arthur's lap he made sure that he looked past his Iseult to Alice Hunt. He spoke:

> Wipe dry these eyes of yours that now are wet
> 'Tis that we do not do that we regret
> The bud of love that never daylight sees,
> The fruit of love we see but fail to seize.

As William closed his eyes he was gratified to see Alice Hunt flutter her own at him. For a moment the corpse of Tristan smiled.

Voice verses of feigning love

William took his bow. He was ready to take another but Hemminges, hand upon his arm, hurried him from the stage.

'Enough, enough. Jesu,' Hemminges said as he bundled William behind the curtain, 'all the clapping has so swelled your head you'll never get that hat off.' He clapped him on the back. 'Good work, Master Shakespeare. They seemed to like it; though, by God, you came near to disaster at the start.'

Hemminges turned away to don his costume for the next scene. He did not, therefore, bear witness to Nightingale striding onto the stage, clipping William's shoulder with his own and sending the newly blooded playwright spinning. William did not care. This petty jealousy from Nightingale was just another kind of applause and equally sweet to him. Besides, he had new business now. He need only find his moment.

William waited impatiently. When all three scenes were done the crowd began to disperse. There was still haggling to be done in the market. The Hunts gathered themselves and set out into the stalls. William dodged round the back of the stage to avoid his father, who was bearing down upon the curtain behind which he had seen his son disappear. William slipped into the crowd.

He slid through the knots of people in the narrow lanes between the stalls, scanning for the Hunts. He found them by a stall with bolts of cloth draped across it and hung from the frame. Hunt's wife fingered them appraisingly while her husband stood bored nearby. As William approached he palmed an apple from a nearby tray. He ducked behind a drape and leaned out to toss the apple.

'*Faugh!* Filthy children,' Hunt cried.

He dabbed at the splashes of mud flung on his hose by the apple's fall into a nearby puddle.

'God's will, Matthew,' said Mistress Hunt. 'Must you fuss so? Go to the well there and wash. I am not yet done here.'

His wife waved him away and, muttering to himself, he went. William had hoped only to distract Hunt; this was better still. He spun round the back of the stall and, hidden by the hanging cloth, edged up to Alice.

'Lord, Alice,' said Mistress Hunt, 'what is with the squawking today?'

'Sorry, Mother,' Alice replied, 'I-I thought I might look over there at the –'

'Yes, yes,' said Mistess Hunt, 'do you not see I am busy?'

Mistress Hunt had not looked up from her business for one moment' not even when William's hand grabbing her daughter's had caused the young woman to give a squeak of shock. William beckoned Alice toward him and disappeared into the crowd.

'You are too bold,' Alice said.

'Did I not tell you?' asked William. 'For you I would dare anything.'

A toying smile played on Alice Hunt's face. She turned away as if to judge the freshness of the fruit nearby.

'You wrote that for me?' she said.

'For you,' William said.

'It was pretty.'

'Pretty?' William felt, unexpectedly, scratched by the compliment. '"Pretty" is a thing of baubles and trinkets,' he said. 'It was a thing far greater. A thing of consequence, an enterprise of honourable-dangerous consequence.'

Alice turned back to William and took a step closer to him. She placed a hand on his arm.

'I know,' she said. 'I meant … I don't have your words.'

William felt, with undisguised pleasure, the presence of her hand clutching the sleeve of his doublet. Noting his gaze she took the hand away and cast her eyes about to see if she'd been seen. William felt the moment ripe. He reached out and touched her arm.

'Say that we can meet tonight,' he said, 'in private.'

Alice shook her head but did not pull from his touch. 'I cannot. It cannot be. We travel home this day.'

'Then I shall follow you there,' William promised.

'Foolish, rash boy,' Alice sighed.

William held her arm more tightly. 'You don't want me to?'

Alice's eyes darted everywhere but William's face. Then they came to rest on his and she spoke smilingly, 'Of course, of course I do. Oh, oh would that I were free to come with you now.'

'Tonight, sweetling,' William answered. 'This very night I will come to you.'

William felt Alice reach for his hand and, twining her fingers in his, squeeze. He leaned down. 'How shall I know your room?'

Alice cast her eyes about in thought. 'I shall leave a candle in the window, and tie a scarf to the frame that you should know it mine. Promise, promise that you will come.'

'I shall, sweet,' William said.

He pulled himself back behind a stall a moment before Matthew Hunt heaved into view.

'Ah, there you are, child. Why must you dally so?'

Hunt pulled his daughter away by the hand. Trailing behind him she turned her head to give one last look to her Tristan. A moment before she disappeared into the throng, she slipped her father's hand and ran to where William hid behind the stall. She grabbed him and planted a fierce kiss on his lips. Without a further word she was gone, leaving him wide eyed with the wonder of a woman found bolder than he had expected. His mind on this, he did not note the danger.

A hand snatched at his shoulder and pitched him to the ground.

A-horseback, ye cuckoo

Ben Nightingale, face red, stood over him.

'Shakespeare, you foul mosquito. Come to latch onto my company.'

William scrabbled to get up. At the prospect of the row the nearby stallholders hurried to cover their goods. Others crept in to catch the entertainment.

'Your company?' William brushed angrily at his mud-splattered clothing. 'Rudesby, be gone. Your delusions are no business of mine.'

'Plague on you.'

'If it pleases the company to use another's words, what basis is that for your ill temper?' William asked.

'You think I don't know your game?' Nightingale spat his question. 'I'll not be replaced. Not by you.'

'Peace, man,' said William.

'Don't speak to me of peace, you cuckoo.' Nightingale tried to advance on William, who slipped back to put a cart between them.

'Peace, child, I should say, since you bawl like one,' said William.

Nightingale growled and lunged but William moved to keep the cart between them.

'I have no interest in your position,' said William. 'Word wrangler to a ragged band of players? All my business with your company is done.'

Nightingale grunted and shook a finger at William. 'See that it is.'

William let out his breath as Nightingale departed.

'Shame that.'

The sudden voice close behind him made William start.

'Jesu, Hemminges?' William clutched at a nearby stall to steady himself as the voice from behind him resolved into the sturdy figure of Hemminges.

'I'd hoped you'd join us. Or have thought about doing so, at least.'

'Would that I could, Master Hemminges. But I have family in Stratford. Camp follower to a travelling player would not suit my wife.'

'Aye. Certainly not with such a – how did you put it? "Ragged band".'

'I only said that to convince Nightingale,' said William.

Hemminges smiled for the first time in William's acquaintance.

'No offence taken. It's true enough. At the moment, at least. But that's the thing about our business. Things can change in a moment. Nick and I could tell you some fine stories to that effect.'

Hemminges' faraway look lasted only a moment before his gaze returned to William's face. He clapped the younger man on the arm. 'Our playing here is done. We leave for London tomorrow. Wanted to thank you.'

'It's I that should thank you,' said William.

'No thanks needed,' replied Hemminges. 'That piece is a good one and will serve as payment enough when we do it again.'

William shook the older man's hand. Hemminges' grip closed on his fingers like a door shutting.

As William watched him depart he wondered what he would have said in answer if Hemminges had been serious about his joining the company. Probably much the same as I did, he thought. Which, by reminding him of his business in Stratford, led him on to thoughts of Alice Hunt, her hot kiss and the tricky question of how to get to her bedroom unseen.

Imagination of some great exploit

Alice looked from the window again. Though the moon was full she could see no sign of William. The field beyond Sir Thomas Lucy's house was edged with wood. Alice strained to pluck forms out of every shifting shadow. She did not dare believe that William would come. She prayed he would.

The stub of candle was nearly burned through. That little piece was all she'd been able to steal on their return from Stratford before her father had ordered her to bed. When it was gone, so would her hopes.

Alice slumped back on her bed and stared at the rafters of the attic. The great house was quiet. Perhaps all are in bed, she thought. She might sneak down to the hall, see if she could find another candle. Though if her father caught her, from her room let alone stealing candles from Sir Thomas Lucy, he'd not spare the rod.

I am the foolish child my father calls me, Alice chided herself, to put my hopes in a rogue of whom I know so little, save that he thinks too much of himself and smiles like a wolf about to spring.

And that he writes plays for me.

Alice smiled and closed her eyes. She saw once more the moment when William had spoken to her from the stage. She felt again the thrill of sitting among a hundred who watched the same traffic of the actors but did not know that she was Iseult, that Tristan spoke to her.

It had not hurt his attractions that all the tedious ride home her father had railed at the wretch Shakespeare and his father, both of whom 'thought themselves too good when they were but barely godly'.

A tap came at the window. Alice sat up. She hurried to open it, nearly knocking the candle to the floor in her haste.

'You came.'

'Did I not promise that I would?'

'God. If you are caught here ...'

'For you I dare all.'

William had prepared a speech based on the theme of his daring. He never got to speak it. His mouth was stopped with kisses.

Hot hounds and hardy chase them at the heels

The baying of hounds drove William splashing through the stream. A cruel contrast from the warm comforts of Alice Hunt's bed in which he had lain until minutes before. Sharp branches reached out from the darkness and cut at his face as he ran. It was a cold morning, sharp tongues of frost licking at William's sweat-drenched head. Yet hunting dogs and stinging branches could not strike the smile from his face. It was a smile of triumph.

William's schoolmaster had forced him to read Aristotle's *Art of Rhetoric*. William recalled only two things from the experience. First, how his schoolmaster had stood over him, cursing William's poor Greek with every haltingly translated line. The second, that when Aristotle turned to talk of the emotions, their causes, their spurs and halters, William had felt himself the great man's master in understanding already.

So it had proved with Alice Hunt. William felt, though he had met her but briefly, he knew who she wanted to be and who she needed him to be. It was not only William that railed at Matthew Hunt's puritan show and longed to snip at his nose for it. The steward had bred a rebel to his own rule. The realisation of his own understanding had been heady; a pleasure greater than those that followed. It was, after all, a love scene that he was writing.

This chase, however, was no part of William's plotting.

He had been lying in Alice's bed, alive with thoughts, just before the dawn, when he heard the heavy tread of Hunt approaching. The Lord alone knew what had alerted the tiresome steward. A question for a quieter moment. He raced to haul on his clothes before the man reached the top of the stairs. God be thanked Matthew Hunt was fat and slow. A tun of man does not move fast even in anger. William went out of the window – the way he came in. Halfway in and halfway out he had found himself grappled. Alice Hunt stole a last kiss from him, then scurried back to her bed to feign innocence again.

William was out of the window in an instant and moving quickly along the roof, heading for the rear of the house. Then a slipping foot on a rain-slick roof tile had sent him tumbling towards the edge. His hands flailed about in search of a grip, his body twisted out over the void, his elbow caught on the pipework, a desperate clutch at the guttering and the slam as his legs swung into the wall below.

It had taken a moment for his head to clear and for him to realise that he hung near face to face with a serving-girl on the other side of a window. Pretty too, even with her mouth gaping open in astonishment. Perhaps particularly so because of it. He had given her his second best smile; the pain in his elbow preventing better. She had screamed.

Pure good fortune to be hanging over a balcony. A short drop and he was back on his way. Skipping over the balcony and scrabbling down the side wall to the ground and then off through the woods. He let out a whoop of excitement. Behind him the sound of shouting and men and dogs being roused to the chase.

William threw himself into the water. Its swirl would keep scent and sign of his passing from his pursuers but, God, it was cold. Two hundred yards further down the stream from where he had entered, he pulled himself up on the far bank and pushed through a wall of reeds. Ahead lay Stratford. Within the hour he was in the rear room of his father's glove shop – stripped before the fire and rubbing himself with a cloth in an effort to restore warmth to ankles that throbbed with pain.

Here was exercise for a March morning. Trouble was sure to follow from this adventure. William found he didn't care. There was, if anything, greater pleasure as a result. The blood stirs more to rouse a lion than to start a hare, he thought.

Dressed again, William sat before the fire. His fingers drummed restlessly on the carved oak arm of the chair. He contemplated the day of work before him. The thought of the endless petty tasks to be completed dragged the smile from his face.

He heard a key turning in the lock.

John Shakespeare closed the shop door behind him. His troublesome son was sitting before the fire, one leg thrown over the arm of the chair.

'Morning, Father.' William twisted round in the chair and smiled.

'I take it there is a reason, other than the desire to purchase gloves,' replied his father, 'that means Matthew Hunt approaches in the company of two of Sir Thomas Lucy's larger gamekeepers?'

Many Jasons come in quest of her

William sprang from the chair.

'Merciful God.'

He was at the door in a moment and opened it a crack to peer into the street. Advancing majestically down the road was a triangle of men, the vast bulk of Hunt in the van. William's father rolled his eyes to heaven.

'Father,' William whispered, 'it would be a good thing if Hunt were not to find me.'

He dashed to the storeroom door and darted inside.

John Shakespeare slowly pulled off his gloves. He took care not to harm the embroidered lace cuffs that adorned them. He shrugged off his heavy cloak and laid it next to the gloves on the countertop. His son popped out of the storeroom, threw his father an embarrassed grimace, raced to the fireplace, picked up a pair of sodden shoes and hurtled back to his hiding place.

John ran thin fingers through greying hair and turned to face the door. Beyond it could be heard the leaden tread of Matthew Hunt approaching.

'Shakespeare!'

William pressed against the wall in the storeroom at the back of the shop, hidden from sight. He heard his father move to the shop door and open it.

'Shakespeare. Where is your son?' Hunt's cheeks wobbled, glutinous with the spittle of righteous indignation.

Hunt bustled forward followed by two men whose faces were weather-cut with a thousand little creases like old leather saddles. John Shakespeare moved slowly aside to allow the three men into the small shop.

'Master Hunt,' said John Shakespeare. 'Good morning to you.'

'I've no time for pleasantries, Master Glover,' said Hunt. 'Your son was caught on my lord's estate this morning. Where is he?'

John Shakespeare drew up his eyebrows and pursed his lips. 'I am at a loss, Master Hunt. You say my son was "caught" on Sir Thomas's estate this morning. Yet you come to me to enquire where he is?'

'Don't bandy with me, Shakespeare,' Hunt said. 'I have not the mood for it. Your son was caught –' The great bellows of his voice declined to a wheeze. His mind sought the right word to describe the circumstances of Shakespeare's visit to Sir Thomas Lucy's estate.

'– poaching.' A grimace of relief at the discovery of this euphemism appeared on Hunt's fleshy features. 'Yes, poaching, for which he has a reputation.'

This last was accompanied by a face of high indignation, chins tilted up, eyes pointing down the nose.

'He managed to fly before we could detain him,' Hunt continued. 'Where is he now? I have come to bring him to Sir Thomas to explain himself.'

'He was caught – in the act?' John asked.

'Faith no!' Hunt said. 'I arrived too late for that. There was no mistaking what had been afoot, though! We'd have had him in the woods too, but he slipped the dogs.'

Hunt was looking around the tidy little shop as he spoke, his nose still thrust up as if he could smell out the presence of the insolent villain Shakespeare.

'I am still unclear as to why you think it was my son that you seek?' John asked. 'Was he seen?'

'The girl as good as confessed it,' Hunt answered.

'The girl?' John Shakespeare said. 'I thought we spoke of poaching?'

When Hunt finally spoke it was as the angry wheezing of steam from cracks in the earth. 'You know full well of what we speak, Shakespeare. This is the fruit of the untrammelled licence of which I spoke at the play. Where is your boy?'

For William, the silence that followed Hunt's demand opened wide as a snare. He knew he had been more burden to his father of late than aid. To defy Lucy, even in the pompous form of his steward Hunt, was no minor matter. William realised he was holding his breath.

'I think you are mistaken, Master Hunt,' John said. 'My son could not have been poaching as you suggest for he has been here at his work all night.'

Hunt made a wet sound of incredulity.

'You doubt me, sir?' John demanded. 'With what reason?' There was a cold timbre to John Shakespeare's voice.

'I know it was him,' Hunt said.

'You did not see him, did not catch him and it is clear by your choice of words that this girl has made no confession,' John Shakespeare responded. 'Who is she? Some scullery maid full of fine fancies?'

'She is no such thing ...' Hunt's voice trailed off.

John said nothing but let the silence grow. William thought his moment ripe.

'How now, Father? Master Hunt.'

William's voice was light as he emerged from the back room and laid cut leather, hastily gathered from the storeroom, upon the counter.

'Whelp, what mischief have you performed?' said Hunt.

William feigned confusion and astonishment at Hunt's question.

'I, sir?'

'Don't play the fool with me, boy,' said Hunt.

'I never play, sir,' William said, 'though I have tried my hand as a player ...'

'You have tried to seduce –' Even as he sought to cut William off, Hunt's voice trailed away at the thought of acknowledging out loud his shame. '– that which I would keep most safe from such as you,' he finished.

William raised an eyebrow. 'Some kind of treasure? A jewel of some kind?'

'Far more than that,' said Hunt.

'A magical item, then,' said William. 'A golden fleece!'

'What?' spluttered Hunt.

William leaned across the counter towards Hunt. 'You should take great care of such things, Master Hunt. For you will find that many Jasons come in quest of the prize and a fleece will not guard itself. It needs a good guard dog.'

'Enough, William,' the older Shakespeare cut his son off.

John Shakespeare turned to Hunt. 'It's clear that you make your accusations without foundation. I say again, my son was at his work all night. Here.'

Hunt made no immediate reply. There were further rumblings from deep within the massy torso. Heat spread up his face. He leaned in and rested meaty hands on the counter, which creaked beneath the weight.

'Very well, very well. This is to be the game?'

He pointed an eloquent finger at the father and son, then turned to leave; no speedy process for so large a man. Eventually the barge of his body turned. As Hunt passed through the door he gave no backward glance but simply repeated his promise from the play.

'I'll not be mocked.'

The grim-visaged gamekeepers followed after.

Unmannerly boy

The slap of his father's hand on the counter snatched William's smile away.

'What has passed here?' his father demanded.

William drew breath to answer but could not speak before his father slapped the counter again.

'Mark you, not one false word. Not one. By God, William, you try me.'

His hand fluttered on the counter where it lay. William could not take his eye from its twitching.

'This is ill done,' his father said.

'It's just a game,' William replied.

He took a step back at the flare that lit in his father's eye.

'What has passed here?' his father repeated.

In hurried words William explained all. When he finished his father's hot eye had been replaced with a pale-faced tremor.

'You have brought disaster on us,' he said.

'That fat fool Hunt has no grounds for accusation,' William protested. 'You said so yourself. 'Sides, what retribution there may be will fall on me.'

'Why? Why do you think that?' John Shakespeare asked. 'You think that Sir Thomas will stand by and see his steward mocked in his own home? The steward's own daughter, by Jesu. You think his eye will fall only on a wayward, unmannerly boy and not on the family that bred him?'

John Shakespeare continued to speak over William's attempt to protest.

'You think Sir Thomas will trouble himself that the evidence of mal-efaction does not sit in his hand? He will reach out and grab what he needs and damn all those caught in his grasp.'

'You overplay this, Father,' said William.

'It is not I that has overplayed my hand, William. And with what stakes. That is the worst of it.' The anger in his voice faded and he placed his head in his hands. 'Selfish child. You brought the enmity of powerful men upon our family for some sordid tumble with a lovestruck girl.'

William saw that his father was crying. He looked away. He could not remember when he had seen that last.

'I had such high hopes,' John said. 'Yet you take your God-given talents and squander them on petty revenges.'

'Father?'

'Did you not think of your wife? Of her shame if the town comes to hear how you treat your vows? Of your mother's anger at your weakness of will? Of what follows for the girl?'

William was silent. He had not thought of these things. He had thought only of the cleverness of his vengeance and his excitement at the chase.

'Sir Thomas is bound to seize on this,' John Shakespeare said.

'Why? Why should he do so?' asked William.

'God's sake, William,' his father answered. 'Enough with your endless whys. What does it matter why? It is enough to know he will.'

'If we knew his reasons we might work on them.'

'Enough.'

'Think, Father.'

'Get out,' John demanded.

'Sir, please.'

'Get out,' repeated his father. 'Think? I can think of only one remedy. You must leave Stratford.'

'No,' said William.

'You will have to,' his father said. 'To stay here will only bring the malice of Hunt upon you and your family.'

'How can I?'

'How can you not?' said John Shakespeare. 'Didn't you think of this? You who always seem to have everything so well planned. Go. Get out.'

But it was not William that left the shop. His father stirred himself and, in his distraction forgetting his gloves, exited, the door closing on a muttered wish: 'I must go and see what may be done.'

Rich gifts wax poor

All that day William waited for retribution to fall upon him. When evening came and the sword had not yet fallen, he breathed again.

The thoughts that haunted him that long day were not of Hunt's revenge or that of his master, Sir Thomas Lucy. He dwelt upon the prospect of duty and where it would lead him.

William's foot had scarcely crossed the threshold when his wife spoke.

'I feared your idleness this week, between revels with the players when they're here and recovery from those revels when they are gone,' said Anne, 'but I see virtuous explanation for our empty bed. You have been busy.'

'What do you mean?' William cast about to see if his mother or father were in the kitchen too. He could not see them. Instead his wife stood there smiling at him.

William shook his head as if to clear it. Anne could not be smiling at his adventures of the night before. Sure, she could not know of them yet for one thing. He hoped she never would. He and Anne understood each other well enough but it would not do to flaunt that understanding in the other's face.

Seeing his bewilderment his wife let out an exasperated sigh. 'The venison, fool,' she said.

Confusion turned to coldness.

'What venison?' William asked.

'Why, the whole beast that hangs in the cellar,' his wife replied. 'A fair piece of meat. We'll dine well on that for a while yet.'

William shot from the room and down to the cellar. There the deer hung, substantial. It was fine and very fresh. He stamped slowly up the stairs and back to his wife.

'I'll not ask how you came by it,' Anne said. 'Was it to be a surprise? If it hadn't been for our daughter playing the little fool and trying to hide in the cellar I'd never have found it for a week.'

William stood, tapping his fingernails against his teeth while his wife spoke.

'I did not kill it,' he said.

'Well, it wasn't your father, now, was it,' said Anne laughing.

'No.'

Seeing his pale face Anne went quiet. William's mind raced. So, this was how it would be done. How Hunt's men had sneaked it into the cellar was a display of skill frightening in itself. A whole deer; no minor play at poaching this. Hunt would see him whipped for it without question, or worse. Caught with the bloody evidence curing in his own cellar. It showed at once both more imagination on Hunt's part and less. He had thought the blow would fall more obliquely. He had counted on it. This was swifter action than his plans contemplated.

'Anne, I must go.'

'What? Wait …'

'This deer is not a gift,' said William. 'Well, a Greek gift, maybe.'

'For God's sake, William, leave your riddles alone for once,' Anne said. 'Tell me what is going on.'

'I have offended.' William was moving through the house. He found his children asleep in the bedroom and kissed each one gently, so as not to wake them.

'William, what is going on?' Anne hissed in his ear as he rummaged through the trunk at the end of the bed to find a shirt and clean hose.

'Too long to explain, Wife.'

He turned and took her by the arm back into the kitchen.

'You're right.' He hugged her waist. 'As always. I am becoming a wastrel.'

'Oh Lord, William. What is this fancy now?' said Anne.

'I am going to London,' William replied.

'What are you talking about?'

'I have done a foolish thing.'

'Wouldn't be the first occasion.'

'True, Anne, true. This time my foolishness threatens consequences for those I care for.'

'What is it, Will?'

'My father and mother will see that you and the children are looked after,' he said, 'till I can write from London and send money.'

He kissed her brow.

'I am sorry for my faults,' he said.

'From London?' said Anne, struggling to keep pace. 'How long will you be gone?'

William did not answer. He had disappeared once more into the cellar. He emerged, staggering under the weight of the deer. He quietly praised his daughter Susanna for an unruly child. She had something of his spirit in her. She'd scarce sit still for a moment, nor would she be ruled by the wisdom of her elders. Yet, had she not played where she should not, he would never have found time to act before Hunt's vengeance fell.

'London, Will?' Anne demanded.

'London, yes. I must hurry.'

William twisted to steer the burden across his shoulders past the frame of the door. Outside his home of twenty years he turned again, reached out and pulled the door gently closed behind him. His hand stayed on the door for a moment before he turned once more and set off.

Anne was still standing in the kitchen open-mouthed when William's father pushed through the front door a few moments after his son had departed out the back.

'Anne, where is William?' said John Shakespeare, 'I have news.'

'Gone out,' Anne answered.

'I think you'll be pleased with my news also.' John bustled about removing his coat. 'I have obtained for William a job, as a teacher, in Lancashire. The pay is good and the family well connected. It is best, I think, that he be absent from Stratford for a while. I will not dwell on the circumstances of his leaving.'

He took up Anne's hand and stared at it as he spoke. 'It will be no hardship for him, nor I think for you and the children that he be gone. I know that you suspect, as I do, that he chafes at the ties that bind him to our little town. It has made him unruly. We shall have some peace with him gone a little while, and he will return to us a steadier man. Did he say when he would be back?'

John looked up. Anne saw his face was wet with tears.

'Oh John, John,' she said. 'Don't fret. Please. An absence will only remind him of the comfort of home.'

He reached out and patted her hand. 'You are a good woman.'

Anne smiled at her father-in-law and thought of the quiet days to come.

'Poor deer,' quoth he, 'thou makest a testament'

William dropped the deer in fright at the sound of his name. His mother stepped out of the darkness into the small yard at the rear of the house.

'Where are you going?' she asked.

William did not think of lying. 'London.'

'Oh, William,' Mary said. 'The sight of you, that should fill me with joy ... Now your father tells me ...' Her voice was cold iron. 'What have you done? Thoughtless, thoughtless even as you use your cunning to weave your plots, thoughtless.'

'Mother –' William said.

'So you have wrought matters that you must go to London.'

'Wrought –' William began.

'Peace, oh, peace.' She shook her head at him. 'To London? Where will your wife go? Or that headstrong Hunt girl? They stay, to face the slights and edged stares of the town.'

'I didn't think –'

'No. No,' his mother said, 'you did not. Think now.'

'I shall make all good,' William promised. 'I wouldn't harm Anne, or the babes, or the girl. Not for all the world.'

'How?' demanded Mary. 'How will you make all good? The time to think of this was earlier. Now, I fear, is too late for such repentance.'

William stood in shame, his mind empty of all but the sadness in his mother's face.

'William,' Mary stroked his cheek, 'your father has often lamented to me that you might have made something of yourself in the glove trade if you were not distracted.'

She pulled him close.

'I lament that you might be something more, much more, in this world. You have a talent. Spend it wisely. The world does not remember those that might have made something of themselves. Only those that did. Go to London. You are not happy here; it doesn't take one of your wit to see that. I pray that you will find good fortune there and return to us.'

She pinched him.

'But be kind, William. Do not spend all your thought on proving yourself clever if that cleverness cuts. A sharp tongue has two edges. Be careful too, William. Choose your friends in London with a care. Trust your own judgment first and do not give yourself over to care of the judgment of others. A mother speaks; a mother knows. And do not borrow money. That has been your father's undoing. Nor lend it neither should you get any.'

She drew a great breath and clasped him close.

'Go, go,' she said. 'Leave the deer here. Your father will deal with it.'

William held his mother's hands. For once he grasped for words but could not find any. He stooped and picked up the deer again.

'I shall write from London,' he said, then turned to face his mother squarely. 'And I shall take the deer. I need it if I am to make good the harm I have done. You will see, it is not too late.'

He was rewarded with a sad smile.

William walked through the darkness.

It had come to him as his mother spoke. The deer was an opportunity. Stratford looked for proof of William's malefaction. Here it was. Yet in proof of this crime it disproved the rumour of another, the shame of which would not fall on William alone. Let my poaching stand confessed by this deer's body, he thought. Let its death disguise another smaller, sweeter death to which no sin should be attached but that men must preach against what they fain would do.

His mother's hurt was before his eyes, her words in his ears still. He had erred in thinking only of his own pleasures and revenges. Let him take the burden of that error on himself. He would spare his wife and Alice Hunt the vicious talk of idle tongues by confession of another sin. He reached his destination and bent down.

William lifted himself from where he had deposited his burden. Through the trees ahead the growing light of a new day revealed Charlecote, the manor-house of Sir Thomas Lucy, hard by. The scene of William's recent adventures. Figures began to emerge from within as the day's work began. He waited till he was seen and known. Then, as if caught where he wished he were not, he ran. Leaving the deer behind.

The path of his travel now successfully aligned with his duty. He went to London with a light heart.

Interlude

Rome, March 1585,
the Villa Montalto

I would think thee a most princely hypocrite

'He's ill. Like to be dead soon. When he is gone I shall be Pope.'

The Cardinal Montalto sat at the head of a long table. It was made of white marble with legs of porphyry stone, the top of each carved to resemble the head of a lion. Its heavy ornamentation was of a piece with the oppressive decoration of the chamber.

The Cardinal himself was gorgeous in his robes, with a tidy white beard combed into two columns and eyes like little black stones glittering above his drooping nose. The little man seemed to disappear within the cushions and carvings of his throne.

At the other end of the long table from the Cardinal sat a tall man dressed in costly raiment, all of black. Giovanni Prospero, Count of Genoa.

'Your Grace speaks with such confidence,' said Prospero, 'a vision from God, perhaps?'

'Better. Discussions with my brother cardinals.'

'I see.'

'And watch your mouth, Giovanni,' the Cardinal said. 'It does not become you to mock visions of the Holy Spirit.'

'Your Grace reproves me to my betterment,' Prospero said.

The Cardinal Montalto ignored the comment. The count was a great provoker and it did not do to notice his little cuts lest he try to worry at them.

'I chafe, Giovanni,' he said.

'It is unseasonably hot, Your Grace, and your robes of office are perhaps a little heavy for the weather.'

Despite the heat and his dark clothing Prospero did not seem discomforted or even to sweat. A thin scar pulled one eyebrow into a permanent arch of mocking inquiry. As he spoke he used a small knife to peel and slice a fig.

'You're in one of your moods, I see,' the Cardinal sighed. 'How trying. It is not my body that chafes, Giovanni. It is my mind. It rubs against the walls of this villa in which I find myself confined. Soon I shall be free and then I shall act.'

'The old Pope need only die for this to be so?' asked Prospero.

'Indeed,' said the Cardinal.

'I shall pray for it,' said the Count.

The Cardinal slapped his hand on the table. 'Enough.'

Prospero paused with a sliver of fig lifted halfway to his thin lips and then popped it in his mouth. The Cardinal's face had grown red to match his robes.

'I have not called you here, my son,' said Cardinal Montalto, 'to have you blaspheme before me. Ugo –' He paused at his use of the name the Pope had been given at birth. 'His Holiness, Pope Gregory,' he corrected himself, lips puckering as they forced the unwelcome title out, 'and I have had our differences, but one does not pray for the death of the Holy Father.'

The Count of Genoa inclined his head in acknowledgement.

'At least, not out loud,' the Cardinal continued.

He pushed himself from his seat and walked to the long wall on one side of the room on which was painted the martyrdom of St Sebastian. The Cardinal gazed up at it.

'You have been of service to me in the past, my son, and will be again when I am Pope,' he said.

The Cardinal looked at Prospero.

'The Papacy of Gregory was devoted to the stick of correction. The excommunication of Elizabeth of England, the destruction of the Huguenots, from his passion for correction not even the calendar was safe but it must be beaten into shape. That is all very well but all stick and no stroking is a poor way to train a horse.'

'Or a whore,' suggested Prospero.

The Cardinal's mouth wrinkled with distaste at the dark man's interruption. 'I bow to your experience in such matters.'

He paused to look back at the painting. 'When I am Pope I shall rebuild Rome, starting with this villa. The glory of God will be visible to all. The heretics will not so much fear to defy us, as Gregory would have it, as long to be with us in that glory I offer them.'

'Your Grace is wise,' said Prospero, 'although, as I recall it, Your Grace has not shied from wielding the stick. Were you not inquisitor in Venice? Did the Signoria of that state not ask that you be recalled because of your harshness?'

'Nonsense. Politics, all politics.'

Prospero relished the sight of the Cardinal's colour rising again. The Cardinal was so easily provoked to anger. A weakness that Prospero had noted early. Only cattle and fools allow themselves to be goaded.

'However,' the Cardinal continued, 'your mention of Venice is to the point. I have a task for you. Two tasks.'

He returned to his seat and settled himself within it. At the other end of the table Prospero sat up.

'Venice,' the Cardinal said. 'You and I, Giovanni, we have both had experience of that troublesome republic. It sits like a leech on St Peter's crown sucking blood from our better endeavours. Rich enough to resist both the rod of Gregory and the glory I intend to offer. That cherished independence is not something that I can permit to continue untouched when I am Pope. There is too much at stake if we are to crush the Turk and return the Church to its proper state.'

Prospero smiled to himself. The Cardinal's sneering nose had wrinkled with ambitions that Prospero considered as foolish as a child's fancies. Crush the Turk? With what arms? The princes of Christendom were too busy fighting each other to trouble the Ottomans. Not that Prospero cared; turbulent times suited him both in temperament and opportunity.

'I am informed that Elizabeth of England sends embassy to Venice,' the Cardinal pronounced.

'Informed?' asked Prospero.

'The source of my information need not concern you, my son. The report is soundly based, be certain of it,' said the Cardinal. 'An embassy to Venice to encourage their support of the Protestant powers.'

'Hardly news,' said Prospero. 'The English have made that their message for a score of years or more.'

'What changes is that now their words are turned to action. Rumour speaks of greater support for rebels against Philip of Spain in the Netherlands.'

'Venice is far from the Netherlands,' Prospero said.

'Venetian coin travels far,' said the Cardinal. 'English merchants further still. The flow of one towards the other would greatly aid the English and discomfort Spain. Meanwhile, it makes corpulent Venice fatter still with foreign money. The English Ambassador brings with him subtle promises to the Signoria that will benefit them and much discomfort us.'

'Us?' asked the Count.

The Cardinal waved his hand in irritation at the question. 'Us. Rome. The Church. What does it matter to you? Your task is simple. That embassy must not succeed.'

'Your Grace intends that I –'

The Cardinal struck the table again. Despite his better will he was finding it hard to contain his anger. 'You know full well what I intend, and that no hint of blame must come near our person.'

Prospero picked up and chewed upon a slice of fig.

The Cardinal looked on him with a vinegar aspect. Must he always make such a performance out of these matters, the Cardinal wondered. He supposed it was some choleric spirit within Prospero. The same spirit that gave him such imagination in the doing of dark deeds. Truly, there was none to match this Count of Genoa in mischief. Were it not so, the Cardinal would not deal with him. Not for the last time the Cardinal worried that the spoon he held was not long enough to dine with such a creature.

'I shall send you Borachio,' the Cardinal said, 'to assist you in your labours.'

'Your Grace is kind but, as you know, I prefer to work alone,' said Prospero. 'Besides, I query if Borachio has the delicate touch required for such tasks.'

'It is not a request, Giovanni,' said the Cardinal. 'If it makes you easier to bear, pretend he is your servant.'

Prospero bowed his head in submission to the Cardinal's command.

'I shall, of course, need funds,' he said.

'You always do,' replied the Cardinal. 'You will find credit awaiting you with my bankers in Venice. By the time you reach them I will have sent word about the English Ambassador's departure and all I know of his train, his route.'

Prospero smiled at the knowledge that the Cardinal, despite his condemnation of Venice, still banked with them. That he hated the Turk yet dressed in robes more opulent than the Sultan's. That he spoke of the glory of Heaven but soiled himself with earthly matters. So much the better, thought Prospero. One always knew where one stood with a hypocrite. It is honest men whose actions defy prediction.

'I am grateful. Death is always so –' Prospero paused, searching for the right word.

'Expensive?' suggested the Cardinal.

He looked with distaste on his assassin and thought with no little pleasure of the moment when he would tie off that particular knot.

'I was going to say "costly", ' replied Prospero, 'but Your Grace's word hits something of the point.'

He finished the last of his fig.

'Your Grace made mention of two tasks?'

The Cardinal shifted in his cushions. 'Yes. This second is a matter more delicate still.'

The Count of Genoa smiled again, for he knew what was coming.

'Vittoria Accoramboni,' said the Cardinal.

There is the name I expected, thought Prospero. Vittoria Accoramboni, more beautiful than any Helen and cause of as much strife among men. Vittoria Accoramboni, once the wife to the Cardinal's nephew, Francesco Perreti. Now widow of the same and married to his murderer. Though, if rumour were believed, the question lay open as to which had dealt the fatal blow, the wife or the now husband. Some even said it was her brother. Such a family, thought Prospero. He suspected they would make merry company at a feast, provided one remembered to eat only from the same dish as they did. As for the dead husband, the Count had met Perreti once. The Cardinal's nephew was a man so dull Prospero had been tempted to kill him himself. Except that it was a fool that offended the Cardinal – and Prospero was no fool.

The Cardinal continued speaking. His face, already so like the gruesome mask of Pulcinella in the *commedia all'improvviso*, was further twisted into that shape by hate.

'She anticipates my elevation and has fled to Venice to seek the protection of the Signoria. She thinks that there my hand cannot reach her. You will prove her wrong in that belief.'

'Your Grace need say no more,' said Prospero.

'You understand what I want?' asked the Cardinal. 'Her and that coward husband of hers, the Duke of Bracciano.'

Prospero relished the venom with which the Cardinal pronounced the word *husband*. How stung he was. How his ridiculous forked beard danced about at talk of his nephew's murderers. Did he even notice the spittle that glistened on the front of his robe?

'To speak the deed to me, Your Grace, is to have it done.'

'But quietly, mark you. Quietly.'

Giovanni Prospero rose and brushed his clothing clean. In truth it remained as spotless as when he had donned it that morning. He pushed back his chair and approached the Cardinal. The black stones of the Cardinal's eyes tracked him as he bent to kiss the fat ring on the Cardinal's hand.

'Am I ever otherwise, Your Grace?'

Act Two

London, April 1585

Such welcome and unwelcome things at once

The broken, mangled bodies were dragged from the pit. Two boys ran out with buckets of sawdust to cover the blood. Henry Carey, Baron Hunsdon, leaned forward in his seat to await the next part of the entertainment. On the verge of his sixtieth year, Hunsdon had a worn look. He played incessantly with the tankard in front of him.

'Disaster. Already disaster.'

Hunsdon's companion, Sir Henry Carr, could barely hear the muttered words against the hubbub of the crowd. The two men sat in a private booth at the Paris Garden, the bear-baiting ring in Southwark just across the river from the City of London. Around the pit at the centre were rows of benches rising up on scaffolds at a steep rake to allow the battle in the ring to be seen. On one side, at the back, were stalls with cushioned seats and curtained privacy for those that could afford it.

'The meeting of the Privy Council went badly?'

Sir Henry's shrewd, round face emerged from a doublet, oddly unkempt, for all it was made of fine cloth and expensive lace. Hunsdon flung up his hands in answer.

'Fools and suitors. All must know there's none to match the Spanish for war. Braggarts, who talk of glory and do not see that once Philip of Spain has crushed the Dutch rebels he will turn to England, surround Her Majesty. Worse yet, she listens to them.'

'You know my thoughts, Hunsdon,' Sir Henry said. 'Venice.'

'*Venice*. Always it is Venice with you, Henry,' Hunsdon said. 'You have your embassy, be content with that.'

The crowd about them rose to a roar. Two fresh dogs were led, snapping and snarling, into the pit at the centre of the wooden O. The bear fixed to the post on the far wall shook its head, flicking sweat and blood from its ears. Its fur was matted here and there with crusting blood from wounds taken before it crushed the backs of the first pair of dogs set against it. It let out a low growl in counter to the dogs' barking.

'The embassy,' said Sir Henry, 'is bootless without matter for the bargaining with Venice.'

'I tell you, Henry, I have wrung from Sir Francis all that I can.' Hunsdon turned to Sir Henry as he stabbed a finger into the wooden rail before him. 'By the Lord, there is too much on foot and too little to spare for frolics.'

'It is because there is so much on foot that we must persuade Walsingham for Venice,' Sir Henry Carr replied.

Below them the dogs were let slip from their leashes. They bounded forward. The bear rose on its hind legs and roared.

'By God, Henry, I despair. I came to you for sound counsel and all you can do is prate at me of Venice.'

Hunsdon swept his hand across the crowd. 'Look at these baying fools, drinking and swiving and all uncaring that England is beset. I need your help, Henry, not your fancies. I need your counsel, talk to me of how I may put an end to this mad suggestion of an army to support the Dutch rebels, of how we may make peace with Spain before he turns his eyes on us. Do not distract me with some Italian folly.'

'Hunsdon, put aside your doubts a moment and listen.'

Below, the two dogs pulled, darted and bit and seemed to swarm the bear as if more than two animals beset it. The bear swung and twisted but could bring neither beast within its reach.

'Venice is all, Hunsdon, all,' Sir Henry said. 'Forge an alliance with Venice, however secret, we gain gold that will pay for men, for ships and for the succour of the Protestant rebels in Holland. More than that, Philip's eyes turn east. When Venice's territories sit right beside his Duchy of Milan they must. How can he not fear that the Spanish road through which pass all his supplies from Spain, through Italy and on to his armies in the Low Countries will be cut?'

One dog darted behind the bear to worry at its heel.

'More than that, the Pope will be much distracted. Venice and the Pope are no friends, and Venice has shown its mettle against a pope's will before,' Sir Henry said. 'With such an ally we may stand. Without them we will surely fall.'

The two dogs twisted apart as the bear's great paws swung and missed. The dogs turned back together as if the two bodies had but one mind. The bear roared as their teeth ripped into its hind legs. The crowd roared with it. The dogs darted back but not before one was raked across the flank by the bear's claws.

'I am too tired to debate with you, Henry,' said Hunsdon. He slumped back against the bench and ploughed his hands through his hair.

'I have the right of it,' said Sir Henry.

'I wish to God it were not so. I wish to God our choices were not so few and so poor.'

'This costs you little, gains you much,' Sir Henry pressed. 'Trust me, Hunsdon. Trust me and lend your weight to mine in this.'

Below them there came a lull in the fight as bear and tormenting dogs drew back and drew breath for the end. The crowd gave a low moan of delight at the gathering storm of the battle ahead.

'The bargaining will be hard. Venice will know its price,' Hunsdon said. 'It will be easy enough to promise attacks on Spanish shipping at the Cape to drive trade back through Venice's arms. Drake and Hawkins need more holding back than setting on. Will it be enough?'

'Maybe not.' Sir Henry leaned his head towards Hunsdon. 'But there is another stake we might place on the table. Our knowledge of papal spies in Venice.'

The crowd roared again as the dogs leaped as one to finish the bear.

'Walsingham will not give that knowledge away,' said Hunsdon.

'He may if he is offered Venice's knowledge of Jesuit spies in England in return,' said Sir Henry.

'Will he be?' Hunsdon's attention was now all on Sir Henry, the fight below forgotten.

Sir Henry scented victory for he had saved the best for last. 'Our gold for theirs. Or so my man in Venice promised me.'

The bear twisted away from the first dog and swung at the second. The second dog was slower than before, its speed and strength seeping from the raking wound down its flank. Where before the bear had struck only air this time it connected. The crack of bones as the dog smashed into the wall of the pit could be heard even over the crowd's halloo. The other dog backed away and the bear strained at the chain about its leg to reach it.

'What else does your man tell you?' Hunsdon asked.

'Very little,' Sir Henry replied. 'A letter reaches me today to say he was found, drowned, at the beginning of March.'

'The Pope?'

'Or Philip of Spain or the Signoria of Venice itself. Or simply drink and a city built on water making for poor bedfellows.' Sir Henry shrugged.

Hunsdon leaned back against the wall of the booth. After a moment he looked down into his tankard and saw it empty in his hands. He put it to one side. 'You'll be looked for in Venice, for certain. The Pope will not sit idly by, not if he learns we may at a stroke unpick all the threads his Jesuits have woven in England. My God, Henry, there's a prize.'

'He'll learn of my embassy, sure, but of my true intent?' answered Sir Henry. 'I am but a simple knight, my concern Venice's pleasures.'

'You'll be watched. The Pope has spies enough to rival even Sir Francis. How will you be free to carry out your business in Venice?'

'I will not be,' said Sir Henry.

'An agent, then?'

'Perhaps.'

'You know the man?' asked Hunsdon.

'Not yet. Such a man would be a lodestone for our enemies' intent. The sacrificial lamb must not have cunning enough to know he is to be sacrificed. Yet, if he is to do good service, he must have cunning enough to live some little time at least.'

The surviving dog darted in again. It twisted past hammering paws to close its jaw about the bear's leg but stayed too long in its triumph. The bear, no longer distracted by the other dog, dug its claws into the dog's back and pinned it. Then it bared its teeth and bent to bite. The second dog's lifeless body was thrown against the pit wall. Hunsdon had already risen.

'You will not stay to see Sackerson fight?' Sir Henry asked.

Hunsdon shook his head. 'I must speak with van Hegan tonight. The Queen will meet with the Dutch soon. I must smooth the way.' He gathered up his cloak. 'I will speak with Walsingham too.'

He turned at the curtain to the booth in which he and Sir Henry had sat.

'I promise nothing.'

A long-tongued, babbling gossip? No, lords, no

William's heart still raced at how close they had come to disaster. Behind him Oldcastle stumbled.

'May God strike me down,' he groaned, 'if ever I turn robber again.'

'Never mind God,' muttered William, 'I shall do so myself.'

The halloo of the Watch could still be heard outside as William pushed his way through the crowd at the Paris Garden, Hemminges and Oldcastle following close behind. Among the gathered multitude the three men disappeared as rain into a river.

'They'll not find us among these many. Take seats. I will get us wine,' William ordered Hemminges and Oldcastle, then disappeared into the crowd. His return some minutes later with a jug of wine was greeted by Oldcastle as the return of the prodigal son. The crowd about William roared their excitement as the bear below threw the last dog against the wall of the bear pit.

'He's leaving.'

'Who is?' asked William as he pushed in beside Oldcastle and Hemminges on the crowded benches.

'Lord Hunsdon,' said Oldcastle.

William peered across the wooden O of the bear pit. He had heard of Lord Hunsdon as a patron of players. He knew him also to be the Queen's cousin. More than that, her half-brother, if rumour were believed, and when was it not? Was there a Boleyn girl that the old King had not lain with? Truly it was good to be the King and so little troubled by the vows of marriage. William's thoughts strayed to Anne and from her to his children, Susanna and the twins, Hamnet and Judith. He missed them.

'The wine, William?' asked Oldcastle, his breath and his appetite regained with remarkable speed.

William scarcely heard him as he passed the jug. He had not reckoned his family would be so present in his thoughts since he came to London. A letter had come from Stratford that day, from his mother. In her terse prose it told him his family were well, thriving. He'd been oddly hurt by the news. How calmly they endured his absence. The same letter brought still less comforting word of the continued rage of Hunt. It was perhaps the distraction of the letter that had led to his agreement to Oldcastle's ill-fated scheme. He tried to dismiss thoughts of Stratford from his mind.

'If our plays ever need a bear,' said Hemminges, 'the part is yours, Will. You shake your head just as that weary beast below.'

'Much to think on,' said William.

In the ring the bear, ragged, bloody and exhausted by its victory, was being hauled from its post. No lull was allowed in the entertainment. As the bear was dragged from the pit two men ran in with baskets of bread. They hurled the loaves into the audience, prompting a small riot of shoving and scrambling as the crowd sought a prize. William watched a fat woman stagger past him wrestling with a much thinner man over one of the loaves.

'Why do we care about Lord Hunsdon coming or going?' William asked, to turn the talk to other topics.

'He's a patron of players,' Oldcastle declared, 'and we are players sorely in need of a patron.'

'There's truth,' said Hemminges. 'We've no talent at robbery. That's certain.'

'We have ended the adventure poorer than we started,' agreed William. 'I am not an experienced thief but I am sure that is not part of the plan.'

'There was a plan?' asked Hemminges.

Oldcastle looked hurt but said nothing. The scheme had been his, a prank on a pompous wool merchant who had offended him. The man was to be fooled into believing he was being robbed by Oldcastle and his companions.

'To fright him from his hubris,' Oldcastle had declared when he laid out the scheme.

Oldcastle had greatly enjoyed the process of dressing up as a highwayman in preparation.

'Do I not resemble the great Tamburlaine himself in all his martial glory?' he demanded of William and Hemminges.

Hemminges had cast his eye over Oldcastle's belly festooned with a multitude of daggers, swords and scabbards. 'You look like the blacksmith's waste heap,' he offered.

A comment that Oldcastle had ignored.

He had paid closer heed to Hemminges' urgent command that the pranksters '*Run!*' when the Watch hove into view. This came just at the point that William realised they were actually robbing the wool merchant rather than simply giving him a fright. The three men had scattered to the musical sound of daggers, swords and various other metal impedimenta clattering to the ground as Oldcastle shed himself of his encumbrances.

In the pit the bread throwers had been replaced by a trio of musicians who were encouraging the crowd to sing along while the arena floor was raked clear of blood and fresh sawdust put down.

William sighed. His arrival in London the previous month had not been followed by many triumphs. None, if he were honest. He'd found no work as a clerk at the Inns of Court in the City, nor found a place in any of the players' companies. His sole piece of good fortune had been to walk past an inn just as Oldcastle had called for ale. No tavern hurly-burly equalled the roar of an Oldcastle deprived of drink. He'd found both Oldcastle and Hemminges within, and they were as entertained to see him as he had been grateful to find friendly faces in a city that had begun to seem set against him.

Hemminges and Oldcastle had proved a mixed blessing. In the first because they could guide him to no work save the chance to earn a few pennies holding the horses of the rich while they attended the plays at the Theatre in Shoreditch. Enough to keep him from sleeping in the rain but little more. In the second because a young man, loosed of family and responsibility in the den of foul licence that was London, could not have found a more unreliable compass of morality than Oldcastle. Nor one better equipped to paint foolish scheme as grand adventure, and William had sorely wanted something grand to justify his exile from Stratford.

'Lord Hunsdon didn't go far,' said William, pointing to where the nobleman had joined another small party further round the ring.

'Oh ho,' said Oldcastle, 'Wingfield and van Hegan.' He turned to William and spoke in conspiratorial tones. 'The rumour of the town has it that Thomas Wingfield is one of Sir Francis Walsingham's hunting dogs. You know who Walsingham is, of course?'

'The Queen's Private Secretary,' said William.

'Say rather the Queen's spymaster,' Oldcastle corrected, 'and chief guardian of our most gracious and Protestant Majesty's virtues and life. Where Wingfield appears it is because Walsingham has put him on the scent. The man he is poking at is a Marcus van Hegan, merchant of the Spanish Netherlands and envoy of Maurice of Nassau. Maurice being, since the murder of his father William the Silent by a Spanish agent, the leader of the rebellion against Spanish rule in the Low Countries.'

'You are remarkably well informed about the affairs of Europe,' said William.

'Shouldn't I be? We are not all country boobs like you, Will,' declared Oldcastle. 'It is my business to portray the great and the good and, therefore, to know of them and their business.'

He paused and steepled his fingers over his prodigious belly. He peered at William out of the corner of his eye.

William stared at Oldcastle, uncomprehending. 'And all this matters because?'

'It matters because of our rebellious Protestant brothers in the Low Countries. They are being crushed beneath the stacked heels of their Spanish masters. And since the Spanish are in ill odour of late, having so foolishly decided to try and snuff out the bright candle of our blessed Queen's life, one suspects that Walsingham intends to add at least a finger's pressure to the Dutch side of the scales. To which end we see his hunting dogs all hugger-mugger with a Dutch carrier pigeon.'

Oldcastle's voice took on a sombre tone. 'England's enemies gather. We are David before the Spanish Goliath. Pray we can find a slingshot in time before war comes to our shores. Oh yes, there is much that our little isle must be concerned with across the waters of the Channel and much to be learned at the bear-baiting. If one only troubles to look.'

'Stop filling the boy's head with nonsense, Nick,' said Hemminges. 'He's trouble enough at his hand without worrying about what the princes of Europe may do.'

Oldcastle gave a snort. 'It surprises me to hear you speak so, Hemminges. You, with your experience.'

'What experience?' William asked.

Both men ignored the question. Oldcastle waved his hand as if to waft away an odour and turned to William.

'Of course, Hemminges has the right of it, as so often. What great ones do, the less will prattle of. In truth, it matters not a jot. Not to us, the humble denizens of London. Not to us, proud Englishmen. These are times of folly and of sport and Christendom is torn with disputes of which that of the Spanish and the Dutch is but one. Yet we sit safe within our fortress isle. Our Channel serving us in the office of a moat.'

'We shall starve in safety,' grunted Hemminges.

'Perhaps not,' said William. 'I have news.'

'You always do,' observed Hemminges.

'Truly you are the Mercury of middle England,' said Oldcastle.

'Hush, Oldcastle,' commanded William. He had waited for this moment and thought of it throughout the chase by the Watch. He would not allow his friends to turn it into a game for wits. 'Have you not lamented of late your lack of employment?'

'We have,' said Oldcastle.

'I have news of fresh work for players,' announced William. 'The word at Court is that the Queen will soon send an embassy to Venice. The Ambassador, Sir Henry Carr, will take a small host with him, including players.'

He looked from Oldcastle to Hemminges but they said nothing.

'This news runs ahead of events,' said William. 'Think, men. You are in a position to present yourselves to this Sir Henry now, before it is generally known and he is drowned in players.'

'It does smack of opportunity,' said Oldcastle.

'Why not *we*?' asked Hemminges.

'What?' asked William.

'Do you not want to be a player?'

'In England maybe, in London certainly,' said William, 'but Venice?'

At this point the conversation was curtailed by a huge roar from the crowd as into the pit was brought a pony with a tiny monkey tied to its back by a chain. The crowd's excitement grew as two bulldogs were loosed into the ring and began to chase the pony, which hurled itself about in fright, desperate to escape. Its thrashings were accompanied by the wild squealings of the monkey clinging to its ears and mane in terror. The sight of which reduced large parts of the audience to tears and howls of laughter.

'What is the source of this gossip?' Hemminges asked over the crowd.

'No one in particular,' replied William.

'Oh hark,' mocked Hemminges, 'the very air itself speaks truths to our country friend.'

'Truly we are blessed, Hemminges, for we stand in the presence of our own English Joan of Arc, who received the voice of God near daily,' pronounced Oldcastle.

'It is well to heed him then, while he lives,' said Hemminges, 'for, as I recall, Joan ended on the fire.'

'You remember right,' said Oldcastle, 'and look, in the reddening of Will's cheek we see the presage of that same fate.'

William cursed his betraying pallor. 'Enough, harpies,' he said. 'A woman told me.'

'Oh ho,' said Oldcastle. 'Her name?'

'Constanza Briaga. She is the daughter of one of the musicians at Court,' said William.

'Oh, we know who she is,' said Hemminges, his brow arched.

'A rare beauty,' said Oldcastle.

'And, through her father, well aware of the news at Court,' said William, ignoring his companions' smiles.

'How came you by this costly songbird's company?' asked Oldcastle.

'Whilst you were doing nothing save rail against fortune, I have been busy,' said William. 'I sought work at the Inns of Court, as a clerk. I found none but I did make the acquaintance of the musicians who play at the barristers' dinners. Through them I met her.'

'There's more to that story than that short telling,' said Hemminges.

'True words, Hemminges,' said Oldcastle, nodding, 'true words.'

'I am lost,' said William. 'I bring you rare intelligence. The chance for employment, for glory on a foreign field. No enthusiasm for the chance. Rather, the messenger mocked.'

'Have a care, Will,' said Hemminges.

'The talk is that Robert Greene has fixed his intent on her and he is a jealous creature,' warned Oldcastle. 'You know Greene?'

'As a playwright,' answered William.

'He is that too,' said Hemminges, 'but chiefly he's a rogue and a dangerous one at that.'

This William had heard already.

'Constanza Briaga is not the only woman in his life,' Oldcastle nodded. 'Greene's wife, if we may grace her with that title, is a notorious bawd. Her brother, a notorious murderer.'

'Greene uses the brother as a guard, though more, I think, for the scandal of it than any need of protection,' added Hemminges.

'Yes, yes, and such scandal too,' added Oldcastle, warming to the gossip. He leaned in to William. 'This murderous brother, Greene's personal praetorian, is known as Cutting Ball because one time he killed a man by –'

'Yes, yes,' interrupted William. 'The warning is well given. I shall be careful. What, though, of the embassy?'

'Do you know Sir Henry Carr?' asked Hemminges.

'No, but by your tone I take it you do,' said William.

'He sits not thirty paces away,' said Oldcastle pointing to the furthest booth. A single figure sat within, small and indistinct. 'Rumour has it that he too is one of Walsingham's hunting dogs, though I do not credit it myself. He lacks the lean look which is their customary apparel.'

'Is that a reason against his patronage?' asked William.

'It is a reason for caution before joining him on an embassy to Venice,' said Hemminges.

'Still,' said Oldcastle, 'gone are the days when we might pick and choose our work. I thank you for the information, Will. We shall think on't.'

William nodded.

'Now, please, I must ask you to be quiet – they are bringing out Sackerson.'

With that instruction Oldcastle turned his attention to the bear pit just as the crowd roared its approval at the entrance of the great bear.

William turned to watch Sackerson brought to the post. The beast's eyes were red-rimmed and sour and it moved with a calm gait quite unlike the other gladiators. It was as if it was too old and experienced to find any relish in its part in the spectacle or fear in the prospect of the battle to come.

William rose to fetch more wine. As he did, his eyes wandered back to the dark alcoves on the far side of the ring. Van Hegan was absorbed by the fight to come. Hunsdon pulled at the beard on his face and leaned back in his seat. Beyond them in the furthest booth sat Sir Henry Carr. Like William, he paid little attention to the bear pit and more to the crowd. William felt a small shudder run through him as it seemed Sir Henry's face turned and held him in its gaze. Then the dogs were released and the crowd surged to its feet in excitement and the face was gone.

According to the statute of the town

Sackerson proved true to his reputation. The great bear brought low four mastiffs before being retired. He had fight still in him but his owners would not risk so famous an attraction. As he left the crowd was treated to a climactic cacophony of fireworks that ended with a rocket fired at a ball suspended in the middle of the arena. It exploded showering apples and pears hidden within it out into the crowd.

William, Oldcastle and Hemminges rose. Being stationed near the back, they were among the first to exit the arena. They stood on Bank Side outside the Paris Garden. The crowd streamed out, flowing round Oldcastle's bulk like water round a rock. Oldcastle was, once again, in full flow to William and oblivious of the obstruction he was causing when the cry came.

'My money, Oldcastle, you fat caitiff.'

An ill-natured and ill-formed ogre with a stye glowing hot beneath his eye confronted them.

'Jesu, Towne,' said Oldcastle under his breath.

'Such good fortune. The debtor, Oldcastle,' cried Towne.

His hands were on his hips and his stye was throbbing. Behind him stood two companions. One was very tall, the other bald and wrinkled; both were rough men with scarred faces.

Towne turned for approval of his observation from his cohorts, who nodded sagely.

'I had thought you fled,' Towne said. 'Where is my money?'

Oldcastle's red features turned a little whey-coloured. He took a faltering step back.

'My dear Master Towne,' he started, 'how good it is to see you and in such fine roaring form.'

'Pox on your verbosity, Oldcastle, you owe me money.'

'Which I shall have for you,' Oldcastle protested. 'This Thursday.'

Towne's fists were clenching and unclenching. He took a step towards Oldcastle. William felt a hand on his shoulder.

Hemminges stepped forward and whispered to William as he passed. 'Be gone, Will. This will grow to a brawl anon.'

Towne pulled up short.

'Sneck up, Hemminges,' he said, 'I've no quarrel with you.'

Towne's eyes were flickering between Hemminges and Oldcastle behind him. The fat man was trying to shuffle back but the press of the crowd, some of whom had stopped to watch this new form of entertainment, prevented him.

'Nor I with you,' answered Hemminges, 'it's been a good day, Towne. Let us have it be a good night also. Nick has said you'll be paid on Thursday.'

'Pox on what he says, Hemminges,' Towne spat. 'Fat guts here has owed me for more than a month now and always on the promise of payment on the morrow. Step aside. I'll have my money or a piece of his flesh.'

Towne looked around for encouragement from his companions. They growled their approval, though William noticed that they hung back. William looked to Hemminges, stood with his arms hanging loosely beside him, and wondered at their caution. To see him was not to know he stood at the centre of a brewing storm. He looked for all the world as if he was simply waiting at the riverside for the fish to bite.

The crowd shoved against William. A cart was emerging from the Bear Garden. It carried a caged bear, sullen and angry from its battles. The carter was trying to force his way through the press of people on Bank Side to get down along the river's edge. The noise and press of people was agitating the beast. As it passed it lurched onto its hind legs, rattled at the cage walls and let out a deep-throated growl.

Heads turned at the noise. One of the scar-faced men with Towne, the tall one, seized on the distraction. With a shout he hurled a wide, clubbing fist at Hemminges. Hemminges ducked slightly and his left fist shot out to slam into the tall man's exposed throat. The tall man staggered back clutching at his neck, hawking and gasping, a noise like a crow cawing. He fell to his knees.

The bald man stepped in, jabbing at Hemminges. Towne thrust out his arms and threw the watching William bodily back against a wall. William's head struck brick and bursts of stars came into his eyes.

Towne turned to join the assault on Hemminges. The bald man threw futilely. Hemminges danced and dodged each blow. He ducked as the bald man charged, slamming two quick hooks into the man's ribs. Little mewls of pain came from the bald man. Hemminges rolled out to the left as the man tried to grapple him close, desperate to still the whirling of those clubbing arms.

Hemminges fought like a graceful demon. In skill he was the match of any one of the two still standing, but Towne and the bald man were no innocents. Though Hemminges skipped and turned they worked to box him in and cut off his movement. Instead of dodging each of the incoming blows, Hemminges was now forced to cover up against them. He turned the strikes off his arms and shoulders as best he could. The bigger men were making their weight tell. Towne, now bleeding from the nose, at last landed a heavy hook that staggered Hemminges, who only just rolled away from another crunching blow that followed.

The tall man's breath was returning and with it thoughts of vengeance. William, shaking his head to bring his battered wits back, saw the tall man push himself up to his knees with one hand while the other reached for a knife hidden in his doublet.

A brawl was about to turn to murder.

With thy sharp teeth this knot intrinsicate

The crowd had parted to form a circle for the combatants. They seemed as happy to roar their approval at the men fighting as they had at bear and dogs. None save William had seen the tall man's knife.

William looked about desperate for aid. His eyes fell on the carter still trying to force his way through the crowd. He ran to the cart and leaped on it, reached around and pulled loose the bolt that held the bear cage shut. The beast burst open the door.

The tall man rose to his feet.

The bear bounded from the cart.

A frightened shrieking came from the crowd, who broke into a fit of shoving as people tried to flee. Hemminges took his moment. He stepped forward, kicking hard. The tall, scarred man was lucky that he had turned at the noise behind him as Hemminges did so. The blow, aimed square between his legs, caught him instead in the thigh. He stumbled back to the ground in pain. Hemminges skipped past him and away from Towne and the bald man.

The tall man picked himself up, looking for Hemminges. Then a roar made him turn.

The bear had been confused by the noise and clatter of the people fleeing. Now it saw before it Towne and his two companions. It set its wrathful heart upon them and reared up to its full height. Long claws still red from the blood of broken dogs were held high above its head. The tall man held his knife before him, eyes bright with horror. A deep and angry growl, rumbling like barrels rolled over cobbles, issued forth from the bear. Towne squealed with fear and turned and fled into the crowd. His equally terrified companions followed. The bear dropped to all fours and loped after them.

The carter was oblivious to the man-made nature of the bear's escape, intent solely on its recapture. William dropped to the ground and worked his way round to where Hemminges stood, breathing hard. Perched on a windowsill above him was Oldcastle.

'An undignified exit. Pursued by a bear,' Oldcastle called out as William approached. 'Did you see Towne run? Did you see?'

Oldcastle was laughing hard though he was in an equally undignified state. It being no easy thing for a man as round as Oldcastle to haul himself up on a narrow ledge and then to cling there.

'How did you get your fat backside up there?' Hemminges enquired of his friend as Oldcastle picked his way down.

'It was a miracle, praise God,' said Oldcastle, 'and thanks be to his servant also, John Hemminges, who like brave Hector before the walls of Troy –'

'Jesu, Nick. Quiet a moment,' said Hemminges.

The words were softly spoken but Oldcastle's mouth shut with a snap. He didn't seem offended.

'You fight very well,' William ventured.

Oldcastle began nodding with enthusiasm. 'Does he not? Yes, yes. Of course, Hemminges was the dancing master to Lord Hunsdon in his time. He moves as quickly and gracefully as the tassel on a spendthrift's purse.'

Hemminges was eyeing William up and down.

'The bear?' he asked.

William nodded; his work.

Hemminges grinned. He turned to Oldcastle. 'For Jesu's sake, pay that lout Towne, will you.'

'That dunghill? That bawd? That scullion?' Oldcastle protested. 'That all-changing word?'

His voice was rising with every spat out name.

Hemminges raised his hands in surrender. 'Enough. You know Towne. You know he'll not let it rest. Will I be there next time?'

'With praetorians such as you and William I fear no enemy,' declared Oldcastle with the boldness that comes from there being no danger at hand.

He clapped his guards about their shoulders and guided them north to the nearest tavern.

These are portents; but yet I hope, I hope

The day after he met with Lord Hunsdon at the Paris Garden Sir Henry had heard nothing. The day after that he received a letter from Walsingham with a single word on it.

'He is agreed,' said Sir Henry to his secretary, Christopher Hall.

'Sir Henry?'

'I have my commission from the Queen and now my cargo from Sir Francis,' said Sir Henry.

Hall coughed. 'The names of the papal spies?' he asked.

'Not in this letter, of course. Sir Francis would not allow such things to be written down. We must meet him at Whitehall. From his mouth to my ear. That is the way of these things.'

Sir Henry looked to his steward, Fallow, who stood before his desk. 'We must make final preparation for the journey to Venice.'

Fallow had fine hair that floated thinly above his pate like weeds wafting in a pond. He carried his ledger with him like a Bible. He was not one for smiles.

'We are advanced in all things, Sir Henry,' his steward answered. 'There is provision for three carts for the journey. The rest will be sent ahead by sea. It must ship within the fortnight if it is to be in Venice before we are.'

'Sir Henry,' Hall ventured in a quiet voice, 'you are certain you do not wish to go by ship?'

'Too dangerous, we would pass too close to Spanish waters,' Sir Henry answered. 'By horseback will do. We must move silently and without drawing attention to our journey.'

He rose from his desk.

'Fetch Watkins please, Christopher,' he said to his secretary. 'You and I must go to Whitehall today.'

Watkins joined Sir Henry and Hall in the hallway of Sir Henry's house.

'Come, Watkins, we must at once to Whitehall to speak to Lord Hunsdon and to Sir Francis Walsingham.' Sir Henry clapped his hands together.

A rare smile came across Watkins' face. It did him no favours since it twisted a face already scarred and broken. A grim face for a manservant but Sir Henry had not employed him for his looks.

'The hoped for news, Sir Henry?' Watkins said.

'Indeed. We are set for Venice. There is much to be done.'

Sir Henry strode for the door with Watkins and Hall following.

'Sir,' Watkins called as he snatched for his sword. 'Let me fetch another man.'

'No time,' Sir Henry said over his shoulder. 'Come, bustle, bustle.'

Sir Henry stepped into the street. It was crowded at this hour. The old man had been given wind by Sir Francis Walsingham's agreement to his plan. He walked with purpose. Sir Henry had feared Hunsdon would be unable to persuade Walsingham. The man was too fixed on the French. Clearly even he had seen the wisdom of Sir Henry's counsel. Pieces in the game breed choices. Who knew to which England might wish to have recourse?

Watkins tried to push ahead, to clear a passage for Sir Henry through the hurly-burly. He struggled to pull on his baldric as he walked. Hall and Sir Henry trailed behind.

'What news of the players?' Sir Henry asked.

'We have not found the right company yet,' Hall replied, steering round a group of apprentices heading to work.

'You have put out the word?'

'I have, Sir Henry, through all routes.'

'Good, good. I must have the right men.' He corrected himself. 'The right man.'

The crush grew greater still as the streets narrowed down towards the River Thames. Watkins was pushed back by the press of the crowd. Sir Henry and Hall slipped on ahead. People filled the gap between them. Watkins struggled against the tide. Sir Henry paused ahead to let a wheelbarrow pass. Watkins closed back on his master. Sir Henry was no more than a sword's length ahead of him.

'What of my friend at Court?' said Sir Henry to Hall in the lull of movement.

'She writes that she has spread the word,' Hall answered.

'No more yet?'

'No.'

'So, so. We must be patient.'

The barrow passed. Sir Henry set off again. Hall struggling to keep pace beside him amid the obstacles of the street, now falling behind, now darting to Sir Henry's side. Ahead lay the river where he would take a boat to Whitehall.

The bell of St Benet's began to ring the hour. Watkins looked up at the sound. He looked back down from the steeple. Ahead a man pressed against the flow of the crowd, heading towards Sir Henry. Watkins felt his teeth grind against each other. The man wore a scarf wrapped round his face, a hat, brim pulled down. Watkins drove against the crowd to catch up to Sir Henry before the masked man reached him. Watkins pushed aside a baker with a tray of buns, ignoring the angry cry. He was too late, the man was at Sir Henry's shoulder.

The man walked past.

Sir Henry's passage was unhindered.

Watkins sighed and slowed and cursed his straining nerves. Then he saw Hall arch and cry.

Watkins started forward.

The masked man turned, took Hall by the shoulder and hauled him to the ground. Sir Henry stared open-mouthed. Iron bloomed in the masked man's fist. His blade came back to strike at Sir Henry. Watkins grappled his arm from behind. The masked man turned and ripped the blade back, scoring Watkins along the palm. The man punched the thin blade at Watkins' gut but Watkins caught his arm and twisted it aside. He cracked his elbow across the man's face. The masked man grunted and pulled his hand back. Watkins went with the pull and drove his knee into the man's stomach. Fingers clawed at Watkins' face. He drove the hand with the blade against the wall, smashing and scraping, ignoring the fingers that reached for his eyes. The knife fell to the ground. Watkins pushed away and reached for his sword. The man leaped after him and Watkins half drew his blade to drive the pommel into the masked man's face. The man staggered back. Watkins drew fully and thrust.

The bell of St Benet's had not yet finished the hour's toll.

The masked man was pinned to the wall. His hands pulled and fluttered at the rapier. Watkins stepped back and kicked him in the gut, pulling his sword free. The masked man slid down the wall. His hands reached feebly for his doublet. Watkins lifted his knee and drove his heel forward into the man's face. He heard bone crack. The masked man moved no more, save slowly to keel over.

Watkins looked about. Sir Henry stood in an empty street that had been full a moment before. At his feet lay his secretary, Christopher Hall. Sir Henry bent to the man. Watkins looked away to scan the road. He could see no other danger. In the distance he heard the cry for the Watch. He bent to search the masked man's body.

'He's dead, Watkins.'

Watkins turned at his name. Sir Henry was kneeling by his secretary's body. His hand held the dead man's.

'So is this one,' Watkins answered.

'Good,' said Sir Henry.

After a moment he continued. 'Good. Though it might have been as well to question him.'

Sir Henry rose and looked up at his manservant. Watkins threw something to him.

'All that he had upon him, Sir Henry. Hidden in his doublet. He reached for it as he lay dying.'

Sir Henry looked at the rosary and then threw it aside. He walked over to where the murderer's blade lay. A thin weapon, all point, a stiletto.

'The back thrust as he passed, Sir Henry,' said Watkins. 'Your good fortune that poor Christopher moved behind you as he struck.'

'Poor Christopher,' said Sir Henry, still looking at the stiletto on the ground.

'I am sorry, Sir Henry, I failed you,' said Watkins as he looked at Hall's body.

Sir Henry did not answer him. He was thinking that the Cardinal Montalto was a worried man.

Live scandalised and foully spoken of

William sat under the stable roof at the Theatre. A smile was on his lips. A horse blanket was pulled around him against an April chill. A stub of quill was in his hand and, balanced on his knee, a small scrap of paper. Onto it William dripped poison line by line.

Towne's rout at the Paris Garden had been but a partial victory. Hemminges had made Oldcastle pay his debt to Towne. That had served to blunt the sharpness of Towne's anger at Oldcastle but had not broken it. William's role in the fight had added him to the list of those against whom Towne took offence. Now, where he could, Towne menaced Oldcastle and William both. Hemminges he gave greater respect, leading Oldcastle to trail after Hemminges like an infant seeking protection under his mother's dress. William had racked his mind for some way to fend Towne off, but none presented itself.

With no plan to defeat the ogre William had settled for petty revenge. He had penned a series of scandalous verses that questioned Towne's parentage and appearance. His favourite had made a strong argument, in rhyme, for Towne's visits to the Paris Garden being born of too great a love for dogs. To find a rhyme for 'unnatural' had been no small matter. William had pinned the poems about Shoreditch where all might read them.

He had expected nothing from the verses but the lustful pleasure of vengeance. For certain, there had been that. Yet more too, and oddly. Towne had seemed cowed by them. Since first William published them a week had passed. In that time, as the poems made him meat for public mockery, Towne had seemed to diminish, eaten up by the contempt of him they generated. He still menaced Oldcastle and William when the chance presented itself. Yet that was less often. Towne ventured abroad less. Nor did his friends seem so many or so willing to support him. William had revelled in the power of his words even as he wondered at it.

That William was the author became known without him publishing the fact. He had used old scraps to write on, bills for plays at the Theatre or the bear-baiting at the Paris Garden. Still, the hand was the same and the rivalry between Oldcastle and Towne well known, as was William's part as Oldcastle's ally. So it was that occasional compliments were sent William's way for a well-turned barb. Compliments that were no argument against the practice either. Even Hemminges, happy to be released from the constant care of Oldcastle by Towne's cowing, had recited a line to William.

'Ho, William, writing to your wife?'

William looked up to see Oldcastle. A pang of guilt went through him. He should be writing to his family. Not penning poems to punish a man more fool than villain. He tucked the scrap away unfinished.

Oldcastle ushered a short man towards him, Sir Henry Carr. William saw him close for the first time. Sir Henry wore a doublet of thick cloth embroidered with gold thread and pearls. Fine lace was stitched to cuff and collar. They were the clothes of a wealthy man. They were askew. William realised that the buttons on the front were in the wrong holes. The man appeared not to have noticed. In appearance he hardly seemed a likely candidate for one of the spymaster Walsingham's brotherhood. Behind Sir Henry, hanging back by the entrance to the courtyard of the Theatre with his hand on the pommel of his sword and his head turning like the swivel gun on a ship's deck, stood a figure more suited to the part. Neither Oldcastle nor Sir Henry introduced him.

Sir Henry peered at William.

'This is your poet, is it, Master Oldcastle?'

'Indeed, Sir Henry, William Shakespeare,' said Oldcastle. 'This is Sir Henry Carr, William, a great patron of our Theatre.'

Sir Henry smiled benignly at Oldcastle's praise.

'Your poem, Shakespeare,' said Sir Henry to William, 'very good. Most entertaining. I hear the hero of it is most cowed by his new fame.'

'Like a whipped cur, Sir Henry,' Oldcastle said. 'William saw where the hurt would lie greatest and stuck his pen in there.'

William wondered that his scraps of poetry should have come to the attention of one such as Sir Henry. He opened his mouth to curb Oldcastle's boasting but Sir Henry, appearing not to notice, spoke on.

'Perhaps you would be so kind as to pen something on my behalf?'

'Of course,' said William. In this flood of conversation it seemed easiest to be swept along.

Sir Henry nodded as if William's agreement was a foregone conclusion. The little man studied him carefully and it was a moment before William realised that Sir Henry did not intend to speak.

'Sir Henry, I am sorry, sir, do you –'

'Yes?'

'Did you have a theme?' William asked.

'Of course, Shakespeare. Love is the theme,' said Sir Henry. 'I am courting and I have come to the view that a love finely expressed in poetry would serve my purpose rather well. It is not a talent that I possess, but Master Oldcastle has convinced me that you do. It should be short.'

'A sonnet?' William asked.

'If you like. As you like. I do not seek to control the muse within you.'

Oldcastle was nodding at Sir Henry's words like a horse trying to shoo away a flea.

'It would be good,' Sir Henry said, 'were the poem to include some unflattering comparisons between my person and that of an importunate rival for my beloved's affections.'

He paused here and looked meaningfully between Oldcastle and William.

'I think you understand, Master Oldcastle,' he said.

'I do, I do, Sir Henry,' said Oldcastle.

'Good, good. Well then, it is settled. Would you fetch it to me the day after tomorrow, at noon? Good. Well done.'

Sir Henry nodded at Oldcastle and William, turned and went. The scarred man at the gate fell in beside him. William stared.

'You may understand what has just happened, Nick, but I have no clue.'

Oldcastle was smiling. 'A patron, you young hawker.' He clapped William on the back. 'What has happened is that you have got yourself a patron and a good one at that. If you don't make a mess of it.'

'He only wants a poem, Nick,' said William.

'Today,' replied Oldcastle, 'today he wants a poem. Tomorrow perhaps more. Make yourself useful to him and who knows what may come of it?'

'Why me?' William asked.

' "Towne's Dropsy", I imagine. Very good, very sharp.' Oldcastle paused to chuckle and hum a line from William's most recent poem.

William rolled his eyes. Such a road to success he was walking.

'What did he mean about the love rival?'

'Ah, yes,' said Oldcastle. 'Sir Henry, for all his years, has a roving eye. He has settled his intent on a lady at the Court. He did not confide in me the lady's name. A beauty no doubt, and educated too. Of course, with a connoisseur's eye, one must expect others to look with interest on the same choice. So it is with Sir Henry.'

'And I am to traduce this rival?' asked William. 'God above, what a way to earn the enmity of powerful men.'

'Oh you'll like this,' said Oldcastle. 'Sir Henry's rival is not another noble.'

'No?'

'Far from it. It is the playwright, Greene.'

'Robert Greene? Jesu, that's worse yet.'

'I know, I know,' Oldcastle chuckled to himself, 'such a temper on that little rampallian. Now another reason for him to take against you to add to your pursuit of Constanza Briaga.'

Oldcastle's eye gleamed at the prospect. 'You've none to blame but yourself,' he said. 'It was your suggestion.'

'Mine?'

'Did you not say that Hemminges and I should speak to Sir Henry about his embassy? And so we did.'

'I thought Hemminges feared to join with the deadly spy.'

'William, William, it is Hemminges' nature to be all caution. But look upon the man, Sir Henry. I ask you, is this the dress of a hell-black intelligencer? 'Sides, I am cut from bolder cloth and Hemminges was swayed by my arguments.'

'So, my news was profitable after all.'

'Not yet, not yet.' Oldcastle waggled a finger. 'Sir Henry must take soundings first. There was much talk about the delicacy of his embassy, the troubled lands we would cross, the dangers and opportunities of

Venice. He demands men he can trust. I ask you, do Hemminges and I not scream trustworthiness in our every breath?'

He did not wait for reply. 'All the more reason to do great work on your poem. It was at my recommendation after all that you received the commission. Do not show my judgment false. Something truly scandalous about Greene is called for. My, how he will rage at you for it.'

William thought Oldcastle's enjoyment at his predicament most unbecoming. Misguided too.

'Greene will not know of my involvement,' he reminded Oldcastle. 'He'll think it Sir Henry's work.'

Oldcastle raised an eyebrow in response. 'Tush, lad. Everyone will know. Sir Henry's care is not to be seen as the best poet but as the man who can hire the best. Oh, Greene will know. Know and care too. Now set to it.'

Their best conscience is not to leave't undone, but keep't unknown

It was a private room, upstairs at the Star on Fleet Street. Small and sparely furnished, the sound of the tavern below and the stink of the River Fleet beyond the window filtering up to fill the space. No one would choose it for romance. It was no blossomed bower with bed of gentle moss. It did, however, have two doors; one reached by the stairs at the front and one by those at the back. Seeing one man enter by the front stairs no one need know another had entered by the back. How Constanza Briaga knew of it William did not like to ask.

William admired her hair, so dark as to seem ripples of ebony. For a moment he forgot they were arguing.

'I would rather you were the subject,' William protested.

'And yet I am not,' said Constanza.

William wished he had never mentioned his commission from Sir Henry. A boast to Constanza had become a battleground. So it had been at each of their meetings. Constanza had a limitless capacity for finding the hidden insult in even the most fulsome praise. To talk of others in her presence was insult in itself. Were she not so fair, William thought, would I endure this Sisyphean courtship? So far there was little to show for it.

Constanza's invitation to meet had reached him at a melancholy moment. Sir Henry's commission weighed upon William. When his poetry had been for his pleasure alone, it flowed from him freely. Writing for another seemed to dam the river. The clock tolled the time till he was supposed to present his poem to Sir Henry; he had nothing to show. It is one thing to think one's hand stayed by the demands of responsibilities and the expectations of parents. It is another to find oneself freed of constraints and the hand still not moving. William's melancholy was the worse for feeling that, in a London full of frustrations and disappointments, opportunity had presented itself and he was unable to seize it.

He had seized instead on the distraction of her invitation. Constanza Briaga was a mystery in which he could lose himself. Strange above all other things was her interest in him. He had seen her the first time shortly after he arrived in London. She had sat quietly listening to the musicians, her father among them, entertain the barristers of the Middle Temple. Dark haired and olive skinned, a bird of exotic plumage. He'd shared a meal with the musicians that night.

'Is it polite to stare?' she'd leaned to his ear to ask him as she passed to her place at the table.

'No,' he'd whispered back, 'but staring at the sun I shall be blinded anyway. The punishment follows the pleasure.'

Not his best line. Not even a good one. He was too busy cursing himself for being caught admiring her to think of better.

She'd laughed anyway. 'Yes, I see your cheeks are already burning.'

When you're discovered, best to be bold, he thought. William had taken his cue.

Now, in the upstairs room of the Star, his cheeks were burning again. This was not how he had hoped the meeting would go. He tried to mollify her.

'Sweetling, you know of great men and their desires, tell me what will please Sir Henry.'

'Why should I know of great men's desires?' Constanza demanded.

'For one, you are a thing much desired,' said William.

'A jewel, perhaps?' she asked.

William saw the danger. 'No, no, sweetling. Not an ornament, not a bauble. No trophy to be displayed.'

'Go on,' said Constanza.

Her eyes were fixed on him. William felt tired. He was not equal to this struggle. He'd hoped for solace from his difficulties. He found himself wrestling with a wolf. No, not a wolf.

'You're like a hawk,' he said, 'prized for her sleek plumage, yes, but desired for the power and the thrill that comes from seeing her fly and fall and strike.'

He had struck his own target. She rewarded him with a smile. Constanza settled back into her chair.

'Do you know this woman that your patron woos?' she asked.

'I don't. That's part of what plagues me. I have nothing to feed off,' William answered.

'Bare imagination is not adequate?'

'So far, no.'

'Take Sir Henry, then, for your inspiration,' she suggested.

William shook his head. 'Worse yet. He's no subject for a poem. Short, addled in manner and in dress. I've scarcely seen him but I hope him wealthy. There's little else to draw a woman in.'

Constanza's fan snapped out and struck him gently on the arm.

'You would be surprised what we women prize,' she said. 'Very well, then, not the lover but the rival.'

'Greene?'

'Now there's a man,' said Constanza.

William thought of his friends' warning. What was Robert Greene to Constanza or she to him? He dared not ask. She was already more dangerous to approach than a sharp-quilled porpentine. He'd only just coaxed a smile from her. Besides, her idea had merit. William longed to see Greene, who it seemed was both his and Sir Henry's rival.

'You are as clever as you are beautiful,' he said.

William took her hand to kiss it. She drew it from him.

'Your hand has other work,' she said. 'The poem will not write itself.'

It seemed she was not entirely soothed.

'I am told,' said Constanza rising from her seat, 'that Robert Greene can oft be found at the George and Dragon in Southwark.'

William rose too but Constanza was already at the door.

'If you hurry, you may find him there while it is still light enough to see him clearly.' She smiled and pulled the door closed behind him.

… most capricious poet, honest Ovid

An argument between lovers is not, in the ordinary way, conducive to the poet's art. Yet, to William's surprise, his muse had seen fit to turn up for the fight. After Constanza's dismissal he had spent a profitless evening trying to find Robert Greene. There was no sign of him at the George and Dragon in Southwark, which was filled with sailors from all the ports of Europe. He had stamped his way home to his lodging in the dark and gone to bed in a foul mood. He had risen with images of nations at war as the guiding conceit for his sonnet turning in his mind. Yet each time he raised his hand to write a word he was prevented by thought that there was a better one.

William distracted himself with a battered copy of Ovid from the small collection of books kept in the Theatre. Here was a poet who understood there were no perfect words or perfect images of love. William need only find one perspective. Better yet, find two and set them in reflection on each other. This frame of mind acquired, the sonnet fell upon his page full-formed.

He took it to Sir Henry.

William finished the recitation, put the page down and looked up at his audience. He stood in the parlour of Sir Henry's house at the centre of a small circle of chairs. To his front, Sir Henry, dishevelled and smiling. To his right, Lord Hunsdon. To his left a third man, stern and pale-faced in black garments. This third man had not smiled since William had entered.

'I like it, Master Shakespeare,' Sir Henry said.

He plucked up the page.

'I take it I am Mars, the God of War?' he said as he scanned it.

'Just so, Sir Henry,' said William, casting his eye about his audience. He had never stood among so many great ones before. Sir Henry had not seen fit to introduce him to the other men before making him speak his poem out loud. He knew Lord Hunsdon by Oldcastle's pointing him out at the Paris Garden. The other's face tickled his remembrance but could not be placed.

'You write a fair hand, Master Shakespeare,' said Sir Henry. 'You speak Latin?'

'Well enough, Sir Henry, though I have not that facility I would wish with it.'

'Greek?' asked Sir Henry.

'Less, Sir Henry.'

'I am surprised, Master Shakespeare,' said Sir Henry. 'You seem to have a facility with language.'

'My schoolmaster thought as you did,' answered William. 'I have considered the issue.'

'Your conclusion?'

'I love our native tongue,' said William. 'Whenever I try to speak in another I think only of how much more eloquently I would express myself in English. It is as though suddenly finding oneself hobbled, a single leg, where a moment before one ran like a greyhound. I dislike the feeling.'

Sir Henry reached out and plucked a sheet of paper from the table. 'Read this,' he said.

William took it from his grasp and saw it was a letter in Latin.

'Out loud, if you please,' said Sir Henry. 'In English.'

William paused and scanned the first line. He longed to know what this mummery was about. Perhaps Sir Henry simply sought to have his paid-for poet perform for his guests. The man's motives were as confused as his clothing.

William began: 'To our beloved and most trusted Henry Carr, Knight. To your special trust ... no, to your special care we entrust this embassy.'

'Thank you,' said Sir Henry.

He reached out and took the letter from William's hand. Placing it down he picked up the poem again and scanned it.

'This should do very well. Very well, indeed. What do you think, Hunsdon?'

Lord Hunsdon nodded, looking at William. 'Yes, it might serve your purpose well, Henry.'

Sir Henry took a purse from his doublet, produced coins and handed them to William.

'I shall need another poem,' Sir Henry said.

'Of course,' replied William, feeling the weight of the coins heavy in his hand.

'Of my rival, though,' Sir Henry said, 'a little too little, I think.'

'He is portrayed as Vulcan, Sir Henry,' said William, put out, 'crippled god, cuckolded husband of Venus, jealous, betrayed.'

'Oh, clever enough, Master Shakespeare,' said Sir Henry, 'and yet –'

'And yet, Sir Henry?' prompted William.

'Will all your audience understand the allusion? Are you perhaps being a little too clever?'

'Too clever?'

'Something a little more direct next time, I think, don't you?' said Sir Henry.

'Of course,' said William.

Of course, for Greene the grudge-bearer, thought William, Sir Henry wants an insult more obvious, a slander more direct. Never mind Robert Greene was a man as well known for the holding of grudges as for the writing of plays. Oh well, William thought as he departed, at least I shall die a poet.

How now? A rat?

Alice Hunt crept down the central staircase of Sir Henry's town house and prayed she was not discovered. She screwed her courage to the sticking place. She had to know why William had come there and why her father hid from him. The hall was empty but she did not wish to be found by any of Sir Henry's servants. Least of all by Watkins, Sir Henry's manservant, whose scarred face with its twisted, broken nose had frightened her from first sight of it. The man moved so quietly she did not dare believe he was not behind her at any moment. Yet she dared not stay above. Not since she had seen William.

Alice had learned to move in silence over many years evading her mother and father. Only by such subtle movements had she held any freedom at all. She moved as close to the door of the parlour as she dared. What was William, the over-bold cause of so much pleasure and punishment, doing in their host's house? What was her father about? The announcement of William's arrival had been like a hawk appearing among doves. Sir Henry, her father's master, Sir Thomas Lucy, and another guest of Sir Henry's, Lord Hunsdon, had set to hurried conversation. At the end of which the three had gone into the parlour and her father had ducked into the alcove in the hall and pulled across the curtain.

As soon as William had left, her father had emerged from behind the arras in the hall and gone into the parlour. She could hear his voice now, excitement warring with anger.

'It is him, Sir Thomas. Out of any doubt, Sir Thomas, it is him.'

'As Walsingham's report suggested,' came a voice she thought to be that of their host, Sir Henry Carr.

Then the dour voice of her father's master, Sir Thomas Lucy. 'If that is so, Sir Henry, have a care. This William Shakespeare is of a family tainted by recusant sympathies, though of his father I have heard only good report. By my man Hunt's witness, Shakespeare is himself of questionable morality.'

'I am always careful, Sir Thomas. That is why I sought to know if you knew aught of the fellow.'

Sir Henry's voice again. He seemed a harmless old man, who'd pinched her cheek when she was introduced to him. Yet, she'd noted, her father was not his usual intemperate self in Sir Henry's presence. Sir Henry's voice had lost some of the gentleness it held when he had spoken to her.

'You had reason to ask.'

A fourth voice that she took to be Lord Hunsdon. Alice had not been introduced to him but she had heard the servants' gossip about him, the Queen's cousin.

'How so?' Sir Thomas asked.

'There have been –' Sir Henry paused, '– oddities of late. That have prompted caution.'

Lord Hunsdon snorted. Sir Henry made no comment on his laughter but continued speaking. 'Walsingham believes the Spanish have agents in the city.'

'Or Montalto.' Lord Hunsdon's voice.

'The Cardinal?' asked Sir Thomas. 'What interest has he in England?'

Sir Henry ignored the question. 'So you see, Sir Thomas, I am grateful for your care, your most gentle care, but all is well in hand.'

'Yes, yes, Hunt. I am quite aware of that.' Sir Thomas again. Her father must have whispered something to him. Alice's curiosity overcame her. Looking about to reassure herself that the hall of the house was empty, she crept closer to the parlour and peered through the crack between door and frame. Her father stood behind Sir Thomas's chair, bent to whisper in his ear. No easy pose for one so massy as her father.

'My steward reminds me that this Shakespeare already stands accused of poaching,' Sir Thomas said.

'And more,' hissed her father.

'Enough, Hunt,' Sir Thomas rebuked him.

Alice could not see her father's face but in the trembling of his frame she could see his anger. For a month now, since the night he had almost caught her with William, her father had kept her at his side. Watching her always. A dog that might stray if not leashed. To be with William had seemed to be finally free of the heavy hand of her father. It had been a freedom brief and passing. Replaced with a shorter chain, a smaller cage.

'There must be some reckoning,' Sir Thomas continued. 'My steward has the right of it there. Justice must be done.'

'I may need him,' said Sir Henry. 'You know how England is beset, Sir Thomas. That is why you and your fellow members of the House of Commons are called to London. The war in the Netherlands, the Spanish unfurling their war banners, the Earl of Leicester's expedition, the French.'

'What do the Dutch or the French or even the Spanish have to do with your embassy to Venice?' Sir Thomas asked.

'I go to seek Venetian aid.'

'Why would papist Venice help Protestant England?'

'For religion Venice has little care. But for commerce? Everything,' Sir Henry answered. 'Venice is wounded. The Turk has harried them from their former holdings in the Mediterranean. Philip has done them harm too. The Spanish route to the Indies round the Cape has cut Venice's monopoly on that trade. If England will promise to set our ships on the Spanish galleons that go south to the Cape then that monopoly is restored and Venice's fortunes with it. They need do little in return save lend us money and be our ally.'

Sir Thomas shook his head. Alice caught a look of frustration pass across Sir Henry's face. Sir Henry shrugged and held out his arms.

'It suffices that there are plans afoot in which the lad Shakespeare may play a role.' Sir Henry looked up at Hunt's heaving bulk. 'If it makes your man content it is a dangerous part this Shakespeare would play, and all unknowing of it.'

'So certain he's the man for your plotting?' Lord Hunsdon asked.

'He has the qualities I sought. Clever, writes a fair hand, a player,' said Sir Henry.

'Yet not to be trusted. His family are known to favour Rome,' interjected Sir Thomas.

'He does not seem religious. And that he comes from popish stock, that may prove to my advantage,' said Sir Henry. 'Being thought he is of doubtful loyalty to his Protestant masters, that he is their agent becomes less apparent.'

Sir Henry looked from Lord Hunsdon to Sir Thomas.

'Gentlemen, I am not so foolish as to fix on him all untried. He will be tested.'

Hunt bent again and hissed in his master's ear loud enough for all to hear. 'There must be justice, Sir Thomas. Where is England if the law yields to expediency?'

'The law or revenge?' Sir Henry asked.

Sir Thomas waved Hunt back and turned to Sir Henry. 'I do not wish to cause your plans to go awry, Sir Henry, but I must insist that this man be held to account. My position in the county would be undermined if it were known I had a poacher in my grasp and let him go.'

Sir Henry gave a bark of frustration. 'What does Warwickshire matter when England is the stake?'

Lord Hunsdon held up his hand for peace. He leaned forward. 'Sir Thomas, you are a Justice of the Peace, what sentence for the poacher of –'

'A deer,' said Sir Thomas, ignoring Hunt's mewl of protestation behind him. 'Whipping.'

'Then why not both at once?' Lord Hunsdon turned to Sir Henry. 'Why not let justice serve your purpose?'

'How so?' Sir Henry asked.

'Is the lad to be trusted, even in the fire? That is what you wish to know, Henry,' said Lord Hunsdon. 'Very well then, give him something precious to guard and see if it can be beaten from him.'

Alice clapped her hand to her mouth.

'A little crude,' said Sir Henry.

'Yet to the point,' Sir Thomas added. 'Yes, I see the sense in it, Lord Hunsdon. I have no doubt it would satisfy my man here.'

Sir Thomas did not turn to see if Hunt was, indeed, sated by the prospect of a beating for William. His eyes remained on Sir Henry, as did Lord Hunsdon's. The little man leaned back in his chair, hands steepled in front of his mouth.

'Hardly justice,' he muttered behind his fingers.

After a moment he nodded. 'The greater good needs must give ear to expedient measure.' He looked up at Hunt. 'It shall be so.'

Alice backed away from the door. She must warn William. She stumbled into something, turned and saw the face of Watkins, Sir Henry's servant, behind her. She gave a strangled squeal and fled upstairs to her room. Watkins watched her go.

And, by that destiny, to perform an act

For the second poem William had tried again to find Greene. Two days of hunting led to no more success on this occasion than the first. The absence of information made the writing of the second poem both easier and harder. Easier in that he did not feel himself constrained by too many points of reference. Harder in that there was no obvious starting point. In the end William played with names. 'Greene' youth and strongly rooted old oak formed the conceit. William found that the theme, once found, gave birth to imagery with little further effort. A drooping willow's branches and the upthrust trunk of the oak happily suggested themselves as contrasts, to the praise of Sir Henry's vigour and the clear slander of Robert Greene's virility. It was not a subtle piece. William doubted that Sir Henry wanted it so.

'Delightful ostentation in the imagery, Master Shakespeare,' said Sir Henry, 'I congratulate you.'

They were in Sir Henry's study. Sir Henry held a distract air. His ruff drooped on one side. A half-played game of chess sat upon his desk beside a plate of half-eaten bread. A crumb could be seen poised on his lip. Sir Henry's eyes did not leave the paper where William's poem was written, even as he fished about within his doublet and pulled out a small velvet bag that he held out to William. Here was something. More coin for writing even if it came by way of ditties to serve an old man's lust. William felt the weight of the little bag. This labour was a marked advance on the shovelling of horse manure.

The rummaging process had left Sir Henry's clothing in still greater disarray. He made no move to straighten it. By his look, William thought, no man would credit Sir Henry as a master of the Court's intrigues. His speech was another thing entirely.

'I shall need another, Master Shakespeare, and quickly too,' said Sir Henry. 'I leave for Venice in a few days. I wish to secure my position before I depart.'

'I understand, Sir Henry,' said William. 'Your embassy has been spoken of to me. As has your need for players –'

Sir Henry interrupted. 'Not just any players, Master Shakespeare. I go as representative of England. The task is delicate, the times, the journey, perilous. I would take with me only those I can trust without question. There is the challenge, for who can trust players? It is their business to dissemble.'

'Some would say it is their business to speak the truth of the part they play,' said William.

'Now we depart into matters philosophical when my concerns are practical,' said Sir Henry. 'Still, no matter. I shall resolve the problem.'

'I am certain of it,' said William, sensing the theme was now closed before, to his frustration, he could plead for his companions' employment.

Sir Henry pointed to a stiff-backed chair beside the desk and took his own seat in a wing-backed chair ornate with carving. His head sank back into the cushioning and the wings of the chair took his face into shadow.

'You are a player?' asked Sir Henry.

'I am of their company, yes.' William supposed that he was entitled to make this answer at least.

'The plays are popular.'

William was not sure if this was a question or a statement. He waited for Sir Henry to come to his point.

'The players' companies have the common ear. Matters may be –' Sir Henry paused to search for the word, '– discussed on a stage that would be addressed too directly otherwise. That is why I like them. I go to see them less for the play itself than to hear at which lines the groundlings roar. People give their unguarded opinion at an entertainment, if one pays attention. And you yourself are a playwright?'

'A beginner only,' William replied with a nod of the head.

'What matter do you write of?'

'Thus far? Love only. The tale of Tristan and Iseult.'

'Strange to take so ancient a tale when there is so much afoot in the world today.'

'The past is prologue to the present. By writing of what went before I might understand what happens now.'

'Such a playwright might prove prognosticator also.' Sir Henry leaned forward and took two other sheets of paper from the desk. As he spoke he began to fold them and prepare the wax for sealing.

'Perhaps you would be so good as to do me a further service, Master Shakespeare?' he asked.

'Your servant, Sir Henry.' William bowed his head.

The older man smiled up at William as he folded closed the poem.

'It would not be seemly for me to be seen to deliver the poem myself,' Sir Henry said, 'my servants' employ is known. Besides which, all are busy with preparation for the embassy. You, however, are a stranger and might, in discretion, deliver the poem you have written.'

'With pleasure, Sir Henry,' William said.

Sir Henry nodded benignly. He folded the paper on the table closed and tucked the folded poem inside. He sealed the paper and held it out to William. As William reached for it Sir Henry pulled it back.

'I can trust your discretion, Master Shakespeare?'

William raised his eyebrows at the question. 'Of course, Sir Henry.'

The packet was proffered again.

'I hope so,' said Sir Henry. 'Your memory is good?

'I believe so,' William replied.

Sir Henry spoke an address. 'See it in the lady's hand and none others.'

'It is done, Sir Henry.'

'I am grateful,' Sir Henry said and watched him go.

After a moment a knock came. Sir Henry looked up. 'All is in readiness?' he asked the figure who looked in.

'I have set a man to trail him, Sir Henry.'

'Call him back. He may make the lad suspect when there is no need. Shakespeare will go by Ludgate. Wait for him there.'

The door closed.

Try what my credit can in Venice do

William pressed himself to the shadows of the stable wall at the Theatre. He had come there straight from Sir Henry's house. He'd taken the short route through the back garden, and thank God, for it had saved him stumbling on unwelcome company.

In the courtyard of the Theatre William saw Towne, cross-armed and smug. Beside him a man, in garments that had once been rich but were now stained and tattered, prodded Oldcastle in the chest with a finger. Oldcastle, despite his bulk, staggered at each sharp thrust. This was Robert Greene, or William was no judge. Towne must have told him of William's role in the first of Sir Henry's poems. An ally for Towne against the vile verses of William's that plagued them both.

Greene finished Oldcastle off with a final thrust of his finger. Then he threw his cloak about his shoulder with a flourish that belied its ragged edge and stalked away. Towne stumped after, grinning. William waited till he was certain both had gone and then stole into the courtyard.

'Damnable twice-faced rogue,' Oldcastle growled. 'A face so tart it would sour good wine.'

Greene, Oldcastle judged, was safely out of hearing him. He gave full vent.

'Ah, Will,' he cried at the sight of William approaching, 'you have just missed my defence of your honour. That scoundrel Greene was here, searching for you. Brave fortune that he should have found me instead and was outfaced. Turned tail and fled before your return.'

Oldcastle gave a great heaving sigh as if sorely tried by the battle with Greene. He sank to a bench nearby and fanned himself.

'Greene, Towne and full two others of Towne's company,' said Oldcastle, 'cowards all in the face of my steel.'

'I saw all, Oldcastle,' said William.

Oldcastle looked quickly up.

'I am conscious of your bravery on my behalf,' said William. 'You must be parched.' He took one of the coins Sir Henry had pressed on him and, calling over a stableboy, sent him to fetch a pot of ale.

'Most kind and most true, Will,' said Oldcastle, relieved as much that his lie would not be presented to him as for the prospect of the ale to come.

Hemminges approached. 'Did I see Robert Greene pass? Trailing Towne behind him like a comet of ill omen.'

'You did,' said Oldcastle. 'The surly dog and six or seven knaves wished me to pass a threatening message on to Will.'

'Six or seven?' William asked.

'Seven at least. All demanding that I pass on their threats to William. I declined to do so. It did Greene no honour to speak it and will do me none to repeat it. Besides, William is not one to be frightened by threats from one such as Greene.'

Oldcastle's own whey complexion suggested that he, on the other hand, might well be.

'Such a day of messages it has been,' Oldcastle continued. 'Not all of them so harshly spoken.'

Oldcastle dug into his doublet and pulled a sealed letter from it. William recognised Constanza Briaga's hand. William slit the seal. It was an invitation to meet her that same day, at the room above the Star.

'It's as well that we will be off to Venice soon,' said Hemminges, 'between Sir Henry's verses and –' he paused to point at the letter, '– other things. If you stay, Will, you're like to be murdered in your bed.'

'Me?' said William. 'I'm not for Venice.'

'You think Sir Henry's interest is only in your poetry?' said Oldcastle. 'I've read your poems, Will.'

William shook his head. 'I'm no player and it's players Sir Henry wants for Venice.'

'You could be,' said Hemminges, 'with work.'

'True,' acknowledged Oldcastle. 'Poor player you may be, yet what might you become? Besides, few players can turn their hand to writing as you can. You are a coin Sir Henry can spend twice.'

'For certain,' said Hemminges, 'if Sir Henry asks for us he will ask for you too.'

'Venice is very far,' William said.

'It is. Venice is the East and mystery and splendour.' Oldcastle sighed at the promised sights. 'All men speak of it, of its wealth and wonders. You would think their fascination witch-born so deep it runs.'

'It's a kind of madness,' Hemminges added. 'You have but to speak the name of Venice and all will stop and listen to you. It's a wonder every other play, every other book is not set in that city.'

Oldcastle nodded in agreement. 'What is the latest play? *The Venetian Comedy*. What that piece had to do with Venice heaven alone knows, or with comedy for that matter. God's wounds, add the name of Venice to aught and, no matter how dull the matter, the common man will flock to see it: *The General of Venice* by Robert Greene. There, 'tis done.'

Hemminges joined the game. 'Duller matter still, *Venice and the Turk*: a tragedy in five acts; *The Tailor of Venice*: a comedy.'

Oldcastle slapped his hand on his thigh, his good humour now restored after Greene's departure, and with this talk of Venice, a great smile spread across his face. 'And this lustre shall be added to ours on our return,' he said, 'no longer Englishmen but Venetians.'

This business at the Theatre had been a distraction. William had a poem to deliver. He was curious to see Sir Henry's lady. Yet to go by Fleet Street was but a small diversion. He left Hemminges and Oldcastle behind but carried their discussion with him. William wanted none of Venice. He had barely left Stratford. He was already far from family.

One half of Sir Henry's money was already spent. The other William had sent to Stratford. With it a letter for his mother with news of his patron and none of his work as a groom at the Theatre. His mother had sent two letters to this one of his. The last again spoke of the quiet contentment of his family. His mother had been frank, shorn of his restless presence there was a calm that had not been there before. Was I so full of self-concern that I did not see how my family suffered for it, thought William? He knew the answer and did not like it.

The thought of Venice troubled him. That Sir Henry would ask him to go now seemed to him probable. How else to explain the strange questioning about his Latin when he delivered the first poem? Or Sir Henry seeking to know if he was a player and a playwright when he delivered the second? William turned into Fleet Street, uncertain if to go to Venice was to seize on fortune's gift or to show himself still restless.

Be Mercury, set feathers to thy heels

'If Sir Henry leaves for Venice I shall have no patron anyway,' said William.

They were again in the small room at the Star. Constanza sat smiling at him. He had made her laugh and she him in turn. The whole course of their meeting had been so fresh and open that William found the burden of his thoughts taken from him and picked over out loud.

'You will find another,' said Constanza, 'talent will out.'

This Constanza of comfort and quiet confidence was a blunt contrast with the manner of his dismissal when last they met. William found her change of mood troubling. He could find no explanation for it.

'What are you doing?' she asked.

William took his hands away from his face where he had pressed them. 'Just making certain it is the same face I had when last we met,' he said.

'Don't be shrewish,' Constanza chided, laughing. 'You have only yourself to blame if on our last meeting I was ill-tempered with you. It does not do to talk of other women, rivals for your affection, in my presence.'

William pressed an astonished hand to his chest. 'I spoke of no such woman. Sir Henry's mistress, not my own, was the poem's subject. My affection, and more, you already have. And if we speak of rivals, what of Greene?'

'What of him?' said Constanza. Her fan flicked out and closed again. She stood and walked to the small window, peering through the panes to the street below.

'Is he my rival as well as Sir Henry's?' said William.

'That depends,' Constanza answered.

'On what?' demanded William, following her to the window.

'On the role you see yourself in.'

'A lover's part.'

He took up her hand and pulled her round to face him.

'It is the playing of parts that I fear,' she said.

She did not pull away. He was able to see her closely. Her eyes were so dark as to seem black. She bent up her head to be kissed and her eyes hid themselves as he bent his.

They broke apart. William felt uncertain. A longed-for moment had come and, for all the pleasure of its instant, something rankled.

'Why are you here?' he said.

'Our embracing was not answer enough?' she said as she raised her head to his. 'Then I shall tell you again.'

This time William let thoughts fall behind him. The tolling of the bell brought him back.

'I must go if I am to deliver this letter,' he said.

'Ah yes, Sir Henry's mistress,' said Constanza, breaking from his embrace. 'Where does this paragon reside?'

'I may not say,' said William, 'though I can assure you she has no place in my heart.'

'Flatterer,' said Constanza. 'I take it she is wealthy? Coleman Street, then, or by the Tower?'

'Truly, I may not say,' said William. 'Not even if speaking would buy me a thousand more of your kisses.'

She tossed her head in annoyance, then smiled again. 'Very well, I would be wiser, I think, to admire your discretion than be piqued by your silence.'

She put her hands up to straighten her hair where his hands had made a happy ruin of its order.

'You will go by Ludgate?' she asked.

'Yes.'

She nodded. 'From here the fastest way to the City. Then to Cheapside?'

'And on,' William said. 'Your route too? I may escort you home?'

'No, I go another way,' Constanza said, 'by boat to Whitehall.'

William made a face of disappointment. She kissed it quickly.

'Give me then leave to leave you,' said William, 'I have my charge.'

'Good luck, messenger.' She pulled him to her and kissed him again.

He reached his arm about her waist to hold her closer but she pulled away. The door shut behind her and William was left in the ungainly pose of a half-completed embrace.

Known but by letter

A light step gave the lover a good pace as he headed east with his charge. The letter was sealed with wax but bore no sign of the sender. To William alone was entrusted the address. He did not recognise it, save that he knew it to be in the City.

William entered London through Ludgate. As he crossed the River Fleet he felt a certain satisfaction. It came from more than the sense of belonging that he began to feel in London. It came from contemplation of his verse. He had been reawakened to the power of poetry by his own efforts. The writing of the ditty for Sir Henry had been a challenge. The balance to be struck not easy. Throughout the writing of it William had wondered why Sir Henry would have another speak for him. William preferred to do his own seducing.

Not everyone thought as he did, he acknowledged. William had been a small child when he first realised the truth of this. His only continual surprise was the recognition that others, far older and more worldly, had still to grasp it.

He was briefly taken by wonder at whether Sir Henry would allow the whole course of the romance to be carried out by agents and deputies. Then by whether he could volunteer for a further role. Best to wait and see the lady before stepping forward, he thought. The Lord alone knew what the strange little man's tastes might be in women.

A man such as Sir Henry must be forced to trust many matters of a private nature to the business of others. A lonely and uncertain life, William thought. To be surrounded by others, forced to place special confidence in them, never knowing if that confidence was safely lodged. Little wonder that the company of rank flatterers was so common among great ones. Would such people prove friends in all weathers? How to know? His mother had been wont to say, when the sea was calm all boats showed themselves alike in floating. William's thoughts turned to Stratford and especially to his parents. He wondered at the strange success of their marriage. His father, confronted by disaster, would wallow in it, unmoving, sinking. His mother, by contrast, was like a sleek ship. Storm winds only drove her forward faster.

Such were William's thoughts when the first man cudgelled the back of his legs.

William sprawled into the mud of Cornhill, pain blazing across his thighs. A second man was dragging his scrabbling body into the darkness of an alley even as he hit the ground. Two men, hooded like the reaper, eyes and faces barely visible, hauled him to his feet and slammed him against the wall. The wind flew from him. Hands fluttered about his person. The velvet purse found and pocketed. Then the letter pulled from the recesses of his doublet and hastily scanned.

'The name?' the hooded man demanded.

William stared dumbly at the hollow dark space beneath the hood. It seemed to him as if a comet passed before his eyes as the hooded man cracked him across the face with the back of his hand. His lungs struggled to suck breath in.

'The name? The address?' the first hooded man demanded again.

'Quickly,' hissed the second.

William felt cold fire of agony across his body. The hands that held him choked him. He shook his head. The cudgel cracked across the front of his legs. William howled, he felt himself sinking into a sea of darkening sight.

The hooded man leaned in. William could make out a nose, twisted as if it had once been broken, within the darkness of the hood.

'The name?' the hood demanded. 'The address?'

William drew breath as if to speak and then spat at his tormentor through bloody teeth. A space opened between them. William slumped down the wall and looked up at the cudgel raised above the hooded man's head, poised to strike.

'William, William.'

How strange, William thought. At this moment I hear my name in the wind itself. Truly my poetic imagination is much awakened.

A man he is of honesty and trust

'He was not pretty to begin with,' said Oldcastle.

'God's sake, hush,' growled Hemminges.

'There's nothing broken, thank God,' Oldcastle said.

'Get him up and out of this stinking hole,' said Hemminges as he bent.

Hands hooked William under the arms and lifted him from his cobblestone bed.

'Can you walk?' asked Hemminges.

William's senses were returning. Slung on the shoulders of his two friends, he was brought from the narrow alley into bright day. Each part of him ached as if his assailants had struck him all over instead of simply twice across the legs and once in the face. He stumbled, each step making muscles knotted with the terror of the blows flinch and recoil anew. It was a blessing when he was deposited on a bench at the nearby tavern and drink put in his hand.

Hemminges sat next to him and spat into the sawdust. 'Jesus Christ,' he muttered, 'William, why were you attacked?'

'No idea . . .' William shook his head and regretted it. 'Wasn't the money.'

He patted his doublet. 'Leastwise, not just the money. Took the letter too.'

'Jesus Christ,' Hemminges spat again, 'and nearly took your head into the bargain.'

William let that selfsame head gently rest against the wall behind him, where it proceeded to swell and contract like the surging of an angry sea.

'What letter?' Hemminges asked.

'Eh? Oh, Sir Henry's to his mistress,' said William.

'Lord knows, I've no time for lovers,' said Hemminges, 'but you've had a savage beating for such an elderly Cupid.'

'I had my revenge,' said William.

'How so?' asked Hemminges.

'Cut the back of his right hand,' William replied.

'That was well done.'

'Very little needed doing,' said William, 'save to put my teeth in the way of the back of his hand when he cracked me across the face.'

Hemminges snorted.

Oldcastle, whose head during this terse exchange had swung back and forth between the two like a weathercock in a gale, took this as the sign for him to contribute.

'You should have seen John,' he said. 'As that myrmidon raised his dreadful trident above you Hemminges flew like Hector to your defence. Seeing him they had no stomach for the fight but turned and fled.'

'False, Nick,' Hemminges said, 'those men had no fear of me. They fled so as not to risk capture by the crowd our hallooing brought.'

Oldcastle clapped Hemminges on the back. 'Tush. They feared your might.' Turning to William, he proclaimed, 'Good fortune indeed that Hemminges and I should have received your message when we did.'

'What message?' asked William. 'I sent you no message.'

'Why, to meet you by Cornhill at this hour.'

'I sent you no message,' said William again.

'You are sure?' asked Oldcastle.

He made a dumb show of William having his thoughts knocked out of him, which William did not enjoy for making him laugh and laughter making him ache anew.

'My head is addled enough as is without worrying about false memory, Nick,' William said.

Oldcastle drew breath to speak but then subsided, silent.

The three men sat quiescent, each considering the import of the morning.

'They questioned you as to her name, her lodging?' asked Sir Henry.

He stood on the staircase in the hall of his house. William, Oldcastle and Hemminges were gathered at the foot of the stairs.

'They did, Sir Henry. Most insistently,' said William. 'Their cudgels marked the questions.'

William stood before Sir Henry like a waning moon, half his face darkening as the bruise began to show.

'You did not tell them?' asked Sir Henry.

'No, but the letter is lost, Sir Henry. I am sorry,' William said.

'Not a word of her name, though? Despite their assault?'

His hand waving at the angry purple of William's face and the way he stood propped against Hemminges was the first sign in the interview that Sir Henry had noticed William's injuries.

'Not a word,' promised William.

Sir Henry looked at him. The sudden appearance of sharp intent on the normally distract face, like a hawk appearing from a cloudy sky, strained William's nerves. Then Sir Henry's eyes slid away from his and onto his companions.

'Master Oldcastle, you I know, but who is your companion?' he asked.

Sir Henry descended to the floor of the hall to view them better.

'John Hemminges, Sir Henry, a player of our company,' William said. 'Were it not for their arrival, I should have been killed in the assault.'

Sir Henry's face broke into a small smile. 'Then we must be grateful to them.'

He beckoned to a liveried servant who stood behind him. The man advanced and deposited a small bag in Sir Henry's outstretched hand. Coins were produced and proffered to Oldcastle and Hemminges.

'Well, it would seem no harm done,' Sir Henry said.

William's wounds, borne in Sir Henry's service, throbbed to hear themselves so lightly dismissed.

'The letter, Sir Henry,' William said, 'the poem.'

'You will write another, Master Shakespeare. Perhaps something a little less ostentatious in its imagery this time, hmm? The important point is that discretion was maintained.'

Hemminges coughed. 'Sir Henry, have you any idea who would seek to steal your correspondence in this way?'

'None,' Sir Henry answered. 'Perhaps they saw me give young Master Shakespeare the purse for the poem and followed him for the money.'

'Yet they questioned William about the letter,' said Hemminges.

'True, true. A mystery, Master Hemminges,' said Sir Henry. 'One I do not have time to ponder, alas. I leave for Venice.'

Sir Henry studied William's friend. 'Hemminges. I know the name. Where from?'

He stepped back, appraising afresh the characters before him and catching Oldcastle in the middle of an inopportune scratching of his hose.

'Sir Henry,' said Oldcastle, taking his cue to recover from the unfortunate impression given by his readjustment, 'you will recall I mentioned Master Hemminges as part of our company of players. In connection with the embassy?'

'Was that it? Perhaps. Of course. The players,' said Sir Henry. 'Well, Master Oldcastle assures me that you know your business in matters of drama, and I have had proof of your constancy to your companions. Do you still wish the commission for Venice?'

Oldcastle looked across at Hemminges and William. 'We do, Sir Henry.'

'And you, Master Shakespeare?' asked Sir Henry. 'You do not signal your assent as your companion does.'

'Forgive me, Sir Henry,' said William, 'my thoughts are too scattered to speak to so great an enterprise. Let me give you my answer anon.'

Sir Henry turned away. As he left he called over his shoulder, 'Do not take too long. We depart three days from now. Master Oldcastle, speak to my steward as to the transport of the accoutrements of your trade and other such necessities.'

The three men stood outside Sir Henry's house. Oldcastle was beaming, Hemminges frowning and William had his face held up to the sky.

'Success, my friends. To Venice.' Oldcastle smoothed his doublet.

'To bed,' William sighed.

'It is a fool that treats that man as the dotard he pretends to be,' said Hemminges. He was staring back at the ornate door. A carved green man, face wrapped in vines, peered back at him.

'He seems harmless enough to me. Perhaps a little scattered in his dress.' Oldcastle patted Hemminges on the shoulder.

'Hemminges has the right of it,' William said. 'There is something here that I do not like.'

William coughed and his lip split afresh. 'Now, if you would be so kind, a bed,' he said.

Oldcastle and Hemminges took William's arms.

'Should have told those villains the address,' said Hemminges. 'Saved yourself a beating.'

'I'll have nothing stolen from me, Hemminges, that I would not freely give,' said William.

'Tell us, then,' Oldcastle panted beneath his load, 'who was this wondrous creature, Sir Henry's mistress?'

'Not to those with sticks. Still less to you, Oldcastle,' replied William.

Oldcastle sighed and Hemminges laughed. Together the three put their worries aside and limped their way north. Alas, worries, like bad dogs and naughty children, will scarce stay where they are put. They come back to bite.

Dangerous conjectures in ill-breeding minds

William winced as the water hit his face. He held the bowl's sides till the pain subsided. Then he thrust his head again into the water. Mud and blood swirled within. He tossed it aside and poured in fresh from the ewer. He wiped at his face and stared in the glass. A grim-visaged creature stared back. One side of his face was swollen, purple and lumpen. His lip pulled up in an unwarranted smile.

For this beating who was to blame? The obvious villain was Greene, who would not pause at violence if it meant he would secure a lady's affection. Or Towne perhaps, brooking no further delay, setting his companions on William. Add to this the strangeness of the message that Oldcastle and Hemminges had received. It had been a sore blow to his head but he was sure enough that he had sent no message to them. Who had? And known to send the two players to Cornhill at that hour? Were they meant to arrive to rescue him or to be parties to the beating?

Too much, too much. It was all too much. No more *coincidence.* There was a hidden hand at work here.

He pulled himself up. Such arrogance. To think that the great men of this world would make it turn on his axis. There was no magic here. He carried a letter from Sir Henry Carr, whose correspondence must be the target of many a curious villain. William began to give greater credit to Sir Henry's rumoured role as a spy.

He lay upon his cot and shifted, trying to find a position that did not drive a bruise into hard wood. Thoughts danced about his head denying him sleep. What did all this mean for the proffered place on the embassy? Venice meant employment and the company of Oldcastle and Hemminges. If Greene was responsible for his beating, then far from London was best for that reason also. William snorted. Sir Henry's company was no refuge. His own glass showed the dangers of that man's company. William was not sure he cared for the thought of the courts of Europe. His business was in London. Now he found himself an intended exile.

How came I to this? One poem saved me from a beating and brought me money, another brought me to a beating and saw me robbed. A third is like either to have me killed or crowned the king of players. That thought carried him to sleep.

I think he hath a very fair warning

'Dear Jesu, your face, your poor, sweet face.'

William sat up in terror and heaved himself back from the cloaked apparition at the end of his bed. His head cracked on the back wall.

'Hell,' he cried.

'Will, calm, calm.' Alice pulled back her hood.

'Calm?' William clutched at his head. He laughed and groaned. 'Calm, Alice Hunt? You may not have noticed it, I hid it well, but I am little surprised to see you here.'

He suddenly sprang from his bed to the door and peered out. The courtyard of the Theatre was quiet. The sun had gone below the horizon and only showed itself by a faint red beyond the wall. He'd slept the afternoon away. William turned back to Alice.

'Is your father here? Does he follow?'

'I think not,' Alice said. 'I hope he thinks me safe abed in Sir Henry Carr's house.'

'Sir Henry Carr's house?' said William.

'Is that a habit of yours?' Alice asked as she rearranged herself on the bed to lean against the stable wall.

'What?'

'Repeating what people say,' said Alice. 'If so, I am disappointed because I thought you a greater master of words.'

'Alice, I tell you truly, I barely feel master of my own wits let alone our English tongue.'

William sat down at the other end of the bed. He touched his sore face.

'Be kind to me, Alice, and tell me, without too many questions needed on my part, why you are here.'

'Sir Thomas Lucy is come to London and stays with Sir Henry Carr. Some business of the State. Where Sir Thomas goes my father follows. Where my father goes I am now brought,' Alice said. 'My propriety is not to be trusted but must be guarded. You should know why.'

'Oh, Alice,' said William. 'I know and am sorry for it.'

'I am not,' said Alice. 'At least, I am not sorry for the night. For the rest, I am sorry for that but it is not your fault that I suffer for it.'

'I should never have brought you into my –' William started but Alice spoke over his words.

'You're pretty. At least you were until –' she pointed to his battered face '– this happened. And you speak prettily too. And, Lord knows, little of this world can I speak of save as pertains to the small part of it I have seen at Sir Thomas's estate. Yet I am not a puppet, Will.'

'I know,' said William.

'Do you?' asked Alice. 'I think there is a little of my father in you. A part that sees others only for how they affect you. Not as actors in a play of their own devising but only as ciphers in your piece.'

William said nothing for a moment.

'I think,' he said eventually, 'that there is a little anger in you.'

'It may be,' Alice laughed.

The laugh was deep and ribald and William thought that it became well the young woman sat on his bed.

'I know now why you are in London,' said William. 'Why are you here in my palatial chambers?'

The laugh left Alice's face. 'Oh, Will, I would I'd been here before tonight. I might have saved you this.'

She reached out and stroked his bruised face. He covered her hand where it lay on his cheek.

'How so?' he asked.

'My father wants you whipped for lying with me. Or rather for the shame he feels that you did so.'

'He's a little late,' said William, 'I've already had one beating.'

'I know. It was at his asking.'

Alice unfolded the story of her spying. The terror of her discovery by Watkins and how she'd been confined to her room for two days after.

'Yet,' she said, 'for my father it was not enough.'

'Not enough,' said William, 'ungrateful, black-scabbed villains all. I would your father'd such a beating to call it "not enough".'

'He wanted more. I think there would have been but that your friends disturbed the business,' said Alice. 'When you three had left, Sir Henry declared himself satisfied and Sir Thomas also, but my father called for more.'

'Dear God, was ever man plagued by such enemies?'

'Come now, Will,' Alice chided, 'you've none to blame but yourself for my father's enmity.'

'True,' said William.

'Besides, all pleasures have a price, and the sweetest pleasures command the highest price.'

This time it was William who laughed. 'Did I mistake you for an innocent flower? I am more fool than even my enemies name me.'

'You get no argument from me,' said Alice, 'but a fair warning. My father railed against the decision of Sir Thomas and Sir Henry to let the matter lie. He dare not go against them openly, but I know him. You are a poison that works and roils within him and he will have you answer for it. Since he has kept me with him I have seen him at his plotting. I know he has spoken to men, dangerous and greedy with it. I think you are in danger.'

William closed his eyes and leaned back against the stable wall. For a long time he said nothing.

'I cannot stay,' said Alice.

'I know,' said William. 'Bless you for coming. For your warning will save me.'

William took her hands. 'Help me again. Tomorrow I will send you a letter.'

'Don't. Anything for me my father would open and read,' said Alice.

'I am counting on it,' said William. 'The message inside will be for him whatever the name it bears. Remember that.'

'I will,' said Alice.

William rose from the bed. 'I'll go with you to Sir Henry's house. The hour is late.'

'No,' said Alice, 'I've a companion for the journey already.'

William looked at her. 'You're blushing prettily.'

'I didn't get out of Sir Henry's house by picking the lock now, did I?' said Alice.

William held up his hands in defeat.

'I ask only that you remain my friend, Alice Hunt,' he said. 'The Lord knows I can afford only one of your family as an enemy and better it should be the weakest among you.'

She kissed him and was gone, leaving him to sit on his bed, to wonder at Sir Henry's tricks and tests and strange talk of William's role in the embassy, and to try to press his tired brain to action before the other Hunt's vengeance fell.

To compass wonders but by help of devils

The morning after Alice's visit had been one of messages and sendings.

When dawn had come William set off for the City to the address Sir Henry had given him for the letter. Returning to the Theatre he found a letter from Sir Henry waiting.

'In Latin,' William cursed. Another test.

It invited him to attend on Sir Henry at the Paris Garden the following day to discuss his participation in the embassy.

'Did I not tell you it would be so?' said Oldcastle now at his breakfast.

'You did,' said William. 'And urged me join you in Venice.'

'You hesitate still?' demanded Hemminges. 'What is there here that holds you?'

'This morning I went to look for a woman,' William answered.

'I know you to be the most frightful lecher of any man your age, Will, yet I pray you have not turned to boasting of it. I assume some connection between your answer and my question,' said Oldcastle, 'though if there is, I lack the wit to know it.'

'Did you find her?' asked Hemminges.

'I did not.' William stared at the ground.

Oldcastle took his thoughtfulness for sadness. He clapped a hand on William's stooped shoulders. 'Plenty of señoritas in fair Venice,' he said.

'Signorinas,' grunted Hemminges.

'What's that, John?' said Oldcastle.

''S'not *señoritas* in Venice,' said Hemminges.

'Really? Good to know. Good to know.' Oldcastle rolled his eyes, taking care that only William could see him do so. 'The point stands,' he continued. 'No need for poxed London whores when the alabaster beauties of Venice await us.'

'I went to see Sir Henry's lover,' said William, 'the lady of the poem.'

'Whatever for?' asked Oldcastle.

'She wasn't there,' said William.

'Where?'

'Where he said she'd be.'

'Who?'

'Keep up, Nick,' said William. 'I mean Sir Henry. I went to find the lady that he commissioned the poem for. The poem I went to deliver when I was set upon.'

'Oh,' said Oldcastle.

'And she was not there,' said William.

'Oh,' said Oldcastle in a tone that indicated he would not pretend to understand what was going on.

'There wasn't even a house at that address,' said William. 'Just an old priory turned to counting house.'

'I do not find the idea that Sir Henry, a man I have seen walk about sucking on an inky quill as if it were a pipe with his shirt scarce buttoned, gave the wrong address as troublesome as you appear to do,' said Oldcastle.

With the authority of a man who had played nobility on many occasions, Oldcastle gave little esteem to a knight that he felt failed to live up to the dignity of his position.

'True. True,' said William. 'Then again, Oldcastle, you do not play chess.'

Oldcastle huffed. 'Here I am trying to console you on your inability to find a woman even in London, a place that teems with them even as a river teems with trout, one need only reach in and tickle one out, and I am rewarded with calumny. Censured for my lack of learning. My inability to play chess hurled against me as though a rock 'gainst the stout walls ...'

'I mean –' William held up a hand to staunch the flow '– that Sir Henry does. Play chess. And that, if you did, you would worry, as I do, that the game you think you are playing is not the one your opponent plays.'

William told his companions Alice's intelligence of the night. It took Oldcastle some minutes to cease his ribald commentary at news of another woman in William's life. At last the sour looks of William and Hemminges penetrated. Oldcastle coughed and subsided.

'Sir Henry set men on you in part to satisfy Sir Thomas Lucy and his man Hunt and in part to test you,' said Hemminges. 'That much is clear from Alice Hunt's tale.'

'What I cannot tell,' said William, 'is how deep the lies run. Was the whole business of Sir Henry's mistress a baseless fabric, draped to gull us, to test us?'

'Greene's taunting in the verses Sir Henry had William pen for him has been real enough,' said Hemminges.

'As is the rogue's anger at William that grew from it,' nodded Oldcastle.

'One thing is clear,' said William. 'There can be no talk of Venice now.'

Oldcastle's eyebrows shot up. 'Why do you say that? Surely Venice is now the certain refuge from Greene's anger and Hunt's revenge.'

'In the company of a liar who would see me beaten as a test?'

'In the company of a careful man. One who weighed the value of his people before trusting them,' said Hemminges with a shrug. 'Before we did not know what Sir Henry was about. Now, thanks to Alice, we do. Neither for the poaching nor for the testing can you fault Sir Henry for the beating.'

'Thank you, Hemminges,' said William.

Hemminges shrugged again. 'I speak as I find. There may be much profit in being Sir Henry's man of special trust. Think on that.'

'Wise Hemminges,' agreed Oldcastle, 'Nestor of our troupe.'

Oldcastle placed his hands on Hemminges' and William's shoulders and turned from one to the other. 'Are we not still poor players, Will? Before we feared the dangers of Europe. Now we know we travel in the company of a cautious man who will not take unnecessary risks with our person.'

Oldcastle returned his hands to rest upon the prodigious bulk of his belly, guarding the precious cargo of his person.

William felt less certain of the value of the knight's move. He fretted. It was a fair guess that any move at all would be bad for the pawns. He had no illusions as to his status in the game. Let his friends do as they will. He would stay in London, where his ambitions lay. Now he needed only consider how he might do so in safety.

William penned two letters. The first in answer to Sir Henry: he would meet him at the Paris Garden. He did not add that it would not be to take any place on his embassy but to throw his plotting in his face. William wished to have the pleasure of that answer facing the knight.

The second to Alice Hunt, returned with the same messenger that took his answer to Sir Henry. That was a bolder message. When it was sent William ran to put in train all those things that would be needed to make good its boldness.

Yet have I in me something dangerous

William carried his ale to a shady corner of the Star, the tavern on Fleet Street where he had met with Constanza. The afternoon after Alice's visit was unseasonably hot. William smeared sweat across his brow with his sleeve. He'd laboured hard in that heat. Now he took his rest and waited for his reward. He did not wait long before it came.

William had spent the time since breakfast in the careful arrangement of a meeting in that private room in the Star. Such a useful room with its two entrances. Now the hour appointed came.

The first guest came in by the back stairs. William could not see him but heard the footsteps on the floor above. Until he felt his stomach unclench he had not realised how he'd waited for that arrival, uncertain it would come.

The next guests arrived by the front door a moment later. Two men, leather jerkins and scabbed knuckles both, shouldered their way into the tavern. Hunt's paid villains. William felt fear flow over him as a cold wave. The thought of these brutes catching him alone made his bruises sting anew. They paid William's shadowed figure in the corner no mind as they strode to the front stairs that climbed towards the private room.

William rose and quickly followed. The thought of missing what would come next was a torture. He saw the two men reach the top of the stairs, shove open the door and enter. William raced up the stairs and pressed himself against the wall outside the room.

'You Shakespeare?' William heard one of the brutes grunt within.

'Most certainly not,' Robert Greene replied. 'Do you take me for some metre ballad-monger?'

The answer caused the pair of villains to set to muttering between themselves. Greene rapped his knuckles on the table to draw their attention. 'Who are you doorstops in human form?' he demanded.

'You a poet?' challenged the brute in answer.

'That I am,' Greene replied. 'Though what business that is to you I cannot think. It bores me to try.'

'You a playwright?' the brute asked.

'What is this? Who are you to question me?'

'You a playwright?' the brute pressed, ignoring Greene's questions.

'I am,' said Greene. 'Again, what that matter is to you I do not know. Now get out, oaf, I am expecting a lady.'

'She's not coming.'

William heard the brute's smile in his voice as he spoke.

'Her father sent my brother and I to pass on a message to the poet, the playwright, the rogue that we should find waiting at the Star to besmirch the honour of a young maid.'

Greene's voice in answer did not rise to the insulting charge. In tones of boredom he asked, 'What message is that?'

William felt the blow land in the sound like a drum being struck, in the grunt as air left Greene's lips, in the stumble of steps as Greene reeled back.

'Damn you,' Greene hissed, 'that hurt.'

'That is the nature of this message,' the brute said. 'We've just started to deliver it.'

Greene coughed and held up his hand before him. 'Wait, Hercules. I take it that it was no part of your message to let my clothes be ruined?'

The brute shrugged. Greene took that for a licence and unlaced his cloak. As he smoothed its folds he spoke, 'You've the wrong man, Hercules.'

'Sure and you've said so,' nodded the brute as he cracked his knuckles. 'You are not Shakespeare. Yet here you are a poet, a playwright and in the place where this Shakespeare said he'd be and at the hour he claimed he'd be there.'

'Oh, I didn't mean that,' said Greene. 'True, I am not Shakespeare but I meant that you had mistaken me for a gudgeon, an innocent.'

Greene shook the cloak. 'I'm not.'

A sudden motion saw Greene toss the cloak over the closest brute's head and with the same sweep, kick up. A howl. The brute fell to the floor, cloak still covering his head, clutching his agonised crotch. His brother stepped over him to hook Greene in the jaw. Greene staggered back into the chair behind him. He gripped the chair back and hefted it like a club.

Painful fingers gripped William's arm from behind and dragged him down the stairs.

'This was not wise, Will,' said Hemminges as he thrust the lad out the tavern door to the sound, from the room above, of wood splintering.

I have seen Sackerson loose twenty times, and have taken him by the chain

As soon hold back a crashing wave as halt Hemminges' driving of him down the street.

'I'm going with you willingly, John,' protested Will.

Hemminges said nothing nor slowed his pace till they had passed through Ludgate. Then, at the river's edge, he stopped.

'Jesu Christ, Will.' Hemminges looked in all directions save at William. 'Jesu Christ.' His eyes finally came to rest on William.

Hemminges had that strange power to compel speech by saying nothing. William found himself making what explanation he could.

'I had two enemies, John. Why not have one confront the other?'

Hemminges shook his head.

'Hunt's paid villains will not come again,' William argued. 'They may even ask of Hunt why he did not warn them of the dangers of poets and playwrights.'

'And Greene?' Hemminges asked.

'Will be wary of a man he dismissed as a "metre ballad-monger" but who has shown himself to be reckoned with.'

'Then you do not know Greene. This is not your small-town rogue, Will. He will not quake at the sound of your boots. He'll dab his split lip and put the bloody handkerchief in a glass case as a symbol of his revenge to come.'

Hemminges paced out to the river's bank. He bent, picked up a stone and hurled it out into the river. He stamped back over to William.

'Clever is not wise, Will. You might have slid below Greene's gaze had you done nothing. Instead you poked the scorpion's nest.'

'I'll outwit him again,' William said.

'No doubt, but why would you need to do so at all but for this business?' Hemminges asked. 'You're clever, Will, but others can be clever too without diminishing you. It need not all be tilts and tournaments.'

Hemminges threw another stone into the river.

'How'd you know?'

'That you'd be at the Star?' said Hemminges. 'Followed you. I saw that look on your face this morning when you sent the message to Sir Henry. Later saw you send the message to Greene. Later still saw Greene go into the tavern where you waited and those two villains follow shortly after.'

'Thank you,' said William.

'For what?'

'For caring.'

Hemminges snorted. 'Where to now?' he asked.

'To the Paris Garden to meet with Sir Henry and to talk of Venice.'

'I'll come with you.'

'To keep me out of trouble?'

Hemminges laughed. 'Trouble is your home as much as the air the birds' or the sea the fishes', but at least if I'm there I might help you out of it.'

One man picked out of ten thousand

Hemminges and William were met at the Paris Garden's gate by Sir Henry's man, Watkins.

'I've seen that nose before,' said William.

Watkins simply pointed to the booth where Sir Henry sat alone.

'The cut on your hand is healing well,' said William as he passed.

Watkins held up that hand to stop Hemminges following. With a shrug, Hemminges tossed his head to show William where he would sit waiting. William passed through the crowd. The show had yet to start. The crowd milled about the ring, yet to settle. William's thoughts were also stirred. He'd been set to bite his thumb at Sir Henry for his tricks and for the beating. Now he was not so sure. Perhaps Greene would not be warned off by the trouble William had brought on him, nor Hunt distracted from his vengeance. Meanwhile, with his friends and patron gone to Venice, what employment would remain for William in London? Was Venice a chance for advancement not to be passed up?

He pulled back the curtain and entered the private booth. Sir Henry sat alone. When William entered he signalled for him to sit.

'You had me beaten.'

'I think you managed to bring that fate on yourself,' Sir Henry answered. His voice was calm contrast to William's heat.

'Your reason?' demanded William.

Sir Henry turned to him. 'You taunted that man Hunt by playing with his daughter. You think nothing follows?'

'Alice Hunt is no plaything.'

'Oh, I know that. A woman of qualities. You may appreciate that now,' said Sir Henry. 'Did you then?'

William said nothing. In the ring below the first bear was brought in and the crowd bayed with excitement for the dogs to be brought. Sir Henry gestured again to the bench. This time William sat.

'You have not been to Europe before?' Sir Henry asked.

'I have not, Sir Henry,' replied William.

'A complicated place.'

'I understand it so.'

'Leaving small Stratford for London has broadened your horizons, Master Shakespeare. Think what sight of Europe may do for your vision.'

Sir Henry gestured to where a tankard sat. William did not reach for it. He was too full of thoughts. Sir Henry studied him.

'You love our Majesty?'

William stiffened. He tried to peer into the darkness of the booth.

'Of course, Sir Henry,' he said.

'She is not loved of many in Europe. There are those bitterly opposed to the course our Sovereign lady takes.'

'These are matters too high to concern one so lowly, Sir Henry.'

'All things concern the playwright. What lessons may our enemies teach, Master Shakespeare? Take Philip of Spain. The man is struck with a holy fervour for England's destruction. His only thought is to bring England's people back under the Pope's control and England's land under Spanish rule. He would tear down every tree in his lands, leave not a forest standing cross Spain and Holland and Italy, if only he could build a bridge with them to get his armies to England. There's a study of a man.'

William looked at Sir Henry's composed and tranquil face. When he spoke his former heat was coloured over with the cast of thought. 'Why set men on me and then call them off?'

Sir Henry shook his head. 'I do not know what you are speaking of, Master Shakespeare. Neither the setting on nor the calling off.'

'You think I do not know that it was you that warned Hemminges and Oldcastle to be at Cornhill?' said William. 'Who else would know the time and place of my undoing but the man who set it in motion?'

'Who indeed?' said Sir Henry. 'I think you sugar o'er my compassion and rate yourself too little in the eyes of others.'

It was William's turn to shake his head in lack of understanding.

'These are troubled times,' Sir Henry said. 'Philip of Spain makes common cause with the Catholic League at Joinville, his assassin strikes dead William the Silent in Delft, the Jesuits slip into England like rats.'

Sir Henry turned and gestured at William's face.

'What is a red face against these terrors?'

'To him that has it, much,' answered William. 'Of my face I know a great deal. Of Spain and Delft and the concerns of great men, nothing.'

'Shakespeare, the state of Europe is fluid. Great powers shift and seethe with alliance and betrayal. As you rightly say, these are not matters of your concern. They concern me. In Venice the Doge is old and ill. Venice is not a single mind but many. It is a place divided against itself. People matter. They pull in one direction and in another. The Pope in Rome pulls with some and we with others. Do you know of the Pope? It is said he spends more on spies than the other princes of Italy spend on all their soldiery.'

It was not clear to William how much of this was spoken to him and how much thoughts spoken aloud. Sir Henry finished his drink.

'Into this maelstrom of intrigues our Sovereign sends my embassy,' Sir Henry said. 'What do you consider will be the greatest obstacle to our success?'

'I do not know, Sir Henry. I do not know the object of your embassy.'

'Why, to add our weight to the scale till the beam turns in Her Majesty's favour,' answered Sir Henry. 'What will obstruct us most in this purpose do you think? The machinations of the Pope? The rigours of the journey? The needs of the Venetian Senate? Come, Master Shakespeare, though report speaks of you for hot-headed rashness, yet have I seen in you a mind. Use it.'

'I confess, Sir Henry, all these seem like great obstacles as you say them. Yet they would not be my first concern.'

'And that would be?' asked Sir Henry.

'That the scale we place our weight in was not defective to begin with,' replied William.

A small chuckle from Sir Henry accompanied a roaring from the crowd at the action below.

'If you were worried that the scale was not true, what would you do?'

'Test it against a known weight first,' said William.

'A good idea, Master Shakespeare. I shall try it.'

In the ring they changed out the first bear, broken at his post, for new.

'You have done well with my patronage, Master Shakespeare. I can use a man with your talent. Come to Venice. There are opportunities in this embassy for one of ambition.'

'Your manservant, Sir Henry?' William ventured.

'Watkins?'

'I feel I have met him before.'

'Perhaps you have. He's been with my family many years. When I find men I trust, men I have been given reason to trust, I value them. I shall hope to have good service from you in Venice.'

Sir Henry smiled as he turned his head back to the fight in the ring below. After a moment he realised William still studied him. The ambassador watched him for a breath before breaking his reverie with a question of his own.

'Tell me, do you, an actor, expect all men to be as they first appear?'

'No,' answered William.

'Nor do I.'

'My worry, Sir Henry, is always that I do not know when I am looking at the player or just the part.'

Sir Henry chuckled again and William's lips bent to a smile. Thus did the two men begin to come to an understanding.

Wounded it is, but with the eyes of a lady

A carriage waited for Sir Henry further along Bank Side where the press of the departing crowd outside the Paris Garden lessened. Sir Henry ambled towards it with William, Watkins and Hemminges in his train. He stopped at the carriage door and turned to William and Hemminges.

'Tomorrow, at my house? We depart as early as our preparations will allow.'

Hemminges nodded. Sir Henry looked to William, who, after a moment, inclined his head in agreement too.

'Your company, ready?' Sir Henry asked.

'It is. The baggage stowed. At least as much as your steward would allow. The rest we've sent ahead by ship,' Hemminges answered.

'Good. Till the morning, then,' said Sir Henry. 'Do not forget my poem, Master Shakespeare.'

'Poem, Sir Henry?'

'Indeed, perhaps something that alludes to my courage in the face of Spanish treachery. That should burnish my armour in the sight of my lady.'

'You jest, Sir Henry.'

'Why do you say that?'

'The prank is up, Sir Henry, we both know there was no lady,' William said, 'only a test. After this evening's entertainments I have had my fill of pranks.'

Sir Henry raised an admonishing finger. 'Oh, there is always a lady.' He signalled to Watkins, who held open the carriage door.

'Doubt not that I shall want the poem, Master Shakespeare. In the morning, if you please. That it might be delivered before we depart.'

Sir Henry climbed in. Watkins shut the door behind him. He signalled to the driver for the off and pulled himself onto the footboard. As the carriage pulled away the curtain of the door twitched. Behind it William caught the briefest glimpse of the smiling face of Constanza Briaga as the carriage clattered away.

William's thoughts flowed back over his talks with Sir Henry and with Constanza. Hearing them again, understanding them again, puzzles unlocking themselves.

'Was that –' said Hemminges behind him.

'It was,' William said.

'Well, well, well.'

'Quite.'

'Come, you must pack.'

'And write a poem too.'

Interlude

Venice, April 1585

The instruments of darkness tell us truths

There are not many gardens in Venice. A city plucked perilously up out of the waters of a lagoon does not spare land lightly. Such gardens are, in consequence, precious jewels jealously guarded and carefully hidden behind high walls. It was, therefore, an understandable curiosity that allowed Isabella Lisarro to accept the anonymous invitation to visit one.

She went knowing it was against her better judgment. At thirty, she had passed enough years in this world to be wary, but hers had never been a backward spirit, to hide from the prospect of adventure at the mere thought of risk. She paused only long enough to inform her maid of her departure and to gather a green cloak about her. Then she stepped into the gondola that accompanied the invitation and was taken away.

Isabella rarely had cause to come to this part of the city. Cannaregio lay in the north-western corner of Venice beyond San Polo and San Marco. The gondola slipped along the shadowed canals. On its cushioned seat she sat with cloak pulled closely around her against an unexpected morning chill. The gondolier behind her oared them forward in silence. Apart from the words that accompanied the invitation he said nothing more until the gondola pulled alongside a small gate set in a long, high wall against the canal's edge.

'We have arrived, signorina,' said the gondolier.

She stepped lightly from the gondola onto the steps. Her cloak fell back, revealing auburn hair whose rich colour the cloak artfully complemented. She did not know who invited her but it never hurt to go armed. Isabella's beauty had ever been one of her strongest weapons. That the gondolier still called her *signorina* showed that age had not blunted its edge yet. She adjusted the fall of her ruff and with a shrug she climbed the steps. The gate swung easily open. With only a moment's hesitation, she pushed and entered.

The walls enclosed a triangle of land edged with bushes bright with spring flowers along two sides. The third was the front of a palace, its windows shuttered against the sun. At the centre of the garden stood a single tree, old and thick, its canopy covering near half the garden in its shade. A blanket was spread across the ground at the base of the trunk. On it a child of four or five years played with a wooden horse.

Isabella looked about but could see no other person. She crossed to the child.

'Hello little one,' she said.

The child, a boy with blue eyes so pale they seemed almost devoid of colour, gazed up at her and slowly held out the horse. She looked about her. She recognised the boy instantly. It was her maid's son, Angelo.

'Is this your horse?' she asked.

Angelo nodded. Isabella gestured at the blanket. Receiving a nod of permission from the boy, she sat beside him.

'It's a noble beast,' she said solemnly to the boy.

'It is,' a voice spoke from behind her.

Isabella started. It was not just its sudden appearance that shook her but the voice itself.

'Giovanni Prospero,' Isabella said, 'I should have known that your return to Venice would be as shrouded in mysteries as your departure.'

The Count of Genoa walked around to sit across from her on the blanket. He laid a silver salver of fruit down. Smiling, he leaned across to pluck a bottle and two glasses from their hiding place behind the tree.

'I left unwillingly and only sent my body,' he said. 'My thoughts remained behind. With you.'

He poured two glasses of *prosecho* and proffered one of them to Isabella. She took it with both hands and brought it to her lips. Her grey-blue eyes held his black ones for a moment. Her lips drew back to reveal perfect white teeth behind the red. She took a sip. She was glad she had not trembled as she did so; though she had been wise to use both hands for fear that using only one would have let the dark man see the sparkling wine shiver in its glass just as she shivered within. Fearing the bitterness of poison, she tasted only the sweetness of the *prosecho*. With relief she saw him take his own sip.

Isabella studied his face. It was changed from her remembrance. The skin a little rougher and touched about with lines at the eyes' edges. The proud nose as sharp as ever. The scar across his face was still there, a little more faded. He smiled and she saw again the young wolf she had known. She wondered how he saw her now. As if reading her innermost thought, he answered.

'You look unchanged, Isabella.'

'I think that unlikely,' she replied. 'How many years has it been?'

'Ten?' he ventured.

'I think fourteen.'

'Impossible.' The Count waved away the idea. 'There are not that many years in your life,' he said. 'You must have made a bargain with the Devil himself. There can be no other explanation for you to look so untouched by time.'

'Oh not so, Giovanni. As you must know.'

'How so?' asked Prospero.

'Why, because you were not here to negotiate the deal on the Devil's behalf,' she replied.

'I am the Devil's lackey, then?'

'Say rather his lawyer.'

'Which is worse,' Prospero said.

Isabella pretended to take his answer for a question. 'The worse of a devil or a lawyer? Easier to answer which is the heavier, the weight of sin or old age.'

'Sin, of course,' the Count answered, 'for old age drags you to the Earth but sin drags you all the way to Hell.'

'Then the lawyer is worse. For knowing that you speak with the Devil may give you the chance to be saved from Hell if not from death, but knowing you speak with a lawyer will save you from neither death nor Hell.'

'You reason as sharply and as prettily as you ever did,' said Prospero. He put down his glass. 'I have missed that.'

The little boy reached across to try and take a piece of fruit. Prospero's hand whipped out and smacked the boy's.

'Patience, Angelo,' the Count admonished to the sound of the boy's cry of pain.

Prospero plucked up the salver. He proffered it to Isabella, who waved it away. He set it down again and took an apple from it. Producing a knife from his shirt he began to peel and slice the fruit. It was a tool ill-suited to the task, a knife made for other work.

'Tell me your latest poem,' Prospero said.

'I have none,' said Isabella.

'None? That is not the Isabella Lisarro of my memory,' he said. 'To let her pen rest idle.'

Isabella shook her head. 'I am not that woman and my life, of late, has not lent itself to verse-making.'

'I had heard of some travails you endured.'

Prospero let his comment fall to silence without glancing at her.

The quiet of this Arcadian scene belied the tumult within Isabella's mind. Of all the people in her life, of all the people in the world, she had thought to see Giovanni Prospero last of all. And least of all was his presence welcome. Foolish, foolish was I when I was young, she thought. And no better now, her rash acceptance of the invitation bitter in her mind.

Prospero cut the first slice from the apple. He held it out to the boy. Just as he reached to take it, the man laughed and popped it into his own mouth. At the child's hurt look he held up his hand in apology. He began to cut another slice.

'Why are you returned to Venice?' Isabella asked.

Of the two questions in Isabella's mind this was not the most pressing. She feared to ask the one to which she most desired the answer. She feared to know what Prospero wanted with her.

'Perhaps I am here to see you,' said the Count.

'If you wanted that you could have achieved it at any point these last fourteen years,' said Isabella. 'No, I think not. Which prompts me to question why you have brought me here to this secluded garden. I warn you, I am not the innocent I once was, to be seduced by you again and set aside.'

'Seduced and set aside,' said Prospero. 'Such a cruel description for our love affair.'

'I realise now there was no love in our affair, Giovanni. At least not on your part. A lover does not depart taking with him the better part of his love's affection and leaving behind only the scorn and contempt of society for her to feed upon.'

Isabella could hear the bitterness that crept into her voice and was angry at it. She did not want to give anything of herself to this man again, least of all an opening into her feelings into which he might once again stick his knives.

Prospero proffered another slice of apple to the boy and, once again, plucked it away to his own mouth before the boy could eat. He laughed at the boy's distress before turning his eyes on Isabella again.

'Have you suffered so terribly, Isabella?'

She did not deign to give his question answer. He had heard, he had said. He must know then, of the state he left her in, of how she clawed her way from it, of the plague that drove her from Venice, the penury she returned to, the false accusations and the inquisition that followed. She had been tested in the fire. Her metal had glowed brightly against the coarse background of her troubles. She had not broken.

The silence built. It was Prospero who broke first.

'Business and affairs of State bring me back to Venice. It is pleasure that brings me back to you.'

'I tell you truly, Giovanni, I want no part of your pleasures any more.'

'You hurt me, Isabella. You did not always answer so.' He spoke lightly but his eyes glittered.

'I see you still wear the ring I gave you,' he said.

Isabella looked down at her hand. She twisted the heavy gold ring with its dark red stone away from sight.

'I understand you better now, Giovanni,' she said. 'What once I was pleased to take as passion I see now was always madness. There is in you something broken. The mechanism turns but to what effect? Not what its maker intended.'

'If so, the fault is not mine. I was born in sin,' said the Count.

'Maybe so. Yet to be a bastard is not all there is to you,' Isabella replied.

'By my own hand is that so.'

'What might that hand do if it were set to honest craft?'

'There's a question to which I have no answer,' Prospero said. 'Nor ever will.'

'You have the answer,' she nodded. 'For well you know, your sin's not accidental, Giovanni. It is your trade.'

On that note their argument paused again. The boy continued to stare eagerly at the apple in Prospero's fingers and the dark man continued to cut slices that he dangled before the child only to consume them himself. This time it was Isabella who broke the silence.

'I want no part in your pleasures nor any in your business in Venice either. If that is the reassurance that you seek.'

The tall man leaned back against the tree. 'I am glad to hear you say so,' he said.

Isabella's heart seized and held in hard grip, knowing she had read him right.

'I doubt there are any in Venice who now remember me,' Prospero smiled, 'save you.'

He leaned forward and tossed the remains of the apple to the boy, Angelo, who seeing it was now nothing but core and seeds angrily threw it aside.

'Such a temper on him,' said Prospero.

'Who is he to you, Giovanni?' asked Isabella.

'No one,' he answered, 'but I know he is someone to you.'

In his voice lay such a pitiless lack of regard that Isabella felt a tear spring, unbidden, to her eye. She understood the boy's presence was Prospero's threat. A sign that he could reach in and take all that she held dear, if he wanted it.

'I leave Venice again shortly for business in Verona, but I shall return. It would be better,' Prospero continued without waiting for reply, 'should we encounter each other while I am in Venice, to be as strangers to each other.'

'There will be no difficulty in that, Giovanni, for I see now that we are and always have been strangers to each other.'

Prospero reached forward and wiped away the tear from her face. His fingers light on her skin.

'How green you are and fresh in this old world, Isabella. Your cloak's colour suits more than your complexion.'

He rose to his feet. He looked down at her.

'For the love I bore you,' he said, 'though you deny it now, I give you this warning. It will be the only one. I will have silence. One way or another.'

He paused. 'Come, Angelo,' he said, drawing the sulky child to him.

'Leave the boy,' Isabella said quietly. 'I will see him home.'

Prospero shrugged. Then he stalked back through the garden and disappeared into the house. Isabella stayed sitting on the blanket till her heart returned to a more sedate beat. Then she rose and brushed her skirt and walked to the canal gate where the gondolier sat waiting for her. The little boy trotted at her heels. All the long ride home she pondered how she might thwart her old lover Prospero, the assassin. She would not let another suffer as she had done.

Act Three

The Road to Venice,

June 1585

Exeunt omnes

William set forth from England in strange company. The small troupe of players had gathered at the house near Ely Place as instructed. Aboard their cart were the pieces of set dressing and the far more valuable collection of costumes that Hemminges and Oldcastle had acquired in their playing careers. William had been surprised by the ostentation of some of the pieces. Nor did the cart bear all their accoutrements. Sir Henry's steward, Fallow, had insisted that to carry all the costumes was an impossibility. Hemminges and Oldcastle had insisted that to perform without costumes was equally inconceivable.

As Arthur had put it in his piping voice, 'I can't be a Queen in a sackcloth, can I?'

A compromise was reached in which some part was sent ahead by ship. Hemminges had clucked over their packing as a hen over her eggs.

Sir Henry had provided a horse and driver for the cart that carried the rest. The horse was an unhappy beast, more ass than horse. The driver, an Irishman by the name of Ben Connor, was copy to the animal he drove and poor company. Save to grunt out his name he exchanged not one word with the players in preparation of departure.

The players occupied one of three carts in the embassy's small train. At its head rode Sir Henry on his palfrey. By his side, astride a small mare, his steward, Fallow. The embassy made for Dover and there took ship to France.

They crossed the Channel in a small and, to William's unseasoned eye, poorly kept ship. The voyage, though turbulent, was swift. The chief entertainment came from the sight of Oldcastle and Hemminges both turning an unusual and unnerving colour of green at the tossing of the sea, prompting many jibes from William. Oldcastle, dignity offended and slow to recover from his seasickness, had refused to speak to William from Calais to the outskirts of Paris. In retrospect, a period of blessed quiet. From Paris, the embassy travelled south through France past Burgundy towards Piedmont. From there to pass through the Duchy of

Savoy and then of Milan and on to Venice. As they went Oldcastle continued his benevolent education of the poor country boob, Shakespeare.

'You're fair enough at a galliard, boy,' Oldcastle said, 'and I have no doubt even in the godforsaken countryside, where you were unfortunate enough to have been born, they offered you sufficient learning to read a prompt-book when it is placed before you. But there is more, far more, to being a player than the spouting of lines and an occasional rustling of the legs in time to a lute. Ours is the careful study of the nature of man.'

In this vein days passed. Not all of William's time was spent listening to Oldcastle wax profound upon the nature of the player's art. Oldcastle and Hemminges took time to run through the parts that he would be expected to play; correcting him on his lines, demanding of him a certain subtlety of delivery. In the evenings, should the opportunity present itself, William would practise his dancing with Hemminges and the boy Arthur while Oldcastle looked on. Then Hemminges would make him fence until the light grew too little for safety. Finally, all would retire to the hearth of the inn. Tired, drilled endlessly and in near constant battle with Oldcastle in word games and wit, William was enjoying the journey greatly.

In their enjoyment of the journey the players stood alone.

Sir Henry sought to keep the passage of his embassy through France secret. He desired no distraction before his destination. Nor did he think it wise for a party of English Protestants to make anything but noiseless progress through France. Such a policy had wisdom but not comfort in it. It meant back roads, small inns and long days. All this burden fell on the carters, the household servants and the grooms. The sight of Oldcastle enthroned on a cart while they trudged beside him, William and Arthur capering of an evening while they sweated over luggage and horses, was the fuel to a building fire. Near Lyons it burst into open flame.

A plague of sighing and grief

As the dark of evening drew in William entered the inn. He was panting and ripe with sweat from his practice with Hemminges in the inn's yard. He collected a mug from the bar, sat at the common table and drank. His seat was furthest from the fireplace, for he and Hemminges had stayed at it long after the others had finished stowing the gear and stabling the horses after the day's journey.

Closest to the fire sat Oldcastle in a tall-backed chair, his feet resting on a small cushioned stool. His face glowed red from the fire and the heat of wine. He talked generously, not caring who received the bounty, but offering it loudly to all.

Sat nearest to Oldcastle was Sir Henry's squire, Hal. A lad of fourteen, the son of a cousin of Sir Henry's. He gave credent and attentive ear to Oldcastle's story.

'Of course, I was there,' said Oldcastle.

'In Brill?' Hal asked.

'Yes, lad. The year our Queen expelled the Gueux from our ports. I was in the Netherlands. I saw them capture Brill from the Spanish. A bloody day that one but a great one.'

'You fought?' said Hal.

'I played my part,' said Oldcastle.

He waved away the anticipated praise. William noted that no detail came of the part Oldcastle had played.

Gathered at the common table were the others of their small embassy: Coll and Jack, the cart drivers; Foulkes, Joiner and Nate, of Sir Henry's household; Francis, Sir Henry's groom; and Ned and Tom Alkin, the brothers who assisted Fallow in his work. They sat in various states of attention to Oldcastle's talk, finishing their meals.

'There's a war that's not yet won. We English shall play our part, mark my words,' Oldcastle continued.

'I should like to fight,' said Hal. He sat up straight on his stool.

Oldcastle gestured at him with his glass. 'Of course you would. There's fire in your eyes, lad.'

He drank.

'Remind me of myself at your age. All pepper and vinegar,' he said.

Not all sat at the common table. The carter, Connor, sat by himself on a stool at one side of the room hunched over his food, a pot of dark beer by his hand. Watkins sat, as was his habit, at one side of the room against the wall. He drank little and watched all. He nodded to William as he entered. Such nods were the extent of their commerce in the three weeks since leaving London.

The lad Arthur was at the kitchen door. He paid no attention to Oldcastle. His interest was taken by the inn's maid. She seemed both flattered and flustered by Arthur's attention. She laughed and pushed at him one moment, tutted and shooed at him the next. William absently admired Arthur's ability to make himself understood to the French girl. For simply by his dumb discoursive show he went about his wooing.

The steward Fallow emerged from the snug of the inn to join the company. Behind him Sir Henry could just be seen. He sat at the table of the small, private room. His dinner finished and Fallow dismissed, Sir Henry studied a chess set. He cradled a small glass of wine in his hand.

In the common room, Oldcastle returned from his reverie on military matters, leaned forward and patted Hal on the knee. 'Do not be so eager for it though, boy. A terrible business, war. Much sadness in it.'

'*Faugh!*' Connor smacked the table and twisted on his stool. 'Stop filling the lad's head with your lies, Oldcastle.'

'Lies?' Oldcastle's feet dropped from the stool and he held his hand to his heart, where Connor's words had wounded him.

'Aye,' said Connor.

'No lies, sirrah,' protested Oldcastle. 'True every word.'

'Give over,' interrupted Coll the carter. 'If you've seen the pointed end of a pike it was only when the bailiff took you in for drunkenness.'

'And what would you know of war, Coll?' demanded Oldcastle.

'More than you, Oldcastle,' the carter replied, 'and all I know of soldiering is what I learned at my grandfather's knee, who was drunk more nights even than you.'

'My grandam was more soldier than you,' joined Connor. 'Soldiering's work and I've seen none of that from you or your troupe these weeks past.'

William watched Connor's face grow red. Now, in the laughter that came from the rest of the company at Connor's words, he heard the dispute grow an edge. So did Fallow, who spoke to curb it.

'Enough of this,' the steward said. 'The players will have work enough when we reach Venice. Yours is the business of the road.'

Connor would not be quieted. 'I'll do my business,' he said, 'but I see no reason, Master Fallow, why I must endure this prating fool's lies while I am about it.'

William looked about him. The company was surly. None spoke in support of Oldcastle. None looked at William. The hush that fell in the room was not the quiet of calm but of the eye of the storm. Oldcastle opened his mouth to speak. William willed him to silence, in vain.

'It does not surprise me, Connor,' said Oldcastle, 'to find you cannot tell lies from truth.'

Connor was up before Oldcastle had finished speaking.

'You fat paunch. Call me liar and, by the Lord, I'll stab you.'

Watkins had risen with Connor. William saw then that Hemminges had entered the inn. He moved quietly to a place behind Connor. His presence emboldened Oldcastle.

'You'd not dare, Connor,' Oldcastle said as he looked about the gathering. 'I've ridden better men than you into the ground.'

'Ride?' said Connor. 'There's proof of a lie. The horse isn't born that could take your weight.'

'I do not shy to be called great, Ben Connor.' Oldcastle rose from his chair and thrust an arm in the air. 'So were the Titans called who came closest to the gods in strength.'

'I know none of that,' said Connor. 'I know only that you are fat. Fat and loud and full of pompous wind.'

Connor's words brought mutterings of agreement from the others.

'Still nimble enough in mind to dance about you, Connor,' said Oldcastle.

'I'd like to see you dance, Oldcastle. Though I fear I'd see your knees crack. We'd have to put you down. Like any horse you'd ridden,' said Connor.

Oldcastle swelled with injured dignity. 'Why, for a penny I'd pitch you in the dust, Connor.'

'I'll wrestle with you and gladly,' said Connor. 'You horseback breaker, you guts, you bag of wind. Best of three falls.'

He looked around for support and finding it turned back to Oldcastle. 'Or are you coward?'

Oldcastle drew himself up to his full height. 'Coward?' he boomed. 'I've seen my death in a cannon's mouth. I've outfaced the Spaniard in his rage. I'll see you overthrown. I'll give you odds – have three for two and still I'll beat you. At dawn we'll see your mettle, Connor. If we see you at all.'

Oldcastle stamped from the room.

The bubble reputation

'I am undone,' Oldcastle groaned.

Hemminges ignored him. He paced the small room the players shared. 'Weeks we shall be in this company. Weeks.'

Hemminges spoke as he walked. 'We've been so wrapped up in our own affairs we've not noticed how little loved we were of the others. Well, now we know. For that alone we can give thanks to your foolishness.'

Oldcastle sat on a bed. William watched from the corner where he stood. Only Arthur was absent. He had matters more pressing than Oldcastle's impending doom to attend.

'A little drink, John. That was all. A little drink and good cheer. It was not me that started to quarrel,' Oldcastle said, his chin pulled down to his chest.

'No, but when it came you pushed it to a higher pitch,' Hemminges said. He stopped before Oldcastle. 'Jesu, Nick, know when is enough.'

Oldcastle hung his head.

'What shall be done?' asked William of the pacing Hemminges.

'I would I knew,' said Hemminges. He looked at Oldcastle. 'Even if he were sober by the morning Connor is half his years and half his girth. He'll crack him like a nut.'

Oldcastle's head flung up. 'I shall submit to him.'

'And have us mocked?' Hemminges rounded on Oldcastle. 'Your brave show has made our small band of players more hated of the rest. Submit now and we'll add cowardice to the list of sins they say besets us. Cowardice and a braggartly nature. No, Nick, no. You'll fight.'

Hemminges ran his fingers through his hair.

'I shall be broken,' Oldcastle moaned. 'He has a vicious and ungentle manner. He'll not spare me.' He looked from Hemminges to William. 'I would I had never drunk a drop. My brain was washed in ale yet feels the fouler for it.'

'Pluck up, Oldcastle,' said Hemminges. 'This is an injury of your own making.'

Hemminges left him to his self-pity. William followed.

'What shall we do, John?' he asked.

Hemminges stood in the inn's yard looking up at the moon. 'No clue,' he answered. 'I'll speak to Watkins. He stands high in the regard of the others. He might persuade Connor to call off the challenge.'

He bit at a fingernail. 'Though I doubt it,' he continued. 'I thought that Connor a coward. He's itched for a fight with our little band since we first met him. He'd never had come against me or you. Against poor old Oldcastle he'll be a Tartar.'

Hemminges rubbed his face. 'There's greater trouble here than Nick's fat mouth and staying the beating that's to come for him,' he said with a sigh. 'We players will have uncomfortable lodging in this embassy unless we mend this rift.'

'Indeed,' came a voice from behind them.

Hemminges rose and William turned at Sir Henry's approach.

'Hemminges, Shakespeare,' Sir Henry nodded to them. He looked out at the yard. 'The poison of division has infected our embassy. It must be drawn.'

He turned to look at the two players. 'Both sides may find release in the morrow's tourney. At the same time, I can't have my player injured, nor my carter. I need them both.'

Hemminges and Shakespeare waited. Sir Henry looked at the yard again.

'Some stratagem is needed,' he said.

'You have some plan in mind, Sir Henry?' Hemminges asked.

'Alas, no,' said Sir Henry. 'I am no Ulysses. Would I were. For when the Greeks could not breach Troy's walls nor the Trojans drive the Greeks from outside them, it was Ulysses who broke the savage balance by making the Trojans think the Greeks were other than they were.'

'Your command could end the strife,' said Hemminges.

'I think not. If I step into the ring then it will be said I take the players' part.'

Sir Henry tapped a hand on the wooden wall of the stable. 'Should be a morning full of events,' he said and turned back to the inn.

Hemminges sighed.

'I'll speak to Watkins,' he said. 'One trouble at a time. If Connor breaks Oldcastle there'll be a breach that has no possibility of repair.'

William put a hand on Hemminges' shoulder. 'A thought has come to me.'

He leaned in and spoke hurriedly to Hemminges.

When he'd finished Hemminges grunted. 'If your cozening works then both men will learn a lesson.'

'And we will be the richer,' said William.

'True. Oldcastle should pay a price for his swaggering.' Hemminges shook his head. 'Sir Henry, at least, will see through the scheme.'

'And if he does?' said William. 'The man as good as suggested the scheme with his talk of Troy.'

Hemminges rubbed his face for the twentieth time.

'A beggar's choice. Very well. I'll speak to Nick. You to Connor.'

William went to work his mischief.

They say he has been fencer to the Sophy

'You're a brave man, Connor.' William clapped the carter on the back. 'I confess I'd not have believed it of you.'

William had found Connor returning through the dark from the privy. 'Brave?' said Connor.

'Aye, brave. To try three falls with Oldcastle.'

'*Hah*,' said Connor. 'One fall will be enough. It will be a wonder if he has the courage to stand in the ring with me.'

William raised an eyebrow. 'Oh ho.' He made to move away.

'Wait,' said Connor. He walked to William. 'What do you say?'

'Nothing,' said William.

Connor gripped William's sleeve. 'Why do you say, "Oh ho"?'

William shrugged. 'No reason. Sure you know already.'

'Know what?' demanded Connor.

'Well, by the arrows you sent towards his bulk, I assume you know that Oldcastle wrestles.'

'What? That paunchy old man?' Connor laughed and spat. 'You're as full as fantastical tales as he is, Shakespeare.'

'You didn't know?' said William.

William sucked air through his teeth as if in pity for Connor's pain to come. 'You know your business, I'm sure,' he said.

A wrinkle of doubt creased Connor's brow as William spoke.

'When Oldcastle put up the idea of wrestling I thought you must have known,' he said. 'Then to challenge him at the very sport. Brave, brave, I thought, but now I see it was mere ignorance.'

Connor said nothing. William pressed on.

'In his youth, I am told, he was a very devil. As a travelling player he tried his mettle at the fair in each town he passed.'

William leaned in. 'I tell you truly,' he said, 'even now I have seen him, in London in his cups and in his rage, hip a man to the dust and break his arm.'

'Oldcastle?' scoffed Connor. 'He's not stirred from the back of the cart these two weeks. He's no devil.'

'Think, man,' William said. 'You spoke of his bulk yourself. Let him set his legs and you'll not move those pillars though you were Samson. Then he'll grapple you at the waist and, well, as I say, I've seen it once: there was a bone as took some setting and a man whose arm thereafter gave him a day's warning of rain.' William winced, as if in memory of it.

Connor looked askance at him. Truly, Oldcastle was no small piece of flesh, he thought.

William pressed the advantage. 'Tell me at least you did not give him odds?'

Connor smacked his fist into his palm. 'The whoreson gamester! He put the quarrel on me purposely and has tricked me to the match. He means to make money by my injury.'

William shook his head. 'So you did give him odds. Jesu mercy, man. I'd say to look to your preparation but I see he has caught you in a catch already.'

Connor clutched at William's arm. 'I'll not be tricked into a challenge I've no chance at. You're a player, speak to him. Persuade him to let the matter drop.'

William took the carter's hand from his arm. 'A bootless task, man. He's incensed against you. The profit from the bout is just savour to the dish. There's no turning him now. If only you had not spoken so churlishly to him.'

'I only gave a voice to the thoughts of many. Damned if I'll be the only one to suffer for it,' Connor said, clutching again at William's arm. 'Tell Oldcastle that he may have his profit if he will spare me the injury,' he pleaded. 'If I'd known he was a wrestler I'd never have spoken so harshly to him.'

William shrugged. 'I will speak to him.'

He finished with another clap of Connor's back. This one in commiseration of the hurt to come. He made sure Connor could not see his smiling face as he went into the inn.

… laid on twelve for nine

The morning came too soon for Connor and Oldcastle.

'You're sure he's agreed?' Oldcastle asked. He stood and shivered in the cold air of morning.

Behind him Hemminges smiled. He worked stiff fingers into Oldcastle's shoulders in preparation for the bout. William stood with the two of them underneath the roof of the stables.

'He's agreed,' William said. 'For his dignity, he says he must make a show but will let you have the first fall then he the second. At that you two will shake and part with honour even.'

Oldcastle nodded. His belly strained the cloth of his undershirt. William did not think the cold of morning accounted for all his shiver.

'You've the money?' asked William.

'Yes. Hemminges, give the boy the purse,' Oldcastle said. He pressed William's hand. 'Thank you, lad.'

William palmed the money. He and Hemminges shared a look behind Oldcastle's back. Then William turned. He strode across the yard.

A circle for the wrestlers' tourney had been scratched in the dust of the inn's yard. On its far side stood Connor. The carters, Coll and Jack, offered him last-minute advice on how to trip Oldcastle. Connor paid it no heed. He stared in growing fright at Oldcastle. Hemminges worked at Oldcastle's muscles with practised fingers as though such matches were a common event for the players. The intensity of Connor's gaze on his opponent Oldcastle mistook for rage. It gave him such cause of fear that he in turn could look at none but Connor. William thought there was a danger they would kill each other by the look, like cockatrices. He approached and beckoned Connor to one side.

'Well?' asked Connor.

'It will be as we agreed last night,' William whispered. 'His honour demands that there be at least one pass, which he will give to you. Then come the second you'll be thrown. Resist not, lest in his passion he use more of his strength than is needed.'

William looked back at Oldcastle as if seeking confirmation the great bear would show restraint.

'Then before the third, with honour on both sides, you'll agree a draw,' he said.

'Bless you, Shakespeare,' whispered Connor.

'All this, of course, turns on the coin,' said William.

William felt the purse pressed into his hand. He nodded at Connor then walked to the centre of the ring. There stood Watkins, who would be marshal of the tourney.

'They'll not be reconciled,' said William. 'Each means to fight.'

Watkins nodded at William's words. Then he held out his hands to call the fighters to the field.

Everyone had risen to see the contest. They now stood round the narrow circle. The outcome of the bout was the subject of eager discussion among them. In the middle Watkins called out the terms of the challenge.

'The best of three falls or the man that first cries *enough*.'

Watkins skipped backwards from the ring. Connor and Oldcastle dropped to a crouch and began to circle. Cries of encouragement rang from the watchers. Both men moved around each other. Connor reached out a hand, Oldcastle snatched at it, Connor pulled it back. Again, they circled. Oldcastle darted a leg, Connor bent to it, Oldcastle danced back. They turned about again.

'Set to it, man.'

'He's afeared of you.'

'Seize him.'

'By the leg, by the leg.'

The wrestlers were proof against the urgings of the crowd. They circled. They darted. They would not close with each other.

'God, William,' whispered Hemminges. 'Have we o'erdone it with our cozening that they should make such a show?'

As Hemminges spoke Connor thrust out his arm. At the same moment Oldcastle thrust out his. Quite by chance, Connor caught Oldcastle. As fingers closed on flesh both men looked at each other in horror. Connor made to pull his arm back. In the terror of the moment he kept his grasp and pulled Oldcastle after him. Unchary of this move Oldcastle unbalanced. He toppled forward onto Connor who, by dint of that great weight stumbling into him, fell back beneath Oldcastle.

'One to the players,' roared Watkins, and the crowd roared with him.

Oldcastle pushed himself hastily up. Connor, the wind knocked quite out of him, lay on the ground a moment. He rolled to his front and slowly got up.

Hemminges clapped Oldcastle on the back. 'Well played, Oldcastle.'

Oldcastle, almost as stunned by the fall as Connor, simply panted.

Hemminges leaned in to his ear. 'Now remember, you were supposed to fall the first time. Since you took him to the ground instead, this time you're to fall.'

Oldcastle turned paler. Watkins gestured. Hemminges shoved Oldcastle back into the ring.

Connor hesitated. His head rang. He felt certain the boy, Shakespeare, had said he was to have the first throw. Had Oldcastle, zealous for the fight, reneged on the deal? Oldcastle watched him with a fixed intent. Connor, misprising Oldcastle's fear for valour, prayed he might be delivered from destruction.

Again the watching company gave call to battle. Reluctantly the two men began to circle. Watkins, conscious of his duty, had been careful to sweep the yard. He had not counted on the earthquake that was a tumbling Oldcastle. A pebble was thrust up in the dust of the field. At his third pass Oldcastle trod on it and howled. Connor, hearing Oldcastle's berserker cry, feared for his life. He closed his eyes, turned to flee, tripped and flung out his arms. Oldcastle, hopping on one foot with pain, was caught by the terrified Connor's flailing arms. He fell to the ground like an axed tree.

'One to the carters,' roared Watkins and again the crowd roared with him.

William picked Connor up and carried him to his corner.

'Faith, Connor, I'd not have known you had it in you,' his fellow carter Jack said and slapped his back. 'That was a rare acrobatic move.'

Connor coughed. His ribs squeaked with bruising. He clutched at William's arm.

'Honour's even, eh?' he wheezed.

William smiled. 'You'll not try the third fall?'

Connor looked at him. 'Tell Oldcastle, I am content to let the matter rest, if he is.'

William nodded at Connor. He straightened and nodded at Coll and Jack. They looked unhappy at this talk of a draw. William walked back to Oldcastle.

'Well done, Oldcastle,' he whispered. 'I really thought you angry. You've a great talent for play-acting.'

Oldcastle was bent double. His hands propped on his knees. 'Thank you, dear boy. Thank you,' he said in heaving breaths. 'Thank God there's no more.'

'You'll not try the third pass?' said William.

Oldcastle looked up at him with round eyes. 'No. No. It was the understanding we'd quit after the second bout.'

William smiled at Hemminges. Then he walked over to Watkins, who listened carefully before beckoning the two combatants to the ring. There the two men shook hands and, wincingly, parted. Hemminges walked over to Connor.

'A fine throw,' Hemminges said.

Coll, the other carter, nodded at the praise.

'Aye, and against a great weight of a man too. No small knock he gave you in the first,' said Coll.

He turned to Hemminges. 'I'd not have credited it of such a soft-handed man as Oldcastle.'

'Soft-handed but hard-headed, eh?' said Hemminges with a laugh.

'*Hah*, true, man, true,' Coll laughed.

'I'd say we've much misprised each other in many things,' said Hemminges. 'We've been busy at our rehearsals and missed your efforts on behalf of all. For that I'm sorry.'

Hemminges tilted his head in Oldcastle's direction. Behind him Oldcastle had found a seat on a small stool and was accepting the praise of young Hal for the first throw and the good-humoured prodding of Foulkes and Joiner at the injury of the second.

'Forgive an old man his pride,' Hemminges said.

'Pride's a sin and no mistake,' said Coll. 'Yet all Christian men should forgive the sins of others as we wish our own forgiven.'

'Wise words, Coll,' Hemminges said. 'Here, let us help with the loading. Then we may yet make our day's allotted journey despite this morning's sport.'

… little of this great world can I speak

The evening of the bout, the day's labour done and supper eaten, Hemminges sat among the company and joined in their good-humoured mocking of Connor and Oldcastle. The former, unhappy at the goading, stamped off to nurse his bruises in his cot. The latter consumed enough wine to care neither for his hurts nor the mocking and joined in it to the laughter of all. William looked on and thought how close they had come to a far worse outcome.

'Sir Henry would speak with you,' Fallow whispered in his ear.

William looked up and saw Fallow gesturing to the inn's private dining room. While the steward joined the rest of the company, now being led in the singing of a round by Oldcastle, William went to see Sir Henry.

The knight was sitting before the chess set. He motioned for William to sit opposite. They began to play. The game was nearly over before Sir Henry spoke.

'Well played, Master Shakespeare,' he said.

William wrinkled his brow at the board. 'You see something I do not, Sir Henry. I think your victory close.'

'I am not speaking about our game of chess.'

William looked up from the board. 'Sir Henry?'

'I speak to you in your Homeric guise,' said Sir Henry. 'As Ulysses.'

It crossed William's mind to feign ignorance of his meaning.

'You are kind to say so, Sir Henry,' he said, 'but the idea was yours.'

'The inspiration maybe,' Sir Henry said as he took William's bishop. 'The execution, however, was all yours. I am glad that my interest in your ability has already been rewarded.'

William looked at the board. His king lay open to attack. Sir Henry gestured at the pieces.

'You attacked boldly,' he said. 'Boldness is all very well. Pointless to attack if you first neglect your defence.'

They played some moments more before Sir Henry's checkmate came. William was frustrated. Each time he'd sought to bring pressure on Sir Henry he'd found himself having to break off the attack to deal with some threat of his opponent's.

'Your strategy was all wrong,' Sir Henry said.

'I would I were a better player,' said William.

'You will be, in time. Your strategy was wrong but it was wrong in the right ways.'

William left this paradox untouched. He was still trying to understand why he was in Sir Henry's presence at all.

'No one springs from the womb playing chess,' Sir Henry continued. 'One learns. Repetition brings improvement. Provided one is open to the education. My steward Fallow, excellent servant. Still plays like he did the first time. All direct lines and open ploys. A straight mind is a fine quality in a steward, essential in a good one I should say, but no grounding for a good gamester.' He began to set the pieces again.

'I find one can tell much about a man from what games he plays and the way he plays,' he said. 'For myself, I prefer chess. The game itself is the diversion of an idle hour but in the play it proves the prompt to other thoughts.'

Sir Henry advanced a pawn.

'Consider the central role that the king plays. Most important piece on the board. Lose him, lose all. Is it not the same in life?'

William looked up from the game to see that the question was not rhetorical. Sir Henry waited for an answer.

'Perhaps, Sir Henry,' he replied.

Sir Henry nodded. Emboldened by the respectful audience to his reply, William spoke again.

'Would Brutus agree? He thought Rome better without a king.'

Sir Henry paused in the movement of his piece.

'Was he right to think so? Look what followed. Caesar dying did not give birth to liberty. Brutus' blow broke open Mars' temple. Turned all to war. Friends and family set against each other. As he lay in his tent, the night before he faced Mark Antony at second Philippi, did he think he had saved Rome or damned her?'

William considered the question while Sir Henry finished his move.

'Truly, I do not know,' William said. 'I am sure it was his hope he'd saved Rome from tyranny.'

'Great hopes and good intentions,' said Sir Henry. He closed his eyes. 'How often they are spoken of. Meanwhile the acts they prompt us to turn all to ash around us.'

He opened his eyes to look at William.

'Our England,' he said and paused again, looking for words. 'Our England is the story of many men. Of many kings. Each thought they were to rule. Lancaster and York contending for their turn to wear the crown. Each finding, in their turn, that crowns make for poor pillows. Little and uneasy rest has a king. And all the while men suffer and die for their ambition. Why? What did it matter to them? What did it matter to those who would be king? Do you know England's history, Master Shakespeare?'

'Some part of it,' William replied.

'There's profit in its study. Seen that with Ulysses, have we not? How much more might we learn from men closer to us in age and country?' Sir Henry said.

He looked down at the board and moved his knight. 'What do you think of the Spanish?'

William was unbalanced by the sudden change in subject. 'I think little of them save to know that they are our enemy,' he replied.

'They are.'

'My Lord knows more than most,' William dared.

'Less than I would wish.'

'What will England do when Spain comes against her in all its strength?' William asked.

'Fight,' said Sir Henry.

'Against the strength of Spain? Against its ships, its soldiers and its gold? Our little England?'

Sir Henry looked up from his study of the board. 'It's will that matters, Master Shakespeare. Will for the fight. Numbers are nothing. Ships, men, gold, nothing. Didn't David slay Goliath? Didn't the Black Prince defy the French at Crécy? King Henry at Agincourt? Those were fearful odds against the French. We English may speak softly in times of peace, but when the trumpet brays for war …'

Sir Henry leaned back in the chair and took up his glass. He pointed to the board. 'You neglect your defence. A common fault. How much easier to think of our own plans and schemes. All the while our enemy plots against us. We face an enemy that will not blanch to strike at our heart. Look at the Dutch when Philip of Spain sent a murderer to strike down William the Silent. Their heart gone, their armies shrink and stumble. Already Philip sends men to England, encouraged by the Pope's edict against Her Majesty. Who are these men? Where will they strike?'

For a moment Sir Henry looked to another place. Then he shook his head and looked back at William. 'How much did Connor give to be spared Master Oldcastle?' he asked.

William shuffled in his seat. 'A shilling. Oldcastle the same.'

'My, my,' said Sir Henry, 'the price of knowledge.'

'The schoolmaster must be paid,' said William.

'Without question,' said Sir Henry.

He turned back to their game. 'You must have a care that Connor does not learn how he was gulled. The great good that has come of their dispute, the growth of harmony within our little band, would be undone. I wouldn't want that. Shall we continue the game?'

William bent his head to study.

Burst of a battle

The new compact in the embassy was sealed a few days later by the whole company fighting as one in a coaching inn on the road to Turin that bore the sign of a cockerel crowing.

There was something about the coaching inn that had made William uncomfortable the instant he entered it. It took him a moment to recognise the source of that unease: there were no women. Not a single serving-girl to leaven the heavy bread of hard-faced men. The English party found themselves sat beside the members of a French merchant's caravan.

William could not say what prompted it. Perhaps it was no single moment but the accumulation of pressures looking for a place to vent. Too many strangers together. Too many nations with their petty rivalries as excuses. Too many tired men, the worse for too much drink for dry, dusty throats. Whatever the cause, tension turned to violence with a rapidity that astonished William.

One moment there had been raised voices in a babble of languages, the next, one of the French was wrestling with Coll and a general melee broke out. In an instant the whole tavern swept into brawl with all set against all. Watkins, Hemminges, William and Oldcastle found themselves trapped in a corner assaulted from all sides. Hemminges and William stood back to back while Oldcastle urged defiance on them from his crouched position behind the table and Watkins pressed his back to the wall.

William swung at a lanky man with a red neck scarf who had aimed a blow at Watkins. He heard a satisfying crack as his hand connected with the man's nose. Watkins cried out a warning and William turned and found a surprisingly hairy Frenchman ('positively Esau reborn', as Oldcastle would describe him in the retelling) lunging at him with a knife a good foot in length and sharp on two sides as well as at the point ('like that with which one imagines Judith took Holofernes' head,' Oldcastle would say, warming to his theme).

William hurled himself backwards, tumbling over a stool and knocking the table with his feet as he went. Wine, beer and food slopped across it. Oldcastle made a wild kick at the knife-wielding Frenchman and missed. Watkins, fortunately for William, was able to reach over and slam a pewter flagon into the temple of the Frenchman. A blow Hemminges followed up by clamping his free hand round the wrist of the man's knife-bearing hand and, using the table as an anvil, hammering the heavy flagon into his hairy knuckles. A combination of events that induced a mighty wail ('like unto that heard from Sodom as the Lord rained fire upon it,' Oldcastle would conclude, still milking the Old Testament for reference), which was only curtailed by William, recovered, whipping a wooden mug across the Frenchman's face. An event that signalled the end of the battle.

The landlord and his sons, armed with metal-bound staves, arrived to separate the combatants. By some miracle, other than the general wastage of food and drink and some dents to a pewter flagon, there was no damage to the inn. For this reason alone the landlord, after a lengthy and loud debate with representatives of both parties and the passage of some coin in his direction, was persuaded to allow the French to depart and the English to sleep, as planned and without the need to disturb Sir Henry.

Though the Crowing Cock had been spared serious harm, the same could not be said for the respective armies. The chief injury was William's. He received a long but shallow cut to his arm from the knife-wielding Frenchman, who in turn had a broken hand and a bloody face. Another of the French contingent had also received a cruel slash to his face from a clay pot that shattered as it struck him. Several of the English nursed ugly bruises to their faces and many on both sides had clothes heavily stained and spattered with wine and food. Oldcastle was furious to discover that his contribution to the fight had resulted in him tearing his hose across the fork.

'Quite, quite ruined,' he muttered as he stumped off to his bed to the sound of the general laughter of the company.

'Some slight disturbance last night, I fancy,' Sir Henry Carr could be heard saying to his steward the following morning.

'A minor altercation, Sir Henry. Quickly resolved,' replied Fallow.

'Honour on both sides, one trusts?'

'Slight advantage to us, I fancy, Sir Henry. Some of the actors appear to do more than play at fighting.'

'Good, good,' said Sir Henry. 'Can't let the French have it all their way, can we now.'

Sir Henry paused his horse by the players' cart and threw a couple of coins down to an astonished and hung-over Oldcastle as he passed.

Recovering, Oldcastle did his best to haul himself to his feet and offer appropriately fawning thanks to the disappearing figure of his patron. The effort was wasted. By the time he was on his feet and had composed a suitably ingratiating response, Sir Henry was a good fifty yards away and Oldcastle was quite out of breath.

Hemminges, loading the last of their belongings onto the cart, took advantage of the unusual silence to collar William as he heaved his sack up.

'Tell me, Will, what do you think happens when the play doesn't please?' he asked.

'I hadn't given it much thought,' confessed William.

'Bloody havoc is what happens,' said Hemminges. 'This is unusual business we're about with this embassy. Soon enough we'll be back to our usual happenstance, and that's to play in any place that will have us. Often enough that's the yard of an inn with an audience of locals who've had drink to go with their entertainment. And if they do not like what they're offered you can forget passing the hat for coins. It's a question of keeping them from burning your set.'

William looked to see if Hemminges was jesting with him, but the man's face held no hint of a smile.

'I know you're no coward, lad,' Hemminges said. 'And we've played at fencing enough that I know you've speed and skill in you. But if a man throws a knife in your direction you can't just fall off your stool and wait for another to set about him while you look on.'

William's face flushed at the memory of his meagre contribution to last night's excitements. Youthful pride made him defiant. 'I fight well enough,' he said.

'No, lad,' said Hemminges. 'At best you duel, like a gentleman does. That's as well for a player to do since he must act the gentleman from time to time. But a knife is not for duelling. A knife's for murder. You need to know how to fight when there are no seconds and no trading clever barbs before each thrust. In a tavern brawl you don't get sent a finely worded challenge full of piss and vinegar in advance. You get some bastard setting upon you when your attention's elsewhere and you're swine-drunk. You have to be ready. The world's full of violence, lad, and it's a holy fool that wanders through it unarmed.'

Hemminges finished his speech with a hard stare. William didn't feel able to do anything but nod. Apparently satisfied, Hemminges broke away and, passing Oldcastle, snatched one of the coins from the fat fingers that were turning Sir Henry's largesse over and over. He bent to finish the packing with a complete disregard for Oldcastle's ensuing ire.

It seemed that Hemminges took William's nod as a licence of a kind. That evening and every evening for the next week there was no dancing or fencing. Instead, Hemminges showed William what he had learned in the experience of more than one tavern brawl. William was taught to scratch an eye, and use a wall, a pot or a hastily snatched cobble to best effect. In the course of his education he received sharp jabs in the armpit, a cruel raking of his shins with the edge of a boot and a crack over the eye from a misjudged demonstration of a head-butt. All of which left him distinctly sour. An emotion heightened by the perpetual giggling of Arthur that accompanied every knock and bruise he received.

William was not, however, proof against the occasional praise Hemminges would dole out after a hard session. The price of the knowledge may have been high in scrapes and cuts, but William was grateful for it.

The mistress court of mighty Europe

Sir Henry checked William again.

'You play well, Master Shakespeare,' Sir Henry said. 'You've an eye for the main chance. You see a stratagem and you work towards it.'

William moved his knight in front of his king. Sir Henry reached out and moved his own, to reveal another check.

Since that first night after Oldcastle and Connor's tourney, Sir Henry had William brought to him after each evening meal and played chess against him. All the while he spoke out loud. William suspected he served as company for a lonely man; the chance to sound out his worries on an inconsequential man possessed of an intelligent mind. William did not object. He learned much. Sir Henry's openness in discussion increasing as he found in William an attentive and willing pupil.

'Yet your play is only good,' Sir Henry said. 'It lacks the touch of greatness. The great players do not look simply to create traps. They work to control the board's shape. To craft the landscape within which their opponent plays.'

William looked at the board. He could see no escape for his king. There had seemed such space for movement. He had ravaged through Sir Henry's pieces. Yet now his own were scattered. Sir Henry's few were all gathered about William's king. William found there was one square he needed. It was denied him. Some moves ago Sir Henry had advanced one of his pawns. The square it threatened had been of such seeming inconsequence to the play of pieces. William had ignored it for the glories that lay elsewhere on the board. Yet slowly, slowly the play had moved across the board and now that square was all. He looked up to see Sir Henry looking at him.

'Even a pawn may be powerful,' Sir Henry said. 'If it is put in the right place.'

William turned his king on its side in resignation. Sir Henry sat back in his chair. Outside the dining room the company could be heard in good-natured revel. Sir Henry refilled his glass and gestured for William to do the same.

'It will not be long before we are in Venice. There we may throw off the fiction we are a private party and stand revealed as Her Majesty's servants. There will our business begin.'

He gestured at William's arm. 'Healing well?' he asked.

'The scab pulls but heals cleanly,' William answered.

'Good, good. Can't have you killed before Venice.'

Sir Henry began to shuffle pieces on the board. 'News has reached me from Rome,' he said. 'There is a new pope now. As expected, the white smoke wafted for the former Cardinal Montalto. He has taken the name "Sixtus". The fifth, I think, of that name.'

Sir Henry took a sip from his glass and resumed his setting of the pieces. 'There's no great news in that. Pope Gregory's death and Montalto's rise to replace him were foreseen.'

'How?' William asked.

'No magic, Master Shakespeare. No scrying glass. The old pope was old. The wonder was he lived as long as he did. As to the new pope. He has many spies, but then, so have we.'

He looked up and studied William. 'You look unhappy. Is it to hear that we have spies or that the Pope does? You think white vestments bespeak a spotless innocence? No more than red hands a fouled conscience, Master Shakespeare.'

William made to protest but Sir Henry held up a hand to stay him.

'These are unstable and uncertain times. You may think a poor player is so far below the concerns of great ones that he need not care for them.'

'I do not, Sir Henry,' said William. 'When great ones storm it is poor sailors drown.'

'An apt metaphor. England is a small boat and steers a rocky and uncharted course,' Sir Henry said. 'Have you ever felt fear, Master Shakespeare? True fear, for your life, for the safety of those you love?'

William shook his head but Sir Henry was no longer looking at him but staring at the chess board as he spoke. 'Philip of Spain is more powerful than any man since the Caesars. His lands, his ships, his men, why all alone he could crush our little island. I fear. I fear what follows.'

He took the white queen and placed it in the centre of the board.

'We stand apart and with few allies,' he said. 'Only the great moat of the Channel defends us, and it is a perilous, narrow thing.'

Sir Henry planted pawns before the queen.

'Meanwhile,' he continued, 'Spain gathers her armies and plots our destruction. Spain is vengeful for Mary, our Queen Elizabeth's sister, the Spanish king's dead wife, the queen that was. Spain fights for their hope of a united Church again. To stem the bleeding of their treasure ships by our Admirals Hawkins and Drake. To stop our meddling in their war in the Low Countries.'

He planted a red queen and bishops, knights and castles in one corner of the board.

'Meanwhile, France ...'

He took the red king and placed it in the other corner of the board.

He pointed. 'King Henry, third of that name. Catholic majesty of France. Sodomite, they say. I know not. I do know that this King Henry has had no children. I know also that since his brother's death in December of last year, he has no heir save Henry of Navarre.'

He placed the white king on the board.

'One trouble only,' he said, his finger resting on the crown of the piece, 'Navarre is a Protestant Huguenot and hated of Catholic France. The Guise ...'

Sir Henry paused and looked at William. 'You know the Guise? No, why should you? The Guise are the most powerful nobles in France. They are fanatics for Rome. They will do anything they can to stop Navarre from becoming king.'

Sir Henry pushed the white king over towards the white queen. 'Think what might be if England no longer stood alone against Rome.'

He pushed the red king over towards the red queen. 'Think what would face England if Spain and France stood together against her.'

Sir Henry emptied his glass. William watched his face and saw his eyes darting back and forth across the board. The little knight reached out and placed two more pieces on the board. A red bishop and a white castle.

'The Pope,' Sir Henry said as he held the red bishop. 'No wonder what he wants. What he will work towards. All united again under Roman rule. Whatever serves to crush the Protestant heresy, to curb England. Yet, Venice ...'

Sir Henry put down the bishop and picked up the rook.

'We need a third colour for this piece,' he said. 'Venice doesn't care for red or white. She cares only for herself. If Venice might be persuaded that her best interests favour peace. That commerce comes when ships are heavy laden with cargo bales, not gunpowder and shot. That, in this, our English ships are better suited ...'

Sir Henry reached out and knocked over the red king and the red bishop with the rook. Then he placed it between the white queen and king, Venice between Elizabeth of England and Henry of Navarre.

'Venice is money and Venice is time. With them England may yet stand. Without them ...'

He and William stared at the board. Sir Henry looked up.

'We've time for one more game before bed, I think,' he said.

Five most vile and ragged foils

The English party made good progress through the south of France. The seventh day after the battle of the Crowing Cock, a month after they had left England, they crossed from France into the Duchy of Savoy and worked their way east past Turin. Azure skies through which no cloud passed to dull the heat of a Mediterranean sun accompanied their journey. The only shade came from the dust cloud kicked up by horses' hooves and carts' wheels as they passed along roads baked dry.

William was uncomfortable. The scab on his arm itched. By the middle of the day the heat was unbearable. Oldcastle was poleaxed by it. He took to lying in the back of the cart, shrouded in a makeshift tent he had constructed from a painted backdrop. From beneath this he could be heard moaning piteously and plaintively crying for water: 'Or sack or beer or sweet, sweet wine.'

Hemminges, temper shortened by the weather, would occasionally hammer on the side of the cart and demand silence from the prostrate figure. To little effect.

Days began earlier in an attempt to take advantage of the relative cool of morning. Still, the heat slowed the party's pace as they were forced to break more regularly to water the horses and to avoid the main heat in the middle of the day. Despite having begun to travel even before light, they had made slow progress through a twisting valley east of Turin. The angry urgings of Sir Henry's steward had failed to prevail against the torpor of the horses, their only effect being to put all in the party on edge. As a result they were late approaching their intended rest for that night and were still a couple of miles from it when they reached the bridge.

The river was not particularly wide or deep at this point in the summer. It was barrier enough though to demand, for the carts' benefit if nothing else, that they use the old Roman bridge. That would be a problem, for sat across the middle of the central span was a cart with a broken axle and an irate man bellowing at a horse. There was no way to pass.

'God's wounds. Will the trials of this day never end,' moaned Oldcastle.

The cart ground to a halt and Oldcastle poked his head out from beneath the sheet to gaze forlornly at the cause of the delay. Squinting and fanning himself vigorously with a hat, he subsided with a sigh as if expiring at the thought of more time spent in the sun.

William and Hemminges took a seat in the long dry grass in the shadow of the cart to await the resolution of the conundrum of the broken cart.

'Odd, isn't it?' said William.

Hemminges looked at him. William pointed at the cart on the bridge. Hemminges followed the finger but could not see what had prompted William's comment.

'To use such a fine horse to pull a cart, I mean,' said William. 'Odd. Still, the people are strange in these parts. Look at that man; no wonder he's angry with such a heavy cloak on such a hot day.'

Hemminges looked again. Ahead, Sir Henry could be seen gesturing his steward forward with quick flicks of his hand to see what might be made of the obstruction. The heat was cruel to Sir Henry. He mopped at his balding pate with a cloth. Some moments passed to the sound of Oldcastle snuffling beneath his canopy and Hemminges grumpily snapping off long-stemmed grass and whipping away at a fly buzzing about him.

Fallow, the steward, having apparently engaged in conversation with the owner of the broken cart to some effect, walked back towards the gathered members of Sir Henry's retinue. He beckoned them onto the bridge. Foulkes, Joiner and the two brothers, Ned and Tom, detached themselves from the small group with no great enthusiasm. They slowly made their way to join Fallow. Reaching the cart, the four bent to assist in lifting the corner with a broken wheel so that the cart might trudge its way off the bridge and out of the path of other traffic.

The owner of the broken cart could be seen mounting his horse as if to urge it to the hauling. As William watched the scene changed. The mounted man gave a shout and dug his heels into the horse. The beast sprang forward, slipping its traces, causing the cart to tip heavily forward. The four Englishmen holding onto the rear of the car were knocked backwards by the same motion.

Hemminges sprang to his feet. 'God above!' he cried.

Emerging from beneath the arch of the bridge near to their side of the bank came two figures carrying crossbows, faces wrapped in red cloth. As Hemminges spoke, they loosed. Coll toppled backward as if plucked at the collar by an unseen hand; a spray of blood twisted through the air. Nate, leaning next to him, gave a surprised yelp as a crossbow quarrel hammered into his chest.

On the bridge two more masked figures emerged from under sacking on the back of the cart, jumped down and fell on the sprawled English. Long knives flashed in summer sunshine. Men trying desperately to rise to their knees were kicked down and stabbed in chest or back. Fallow, who had been guiding operations and was not knocked over by the cart, stood a moment in astonishment before he came to his senses. He began to stumble backwards across the bridge. He turned to run. William watched as the two masked figures on the bridge took crossbows from the back of the cart. One fired, the quarrel looping into Fallow's back. The steward fell forward with a surprised O on his mouth. Sir Henry's horse, startled by the shouts of terror from the men about him, had begun to prance and twist. The old man struggled to bring the frightened mare under control. The other's quarrel, surely intended for the rider, found instead the flank of Sir Henry's horse. The mare reared and tossed its rider to the ground before sprinting away in agonised terror.

In a matter of moments more than half the English party were cut down. The four masked men drew swords and advanced on the remainder. Frightened men ran in several directions. A brave pair pulled weapons of their own and moved to protect the moaning figure of Sir Henry, who lay stunned by his fall. Watkins was one, Sir Henry's squire Hal the other. Of the two only Hal had a sword. He drew it.

The two men from the bridge were the first to reach them. Watkins braced himself. Yet for all his bravery and skill, he could offer only a knife against the extra reach of a sword. The masked man feinted an overhead cut and then flicked it calmly round the rising guard of the knife to catch the man in the armpit in a backhanded cut that lifted Watkins bodily from the ground.

Hal hurled himself on the other man with a terrified shout. His thrust was knocked aside with the dagger held in the masked man's left hand. The sword in the right hand was sent straight into the boy's chest. Hal sank to his knees, impaled. The masked man stepped forward and kicked him off the point. The boy lay awkwardly, bent on his back with knees folded under him; his chest made a wet sound as he drew air in ever shallower breaths.

'The cart. Get on the goddamned cart,' Hemminges yelled.

Hemminges' hand yanked William away from his reverie at the bloody scene before him. Hemminges pushed him onto the back of the cart and across Oldcastle. The driver, Connor, was already trying to turn the little cart around. His whip was flying back and forth upon the horse's back. Stung by its effects the horse was jerking forward trying to escape the harsh pull on its bit. Oldcastle had popped his head from his tent and was staring at the unfolding tragedy with his mouth sagging open. As William landed on him the air blew from Oldcastle's lungs. Then his head rapped sharply against the cart as it surged suddenly forward, stunning him. Arthur was pressed into the back, screeching with fright.

Hemminges was running down towards the river. William hauled himself up to the driver's box. He stared back at the four masked men who were continuing their butchery with casual efficiency. Great wails could be heard coming from unseen victims as the four spread out in search of the other members of the English party. Into the gap Hemminges raced. William watched him reach Sir Henry. Hemminges bent and hauled him across his shoulder. He turned and began to run back to the cart.

'Hold, Connor, hold. Hemminges is not with us,' William shouted at the terrified man. Connor paid him no heed.

William bounded from the back of the cart. 'Hold the cart, Nick,' he screamed at Oldcastle.

He started to run towards Hemminges. Oldcastle, finally following events, levered himself up and began to wrestle with a wild-eyed Connor, while the horse bucked and twisted in its traces. The nearest of the masked men saw them. He began shouting in a strange dialect to his companions and gesturing with his sword at Hemminges.

Hemminges was waving William back to the cart when the quarrel clipped him in the arm, spinning him to the ground. William slid in beside him and dragged him to his feet. The body of Sir Henry had crunched heavily to the ground as Hemminges fell. Now Sir Henry let out a piteous moan as William heaved him onto his own back. William and Hemminges, white in the face, staggered towards the cart. Oldcastle had a meaty hand on the collar of Connor, who was trying to free himself from the big man's grip by flicking his whip blindly behind him. William flung the semi-conscious Sir Henry onto the back. Hemminges crawled in beside him. William vaulted into the driver's box next to the carter.

'Drive, man, drive,' he cried.

All were now of one mind. The former struggle between Oldcastle and Connor was forgotten. The horse was whipped to action and lurched to haul the cart forward. A quarrel slammed into the side wall of the cart, punching through to embed in the side of a chest of costumes. Connor, hunched as low as he could manage, urged the horse forward with desperate shrieks. William heard the whine of another quarrel skimming low above the cart as it began to gather speed. Hiding low on the cart, William risked a glance behind him.

The horseman whose sudden shout had signalled the beginning of the attack was now swimming his horse back across the shallow river. His companions were cranking back their bows and gesturing at the escaping cart.

A false quiet fell. The only sounds that broke the silence were the panting breaths of Hemminges and Connor's sobbing voice whispering, 'Oh Lord, Oh Mary,' again and again.

William turned his gaze back to the cart. Hemminges lay to one side. Cradled across his legs was Arthur. The boy's eyes stared emptily at the sky. The fletches of a quarrel stuck from his neck.

Goodnight sweet prince

Connor urged the cart on with wild cries. It heaved over a stony hill and into the forested plain beyond. Connor's whip flicked back and forth across the horse's back like an adder's tongue. The cart lurched wildly across the stone-strewn path.

'For God's sake be calm, be calm,' called Hemminges.

He laid Arthur's dead body aside and hauled himself towards Connor.

'You'll snap the axle-tree, you fool,' he cried.

Connor ignored him. Hemminges tried to catch his whip arm as it danced about. Connor, fear-strengthened, flung his arm back and caught Hemminges across the mouth, knocking him into the well of the cart. The horse roared on, mouth foam-flecked.

Proof of Hemminges' prophecy came in that same instant. The cart began to slide, a wheel caught in a rut, there was a noise like Jove's thunderbolt. With a terrible heave the cart spat forth its contents. William saw the sky flash blue above his tumbling head and cracked the ground, rolling into the grass. Again a silence fell, but only for a moment.

'Up! Up!' Hemminges was hauling Oldcastle to his feet.

The great man stood pale and swaying. His eyes fixed on the lifeless form of Arthur. He sat heavily down again.

William scrambled across the grass to where Sir Henry lay motionless. The man's face was bloodied. He stared up at William and groaned.

'His leg is broke. Maybe more,' William called out.

Tears of pain ran from the corner of Sir Henry's eyes.

'He lives,' William muttered.

He turned to see Hemminges staring behind them. At the crest of the hill a silhouetted horseman appeared. As William watched, the figure swirled a signalling sword in the air and set his horse to the canter. Connor wasted no time on his passengers. He drew a knife, cut the traces and vaulted onto the back of the dray horse. He urged the terrified beast away.

'Stop him, Hemminges. He has the horse,' William shouted and lurched to his feet.

Hemminges did not move. The horseman closed on the cart. Hemminges stepped back to put the broken vehicle between him and the mounted man. The figure slowed as he approached. William could see little in the shadow between the brim of the hat and the red scarf wrapped about his face. To William's surprise the horseman did not stop.

Cantering past, he closed upon Connor ahead. The dray horse, tired from a hot day hauling the players' cart and driven to distraction by fear and Connor's whip, was easily overtaken. The sword flicked out. It was in the casualness of the slaughter that the horror lay. As Connor slid from the dray horse's back the swordsman swung his own horse round. He began to trot back towards the players.

Hemminges pushed Oldcastle. 'Get away, Nick.'

The fat man was too stunned to move. He sat heavily upon the ground.

'William, help him. Hurry, lad. Hurry …' Hemminges' voice was high-pitched.

William reached under Oldcastle's arms and tried to pull him to his feet. As well try to move a millstone. Hemminges kicked. Oldcastle screeched.

'Up and live, quickly, you fat fool,' cried Hemminges.

It was too late. The swordsman was near. He urged his horse to the canter. The sword was held, pointed in front of the animal's head, and William saw in it the death of all. He thought he heard a whispered word from Hemminges.

'Hopeless.'

Hemminges looked to William and Oldcastle and back to the horseman. Then the passage of time halted. What followed William saw as if in a series of embroidered moments: Hemminges standing breast bared as his murderer bore down upon him. Hemminges dart, swifter than a swallow, across the horse's path to catch the man's leg as he passed. The killer's sword-hand seeking to follow but, the horse's neck obstructing, rise and fall. It turning as it moved so that not the blade but the basket hilt cracked Hemminges' head. Hemminges' hands, tighter than iron on the man's leg, drag both to the ground as the horse rode heedless on. The swirl of cloak and sword as the two tumbled on the ground. The rise and fall of the heavy sword hilt as it hammered. Hemminges on his back and his murderer rearing up above him. The great groan from Hemminges and then the lion's roar from Oldcastle.

The anguish in Oldcastle's voice was outmatched by the fury. Oldcastle, with a broken spar of axle, loomed up behind the cloaked figure and struck. The masked man's skull turned to bloody, broken shards. Only William's restraining hand ended the assault. Whereupon Oldcastle ran to Hemminges. He knelt slowly by his friend and wept.

A curtain of blood had fallen across Hemminges face. He made no movement. Oldcastle stroked his friend's face.

'Oh, stay a while. Stay a while,' he whispered.

William could barely hear Oldcastle's voice.

'He's dead,' Oldcastle cried out. 'I might have saved him. Now he's gone forever.'

His howl was terrible to hear. He hugged Hemminges to him. Hemminges' body lolled in Oldcastle's arms. William did not know where to look. Oldcastle howled again. He drew breath. He looked up at William.

'He's yet alive,' he said. 'Quick, get me a glass from the baggage.'

'Nick, Nick, we must be away,' said William. 'The others will be upon us.'

Oldcastle snatched dry grass and held it in front of Hemminges' mouth.

'Look, look. His breath lifts the grass. He lives. He lives.'

William pulled gently at Oldcastle's shoulder but the anguished man threw him off.

'He said something before – before the villain was on him,' said Oldcastle. 'What was it? Did you hear it?'

William was no longer sure what he had heard in Hemminges' whisper. He knew only that he could bear to look upon the tragic scene no more.

He stumbled over to the figure of Sir Henry. The old man was groaning through clenched teeth. The dray horse, terror abating, had ambled back to the cart. William looked up to the crest of the hill. No one could be seen there yet but it could be only moments more before the other men, their bloody business finished, arrived. William hauled the little knight to his shoulder and staggered over to the dray horse. He shoved the old man over the horse's back to the tune of groans. He grabbed the severed reins to drag the horse's head round. On the crest of the hill figures appeared.

'Nick, we must go,' William said.

'No. No. There's breath yet in him.'

'Oldcastle, he's gone.'

'Please,' said Oldcastle.

'Nick, we'll all be dead unless we go,' said William. 'Now.'

William's stern command seemed to bring Oldcastle to his feet. He cast a final look at his friend and strode to the cart. Snatching from it two tied bags he joined William.

'Disguise.' He nodded at the bags.

Oldcastle and William moved off into the wood dragging the reluctant horse and its moaning load with them. Behind they left a scene to delight any butcher, bright red on green.

The first of the flies beginning to descend.

Upon the pikes o' the hunters

'We're hunted, Nick,' said William. 'We must lose the horse.'

'We cannot carry him,' Oldcastle said and gestured at the stricken knight.

'I know it. I know it. Trust me,' said William.

Oldcastle's face was streaked with grime and blood cut by tracks of tears but his voice was calm. Here was a man who had put his grief in a box. There it might stay, safely locked, until some more prosperous time allowed it to be taken out and treasured. William, too, felt cold and numb, a stony image of his morning's self. His only thought was safety.

'They will track us by the horse,' explained William. 'So, we take Sir Henry off and secrete him nearby while the horse is sent to lead them astray. Then we make our way to refuge and to succour.'

Oldcastle shrugged, past caring. William set to pulling Sir Henry from the horse. Oldcastle dragged the horse off to set the trail.

William lifted the little knight and carried him away, deeper into the wood. When they had gone fifty yards William laid him on the ground and dragged him into the cover of a thick bush. He turned to drag brush over the gaps.

Sir Henry's eyes flickered open.

'Watkins?' he said into the darkness beneath the bush's canopy.

'No, Sir Henry. William.'

'Shakespeare?'

William could hardly hear the hollow voice.

'The same, Sir Henry,' he said.

William heard laughter crackle in the knight's chest.

'The sacrificial lamb is become the shepherd,' Sir Henry said.

William stared at the knight. In the shadows of the bush Sir Henry's face could barely be made out.

'We are both sheep now, Sir Henry,' William said, 'and fly from hunger-starved wolves.'

'Not me, Master Shakespeare. My running is done.'

Sir Henry's hands fluttered over his leg. A great sob of pain wracked him. 'You must run for me.'

'Hush, Sir Henry,' said William. 'We'll not leave you but we cannot carry you. You must stay hidden here till aid can be found and brought.'

'You'll not leave me but I will leave you,' said Sir Henry. 'I feel myself going.'

The knight grabbed William with an urgent hand. 'Listen. All is changed but you must do this.'

He scrabbled about within his coat and pulled from it a package wrapped in a leather wallet. 'These are for Venice from England,' he said. 'See that they reach him.'

'Sir Henry, there's time enow.'

'There's never time. Do this. Do this. Venice must agree, our names for theirs.' Sir Henry's voice was urgent.

'Names, Sir Henry?'

'Yes, the names. You need the names. The letters too.'

Sir Henry's body shook. He clutched at his leg. His eyes stared wildly about him. His voice came in coughs and starts. 'The letters, Adam, the letters.'

He pressed the wallet into William's hand. 'Stay at the House of the White Lion. Watkins. We are known there,' he said.

'Sir Henry, I don't know what you want ...'

The grabbing hand pulled William close. 'For the Doge. The letters, for the Doge and none other. The names go with the sign of the Lion of St Mark. All turns on this. Promise me.'

'I do.'

'Swear it,' Sir Henry pressed.

'I do.'

William felt the breath shortening in Sir Henry's body.

'I have sinned,' Sir Henry said.

A little whispered voice in dying echoes ... 'Bless me, Lord, I have sinned.'

And all was silence.

'Oldcastle,' whispered William. 'Over here.'

'God's blood, William,' said Oldcastle clutching his chest in fright at William's voice from the darkness, 'I nearly soiled myself. The horse is gone and leads our pursuers a merry chase. Where is Sir Henry?'

'Gone too,' said William.

'Holy God,' moaned Oldcastle. 'We are undone.'

'Enough of that, Oldcastle. We still live. Darkness comes. We must find safety.'

'Darkness comes?' Oldcastle nodded. 'Yes, all's darkness now. Cheerless, dark and deadly.' He turned sad eyes on William and gestured: 'Lead on. Let us see what safety may be left us.'

With what manners …

Ahead lay welcoming lights. The pair had made their way circuitously to the road and headed west in the gathering dark until they saw ahead a coaching inn. Three sides of building and a high stone wall sealed off a courtyard. The inn seemed more keep than lodging. No wonder, for it sat alone in a grey swathe of road.

'Here's refuge,' said William.

'Thank God,' Oldcastle responded.

Oldcastle was a broken staff. William had hauled him much of the last mile.

'Why do we wait?' said Oldcastle. 'Let us be in. Welcome, ale, food.'

William forgave the note of petulance in Oldcastle's voice.

'What if the men that attacked us have gone ahead to this place?' he cautioned.

'Vagabond kites?' said Oldcastle. 'Crows? They're flown back to their nest. May they be buried in it.'

William did not think so. Carrion birds do not set traps or hunt the living and leave the dead. These were wolves. He hurried after Oldcastle, who had been given new spirit by the thought of wine nearby.

'Wait a moment, Nick,' William urged. 'At least, let me go first and see how the land lies.'

Oldcastle grunted but made no further protest. He sat in the shadow of a tree and waved William on to approach the inn.

'Open the gate there, ho!' he cried.

William hammered at the door. After a moment a voice called out from above. He looked up. A cautious face peered over the wall of the inn's yard. Again the voice addressed him, but in a language that William did not know.

'A little help here,' William tried again in timid Latin.

'What's your business?' a voice called down.

William gave a little prayer of thanks that he was understood.

'We have been attacked,' he said. 'On the road. All my company are dead save myself and one other. Help please.'

'Get away,' the voice said. 'You think we're fools to open our doors to you and your thieving friends.'

William's mouth gaped. Of all the welcomes he had thought to receive, to be taken as a robber was not one.

'I'm no thief,' he said.

'You're no honest man either,' answered the voice. 'Look at your rags. Get away. We'll not be fooled again.' The voice above snorted. 'Open the door and have your fellows set upon us.'

'I am alone,' protested William.

'I catch you in your lies already, thief. You said you had a friend.'

It was William's turn to snort. 'I do. He's injured and resting over there.'

William's mind was turning. He had approached the inn fearing that the embassy's attackers would be there already. That was no more his worry. Now he feared they would not be given the safety of the inn. How to reassure the gatekeeper he was an honest man? He began to fear that he and Oldcastle would have fitful sleep beneath the tree that night, if they were not attacked again.

'I tell you we were set upon,' said William. 'My "rags" are clothes stained with the blood of friends.'

'Away, thief. I'll no more of you,' the head said and ducked back into the darkness.

'Go to,' William muttered, then louder: 'There's coin here. My master is a noble man. Give succour and be rewarded.'

Another snort came from above but the face returned.

'Please,' said William at the sight. 'I shall return with my master, you'll see. A knight.'

'*Hah!* Very well, bring your knight. I'll wait,' said the voice.

William cursed under his breath and turned away to the sound of mocking laughter.

'Never,' said Oldcastle.

'We have no other choice, Nick,' said William.

'It's madness. And capital offence if we're discovered.'

'It's not just a cold night beneath the stars we face but those that hunt us. We must have safety. Safety lies at the inn. They will not let us enter if we seem not better than we are,' William said. 'In the morning we are gone and none are the wiser.'

'Why must we pretend to be other than we are?' asked Oldcastle. 'Will they not let poor players in?'

'They will not.'

'There's Christian charity for you,' huffed Oldcastle.

'There's caution on a dark road in difficult times,' replied William.

Oldcastle blew air between his lips. '*Faugh!* Say rather there's no profit in the saving of players but much in the saving of a gentleman.'

'True. And still,' William said.

He waited. Distantly, within the wood behind, the faint howl of a wolf cut the silence of the night. Oldcastle's head turned to the noise, then back to William.

'They will never believe us,' said Oldcastle.

William smiled. 'What? Have you never played a knight before?'

'Of course,' Oldcastle said.

'Was not believed by those who saw it?' William asked.

Oldcastle's chest swelled. 'Was met with roars and the stamping of feet.'

'Well then.'

Oldcastle rose unsteadily to his feet. 'It seems I was right to bring disguise,' he said.

With great dignity Oldcastle bowed to William and, taking the bundle of clothes snatched from the cart, strode behind the tree to don the mantle of a knight. William spoke to the gloom as Oldcastle dressed.

'I'll be your steward and you the knight,' he said. 'We've no money between us so our credit depends on your performance.'

'Never doubt me, William.'

'I do not,' his friend replied.

'What is our theme?' asked Oldcastle.

'We'll play the parts we know, Sir Henry and his embassy,' said William. 'In that way we are like to find ourselves constant in the telling.'

Oldcastle emerged. He had shed the bloody doublet and donned a costume of rich red raiment. A feathered cap sat at a jaunty angle.

'Will't serve?' he asked.

William turned towards the inn. 'Let's find out,' he said.

'What knight speaks so little Latin and so poorly?' the voice demanded.

William sighed inwardly at Oldcastle's lack of learning. There was at least easy explanation.

'An English knight,' he called up.

William feared that Oldcastle would never get the chance to play the part, unless by moonlight from ten paces distant.

'Who's that below?'

A second voice, refined and clear where there first was coarse and suspicious, joined in.

'I do not know, my lord,' the first voice said, now obsequious. 'They claim to be an English knight and his servant. Robbed by the road.'

'Well, fellow, let them in,' the second voice said.

'I fear an ambush, my lord. There are bandits on these roads would try to trick us.'

William saw his chance.

'Yes,' he called up. 'Bandits that have attacked our party. Look at us. Do we look as if we have the strength for robbery?'

A muttered conversation from above was followed by the sound of bolts being drawn. Light from the courtyard spilled out from the open gate through which walked William and his false knight.

Stands on a tickle point

In the courtyard stood four men. Though the three servants of the inn stood with swords in hand, the eye was drawn only to the fourth, whose splendour cast all others into shadow. As different in appearance from the others as the night the day.

'I am Giovanni Prospero, Count of Genoa,' the splendid man said.

'Your servant, my lord,' said William. 'My master, Sir Henry Carr.'

William gestured at Oldcastle as he bowed.

'I am his steward, Fallow,' said William.

'You're hurt?' the Count asked.

The voice mellifluous from thin, bloodless lips. The brow arched in polite enquiry above an eagle's beak. A handsome face against whose sharp features William imagined many maidens' ships had found a rocky end.

'The blood is not ours, my lord,' William replied. The proud manner of the man before him made William disdain himself. Next to such gathered majesty William felt every patch and thread in his muddied and bloody clothing.

'What's he say?' Oldcastle enquired with a formal nod to the man.

'He's asking if we're hurt, Sir Henry,' said William.

'Most gracious, most gracious,' Oldcastle said.

Oldcastle did his best against the bruises of the day to bow. He embarked on conversation of his own. His Latin as beaten as himself.

'You, sir, are a man of true nobility,' said Oldcastle. 'It has been a terrible day, an awful day.'

For a moment Oldcastle's voice caught in his throat. He recovered.

'Finally, we are returned to civilisation, to comfort,' he said in English. 'I am undone with tiredness.'

Oldcastle staggered. William did not think it all play-acting.

One of the landlord's men sheathed his sword and made to help Oldcastle to a chair, then halted. He held himself a moment until a slight nod from the dark figure of the Count released him to assist. William and the servant steadied Oldcastle.

'I do not speak English,' the Count said.

The man's tone made clear he did not consider the difficulties in communication were his failing.

'My master, Sir Henry Carr,' said William, 'is expressing his gratitude to you and to the owner of the inn, my lord.'

'Quite so,' replied Prospero.

The party moved to the comfort of the inn. William sat down on a bench and was handed a glass of wine. His hand shook to take it. The tension of the day, held at bay by the demands of that awful afternoon and evening, were freed to flicker through him. He looked across at Oldcastle. He seemed shrunken.

In a high-backed chair beside the low fire sat Prospero. His legs, dressed in fine black cloth, stretched before him, crossed at the ankle. He reached out and received a glass of wine from the landlord without his eyes leaving William and Oldcastle.

'So,' said Prospero.

'My lord?' a tired William replied.

The man had a sharp and hungry look. William did not like it.

'How came you to this perilous pass?' asked Prospero.

William bristled. The question was understandable, expected. The offence lay, rather, in the manner of its asking. It spoke of amusement, not sympathy. William noted a small scar that ran across the socket of the man's eye from cheek to brow. Its presence pulled the man's eyebrow up, a further mockery.

'Our party was on course for Venice,' said William. 'As we rode towards our planned night's lodging we were set upon. Our party murdered.'

'All dead?' Prospero interrupted.

'All.'

'Save yourselves,' said Prospero.

'By God's grace and only by a hair's breadth,' answered William. 'And at great cost. They killed our company, children and all.'

'Innocents 'scape not the thunderbolts of Heaven.' Prospero smiled sadly to accompany his saying. The sorrow did not reach so high as his eyes. 'Tell me what happened.'

William felt he began to understand the man. Dull is the life of those to whom all is given, for there is no exercise in it. Some address the boredom with adventures and high deeds. Others, and this surely was one, live in the lives of others. William had no desire to be entertainment for a bored lord or pass his losses before a stranger's eyes to dazzle them. He told the tale of their assault in swift, short statements.

'And so we find ourselves here, my lord,' said William. 'At the mercy of our host's kindness.'

William had finished his tale.

'Not at all,' said Prospero with a wave of his hand. 'I consider it my duty to offer you succour and our host his true recompense.'

Oldcastle, unable to follow the full flow of conversation, was turning his head from William to Prospero in a vain attempt to gather what was happening. He saw William's surprise.

'What's happening now?' he asked.

'The Count has paid our lodging for the night,' William said in English.

'That's uncommon kind of him,' said Oldcastle.

'It is, it is,' acknowledged William.

Prospero smiled graciously as Oldcastle stood unsteadily and bowed to him before sitting heavily back down.

'You will return now to England? Or on to Venice?' asked the Count.

William realised he had no answer to this question. For some hours he had thought only of immediate horrors, not of the next day. He turned to Oldcastle.

'He wants to know if we are returning to England now.'

'I understood that much,' said Oldcastle. 'Well, not now. I must sleep first.'

'No. Not now, Sir Henry,' said William, wishing Oldcastle's had his wits more about him. 'In the morning. Where do we go?'

'Well, England, of course,' said Oldcastle.

William paused. He was aware of the scrutiny of the Count on him as he and Oldcastle deliberated. He wished they could have privacy.

'I don't think we can go to England straight,' said William.

'No, of course not. You're right,' Oldcastle said. 'We must try to find poor John's body and give him a Christian burial.'

William nodded. 'Yes, but I think we must go also to Venice.'

'What? Whatever for?'

'You have something you must deliver,' said William.

'I do? No, I don't,' said Oldcastle.

'Are you sure? Sir Henry?'

Oldcastle looked puzzled but William was thinking of the weight of Sir Henry's packet of letters in his doublet. He had intended simply to dispose of them as he passed through the woods. That he had paused was not just in memory of the droll little knight but in fear of what would be asked of the survivors of the massacre. How had they alone survived when all the others were murdered? To whom would explanation have to be given? Who had set men upon them? William did not think they were the victims of ragged bandits, though the woods were full of such people. Poor thieves did not come armed with crossbows and fine swords. These were hunting dogs and William did not know who held the leash. These fears made him think that the better part of valour lay in completion of the task given to him by Sir Henry. More than that, such a deed might, if not explanation make, then fair excuse when he and Oldcastle returned to England.

Oldcastle did not follow William's thoughts but he caught on quick enough to the possibility that William understood something he did not. Prospero, whose eyes had not left Oldcastle, clearly waited an answer.

'Ah yes. You are right, Fallow. We must to Venice.' Oldcastle nodded at Prospero and then muttered, 'When our wits are quite recollected.'

William translated. Prospero smiled, revealing sharp little canines set at an odd angle within his mouth.

'What a fine pass of fortune,' the Count declared. 'Had you been for Verona or for England I should have been forced to leave you. But I travel to Venice myself. It would be an honour to accompany you.'

William moved to fend off Prospero's goodwill.

'Most kind, my lord, but beyond the call of courtesy,' he said.

'I did not ask you,' the Count said. The eagle's beak swung to William. 'I asked your master. Do not interrupt me again but do your office and translate between your betters.'

William had thoughts on the subject of superiors. It was with an effort of will he pressed them from his mouth. To express the hot touch of choler would do him no good. As like light the gunpowder on which all sat; harm one, harm all.

'Sir Henry,' said William, 'the Count offers to accompany us on our journey to Venice.'

'Really? That's very kind of him,' Oldcastle said in English.

If only Oldcastle's brain was not befuddled by the day. William rolled his eyes. Fortunately neither Prospero nor Oldcastle were looking at him. The former watching the latter and the latter's eyes slumping to the table with tiredness. Prospero may not have understood Oldcastle's words but he had no expectation but acquiescence to his suggestion and took Oldcastle as having offered it.

'Very good. You and your party,' he did not look at William when he said this, 'are clearly not capable of completing the journey without assistance.'

Oldcastle spoke again, this time once more in his limp Latin. 'My lord, forgive us. We are broken men and must to our beds.'

'Of course,' Prospero said. He rose and bowed to Sir Henry. 'Please convey to your master my wishes for a bountiful rest. We shall have a long day of travel in the morning, but the day after, Venice.'

In the cup a spider steeped

William and Oldcastle were shown to a small bedroom at the back of the inn in which two cots were made up with linens. The innkeeper left them with a stub of candle and a peevish bow. The door shut behind them.

William and Oldcastle sat on their cots across from each other, their heads bowed low together in conversation.

'I'm sorry,' said Oldcastle.

'We've no choice now,' said William. 'Refuse his hospitality and he'll grow suspicious.'

'I should have thought more carefully. It's one thing to fool a man for a night, it's quite another to maintain the illusion over many days.' Oldcastle's voice was tight with tension and exhaustion. 'Our cozening will be discovered. Then what? Nothing good.'

'You're right, Oldcastle. This performance will define us.'

'No doubt. Fail in it and it will be our lives,' said Oldcastle.

'Let us just to Venice,' William offered, 'then we can find excuse to part ways, deliver the packet and be gone.'

'We cannot linger in Venice, William,' Oldcastle said. 'I haven't the stomach for it.'

'You've stomach to spare, Nick.'

'William. I'm serious,' Oldcastle answered.

'Forgive me, Nick. Forgive me,' William said. 'A serious day, with serious business in't.' He held up a weary hand even as his head drooped. 'To Venice and then gone.'

The two undressed and lay on their cots. After a moment Oldcastle spoke into the darkness.

'I never thought to see Hemminges fall. I've seen him best better before.'

'The man was armed and horsed,' William said.

'Still.'

'Even Hercules must yield to odds.' William spoke gently.

'So,' said Oldcastle.

The sad conversation faltered. After a pause they said more in whispers, but it was not clear if it was to each other or to the darkness.

'By the Mass, I'd swear he lived, yet,' said Oldcastle.

'It was the saddest scene,' William said.

Oldcastle sighed. 'I can't believe him gone.'

William heard Oldcastle try to choke his sob with a cough.

'I think I shall sleep,' Oldcastle said. 'Sleep may mend this care.'

They said no more till morning.

Outside in the courtyard Prospero could be seen, had any been awake to view the meeting, talking by the gate. He spoke to a squat man with a broad-brimmed hat and a red scarf just visible between the folds of his cloak.

'You've failed, Borachio,' the Count said.

'My lord, you know?' replied Borachio.

'That the English Ambassador escaped your ambush? I do.'

'How?'

'How, *my lord*,' Prospero reproved him with a wiggled finger. 'He's here with his steward.'

'I'll deal with him straight, my lord,' said Borachio.

The Count stopped him. 'You'll do no such thing.'

'My lord?'

'Even this wantwit of an innkeeper will notice if his guests go to bed whole but in the morning are to be found only in parts. No, no. You are a good, blunt instrument Borachio. This, however, calls less for the club than the poniard.'

'As you say, my lord,' said Borachio.

'Don't bristle, Borachio,' admonished the Count. 'You're not a hedge-hog.' Prospero smiled a wicked smile, all teeth. 'And if you were, your spines would not even dent the leather of my shoes were I to step on you.'

Borachio felt the night grow colder.

'My lord, the failure was not mine,' he said. 'All went according to the scheme save that headstrong child Conrad charged after the 'scaping party and was killed in the chase.'

'Then he has paid for his fault has he not?' said Prospero.

The sullen Borachio made no reply.

'Were you not the leader, Borachio?' asked the Count. 'Was not the scheme yours?'

The Count took silence for assent to his questions. 'Then do not seek to pass the responsibility for its failure on to others.'

'I do not, my lord,' said Borachio.

The noise that the Count made through his pursing lips indicated that he remained to be convinced. 'It's no matter, Borachio,' he said. 'There will be opportunity enough to make recompense in the days to come.'

Prospero's attention shifted from the pleasures of unnerving his brutish servant. 'All dead save these two in the inn?'

'All, by my count.'

'A shame that our man amongst the embassy was killed.'

'That was the scheme. No chance for double-dealing. The Cardinal ordered it.'

'The scheme had the Ambassador dead too. Living, a spy still in his party would have had use.'

Borachio shrugged.

'You searched the dead?' Prospero asked.

'We did,' Borachio replied.

'By your silence I take it you did not find the letters.'

'We did not.'

'The bodies?' the Count asked.

'Buried.'

Prospero paced a little, tapping his lips with a finger as he moved.

'Your failure to obtain the letters is most unfortunate. Who knows what else you have missed. This English Ambassador is a curious creature. How oddly he is suited. I have never seen the like before. I think he bought his doublet in Italy, his hose in France, his bonnet in Germany, and his behaviour? Everywhere.'

Prospero stopped next to his servant and turned dancing eyes on him. 'There is something unseen here. For that reason alone we should stay our hands.'

He tapped at his teeth. 'Even if it were not so, my spirit wills it,' he said. 'The arrival of the Ambassador into my care presents many opportunities.'

'I thought our orders were to have him killed,' said Borachio.

'Thought? Thought? Oh, my dear Borachio. It is not for your thinking that you are employed, and if it were then you are sore overpaid.'

Prospero's mind dismissed Borachio and travelled through schemes and stratagems choosing one that best suited his purpose and his artistry. Borachio interrupted him.

'His Holiness will wish to know how matters proceed,' Borachio said.

Prospero turned his cynic's brow on the sturdy little man. He wondered, not for the first time, whether Borachio planned to betray him with a behind-hand stab. If he did so, would it be at the expressed wish of the new Pope? Oh Borachio, you are such a useful villain, Prospero thought. Were it not so, I'd kill you here and now. As it is, I shall wait until your use is all used up. Then will I serve the servant for his double-dealing.

In the shadow of evening Prospero's features, smiling wickedly, stood sharp set. Being caught in that gaze, Borachio wondered what thoughts lay behind it. He was angry with himself at the fear that shivered him.

'Leave this to me, Borachio,' said Prospero. 'We have a double mission and this fat fool of an ambassador may serve me in both before we make disposal of him.'

'As you will it, my lord,' said Borachio.

'Always, Borachio. Always.'

What may man within him hide

William woke to discover Oldcastle already risen. Oldcastle up at such an hour was a sight rarer than the phoenix. William was about to make play of it when something in the way that Oldcastle stood stopped him. The old man had never looked older than he did in that moment. The great frame was braced against the window's ledge. Though it seemed as if the scene surveyed beyond his bowed head suggested his thoughts were elsewhere.

'Nick?' William said.

Oldcastle straightened. He let out a sigh. Then, after a moment, slapped his hand upon the ledge.

'Up, lad,' he said. 'I'll have no slovenly fellows in my service. We must be about our business.'

When he turned to William he had a smile on his face for all that his eyes were still red-rimmed. William threw off the thin sheet of his cot and pulled on his shoes.

Downstairs Prospero was already at his breakfast. He rose and acknowledged Sir Henry's presence with a bow. A hand pointed to the vacant seat beside him. Oldcastle gratefully took it and managed to suppress a look of disappointment at the strange fare put before him in place of his beloved sausage and eggs. William sat next to him. Prospero's other eyebrow rose to match its fellow's level. He turned pointedly to speak to Oldcastle.

'Is it customary in England for the servants to dine with their masters?'

William cursed inwardly. He had forgot himself and his place. Fortunate for him that Oldcastle was more alert that morning.

'Not in the ordinary course, my lord,' answered Oldcastle. 'However, Fallow, in addition to being my steward, is also my bastard and I indulge him.'

'I thought he seemed young to hold such a position in your household,' said Prospero.

Was it William's fancy or did Prospero seem to soften slightly in his attitude to William. It was hard to tell from his tone of voice. There seemed for a moment to be a genuine smile on the face that had, till then, born only a sardonic one.

'Do you smell a fault in it?' Oldcastle beamed good-heartedly. 'True he came too saucily into this world before he was called for, but his mother had a merry eye and there was good sport in his making.'

Oldcastle paused to gaze on William as if reliving the moment of his conception in his mind.

'Would that her field had been as barren as her name had promised,' he said. 'Still, we must acknowledge our sins if we are to be forgiven them, and the bastard must be recognised. "There's no pleasure in permitted sin. Forbidden things are most desired", as the poet says.'

Oldcastle turned a smug regard on William as he deployed words of Ovid that William had once admonished him with outside a Shoreditch brothel. William restrained a rolling of his eyes only by a titanic effort of will. Oldcastle rounded his speech off by ruffling William's hair, to the irritation of William and the great amusement of Prospero.

'One cannot wish the fault undone when the issue is so proper,' Prospero said with a nod to William. 'I know something of bastards. Why treat a man as base when his mind's as sharp and frame as firm as legitimate issue? I have no time for customs when that custom leads us false.'

At that moment the travellers' breakfast was interrupted by the arrival of a solid man with a surly look. Ugly, as if his maker had carelessly reached out a hand and smudged the clay of his face before it baked.

'My lord, the horses stand in readiness,' said Borachio.

The ugly man stared with impertinent intensity at Oldcastle and William. Prospero seemed not to notice his servant's ill manners.

'Good, Borachio.' Prospero stood and wiped his lips with a linen handkerchief. 'Then we must be off. We have some way to ride before we reach the barge that will carry us the rest of the way.'

Oldcastle sat like a sack of suet on his horse. There had been a moment when William feared that Oldcastle's poor seat would give their counterfeit away. Oldcastle, whose mind seemed to be working with a clearness that William was not used to, had excused himself by reference to injuries taken in the previous day's tumult. An explanation that seemed to satisfy both the Count and his servant.

William had taken an instant dislike to the servant, Borachio. There was nothing on which to pin this dislike. William was not so foolish as to take the man's ugliness for an ugly nature. Yet he distrusted him, and that mistrust built when the small party rode past the place of the previous day's battle and found it empty.

'It was here he fell, I'll swear it,' Oldcastle said as he looked about. 'There, upon the trampled ground, blood still.'

Of all other signs of battle there were none. Even the players' cart had disappeared.

'Where can it be?' Oldcastle said. He trammelled the sides of his horse, seeking to move it deeper into the woods in search of Hemminges' body.

Prospero looked bored.

'No doubt the robbers sought to hide the signs of their misdeeds,' the Count offered.

Whatever softening there had been in Prospero at breakfast had been replaced with the same disdain William had noted at their first meeting. It made him wonder what made the Count wish to share his journey with the English Ambassador. Christian charity? The bond of nobles? Simple curiosity? William doubted each.

'Robbers do this? I think not, my lord,' said William. 'Take and run I warrant you is your highway robber's business. Not this. Not disguises and ambuscades.'

William could not understand it. He had already ridden to the ridge and seen that ahead too there was no sign of the English party, neither baggage nor body. That robbers might steal the carts and the luggage he could understand, but not that they would trouble themselves to remove the bodies.

'As you wish, Master Fallow,' replied the Count. 'Perhaps you have had more experience with thieves.'

William drew breath to give this barb sharp reply but Borachio cut across him to speak in Latin more crumpled than Oldcastle's.

'Wolves.'

'What's he say?' Oldcastle had rejoined the group. William looked at Borachio without speaking. The man had a smirking smile on his face.

'Wolves, my lords,' said Borachio. 'They will drag the bodies to their den to feast upon them at their leisure.'

'What's he say, William?' asked Oldcastle. 'What's this talk of "wolves"?'

Vicious little man, thought William. To proffer this suggestion when he knows both that it must be false and that the thought of it alone will give much sadness to the distressed man before him. William was glad that between Borachio and Oldcastle lay so little learning that each could understand but one word in five of the other.

'Nothing, Sir Henry,' said William. No purpose to upsetting Oldcastle further. 'He says he does not know. He says it cannot be wolves, for there are none in these parts.'

Impatient for the off, Prospero spoke. 'Come, Sir Henry. If this sad business is concluded, as it is clear it must be, then we should ride.'

Oldcastle nodded but did not move, his head still scanning the scene for sign of Hemminges' body. Prospero waited a moment more and then simply turned his horse and began to trot along the road. The sound of hoofbeats on the earth stirred Oldcastle and with a final glance at the ill-fated woods he drew a great breath and spurred his horse's sides, trotting after Prospero. William was left with the smirking Borachio. The man's arms were propped across the horn of his saddle. Borachio slowly raised one to make an obsequious gesture that William lead off. William did.

As he rode William tried to decide whether he would be the better man for finding a way to wipe that smirk from Borachio's face or for rising above his provocation. He knew which would give him the greater pleasure. He passed the rest of the day's ride in contemplation of it.

The brief and the tedious of it

Prospero, not confined by the need to travel with a great train of baggage and with discretion as Sir Henry had been, chose to use the canals that crossed Italy to travel to Venice. A few hours' ride from the fateful woods, the small party had changed from horses to a barge. In the company of two Savoyard merchants who joined with goods for the markets of Venice, the barge hauled them forth while Prospero reclined in cushioned comfort and Oldcastle made small and stilted conversation through the medium of William.

The closeness of their travelling arrangements, the three men tucked neatly into a cabin at the front of the barge, along with chairs, tables and, strangely, an elaborately painted chest, added to William's unease. He noticed for the first time that Prospero was delightfully perfumed. William distrusted it. No man should smell so good. He was also conscious of his own rank sweat and resented the contrast. He resented more finding himself put in the role of secretary of small value save as a mouthpiece for Oldcastle when his Latin failed him. That burden greater since Oldcastle, growing melancholic, had been robbed of the ability to make more than the briefest of answers, which William felt obliged to supplement for fear of offending their host.

In that ambition William seemed destined for failure. At least with respect to his own presence, which Prospero appeared to find increasingly irritating.

'Scribble, scribble, scribble, Master Fallow. What is't with you and your constant scratchings?'

William looked up as Prospero loomed over him.

'My commonplace book, my lord,' William said.

'And what is that?' asked Prospero.

'A book in which I make note of matters of interest. It is a habit I acquired at school and have carried with me ever since. I find my thoughts find form and substance as I write them, when in my head they remained only ghosts.'

William gave greater explanation than he had intended. He was annoyed with himself that he did so in an attempt to win over the goodwill of the arrogant prince who stood before him. The more so since it had no effect.

'Are you still a schoolboy, then?' said Prospero.

'Of course not, my lord,' answered William.

Prospero cut him off. 'Then kindly do not weary me with your schoolboy antics.'

William tried one more tack. 'I have also made some attempts at poetry.'

'*Faugh!*' Prospero interrupted. 'An art I cannot bear. A dry wheel grating in an axle-tree is kinder to my ear than mincing poetry. I counsel against it, Master Fallow. There is no profit in poetry.'

The journey was thus both faster than the slow march of Sir Henry's travelling embassy and more comfortable, at least in the method of travel. The strange company and perilous position William and Oldcastle found themselves in prevented true repose.

Almost as unhappy and uncomfortable in the journey was Borachio. Nightly on their three-day journey he pleaded with Prospero that they might make an end of the English.

'I tell you there is something strange about this pair,' said Borachio. 'I'll swear the English knight was not this great weight of man we carry with us now.'

'You'll swear it?' Prospero asked.

'I've told you I didn't see him close but –' Borachio broke off, '– I'll swear he was smaller. More like the steward in size than the knight. What does it matter? Let us kill them and have done with it.'

'I've told you no, Borachio,' Prospero said and dismissed him with a wave. 'My patience withers. Do not ask again. I see for these Englishmen much use.'

'If they reach Venice we may lose them,' said Borachio. 'Here they can be done and the bodies in the canal before the sun rises.'

'You've found the letters, then,' the Count said.

'They are not in their cabin,' Borachio replied. 'Surely the fat one or his steward has them on his person. Kill them and then search the bodies.'

Prospero looked down at the beautifully carved travelling chess set open before him.

'If they are not on them, what then?' he said. 'Will you ask their corpses where the letters have gone?'

'Put them to the question first, then.'

'Even if we could put them to the question without drawing attention on ourselves, what lies will we hear from tortured lips? And the proof far from us.'

'Leave that to me; they'll not gull us while hot iron waits and will do no more than whisper.'

'I tell you no.'

'My lord –'

'No. You're a fool, Borachio. Impatient and coarse.'

'My lord has no need to insult me,' Borachio said.

'Oh but I do, Borachio,' the Count replied looking up. 'First, because it pleases me to do so. Second, because it seems I must hammer home my words in terms hard as iron nails or they will not enter your thick skull. I say again, I have plans for these Englishmen. In Venice.'

Interlude

Venice, June 1585

Made him give battle to the lioness

'Madonna. For the sake of us all, sit still.'

Isabella paused in her pacing but did not sit. Her mind was in a motion perpetual and her body matched it. Her striding was replaced with the fluttering of a fan.

'Mother of God. I cannot bear this fidgeting,' the old man said as he slapped his palette down.

He began to clamber down the scaffold. Behind him, far from finished, lay his latest work. It was destined for the Salla della Scrutinio in the Doge's Palace. One of several showing the triumphs of Venice as she built her empire. *The Capture of Zara from the Hungarians in 1346 amid a Hurricane of Missiles*; this was but a working title. He would think of something more succinct, more pithy, in time. Or maybe not. People would call it what they will. He had never really cared for titles. After all, he had been born Jacopo Comin, but everyone called him something different now, Tintoretto. Except for the lady, except for Isabella Lisarro. In this, as in so many things, she was exceptional.

Isabella snapped her fan shut. The noise loud in the space of his workshop.

'How can I sit still when he is out there?' she said. 'I know nothing, Jacopo. Nothing.'

She slapped her fan against her hand. She wore high britches that day, aping a man's style. It was the fashion in Venice for the women, at least the more daring among them, to dress in men's clothes. The dark green silk of the britches was complemented by a jacket of white silk. It bore a high-collared ruff of pearl and lace that plunged low and was a source of considerable distraction to the painter.

'Be patient, Isabella, and all will be well,' he said.

'You can say this,' she retorted. 'You, whose imagination can expand to encompass that possibility. I cannot. How can the stomach be filled by bare imagination of a feast? How can I make all well by the mere thinking of it so?'

'Often have I heard you make this argument,' he replied. 'I know it false as I know your claim to lack imagination false. Be calm and put your mind to work.'

Tintoretto was in an unhappy mood. Ordinarily he would welcome a visit from his friend, but Isabella had been of late as changeable and dangerous as a lion with a thorn in its paw. Tintoretto loved women and, of all women, he loved those with wit and creativity and the spark of danger in them most. He thought of his daughter, Marietta. She had that to her. She was a painter of rare skill; skill greater than that of his son Domenico, poor boy. A smile, infrequently seen on the intense little man, creased his face and lifted the drooping eyes for a moment.

He wanted Isabella to sit still for a moment so that he could have calm to resume his work, but he also wanted to watch her walk and see the long tails of her jacket flare as she turned revealing the stockinged calves in all their slender glory. He wanted to watch the single thread of rose-gold hair that had broken loose from her carefully piled tresses flash past, a dragon's tongue hissing. It was everything he loved in a painting, colours and movement and, yes, fury and power.

Madonna, but she was still beautiful, especially in her fury. Her brow furrowed with concentration and the full lips that always seemed to promise they would whisper you secrets if you were only fortunate enough to be allowed close, slightly parted to reveal such white teeth, set with determination. Tintoretto sighed.

'Isabella. This is not you,' he said.

'What do you mean?'

'To dash about like a frightened mouse,' said Tintoretto. 'You are the lion. You don't scurry about, you wait and then you pounce.'

He twisted his hand as if turning a glass of wine to find the light.

'To see you like this, I find it hard to reconcile you with the Isabella who quelled the Inquisitors of Venice with a single glance or brought King Henry of France to his knees as if her smile were a wrestler's throw.'

Isabella paused and pointed at the painter with her fan.

'You are right,' she said, 'as always.'

She strode across the floor of the workshop and kissed him on the forehead.

'I am all activity but without result,' she said. 'It is true I know nothing. Now how to remedy that? That is the question. I fear the assassin but he does not fear me.'

Tintoretto had wandered over to the window. He picked up a small knife and began to scrape paint from a palette.

'Why do you laugh?' Isabella turned at the sound from the window.

'I am just recalling those I have painted,' he replied. 'Do you remember Aretino?'

'No,' Isabella said.

'Of course not, you were a child when he died, if you were alive at all,' said Tintoretto. 'Sweet mother, he was a scourge. He made his living by being the poisoned pen of many a man and as many paid him just so that he would not direct his barbs in their direction. He asked me to paint him once, though he knew I did not like him.'

'And why does that make you laugh?' Isabella asked.

Tinteretto held up the small paint-covered knife. 'I was reminded by this,' he said. 'When I finally agreed I went to his house for the sitting, but each time I took the measure of him for the painting, to ensure I had the scale right, you understand?'

The painter held up his thumb and squinted at Isabella past it, showing how he took the proportions of his subject by reference to the constant of his thumb.

'Each time,' he went on, 'instead of my thumb or brush, I held up the blade of a stiletto. He knew then I had his measure. He was the most civil of all my subjects.'

'Save I alone,' said Isabella.

'Oh my dearest one,' said Tintoretto. 'You are many things, but I would never sully you with the simple word *civil*. Nor dare to show you a dagger.'

Isabella laughed. 'I shall leave you, Jacopo. I have my answer now. You have given it to me.'

'I have?'

'You have,' Isabella said. 'You're right. I am not the mouse. I am the lion. No, not the lion, to sit and preen and be admired, but a lioness. The one who hunts.'

She paused at the door and tapped her fan on the frame.

'Yes, you're right,' she said. 'I am not the hunted but the hunter. I know my prey and I shall take his measure with my stiletto.'

Act Four

Venice, July 1585

Speak of thee as the traveller doth of Venice

'Venice the Wise. Venice the Just. Venice the Rich.'

Prospero rose and the gondola shifted under him. William and Oldcastle sat under the canopy, Oldcastle clutching at the rocking sides. Prospero moved to the prow and swept his hand out over the vista.

'Trapped between the Turk and France. A liminal place, eh, Sir Henry? A place of borders and opportunities, of doors opening and others shutting,' Prospero said.

He paused to sniff the air, as if smelling the fortunes that floated on the breeze. William's nose detected only the hot stink of rubbish floating past the gondola. The smell was nothing compared to London but it was not a cause for wonder. Against Oldcastle's muttered curses that he be still, William struggled to his feet.

Finally, he saw Venice.

The city emerged in silhouette, rose-gold in the light of morning. Venice the Magnificent. Domes jostled above the white and pink squares of palaces. Tall chimneys, strangely capped, thrust up everywhere, an army of mitred bishops observing the tumult of commerce below. The green waters of the lagoon were flecked black with gondola and *traghetti*, those uglier but more practical boats of commerce, silently oaring their way.

Their gondola turned a curve and passed the obscuring edge of a palace to reveal ahead the Piazzetta di San Marco, the public square outside the Ducal Palace. The gondola drew towards its mooring between two statue-capped columns.

To William's right rose the Ducal Palace, a vast building of pink and white porticos and arches. It stretched away to another square beyond. Past the Doge's Palace lay the Basilica di San Marco itself, five great green domes floating above five arches in which could be seen the flash of painted golden figures. For scale, William could think of nothing to match what he saw.

'*Hah!* Your steward is like a cat at a window, Sir Henry,' said Prospero. 'Caught by the view.'

Prospero's permanently arched eyebrow was turned on William.

'Tell me,' he said, 'has your England anything to compare to this?'

William could truthfully answer that if it did he had not seen it.

'Such is the power of Venice. They know it too,' Prospero said, nodding with respect touched with disdain.

'You see the horses above the western face of the basilica?' Prospero pointed. 'Rampant are they not? A symbol of the Venice that tramples the interests of all others before them. We Genoese have a saying, there can be no peace between our cities until those horses are bridled.'

William's eyes travelled up to the rearing beasts and then on. To the north the square was bounded by a long arcade of buildings; to the south its edge was a scene of industry, scaffolding and broken walls, though whether the building work was putting up or tearing down William could not tell. Rising above all on that southern side, opposite the basilica, was a red-brick tower capped in a pyramid, an obelisk many storeys high, the Campanile.

Prospero was loudly naming the sights to an uncaring Oldcastle who sat, bilious, in the bottom of the gondola. William was rapt. Here was a beauty, a lightness, that he had never encountered before. It held him.

'Enough of this,' said Prospero abruptly. 'One could spend many hours admiring Venice as your servant does. He will start scribbling in his little book again if we give him the chance. However, we all have business in the city and we must to that, no?'

Prospero hopped lightly to the quay as the gondola pulled alongside. William and Oldcastle hurried to follow. An unsteady Oldcastle even accepting a helping hand, reluctantly proffered, by the crouching figure of Prospero's servant, Borachio.

Amid the already bustling activity of the square Prospero renewed his attempt to convince Oldcastle to accept the hospitality of his own lodgings in the city. Oldcastle, schooled by William, repeated both his gratitude for the offer and his refusal. The English had lodging ready for them that they must use. Prospero gave way.

'Very well. Do you see there?' Prospero pointed out towards an arch above which was set an ornate clock tower. 'That is the route to the *sestiere* of San Polo and it is there that you will find your lodging, the House of the White Lion.'

He bowed to Oldcastle, who responded in ornate style. William was impressed. He didn't think Oldcastle could still bend in that part of his body.

'I look forward to our further meeting, Sir Henry,' said Prospero. 'If I might be of assistance at any point, I am your servant. Your man knows where to find me.'

With a further bow Prospero swept off into the crowd trailed by the surly figure of Borachio.

'Do you know where to find him, Will?' asked Oldcastle.

'Of course,' replied William. 'Under some dark stone.'

'Quite. Best left there I would say.'

'It is for these points of judgment, Sir Henry,' said William, 'that Her Majesty has found you worthy to be her representative in Venice.'

'Her Majesty's judgment approaches mine in perspicacity,' Oldcastle said. 'The Lord knows she certainly didn't choose me for the quality of my retinue.'

'Calumny,' cried William.

'An efficient steward,' said Oldcastle, 'would have already disposed of these troublesome letters, that his master might take his well-deserved repose.'

'Let me remedy the fault,' said William.

The two men walked with purpose towards the long arcade of offices on the north side of the square. Prospero had identified these buildings as the Procuratie Vecchie, home of the Procurators of St Mark, the officers of the government of Venice. They were the route by which William and Oldcastle would be brought to the presence of the Doge, the ruler of Venice.

Arrange the delivery of England's letters to the Doge and then depart, was William and Oldcastle's thought. Though their deception would be tested once again, the two men approached the task with lightness in their steps. Each thinking the end of a hard road was in sight. A very little, little let them do and all was done, free men again. With such foolish thoughts do great and arduous enterprises begin.

'Quite impossible, my lord.' The clerk shook his head.

He made a sad face and turned it towards William and Oldcastle in turn.

'You don't understand,' said William. 'It is vital that we be granted an audience with the Doge as soon as possible. We bear,' William paused, realising that he didn't know what was in the sealed packet of letters, 'missives from Her Majesty Queen Elizabeth of England.'

'It cannot be done,' said the clerk.

The words were not clear to Oldcastle but the functionary's demeanour carried its own message. To an Oldcastle desperate of England, such an attitude was unacceptable.

'What's he say?' he demanded of William.

'He says that we cannot have an audience with the Doge,' said William.

Oldcastle drew himself up. 'Inform him that England will take it ill if she is slighted thus. Tell him, William. Tell him.'

'Calm yourself, Nick,' pleaded William.

'I am as calm as the Thames on a windless day, William. Yet tell this minor magnifico that when the wind blows that great river may overflow its banks to the destruction of all.'

The clerk could understand Oldcastle no better than Oldcastle him but the reddening of Oldcastle's face told its own story. The clerk hastened to quench the bombard before it fired.

'You misunderstand me, my lords,' he said. 'No insult is intended. It is not that we deny England audience with the Doge. It is that, I am devastated to say, there is no doge to give audience. The Doge is dead.'

'Dead?' said William.

'What's he say?' asked Oldcastle.

'He says the Doge is dead,' replied William.

'Contempt,' cried Oldcastle. 'Mockery. This beslubberly knave thinks to fool us as though we were mere country bumpkins to be cozened out of their coins. Does he not understand that we stand here for England?'

William was concerned that Oldcastle had begun to forget he but played a part. Nonetheless he too was curious and surprised.

'Forgive us,' William said. 'We have seen no signs of mourning at the death of your ruler.'

The clerk smiled. 'Oh, my lord, the Doge does not rule.'

His look said much of the pity he felt for the inhabitants of such backward states as England. Cursed with a queen when they might be members of a beneficent republic. In profound tones he spoke in Italian, '*Si è morto il Doge, no la Signoria.*' 'The Doge is dead, but the Signoria is living. The Republic is not ruled by one man but by our senate, the Minor Consiglio and the Quarantia. It is a system of government that has served Venice well for many years.'

William could see that, unless swiftly curtailed, he was like to be treated to a lengthy discourse on the Venetian polity.

'I understand, of course,' he said. 'Well, when may my master be presented to the Signoria?'

'Oh, not until the new doge has been elected,' replied the clerk.

'Lord, these clerks must be born with one leg shorter than the other that they should run in circles thus,' Oldcastle grunted. 'Well, when is this doge elected?'

Not for another fortnight at the soonest, it appeared. He would then be presented formally to the citizens of the Republic. The opportunity to have audience would come during the many celebrations that would accompany his elevation.

Outside the Procuratie Vecchie Oldcastle slumped on a bench.

'Jesu's sake, Will,' he said. 'Another fortnight at least while we await discovery and destruction. My nerves cannot bear it. My purse cannot wear it.'

William understood Oldcastle's mood. Yet there was a part of him that was pleased. Here was a city of wonders worth the strain of two short weeks play-acting more.

Oldcastle mopped a dewy brow. 'I don't understand why we can't just leave the damnable letters with that clerk and be done with it,' he said.

'I've told you why, Nick,' answered William. 'Sir Henry was insistent it be to the Doge and no other's hand.'

'We are bound to be discovered.'

'We must try.'

Impossible to convey to Oldcastle the same urgent charge that Sir Henry had laid on him. William would not say he had understood all that Sir Henry had spoken of during the long journey from England. The wars and rivalries of Europe were too great and too twisted for so brief an education. He understood this, that Sir Henry feared for England and placed his hopes in his embassy. That in these letters and their delivery Sir Henry believed lay the safety of many lives. Now William stood here for him and for those hopes. He wondered how much of Sir Henry's thinking had turned on the character of the old doge and whether the new doge would prove as welcoming to England's wooing. 'Dead it is then,' said Oldcastle.

He let his head rest on the wall behind him.

'I can't even say it has been a good life, well lived,' he said. 'Hanged in Venice. Or worse, some torture they have learned of the Turk. Hot oil. Or more of that poisonous food they serve. A hundred dishes, each smaller than the last. Give me good capon.'

Oldcastle pushed himself to his feet. 'Come,' he commanded. 'Lead me to our lodgings. If I am to be killed for lying, let it be while I am drunk. The wine, at least, is good.'

Behind them Borachio peeled himself away from the shadow of a column and followed.

What is the city but the people?

Venice thronged with people. William and Oldcastle pushed slowly through the narrow streets towards Rialto. Men of all colours and fashions of attire, speaking all the languages of Christendom and the barbarous tongues of lands beyond, were gathered there. Even to one such as Oldcastle, used to the bustle of London, the sight was worthy of comment.

'God's wounds, Will. Did you ever see such a body of men?'

Oldcastle's great girth made his passage through the crowds as slow and painful as the passing of a stone. Sweltering in the heat his face was fixed with a manic grin as he noddingly acknowledged the curses of those Venetians whose passage he obstructed. William did his best to travel in Oldcastle's wake.

'All the world is here,' William agreed, dodging a scampering boy toting a crate of bottles.

'Truly,' Oldcastle said as he heaved himself through a gap between two groups of arguing merchants like a camel threading the eye of a needle. A moment later William and Oldcastle found themselves pressed back against the walls by a knot of liveried men, with, at their centre, a richly dressed man in a black gabardine coat. One of the Venetian senators, William surmised.

'It is rather *Orbis* than *Urbis* forum,' offered William from behind Oldcastle.

'Is that Latin?' said Oldcastle. 'Are you being clever in Latin? I wish you wouldn't.'

Oldcastle's mood was deteriorating with the press of bodies. The fixed grin beginning to take on the semblance of a snarl.

'Your perpetual punning is draining to the soul, William,' he said, 'even in English.'

In this manner did the pair make their way to the House of the White Lion.

The *osteria* was a four-storeyed building of red plaster. It backed onto the Canal Grande. It was with some surprise that the owner, one Salarino, greeted Oldcastle and William on the street entrance. He was a short, plump man dressed in a loose linen shirt that failed to disguise the strain his flesh placed it under. Throughout his conversation his hands never ceased to tumble over each other, save when they sought to slick down the remaining thin strands of hair upon his head.

'My lords, you are expected, yes, yes, but not in such few numbers and not by the street,' he said. 'Why did you not come by gondola?'

He glanced unhappily down at William and Oldcastle's legs, their already tattered weeds now muddied from the Venetian alleys.

'Never mind the manner of our arrival, man,' commanded Oldcastle. 'Show us to our lodging.'

William suppressed a smile as Oldcastle grew to his role as imperious knight, but still thought it wise to intervene.

'Good Master Salarino,' William said, 'the manner of our arrival reflects the troubles of our journey. Spare us the need for explanation until such time as we have recovered ourselves. You say we are expected.'

'Of course, letter of credit for your accommodation, Sir Henry, arrived some three weeks since,' said Salarino. 'As did some chests of clothing and other things. They are in the storeroom, safely locked. Your arrival, however, was not spoken of until a week hence.'

'Circumstance accelerated our arrival even as it diminished our company,' explained William.

Salarino's discomfort was manifest in an increased tumbling of his hands. His head bowed almost to his waist in a curve of abject embarrassment.

'I am devastated to say that in consequence of your early arrival your suite is not yet prepared.'

'What's he say? *Non* what?' Oldcastle tapped William impatiently on the shoulder.

'That there is no room at the inn,' William said.

For the second time that day a Venetian witnessed the near miraculous sight of Oldcastle swelling with fury. The response of Venice to English displeasure was just as panicked on this occasion as the last.

'Of course,' said Salarino, 'if you will grant me the space of a few days, my honoured lords, your rooms will be freed – freed and readied for your lodging to the finest standards. In the meantime, I would be pleased, pleased, yes, yes, to offer you my own quarters as if they were your own.'

It was with relief that Salarino saw the translated words deflate the English knight before he burst.

The two men were shown to a large room on the second floor of the *osteria* that looked out over the Canal Grande beyond. The shutters were closed against the heat of the day and there was a stale odour to the room. Oldcastle, worn from the climb to the second floor, sat heavily on the bed. A violent shriek rent the air and Oldcastle sprang back up. An outraged cat, nearly the thinner by a deathly margin, shot from its nest in the bed and out of the door. Oldcastle's hands let go his breast where they had leaped and he breathed out heavily.

'Lord, William, I think I've soiled myself,' he said.

William spoke quickly to Salarino to hide his laughter.

'It will do, I suppose.'

Apologies still flowing from his lips, the Venetian left the room. William turned to Oldcastle.

'Well then, now what?'

Defer no time; delays have dangerous ends

Prospero sat behind a desk of gilded walnut, his feet flung carelessly up on the surface. He stared out of the windows that overlooked the Canal Grande. The room was dark compared to the brightness beyond. A small knife that he used to open letters spun in his hands and glimmered as the light caught it. Like a cat caught by the sight of a dancing string, Borachio found it hard to look anywhere else.

'Well then, my lord, now what?' he asked when he had made report of his intelligence. He shifted uncomfortably.

'Must you make that sound?' demanded Prospero.

'My stomach plagues me,' Borachio answered. 'Has done this fortnight past. Damned Venetian food.'

Prospero gestured to a glass set on the table. 'Then take a little wine and be quiet, that I may think.'

Prospero tapped the knife against his bloodless lips and smiled.

'There are four objectives we must attend to, Borachio,' said the Count. 'Each demands of us a certain cunning if we are to achieve our goal. First, the destruction of Vittoria Accoramboni, who has given our master, the Pope, such cause for dislike. Her lodging is known to us but so is the Holy Father's vengeful intent known to her. More than that, someone has given her warning that the time of the Pope's revenge approaches. How we are known I cannot fathom but that we are is certain. She is now more strongly guarded than when first we came to Venice. How then to distract her watchful eye?

'Second,' he continued, 'the destruction of the English fools. A simpler matter for they are guarded by nothing, unless their rags hide armour. By your good report, they lie open to our hand, and for at least the next fortnight till Venice has a doge. Time and enough when we need only close our fingers round them and they are gone.'

Borachio broke in. 'Tonight then? Let this be done at least.'

Prospero's eyes swung up, and he gave the tiniest shake of his head. 'Where is the sport in that?' he said.

He looked again at the canal beyond and continued as if Borachio had not spoken.

'Third, the obtaining of the letters from England to Venice. As you have taken pains to argue, surely these are held on the person of the English Ambassador. Or, as likely, his steward, Fallow. They lack the luggage to have hid them elsewhere. So then, take them before disposing of the men? A tricksy task to do unnoticed. Yet strike them down and in the general halloo that follows we may lose our chance to get the letters. Finally, what if we are wrong in our surmise and they do not have the letters? How to resolve all these?'

Borachio stared at his master, suddenly concerned that Prospero required an answer of him. Prospero shook his head in resignation.

'I shall set the first against the second to their mutual destruction. Whilst they are thus distracted we will have the opportunity for you to achieve the third, the purloining of the letters.'

'I am to do it?' asked Borachio. 'Why me?'

'Why?' replied the Count. 'Because of our fourth objective, Borachio. Which is that, throughout, I remain unharmed and happy. To which end let the Roman bitch and the English mastiff chew at each other for my amusement while you, my loyal hound, sniff out your way to those letters.'

With these words Prospero turned to his desk and drew pen and paper to him. He began to write. The smile on his thin lips growing broader as he did so.

When Borachio had departed with the letter, the Count remained in quiet contemplation for some time. There were yet some streaks of day in the west and he did not light the candles to fend off the dark. He often found the fading light of evening brought with it melancholy. A mood that had plagued him all his life. It was at its worst in Venice. Something about the city and its memories kindled it within him.

He thought of the English embassy. The fat Ambassador was a fool but he rather liked the bastard son, Fallow. The lad had a sharper wit than his age might credit and saw with surprising wisdom. He rather wondered if this Fallow had not discerned his malign intent. If so, so much the better. Prospero preferred his prey to be aware they were hunted so that they might realise they struggled in vain to free themselves of the trap. As to his liking him, that little mattered. He'd killed even those he loved in his time. Maybe, this time, he would hold off his hand, he thought. After all, it was only the Ambassador himself that mattered.

Prospero spent a moment thinking of that problem and then put it away in a part of his mind for later contemplation. What worried him most was not how to deal with the English embassy, it was that his scheming did not seem to lift his melancholy as it had always in the past. From this, in succession swifter than a line of kings, came thought of Isabella Lisarro. His melancholy mood darkened. Isabella was a symbol of too many things. He turned his mind from her to Vittoria Accoramboni.

Prospero imagined Vittoria's relief as she slew the English, thinking as she did so that she stopped the deadly hand cast against her. Imagine her gratitude to Prospero, who had showed her where the danger lay. How might such gratitude manifest itself in one so beautiful and so scant of moral qualm? How would her face change when she realised the person she drew close to was her true betrayer? Here, at last, were thoughts to distract him from his sadness. He stayed with them till darkness fell.

As the evening wore down the streets of Venice thronged still with people. Truly, of that crowd it seemed as if one half were set in watch over the other half. From where she sat by the canal, with a basket of lace at her feet, the young girl rose and gathered her belongings tidily about her. She had made few sales that day and yet much profit from her toil. Her mistress, Isabella, would reward her. Slowly she threaded her way home taking with her the news that Prospero was returned to Venice.

... three things that women highly hold in hate

'We are safe here in Venice. That is why we came,' Vittoria Accoramboni, the Duchess of Bracciano, said to Isabella as she waved away her servant.

Isabella paced in front of the windows of the Duchess's small study in the Ca' Bracciano. When she had learned Prospero had business in Venice, Isabella had set her mind to fathom his purpose. A death, that was certain, but whose? Then she had heard of the arrival in Venice of the Duke and Duchess of Bracciano. Such scandal attended them. She had learned that Vittoria Accoramboni had fled with her new husband to Venice in fear of the Pope's vengeance. There was her answer. Prospero had ever been the Cardinal Montalto's man. In this only had he shown any constancy. Surely, if he served the Pope still, this woman and her husband were Prospero's targets.

Isabella had gone straight to Vittoria, relying on her fame as a courtesan to admit her entry. To Isabella's frustration Vittoria had given little credence to her warnings. Now, with news of Prospero's return to Venice, Isabella tried again.

The serving-man carried the silver salver across to Isabella. She did not spare a glance for the gorgeous sweetmeats on offer. She too waved the man away. When they were alone again Isabella returned to her theme.

'You are too confident of Venice,' she said to Vittoria.

'Should I not be?' Vittoria asked. 'In all Italy, in all the world, Venice is famous for three things: commerce, justice and the reach of the agents of the Signoria.' She gave a little smile. 'I am told the Signoria has more spies than the lagoon has fish. Yet we have had no word of danger. Save yours.'

And is mine not enough, wondered Isabella.

The Duchess smiled at her and gestured to the windows beyond.

'The Pope is angry,' said Vittoria, 'little matter that his anger is misguided. Yet the Pope dare not offend Venice by threatening me, here in the city.'

Isabella looked to the ceiling. Its central oval bore a depiction of the Last Judgment. If Isabella hoped to find in it some inspiration to persuade Vittoria Accoramboni of the threat, she did so in vain. When she lowered her gaze she saw the Duchess staring intently at her. The vast eyes were filled with curiosity.

'Have you heard more than when you first came to me?' she asked. 'You have had some information that the Signoria has not?'

Isabella came and sat by her. 'None. I know only that Prospero is returned and in strange company. Oh, lady, believe me. If he is here then he brings death with him.'

Vittoria leaned back to take a better view of Isabella.

'I met your Count of Genoa once,' Vittoria said. 'In Rome. I do not think I told you this at our last meeting.' She fanned herself a little. 'A very handsome man.'

Isabella waited to see what road the other woman travelled. Vittoria tapped the back of Isabella's hand with her fan. 'How long were you lovers?'

Isabella stood. Her face was flushed with anger. 'Forgive me if I speak hotly. My warning to you, I promise you this, is not born of heartbreak at a lover's betrayal.'

The Duchess held up her hands. 'Do not be so proud, Isabella. Though I am younger than you I know something of love. Let me advise you. The stronger fuel we women are, the brighter burn men's fires. I see your strength and do not wonder that the Count's love flared in your presence. Is he all to blame that you were burned by the heat?'

'I do not doubt that you know more of love than me, for all your youth,' Isabella answered. 'The courtesan does not advise the wife about love. Yet let me speak to what I do know. Your marriage sets the seal on the Pope's humiliation. To see his nephew dead is one thing, to see his widow married to the man he thinks his nephew's murderer, still another. He will hunt you, even here. You think you know Prospero? I have seen his secret heart, lady. It is black, lady, black and deadly.'

'Forgive me, Isabella, but to hear you speak of this man, in these terms, you must have loved him dearly then to hate him so now.'

Isabella turned to the window. How had she failed so completely in her task? This woman, whom she had hoped to frighten into safety, saw in Isabella's passion only a misprised mirror of her own for her new husband. Vittoria thought Isabella spoke hotly because of love. How often we see in others only our own reflection.

'I see you'll not be persuaded,' Isabella said turning back. She bowed to leave. 'I have warned you. I can do no more if you are not willing.'

'Wait, wait.' The Duchess gestured for Isabella to sit. 'I do not dismiss your talk of danger. You see, I am here surrounded by my husband's men.'

Vittoria spoke the word *husband* with relish. That status only so recently gained; no longer merely mistress.

'Full of wise care for my safety is your counsel, Isabella.' She caught the other woman's hand. 'I am to hold a banquet three days from now. Let us invite your demon lover and his companions. Then we may see them close and gauge them.'

'Oh that is madness. Let him within a knife's thrust of you?' Isabella said. She pressed the young woman's hand that had taken hers. 'Prospero is not my lover. It's not his love I tremble at.'

Isabella saw the doubt in Vittoria's look. 'Foolish child, what must I say to have you trust me when I say he wishes you only ill?'

'Dare you?' Vittoria shouted and snatched her hand back.

Isabella recoiled from the sudden show of rage.

'Do not overstep yourself to call me "child",' Vittoria said.

She took a long breath to calm herself.

'I know you speak only from care for me,' she said. 'I am sensible of it. But I will not quake at rumours. Bring me something to prove your fears more than imagination.'

Isabella did not trust herself to speak. She rose and bowed and left.

After Isabella had departed Vittoria rang a small bell by her hand.

'Send for Antonio,' she told the servant who attended her call.

While she waited for Antonio, captain of her guard, to come, Vittoria thought on Isabella Lisarro. Still beautiful even at thirty. She must have been something remarkable at twenty. Fierce too; though she was but little. Of undoubted cleverness, to have forged her own honours in this world. Vittoria wondered if others would say the same of her when she was Isabella's age. If her own efforts could make it so, they would. Indeed, in titles and wealth she had already surpassed the courtesan tenfold. Some greater respect was due. How dare Isabella Lisarro call her child? Vittoria felt the sudden flare of anger and fought for calm. How easily I am transported, she thought. What of it, if I am? I act where others cower.

The door opened to reveal a tall man, stiff, straight and grey as a gun. He bowed.

'My lady?' Antonio said.

'I have again received warning of a plot,' Vittoria said.

'The same source?' the captain asked.

'The same,' Vittoria said.

'With what new information?'

'None.'

'My lady, should we tell your husband of this?'

'No. He will only fret. I shall deal with this myself,' Vittoria answered.

'My lady –' the captain began, but she cut him off.

'No. When he returns from our estates in Salo then we shall tell him, and tell him too that the danger, such as it may be, I have dealt with.'

The captain turned to the window and gazed at the commerce on the canal below.

'My lady, I beg you to reconsider,' he said quietly. 'The courtesan's warning may be well given.'

The Duchess waved his concern away with her fan.

'Trust me, Antonio,' she said. 'That warning is bred of something other than reason. I know love turned to hate too well to miss its signs in others. Besides, we have the letter from Prospero, Count of Genoa.'

'True.' The captain kept his unhappy look.

'We have discussed this before,' Vittoria said, rose spots of gathering anger blossoming on her cheek at the thought that the captain of her own guard still questioned her judgment. 'What assassin writes to warn his victim?'

Antonio raised his hands to show them empty of weapons, as he would to reassure a wary man he was no enemy.

'It is strange, past question,' he answered. 'That only increases my mistrust of it.'

Vittoria drew Prospero's letter from her dress. She cast her eye across it again. It warned of imminent danger and promised information about an embassy from England, false and mortal in intent to her. Prospero, the Count of Genoa, asked that he give the warning in person for he dare not trust his news in full to paper.

Vittoria's heart raced. She dismissed her captain's caution. Vittoria felt the sweet drug of danger flood her. Here would be some entertainment just as Venice began to pall. What is life without risk? She longed to see Giovanni Prospero and Isabella Lisarro together. If talk of him alone would make Isabella hot, a meeting would surely blow the coals to leaping flame. What of Prospero himself? How would he view his former lover?

Yet to be bold is not to be foolhardy, Vittoria thought. So many warnings of impending doom. They must be sounded out, precautions taken. The invitations to the feast in three days' time were already sent. Such guests there would be. Such a banquet, with so many things to taste. She turned to the captain.

'Here is my plan, Antonio,' Vittoria said.

With surety stronger than Achilles' arm

The light of dawn through the shuttered windows had drawn William forth like a moth. When it had first become clear that he would visit Venice, he had sought to find out more of the city from such report as had come to England. Now he was eager to satisfy his eyes with sight of the memorials and the things of fame that hitherto he had only read about. He had not made the door before Salarino was on him, hands wringing with anxiety.

'My lord,' said Salarino, 'you cannot walk abroad in such a state, no, no. Heaven spare us, your dignity and the dignity of this house will be offended.'

'Alas, I have no other garments,' William said, 'and my master and I, having been robbed, are out of funds.'

News of a robbery set Salarino into such a caterwauling in Venetian that William became quite concerned for the man and the rousing of the other residents of the *osteria*. When finally order was restored, Salarino, face wet with tears for the misfortune of his guests, clapped his soft little hands together with surprising loudness. A scurrying maidservant rushed to call a gondola to the canal entrance of the house. William was then brought out into the sun. He was guided to a seat in the waiting boat. Salarino addressed him from the jetty.

'Now, please, my lord, I shall join you and direct you at once to your bankers. Oh devastation that you should have been so set upon. I curse them, yes, yes, curse them from the heights of my propriety to the depths of their iniquity.'

He smoothed the wildly wafting locks of hair upon his head and, calmed, stepped aboard. He gave directions to the gondolier.

'When you are in funds again, my lord,' Salarino said, 'please, please, to go with me to the tailor and obtain fresh garments for you and your master. We have, you know, the finest cloth in Europe here in Venice. Why do you laugh?'

Salarino's anxious face stilled William's chuckling.

'Nothing good Master Salarino,' William said. 'I am simply pleased that I shall, today, meet the Tailor of Venice.'

*

It was past noon when William returned to the House of the White Lion to find Oldcastle still nestled in his burrow of sheets.

'Fie, you slug-a-bed,' said William. 'Not up yet? When I have seen the world in a city?'

'Pipe down, Will,' said Oldcastle. 'I have been engaged in strenuous thought whilst you were gadding about.'

'"Thought" you call it now,' said William, eyebrow arched. 'Truly, I see the strain writ on your face. What thoughts did you generate with your efforts?'

'Your own thoughts are as low as your birth, William. My thinking is as yesterday. We were best gone before we are discovered.'

Oldcastle sat up in the bed and stared. 'What are you wearing?' he asked.

'The fruits of this morning's labour,' said William.

He spun about to allow Oldcastle to admire the flare of the cloak. 'Courtesy of the English Ambassador's funds,' he said.

Oldcastle let out a moan. 'We are undone. Undone! It is one thing to play the Ambassador to 'scape danger. It is another thing entirely to spend his money.'

'Be calm, Oldcastle,' said William. 'If we do not draw on the ambassador's credit to dress ourselves out as fitting to our rank and station then we are questioned for it and our deceit discovered.'

For response Oldcastle simply moaned again and clutched at his fraying beard. William ignored his wailings. 'Nor do I think we will be begrudged some small sum if we succeed in our mission. Come man. Dare do all that we may win all.'

There was a rap at the door. William answered it to find Salarino beyond.

'My lord, the tailor is here to measure the worthy Ambassador,' said Salarino.

At this news William turned and smiled at the blanching figure of Oldcastle. The figure of the worthy ambassador groaned and rolled deeper into the bed. Salarino came bustling past William with the tailor in his train. Oldcastle was soon mounted on the truckle bed, his measure being taken. Salarino smiled with satisfaction at the sight. He turned to William and handed him a letter.

'For the English Ambassador, my lord,' Salarino explained. 'It came this morning while we were out.'

William slit it open with the dagger from his belt and scanned it.

'Well?' demanded Oldcastle. 'What is it? Are we betrayed? Orders from England? Spit it out, William, for the good Lord's sake.'

'It's an invitation,' said William.

'An invitation?' said Oldcastle.

'We're going to a feast.'

A golden mesh to entrap the hearts of men

Three days later William and Oldcastle stood in the courtyard of the Ca' Bracciano in readiness for Vittoria Accoramboni's feast.

It was early evening but the light was still clear and with that quality that made all things more beautiful to the eye. The white Istrian stone with which each storey of the palazzo was adorned glittered with a golden coat of sun. Each storey of the courtyard, tiers of sharply pointed arches and windows each ornately decorated, pulled the eye upward to a lapis sky.

Oldcastle stood sweating in more finery than he could recall wearing in his life, even when he had played King Solomon. William was next to him, also draped in gorgeous weeds. William flicked a mote from Oldcastle's doublet.

'Do at least try and look like the worthy Ambassador of England,' he said, 'rather than a hogshead in a sack.'

William was once again cloaked, which he disliked, but he accepted its weight as the price for the fine figure he cut. He flicked his cloak back and flexed a calf. Oldcastle rolled his eyes.

'Your self-love rivals Narcissus,' he said.

'Self-love is not so great a sin as self-neglect, your Excellency,' responded William.

He felt calm and cool. He was enjoying the sweet, salt smell of the sea that blew in across the lagoon. The evening was mild. William suspected Oldcastle's sheen owed more to a heated spirit than a heated climate.

'This is madness, William,' Oldcastle hissed. 'No, say not that. Were madness doubled still it would know well enough not to come here.'

'Gather your courage, Nick,' said William. 'We but play a part tonight. You yourself have told me that the playing is all. People will see what they expect to see. The danger lies only in refusing to perform at all.'

William was torn. There was sympathy for the lingering effect of Hemminges' death on Oldcastle's spirit. The old man was not sad without cause. Still, it had taken all courage from Oldcastle and put fright in its place, as a dog caught in black rain is cowed and scurries beneath a cart, refusing to emerge until better weather. William's sympathy warred with his frustration. His friend had never previously shirked adventure.

'If we hide in our chambers and shun society it will be asked, why?' William said. 'What mischief do the English plan that they hide it from men's eyes?'

'What will they say to see our motley?' Oldcastle gestured at his own cloak.

The tailor had worked as if pursued by a demon. Even so, not all could be prepared in the time. Both William and Oldcastle had been forced to supplement their Venetian clothes with pieces from the chests of costumes sent ahead from England. Though Oldcastle fretted now, the viewing of the costumes had briefly lifted the clouds that hung over him. He had displayed with pride a cloak, 'as cost me more than all your meagre worth, Will.'

William prayed they would withstand close viewing.

Behind the two men the sudden slap of water on stone announced the arrival of a new gondola at the water entrance to the palazzo. Liveried servants advanced; shunning their assistance Prospero stepped lightly from the gondola. He strode through the crowding guests, who parted before him as weeds before a ship's prow.

'Your Excellency,' Prospero bowed to Oldcastle and then turned to offer a shallower nod to William.

His dark hair shone black as a beetle's shell.

'So soon in Venice and already at the centre of society,' Prospero said.

His sharp-toothed smile cut through the neatly trimmed beard. William could see that Oldcastle's own smile was as fragile as glass and like to shatter at the smallest knock.

'Tell him I'd rather be in my bed in the company of a cup of sack than here among all the princes of Europe,' muttered Oldcastle.

'I shall do no such thing,' said William, smiling at Prospero as he and Oldcastle spoke in English. 'Screw your courage to the sticking place, your Excellency, or you will undo us.'

'Then you banter with this coxcomb knave. I am done,' Oldcastle said.

He bowed to Prospero as if completing a compliment.

William, whose own smile had grown the broader and more fixed through the exchange, turned to Prospero and his taunting brow. He did his best to disguise Oldcastle's dangerous mood.

'My lord,' he said to Prospero, 'enquires if you are well, and begs you to forgive him. He has not that facility for idle talk that he would wish. It is not just that he must speak in a strange tongue. The food in Venice is strange to him also. Having surfeited on squid at noon he finds himself now distract. His shame, he wishes to convey, is only made worse by comparison with your own magnificence.'

Prospero laughed. 'He said all that, did he? In so few words of English. Truly it is an expressive language.'

'We have words to suit all occasions and persons,' said William. 'And where we do not, we find no shame in taking them from other sources. Latin for example.'

'I shall have to learn it,' said the Count. 'Very well then. We must ensure that your master is provided with food of more bland complexion than the heavy fare of Venice.'

As he spoke the party had found itself moving within the press of guests towards the entrance of the palazzo. The three men moved within and climbed the stairs to the first floor: the *piano nobile*. Viewed through the high windows of the long gallery room, the solemn churches and gorgeous palaces lining the Canal Grande formed a backdrop of reds, whites and golds cut by the green of the canal.

The feasting room was richly decorated, the ceiling fretted with golden cherubim. Yet all its ornament and the splendour of the view beyond could not draw the eye. Not when at the centre of the room stood the most exquisite creature William had ever seen.

She stood, draped in white and gold, welcoming her guests. Vittoria Accoramboni, Duchess of Bracciano. Golden hair, near white, pulled into the tightly bound curling horns that were the Venetian fashion and from which two tangled curls hung artfully down the slender neck. Her dress, also in the Venetian fashion, had a bodice like a dagger that cut sharply down to flaring skirts. The bosom draped in fine lace and pearls through which it seemed at any moment all the treasures of the world might be glimpsed.

Prospero ushered Oldcastle and William forward, whispering as he went. 'The scandalous Vittoria Accoramboni, gentlemen. Deny it if you will, but having seen her, do you not understand a murderer's desire? For myself I think it only right that any husband should be tested if he wished to keep such a trophy. None but the strong deserve the fair.'

William and Oldcastle understood Prospero's allusion. When William had revealed to Oldcastle that they were invited to a feast at the Ca' Bracciano in three days' time their host, Salarino, near fainted with excitement. How thrilling for his honoured guests to be invited to the foremost social event, and yet how scandalous too. Dare the English Ambassador accept the invitation of the notorious Vittoria Accoramboni and her new husband, who, rumour had it, was also the murderer of the old? Of course, yes. Such rumours were no more than that. Envy of the beautiful Duchess, so beautiful, and her new husband, so lucky. Doubtless the wicked rumour's origin lay only in the speed with which the Duchess had married her new husband on the expiry of the old. For Salarino this was nothing more than thrift. The funeral meats had, coldly served, formed the wedding feast. Thrift only. And envy. Oh, and such people would attend, the finest in Venice. Yes, yes, they must be there to see and to be seen. Salarino had then broken into a torrent of Venetian dialect directed at the tailor. The little figure had moaned and clutched his temples and then applied himself with even greater vigour to the caparisoning of Oldcastle.

Now they stood before her and William was not disappointed in his imaginings.

'Your Grace, may I introduce the English Ambassador, Sir Henry Carr, and his son, Fallow,' said the Count.

William was surprised to hear himself described as Sir Henry's son. He wondered if Prospero did it to elevate him from his status as a steward or to set a trap of indelicacy should he have to explain that he was Sir Henry's bastard.

'These are the men you talked of, Count?' The Duchess spoke in Latin. In her mouth it had a musical quality.

'They are, Your Grace,' Prospero answered.

The beautiful creature turned her gaze on William and Oldcastle. At first the coldness of the fair white face and pale gold hair took William aback. Yet, as he felt himself being weighed and measured, her face broke into a smile of pearl-white teeth and frost-pink lips, so dazzling it was as if they had seen winter turn to summer in the passage of an instant.

'You are very welcome, England,' said Vittoria Accoramboni.

William spoke for an Oldcastle whose strings, strained taut already, had been quite frayed and snapped by the appearance of this ice queen and the sudden passage from cold regard to smiling warmth.

'Your Grace's kindness and hospitality are matched only by her beauty and generosity,' William said.

'He's silver-tongued, Count, this son of England,' Vittoria laughed.

'I would that I were golden-tongued, Your Grace, to give you due repayment for the pleasure of your company,' said William. 'As it is, my lord's embassy begins as it had not hoped to, in Venice's debt. For having given us sight of you.'

'Enough, England,' said Vittoria. 'Too much of flattery and I see already this is a game in which you are my master. You're welcome and the debt is ours, that we should have the pleasure of your company.'

A slight nod of the head to the three men signalled the end of the audience and she turned to the next in line to greet them. As the three men moved away William glanced back to see Vittoria glancing back at him. Such a look as the hawk gives.

Honour, clock to itself

A comely lad in a cream-coloured doublet of good cloth approached and thrust a silver tray of sweetmeats in front of the trio. Prospero's hand hovered for a moment and then struck down upon a delicate-looking curl of fish and tomatoes that rode on a small wafer of bread. Oldcastle, still recovering, simply seized two large pastry baskets filled with chopped and spiced meats and plopped them into his mouth for sustenance of his nerves. William, taking nothing, waved the beautiful servant away. He looked around the gathering and saw that all of those serving were, in their own way, as ornamental as the room. Prospero, smiling, begged that Oldcastle and William excuse him a moment while he spoke to an old friend and slid away.

William and Oldcastle found themselves alone within a whirlpool of people. Their fellow guests had clapped to each other with loud talk and laughter and the heavy revel that good wine at others' expense will feed. Amid so many strangers and the chatter of so many voices, all in tongues unknown, William abruptly felt himself lost and far from home. In Stratford he had railed against the wearisome familiarity of each day. Now every moment was an assault of novelties.

William opened his mouth to confess to Oldcastle that he began to think the old man's fears had something in them. Before he could utter a word he and Oldcastle were surrounded.

'My lord of England, I am Enrico Dandolo and this my son, Lucio. You are recently arrived in Venice?' A grey-haired man gestured with a hand thick with jewelled rings at himself and the young man beside him.

As he did so, three more men joined the circle.

'Sir Henry, I am Mauro Foscari,' said one of the three. 'This is my brother Giovanni and his son Pietro. I trust you have found Venice to your liking.'

A young man wedged himself into the growing circle, gorgeously garbed in flame-coloured stock, long hair slicked back from a dark face.

'Introduce me to the Ambassador of England,' he demanded. 'I am Francesco Tiepolo.'

The heavily jewelled man spoke again, through tight teeth. 'Peace, Tiepolo, the Ambassador's man has yet to translate on our behalf.'

'I see no need to wait, Dandolo,' said Francesco Tiepolo. 'Nor will England find much profit in waiting on Dandolo business. Let the order of introduction stand not on the time but the value.'

'I see you ever the foul-mouthed and calumnious knave, Francesco. It cannot be helped. It is in the breeding,' the younger Dandolo said and rested his hand on an ornamental dagger at his belt.

'At least I know my breeding, Lucio,' replied Francesco Tiepolo.

William withered before the tumult of translation and ill-will. Oldcastle stared around the circle like a bear at bay. What was this sudden show of rivalries?

From behind William a voice whispered, 'I imagine England's business will be conducted in the morning. The evening is for pleasure.'

William turned his head and caught a trace of perfumed air. He had no time to dwell on it. The hint was well taken. He rushed to damp the fire building before him.

'My lords, you are all welcome,' said William. 'It is my master's policy not to mingle business and pleasure. You will find him at our lodging in the morning. At which time we shall be happy to speak with you all.'

He nodded at each group of men and then added in heavier tones, 'In the order of your arrival.'

Oldcastle seized the excuse and offered his own addition. 'Against the noise and tumult of the feast my poor Latin will serve only to make strangers out of the strangeness of your words. I would rather we spoke in the quiet of a different setting. Forgive me.'

His stumbling words themselves gave the ring of truth to his message.

'Of course, forgive us. Till the morning,' said Enrico Dandolo. He gripped his son's arm and turned them away.

The Foscari three proffered some further pleasantries before also turning away. Only the bold young Francesco Tiepolo remained, though only for a moment, during which time he allowed his eye to travel with insulting slowness across the figures of William and Oldcastle. Then he bowed and departed into the tumult without a word.

William drew breath and was once again aware of a perfume in the air. A woman stepped before him. William took in red hair and green silk and fine, strong features and thought of the profligacy of Venice, that it baited its traps with such wonders.

Ne'er saw her match since first the world begun

'S-ciào vostro,' the woman greeted them both.

William had been scant four days in the city and he had already seen two women more beautiful than he suspected lived in all of England. Such variety of beauty too. Where Vittoria Accoramboni had been a youthful creature of air and ice, this figure before him was a woman made of different elements, of earth and fire. They suited him better, much better. The woman stood before him in clothing that aped a man's. It showed to William's eye a scandalous extent of leg. The voice was the same that had hinted his excuse to him. At his silence the woman smiled.

'Forgive me, sir, you don't speak our Venetian dialect?' she said in Latin.

The wheel of William's brain struggled to turn in the current. Getting no answer she broke into Greek. William fought to follow her meaning with his schoolboy Greek as she seemed to talk about a pipe with a broken reed.

'No, lady, Latin, lady. Latin is best for me. For us,' said William.

Recovering some of his poise, he gestured at Oldcastle. The great man, royal lord of any tavern in England, now stood with a crumb of pastry poised upon the corner of his lips.

'Then in Latin I may say that I am pleased to make your acquaintance. I am Isabella Lisarro,' she said.

She paused in expectation. William, aghast to realise his discourtesy, hurried to make his introductions. Isabella studied him as he did so.

Her spies and servants had reported Prospero's arrival in the company of two Englishmen. A young man and his master, whom rumour called the English Ambassador. The two did not appear in either number or appearance fitted to such a task. Strange company for the Pope's assassin. Knowing of Prospero's return was but one part of her task. She needed to know his business and prove it too. Isabella was certain that Vittoria was some part of Prospero's schemes; surely this motley companionship must form some part of that plan. But, she thought looking at William and Oldcastle, were they part of the business or another of its objects? The old man seemed harmless. Unless too much love of food and good living were signs of ill intent, in which case he were the very Devil. The lad was harder to gauge. He had a sharp face that would be called handsome without being worthy of further comment were it not for two very dark eyes that moved in constant observation of the world. Those were clever eyes.

It was a rash act to have come tonight, she thought. Prospero would see her. It could not be helped. Vittoria had as good as demanded it. Besides, there was only so much she could learn from report of others. These English, were they mere ciphers or the clasps that would unlock the book of the assassin's intent? She would know.

'You have come far?' Isabella asked.

William answered for his master. 'From England.'

The answer had seemed bland enough but Oldcastle, whose spirits had been swept this way and that by the tensions of the last few encounters, at the name of England heaved such a sigh and seemed to wipe his eyes of sudden tears. William in astonished embarrassment held his breath. Often he had heard it said that grief softened the mind and made it fearful. Here was proof.

It was Isabella that rescued him.

'The good knight seems troubled by the heat,' she said. 'Perhaps he might welcome refreshment. Shall we fetch it for him?'

Oldcastle swiped at his brow with a lace ruff and then endeavoured to hide the gesture by hiding the arm itself behind his body. When William suggested that he go with Isabella to find something more substantial for him to drink, his head bobbed in grateful assent. Oldcastle ploughed his way to the edge of the galleried room and there sat heavily on a chair.

Isabella plunged into the crowd with William in the chase. She moved ahead in haste, to disguise her own amazement. So mild a question should not have produced so bitter a response. How to fit this into the puzzle of the English, she thought. So wrapped was she in her own contemplations she did not see the flaming Tiepolo step in front of her.

'Isabella Lisarro. I thought you retired?' he said.

Francesco Tiepolo's chest was swollen like a game-cock as he strutted up to Isabella. She sighed inwardly. If pride were money, Francesco Tiepolo would be the wealthiest man in Venice. If sense and judgment credit, the poorest in the world. Once, just once, some years ago, he had sought her out. More fool her, flattered by a younger man's pursuit, she had allowed it, thinking to let him down gently with none the worse for the diversion of a pleasant month. He had not seen it as she did. Too much pride is men's folly; too little, women's. Well, his pricked pride was his problem, not hers. She had too much business on foot to take the time to smooth the ruffled feathers of this cockerel.

'Retired?' she asked.

'From the field of combat.'

'Then your eye fails you for all you squint with it, for you see me here before you, do you not?'

'I see you standing,' said Francesco. 'I understood in contests of your kind to be in play was to lie on your back and to be retired was to be back on your feet.'

Francesco Tiepolo looked about in braggartly pleasure. He hoped for an audience for what he was sure was a hit, a very palpable hit on Isabella Lisarro, who had dared to deny him. From the corner of his eye he noted with satisfaction that one or two of his companions were watching. His satisfaction turned to instant gall at Isabella's turning of his thrust.

'You are mistaken, sir,' she replied. 'I am at my most potent when standing and sadly diminished when flat. Though I understand your confusion on the subject, for the idle prattle of the city has it that you are not familiar with the former state.'

A most indicative movement of fingers accompanied Isabella's words. Hands flew to mouths in those watching as laughter was stifled. Francesco Tiepolo's face grew as red as his flame-coloured stock.

'My eye holds scant regard for a bird so old as you,' he said.

'There's a leer that wounds like a leaden sword,' said Isabella. 'Go boy, old birds are too tough for your milk teeth to chew on.'

William had not followed the exchange of barbs, which had been conducted in the dialect of Venice with pace and venom. He had no difficulty, however, in recognising the growing colour in the man. Nor was there any mistaking the message of the clenching fists. He stepped between the two and spoke to the man.

'Sir,' said William, 'my master, Sir Henry, has sent me to inform you that he would, of course, be pleased to speak to you in private in the morning.'

With an effort Francesco Tiepolo dragged his eyes from Isabella Lisarro's hot regard to the black-eyed Englishman before him.

'You gave this message already,' he hissed.

'Did I?' said William. 'I am sorry, then. I was distracted by so many voices at one time. Forgive me. In the morning, then.'

He turned to Isabella Lisarro. 'My lady, you were showing me where I might find a cordial for my master?'

At William's gesture Isabella inclined her head and led the two away. Behind them Francesco Tiepolo made to follow and then recovered himself. The moment had passed but not the sensation. Twice now, and this time most publicly, that woman had slighted him. It would not stand. He grabbed a full glass of wine from a passing servant. With false cheer he rejoined his companions, who had the sense not to offer comment on what had passed.

As William and Isabella moved through the crowd William whispered, 'What unlooked for excitements Venice holds. If this is what Venice is like at a feast, I dread to think what it is like when at war.'

'For certain, you must be ready for any happenstance in this city,' she whispered back.

'Or have a strong protector,' said William. 'You have no hidden dagger, my lady? I am already frightened of your words. I would not see you armed as well.'

She laughed. 'Quick wit and quicker actions, such as you have, will see you safe even from my weapons.'

It was his turn to laugh.

Scoff on, vile fiend and shameless courtesan

Across the room Prospero glared. He saw Isabella laugh at something said and rest her hand for a moment on the boy Fallow's arm. His heart danced but not with joy, not joy. The Duchess of Bracciano studied him in his distraction.

'Something has unsettled your eye, Count?' she asked.

With an effort Prospero tore himself from the sight of the steward Fallow and Isabella Lisarro, so close in conversation as to seem to be meeting noses.

'I am simply surprised to see you admit courtesans to your feast,' he said.

'Should I not? *Cortigiana onesta*, the "honest courtesans", are they not part of the special charms of Venice? I am surprised to find you so –' Vittoria Accoramboni's eyes sparkled with immodest delight as she sought the right words, '– to find your thoughts so dry in appreciation of their delights.'

'My thoughts are turned to only one concern,' said Prospero. 'Your safety, Your Grace.'

Prospero let the intensity of his sudden anger appear as fierce regard for the woman before him. She smiled back at him and laid a hand, light as a leaf on water, on his arm.

'That I was in danger I knew and accepted,' she said. 'Thanks to you I now know the direction from which that danger comes. You may trust that I will defend myself.'

The pressure on his arm increased as she said, 'And trust that I will not forget to whom I owe thanks for my safety.'

Prospero let his eye travel down to the pale pink hand and then back to the Duchess's face. He bowed.

The honest courtesan and the false steward stood at the edge of the gathered company. They waited for the return of a swan-necked serving-girl, sent to bring them a draught of cordial comfort for Oldcastle.

A silence had arrived with the departure of the girl on her errand. Isabella smiled at William. She would not profess to have the measure of him on so short an acquaintance but, she would admit it, he had a sweet wit to him. He had made her laugh more in the past minutes than she had in all the three months since Prospero had returned to her life. William returned her smile and then, having no better thought, turned his head to look past the marble columns of the windows to the lights of the city beyond.

'I have never seen so many lights at night,' he said.

'The *ancone*. The shrines. You have seen them? The city pays for the lamps to be lit each night,' Isabella answered.

'Aah. I wondered at their purpose as I wandered this morning,' William said. 'So many of them, on every corner. Now I see. I thought them simply ornaments. I am beginning to realise that nothing in this city is done without purpose.'

'The sun may set on Venice but the city does not let the light depart,' Isabella said.

'"The sun may set and yet rise again,"' William said to himself in answer to her words.

'Catullus?' she asked.

William looked up. 'You know it?'

'I do,' she said and, at his raised brow, quoted back to him, '"Once our light, that briefly shone, sets, we rest in a night without end."'

Isabella's head tilted. She looked again at the young man who quoted Catullus.

'Venice pleases you?' she asked.

'There are many things here that, in outward show at least, are beautiful,' he replied.

Isabella studied William's face.

'Sometimes the interior proves more interesting than all the outward show,' she said.

'I have often suspected so.'

'Do you know the church of San Rocco in the *sestiere* of San Polo?' Isabella gestured beyond the windows to the city with her fan.

'I do not.'

'You should visit,' she said. 'Inside there is more, much more that would profit the curious and discerning visitor than the exterior, for all its magnificence, ever could.'

This time it was William who paused before answering. 'A suggestion from a woman of your beauty is as good as a command.'

She smiled. 'I shall be careful then for fear I will lead you astray, now that I know your judgment extends no further than a fair show of face.'

Protest at the challenge to his judgment was prevented by the return of the servant with the cordial. William took it. Isabella gestured to the drink. 'What lies within is not always sweeter. You should remember, sir, that even in a gold cup there may be a spider steeped. I hope your master's health and humour are much recovered by the cordial.'

Isabella bowed her head and turned away before William had even completed his own bow in return. His gaze followed her as she moved through the guests and disappeared into the gathering.

William was no chaste and anxious boy. No stranger to women. He had not seen this woman's like before. How this Isabella had outfaced that peacock wretch as if he were a cipher, no more, a very nothing. His blows parried and returned. His threatening look met with hot regard and hotter wit. William's own sallies, his talk of Catullus met and matched and more. Such a creature was a wonder to him. She burned with a fierce, fast fire that matched his own. She was of his humour. It made him think of his mother and her strong will, of Anne and her quiet confident calm, of Alice and her boldness, Constanza and her beauty. Oh, he might admire or speak in praise of others. Here was something he might love.

William cursed the memory of his clumsy compliments. A woman like Isabella Lisarro knew her beauty. She did not need him to remind her of it. He would have to do better. And doing better he might do much. What was it that Prospero had said? 'None but the strong deserve the fair'? Well, in this game of wits, he would prove himself no green and backward boy.

William turned to bring the cordial to Oldcastle. Then he would gather him up and help him home. The English embassy had done due service by their hosts. They might, with honour, retire from the field. The fear their false status would be discovered had hung over William like a threatening cloud the whole feast. He would be glad for the shelter of the House of the White Lion.

Oldcastle was lingering, morose, by the window. He studiously avoided the eyes of others. As William joined him so did Prospero. Prospero's face was clouded; his thin lips were pressed as straight as a line of pikes before the battle starts.

'Beware, my lords,' the Count said.

William looked at him in astonishment, at the anger in the voice of the man whose seeming depthless calm was turned to spleen.

'That one is not to be trusted,' the Count continued.

'Who, my lord, who is not to be trusted?' William interrupted.

'That woman with whom you spoke but a moment ago.'

'Surely you are mistaken, my lord,' said William, 'that lady was a diverting conversation and nothing more.'

'That is no lady but a whore,' said Prospero.

William gaped, as much to hear Prospero speak in such terms as at the venom in his voice.

'Though some seek to gild that truth with false titles,' the Count went on. '"Honest courtesans" they call themselves. What is a courtesan if not a whore? And what is an honest whore if not a paradox that transforms beauty into a bawd? That mistakes brazen talk for truth. I say again, beware.'

The initial storm of his words subsided. The former Prospero of still waters began to return. The ripples from whatever stone had disturbed his calm began to fade. Prospero pulled a smile back to his lips.

'I am sorry to speak with such harshness,' he said. 'Venice is baited with beauty to trap the unwary. I would spare you its dangers, if I may.'

William, mind again at a whirl, seeking to bring all this new matter into focus, bowed. He gestured to Oldcastle. Grateful that his torture was at an end, Oldcastle drained his glass and led them from the palace.

Too hot, too hot!

This time it was Prospero who stood and watched as others departed. He had warned Isabella had he not? This was how she rewarded his forbearance? Why did she take these steps against him? He cast his mind back fourteen years and replayed incident after incident in his mind. No man could say he had not tried to save her, to protect her from the dangers that surrounded her. Then and now, then and now. If she had only chosen differently, how different both their lives might have been. He had seen the ring she still wore. The ring he had given her. She might deny it now but he knew her true feelings then. Did she owe him nothing? His fingers ground against each other.

His anger at Isabella was matched only by his anger at himself. Such an unseemly loss of control; so much revealed and to that cunning boy Fallow who thought too much. He breathed out a sigh to still the whirlwind in his chest. He had a *tremor cordis* on him. Be calm, be calm, he thought.

He had spoken with Vittoria Accoramboni. He had set her in motion and she would be the wheel that would grind up the English. When they were done and Accoramboni and her husband in their turn taken and turned to chaff then, then, he would deal with Isabella. Patience. Would he had it, he thought, to sit like a statue staring at the very thing that stirred him, unmoving.

A loud laugh drew Prospero's attention. A knot of young men, deep in their cups, were neighing and snorting and stamping their feet at some tale. Their brilliant particoloured hose showed them to be members of the *Compagnie della Calza*, a society Prospero knew to be popular with the wealthy youth of Venice and much resented by all others. They distinguished themselves by their ostentatious dress and their prideful displays of conspicuous wealth. At the heart of the group stood the long-haired boy that had accosted Isabella earlier. An idea began to form in Prospero's mind. A vengeful thought. A cruel thought. A thought that like an icicle, drop by drop, grew until, full-formed, its cold weight snapped and fell.

He need not wait. He might achieve all at once. Prospero walked across the room and began to engage the young man in conversation.

Let heaven see the pranks

William barely slept.

The first hint of light through the shutters had driven from him all hope of sleep. All that had occurred at the feast occupied his thoughts. He had the knowledge but not the understanding of it. It nagged at him like a poem in which he knew the words but could not make them fit the metre. It was too early to be abroad but he could not lie still. He kicked at Oldcastle's bed to wake him and discuss the matter.

'Pestilential toad,' Oldcastle howled at William. He flapped his hands at the boy from within a mound of sheets. 'Is it not enough that you drag me to this nightmarish, topsy-turvy city but you will not let me sleep through it?'

Oldcastle subsided to muttering. 'Roads are rivers, women dressed as men, feasts turn to brawls. It is enough to turn a man mad.'

'Be cheerful, Nick,' said William.

These words were barely out of William's mouth before Oldcastle sat upright in the bed. He pointed an accusing finger.

'Zounds! What foolish prating advice is this? You command me be cheerful? Command me? As if a mood were a dog or a horse to be called by its master's voice? I am not cheerful nor will I become so by being told to be so. I am sick of heart and sick of stomach and I will not be cheerful. For certain, not at the command of some want-beard boy. Begone flibbertigibbet, let a troubled soul rest.'

William flung up his hands. Oldcastle, glaring, fell back, rolled over to face the wall and pulled the sheets about his head. With much noise and sighing, William pulled on his clothes and stamped out of the room.

William walked an hour through the city before his temper cooled. Was it not enough that he must unpick the hemp that tangled him and Oldcastle? Must he do it with the old man's calumnious contempt for company?

He sighed at his own distemper. Hemminges' death was the cause of Oldcastle's mood. His was the poison of deep grief that has no cure but time. William's own was derived as much from frustration at how little he could aid Oldcastle as any true fault of the old man's.

William passed south through Rialto and its markets. He stopped to buy food. He nodded to the stall owner at the offer to dress a plate of polenta with a hash of salted cod. On his first visit to the market on his way to the banker and tailor he had tried this *baccalà mantecato* reluctantly and at Salarino's insistence. Now he sought it out. As he ate he conversed with the stallholder as best he could, less a matter of Latin and more of gestures. Sated, William walked away along the edge of the Canal Grande. The trouble with actors, William mused of Oldcastle as he walked, is that they are not content simply to have a feeling. They must parade it before an audience to have it noted and applauded.

William turned into the back streets and followed the path of small canals. The light reflecting from the water sent ornate patterns dancing high on the red plastered walls of houses. Oldcastle had the right of it, of course, he thought. One could no more command one's humours than the wind or sea. Moods came at their own prompting. Though gall and melancholy could be fed, as Oldcastle seemed to do, with too much wine and heavy food to thicken the blood. The all-present water of Venice, ever lapping at the walls and casting strange lights, played its part. It turned thoughts rolling inwards in the mind.

William looked up at the roofs of the houses opposite. Above them the *campanile*, the bell towers of Venice's many churches, overpeered the city. He set his eye on one he recognised and set out for it.

He flicked a loose pebble into the canal as he passed and watched the water close over it. What had brought about the sudden ill humour in Prospero? The Count was no actor to parade his feelings wantonly. Something had dragged his ill temper out into the open.

William came to a bridge. It had, set in the floor of its central span, four white marble footprints. One was placed in each corner, as if four men had stood and dug their rear heels into the stone of the bridge. This must be one of the Ponte dei Pugni, the Bridge of Fists, that Salarino had told him about. At the winter celebrations, Salarino had explained, the clans of Venice would meet, one either side of the canal. Their champions would come and stand facing each other in the centre of the bridge, their feet set on the marble footprints. Then the two sides would fight each other until one side was driven back or all thrown into the canal. That's one way to prevent more general riot, William thought. Such is the outward triumph of Venice that its people now war against each other.

He walked over to one of the four marble footprints. Here I stand with Oldcastle, he thought, waiting to deliver my charge to the Signoria and leave the city. He paced to his left and the next of the marble footprints. Here stood Prospero. Was he just walking beside them? Or was he a dog at their heels?

Who stood opposite them? William walked to the other side of the bridge and stared at the third footprint. The Duchess of Bracciano, Vittoria Accoramboni: what was he to her or she to him? Prospero had some business with her. William had not been so distracted by Isabella Lisarro as to fail to observe Prospero and Vittoria with their heads bowed together in conversation of great pith and moment. Nor had he failed to observe Vittoria's touch upon Prospero's arm.

He crossed to the last of the marble footsteps. What of Isabella Lisarro? Where came her interest in William and Oldcastle? Were he and Oldcastle just curious pleasures, toys for a cat to play with? Was her interest in them, or in the company they kept?

William took a last look at the prints and resumed his walking. He thought of England. What would his daughter Susanna think of Venice and its wonders? Anne he felt, would have been of Oldcastle's humour, longing for the comfort of the familiar. What was it that made some rejoice in new experience and others flee from it?

He returned to his first thought. Whence came Prospero's anger at the finish of the night? What of his warning? Did he know Lisarro of old? Had they been lovers? Sure, that was an answer in which lay much explanation. Seeing William and her in conversation he had assumed much more than had occurred. What matter that there had been nothing to offend in it? Trifles light as air are to jealous minds confirmations strong as proofs of holy writ. Nor could William deny that Isabella Lisarro had been in his dreams that night.

He emerged from an alley onto the Fondamenta della Zattere, the long street alongside the Canale della Giudecca. Ahead of him was a white-fronted church. He walked up to admire the three statues at the top of the front of the building, a statue of Jesus and two saints he did not recognise. As he came closer to the church he saw there was a small carved lion's head set in the wall with a Latin inscription above it: 'For the Magistrates of Public Health, the *sestiere* of Dorsoduro'. A hole yawned in the mouth of the carved lion, one of the *bocca di leone*, the places where anonymous accusations could be placed for the attention of the Signoria.

He thought for a moment of returning to the House of the White Lion, fetching the packet of letters, pushing it into the mouth of the *bocca di leone* and having done with Venice and its mysteries. Oldcastle would be glad if he did. William stared at the carved lion and thought again of one of his mother's sayings: the blood stirs more to rouse a lion than to start a hare. Truly, Venice had much to stir him. Isabella Lisarro being one part of it.

If William were right in his speculation of Prospero's jealousy, then Prospero's anger lay as much with William as with Lisarro. In that much danger. Yet Prospero had done Oldcastle and he much service on the road, and that did not speak of ill intent. Not at first.

Too many questions, he thought, and too few answers. William kept walking.

You laugh when boys or women tell their dreams

'You see. Despite the foretold dangers of the feast, I live still,' said Vittoria Accoramboni.

'I thank Heaven for it,' said Isabella.

'Heaven had naught to do with it,' Vittoria responded.

The two women were once again ensconced in the Duchess's study.

Vittoria paced before the windows. Isabella sat in an ornate chair. She watched Vittoria flutter about the room and wondered at it.

'Lady, something has happened?' Isabella asked.

Vittoria threw up her hands. She came and sat by Isabella.

'The Signoria,' Vittoria began and then stopped to smooth her dress.

'Yes?'

'The Signoria informs my husband that the Pope has sent assassins to Venice.' She did not look at Isabella.

Isabella fought her urge to trumpet the confirmation of her suspicions. At last, her warning would be acknowledged.

'They know no more than that,' Vittoria continued. 'They say only that the Pope has been heard to boast that he will not be long defied. That justice will be served for his nephew. The rest they guess at.'

Vittoria could not sit still. She rose to resume her pacing.

'Justice? *Hah!*' she said. 'What does that wicked man know of justice?'

Vittoria crushed her hand into a fist. She shook it at the window, at Rome. 'Would I had this Pope's throat within my hand's reach. I'd show him such a deal of justice.' She took a great breath.

Gathering herself, Vittoria turned and took her place by Isabella's seat. She took up her glass and gestured at Isabella, who had remained silent.

'Tell me, did you learn anything at the feast?'

Isabella studied the other woman. The calm in her words were as fragile as an egg's shell. Vittoria's glass of wine was nearly drained in one swallow.

'Lady, you are frightened. There's no –'

'Frightened?' Vittoria Accoramboni's voice rose. 'Angry, yes. Frightened, no. Do not confuse one for the other.'

Isabella did not think she had it wrong. 'Forgive me,' she said. 'I would have such fears in me were I you. I attributed my weakness to you.'

Isabella saw the other woman mollified. For herself, she did not think fear weakness. Fear leads to caution. Caution before a threat of murder is no more than sense.

'I spent much time talking to the Count of Genoa's companions. The English,' said Isabella. 'They are strange. The older man seemed much distract. I could not discern the cause. There seemed none. The younger was full of fine words and fancies. The difference 'twixt his mood and his fellow's was, itself, a curiosity. I did not discern in them malice.'

'Was your commerce with them long? That you might safely make that judgment?' Vittoria said.

Isabella heard in her question some admonition. She bridled at the tone. 'The youth and I spoke of many things,' she said. 'Of Venice, of England, of his companion, of poetry.'

'Poetry?' Vittoria broke in scornfully. 'I see it was a deep examination.'

'I would do more,' Isabella replied, 'if time permitted. I have arranged to meet with him again.' Feeling unaccountably attacked, she sought to defend herself. 'I think a man inclined to poetry is less inclined to murder.'

'Then you are the more deceived,' Vittoria said, her brow rising in triumph. 'Whilst you have been engaged in questions of metre and rhyme, I have made more solid investigation of my own. My spies tell me that these English, if they are truly English, lie at the heart of the threat to me and my husband.'

'Prospero is at the heart.' Isabella was sure of it. 'If these English are some part of his scheme, I know not. Never think, though, that the Count of Genoa is not behind them.'

'So you say. What proof have I of this?' Vittoria said. 'Only the word of an abandoned lover.' She rose to pace again.

'What I do know is that Prospero himself has given me warning of the English,' she rounded on Isabella. 'Is that not strange behaviour for an assassin?'

Isabella rose and her voice rose with her. 'Your spies are Prospero?' she said. 'That is your proof? Oh lady, he distracts you. Makes you turn to look in another direction. Then strikes your back.'

'Makes me lower my guard by warning of attack?' Vittoria scoffed. She threw back her head and cried out in frustration, 'Is there no one that can see past their own concerns to my safety?'

The two women glared at each other. Isabella fought for calm.

'You may have the right of it, lady,' she said. 'Let me have time to take the measure of the English. It may be that I can discover from them some aspect of their plan that advantages you in your defence.'

Vittoria still swelled but said nothing.

'I beg you,' Isabella pleaded, 'beware the Count. I know you think I am poisoned against him by my past. Consider that the poison that infects me may stem from knowledge of the man. I will not see him do to another what was done to me, or worse, as I know he has done to others.'

'I will not stand idle. Not while danger gathers itself,' Vittoria said.

'I do not ask you to,' said Isabella. 'Only that you do nothing precipitate.'

Isabella watched the young woman wrestle with her better judgment before she nodded her agreement.

When Isabella had departed Vittoria rang her little bell. The door opened to admit Antonio.

'You heard?' she asked.

'I was at the door,' he replied. 'I heard all.'

'Your thoughts?' Vittoria demanded.

'If my lady's information is sound then we should not wait on the courtesan. Let me send men to follow the English, to mark their passage, who they meet.'

'Agreed.' The Duchess, her face and chest flushed, flicked her fan open. 'These matters distress me.'

When the captain did not leave at once Vittoria looked up at him. 'Yes, Antonio?'

'I second the courtesan's advice,' he said. 'Till we know more we should show caution with the man Prospero.'

'You think I do not realise that?' Vittoria Accoramboni cried. She clenched her fist in front of her, her rage making the tendons of the slender hand stand out as stark as battlements.

'Do you think I am a fool, Antonio?' She forced out the words against the set of her teeth. 'Do you think I have not considered the danger Prospero presents?'

Antonio saw the rising anger in his mistress. In such a mood, to say more to her was provocation only. He bowed and left.

The tremors within Vittoria began to subside. She finished the wine in the glass beside her and fanned herself to cool a little of her choler. She cast her mind out to more pleasant thoughts.

The feast had been every bit as delicious as she had hoped. To see the anger provoked in Prospero by mere sight of Isabella Lisarro. To witness his struggle to control himself. Sweet delight, she thought. How Prospero had pressed her hand as he spoke. Vittoria had felt the passion pass along it to her breast. One delight among many.

Even the Tiepolo boy, whose attention to Vittoria since she came to Venice had been alternately flattering and dull, had justified his inclusion at the feast by his hapless jousting with Isabella Lisarro. The glorious moment when it had seemed he would be pushed to violence there, at her feast, the scandal it promised. She thrilled at the thought of it; how close it had come. Such games were enough to satisfy even her wanton spirit.

And Lisarro, such courage, such wit; they were so alike, the courtesan and her. It hurt her that Isabella did not see it but treated her still as a child. Well, Vittoria would be pleased to see how the courtesan's maturity handled the English suit. She thought Isabella's judgment of their merit much clouded. Poetry, *faugh*! What a standard by which to judge the world.

Vittoria Accoramboni waited for the moment that Isabella Lisarro understood that love could be made to rhyme with murder.

The news from the Signoria was a dark blot amid all this. The talk of plots and murderers had seemed more sport than threat till this confirmation; now a cold fear thrilled through her veins. Cruel tokens of real consequence had been placed onto the betting table. So be it. She would not stand idle. As she had done before, as she had warned Isabella she would, she would act.

Love all, trust a few

The invitation to attend the gathering at the Ca' Venier had come at breakfast one week after they arrived in Venice and two days after the feast at the Ca' Bracciano.

The previous day of walking had revealed much of the city to William. He began to have some feel for the relationships and rivalries that formed the currents and unseen eddies in the lagoon. Yet on returning to the House of the White Lion the night before there had been no moment to speak of what he had learned before Oldcastle had turned again to his plaintive requests that they leave for England. William was in no mood to listen.

When the invitation came William did not trouble to wake Oldcastle. He went alone.

The tailor of Venice still laboured hastily on William's behalf but quality will not be rushed. Therefore, William was once again dressed in motley: half the work of Venice's workshop, half the work of England's stage. The whole, William hoped, would suffice. There was a part of him that thought it madness to expose his false status to examination. That part was shouted down by a desire to see the wonders of Venice. That he had not been revealed as false at Vittoria Accoramboni's feast had given him confidence. If he behaved modestly, he thought, and shunned the light, he should be safe.

William stepped from the gondola to the canal entrance of the Ca' Venier. Where the Ca' Bracciano had impressed by dint of its scale and sumptuous decoration, this palace intimidated by its reek of ancient power and privilege. The noon sun struck a multitude of statues and the circular plaques that William now recognised as Byzantine. The tattered naval banners hung from the ceiling showed their source, the plunder of Constantinople.

'Sir William Fallow,' called a voice.

William turned at his name. A man bore down on him dressed in the black robes of a Venetian senator.

'You are very welcome, Sir William,' said the man.

The man's broad smile of welcome was accompanied by two hands that reached out and engulfed William's own.

'Marco Venier,' he said. 'Welcome, welcome to my house. Delighted to meet you. We have been warned already that you will be a potent addition to our contests.'

William struggled to keep up.

'Forgive me, sir,' he said. 'You've lost me. I am no knight but plain William and I do not know what contests you talk about.'

'You are not Sir Henry's son?'

'Well, yes,' said William recalling his part as Oldcastle's bastard, 'but no knight, sir.'

Marco Venier shrugged.

'No matter,' he said. 'We are not ones for titles here in Venice.' He laughed. 'Well, not those kinds of titles.'

He reached out his arm and swept it round William's shoulder. 'As for the contests, I mean, of course, the contests of wit and poetry for which my house is famous.'

Marco Venier ushered William into the palazzo and up marble steps to the *piano nobile*. When the invitation had arrived William had been anxious to be out, desiring to avoid Oldcastle, and had taken no time to consider further. Now here, he realised he had no idea what lay behind the invitation.

At Marco Venier's approach two servants pushed open the doors to the great room. A dozen of the nobles and finer people of Venice stood there already. They turned as one at William's entrance. The collective weight of their gaze pressed him to a halt. Marco Venier, ahead of him by some paces, turned, held out his arms and announced, 'Sir William Fallow, of the English Embassy.'

William winced to hear the undeserved title repeated. He made a bow. Marco Venier was beckoning him forward to make introductions. William tried to take in the names. He recognised no one save one, Isabella Lisarro. She was as beautiful as he remembered. Daylight showed her older than he had thought. She smiled. He saw that one of her teeth was slightly crooked. He thought her more beautiful still. The slight flaw showing him the perfection of the rest.

'*Hah!*' Marco Venier clapped him on the back. 'I see you have already met the beauteous Isabella.'

Venier leaned in and in a whisper more suited to the stage than discretion said, 'Do not worry, Sir William. We are all caught staring when Isabella is present.'

William blushed and the rest of the company joined with Marco Venier in laughter. Venier clapped his hands, servants scurried, a glass of wine was put in William's hands. William turned to remind his host that he was no knight. He found Marco Venier already three strides across the room greeting a new arrival.

Isabella watched William twist about. The young man was strangely dressed. His hose and shoes were new and finely made. His short cloak the fashion of fifty years past. William and Isabella's eyes met and the pattern of her smiling and his blushing rewove itself. If he was an assassin he made good hiding of it, Isabella thought.

She counselled herself to caution. The flattery of a young man's attention was not new to her. That did not mean, even after all these years, it was unwelcome. Nor that it was incapable of distracting her from a true appreciation of his merit.

As William stood, daring to admire Isabella, he was approached by one of the noblewomen, a tall, dark-haired woman in a red dress.

'Pay Marco no mind,' she said to William. 'His nickname in our little society is "the Ladle". He so loves to stir the pot.'

'I thought we called him "the Witch", Faustina.' A fat little man in black, his belly draped with a thick gold chain, stepped over to join William and Faustina. 'Since he is always brewing trouble.'

'Oh very good, Andrea,' Faustina said to the fat man. 'That little jibe must have been weeks in the preparation.'

Andrea played with his chain. 'It's for remarks like that, Faustina, that you are known as "the Cat".'

'As well as for her whiskers,' he hissed at William.

Faustina scowled. 'Cat I may be, Andrea, but you are simply a burr beneath our seats. Save your jibes for the contests, Andrea, you have few enough to spend as it is that you should so waste them.'

'Now, now good madam, good sir,' William said to the pair. 'I can scarce believe either name deserved. For your height, your colour and your far-sightedness, madam, I am sure you're styled the "*Campanile*" of this society. You, sir, by your quiet contemplation and your obvious wealth must be the "Patriarch".'

'Excellent, excellent well.' Marco Venier returned bringing with him a new guest. 'You see, Francesco, this Englishman, Sir William, is quite the equal of us all in wit. And worth two of you in flattery.'

Venier spoke to the new arrival, Francesco Tiepolo, the surly young man from the feast at the Ca' Bracciano who had battled with Isabella and lost. His attire was as gorgeous as before and his manner as ugly. Francesco bowed his head low in greeting, which did not quite disguise his sneer. On raising his head he looked around the rest of the room with studied disinterest in William. Save that any praise of others savoured sourly to this Francesco, William could think of no reason for this surly show. Marco Venier seemed not to see the insult. He clapped his hands and gestured.

'Come, my friends, it is time for the contests of wit, the courts of love,' he said as he ushered his guests to the end of the room.

The company began to move towards a circle of chairs.

William felt his arm caught and scented violets.

'So it begins, Englishman,' Isabella said. 'Are you ready for the battle?'

'I thought to play not fight. I've come unarmed and unarmoured,' William said.

'Sadness,' Isabella said and looked aside at him as they walked together towards their seats. 'Then you are not likely to remain unhurt.'

By Heaven, I do love, and it hath taught me to rhyme

Marco Venier stood before the fireplace. Arranged around him were his guests. William sat between the tall woman, Faustina, and a swart man who, by his dress, hailed from the East. He had been introduced to William as he was shown to his seat by Marco Venier. 'This is the great Iseppo da Nicosia. Careful with this one, Sir William. Make no bargains with him if you wish England to stay wealthy.'

Francesco Tiepolo had refused a seat. He prowled the outside of the circle. Isabella had moved to sit near where Marco Venier stood. By Isabella sat fat Andrea, playing with his chain and whispering at her. Isabella paid no attention to him or to the rest but gave attentive ear to her host.

Marco Venier swept his arm out to encompass them all. 'Welcome, my friends.'

As the arc of his arm reached Francesco he paused his hand and signalled, 'maybe'. A gesture that received the sought-for laugh from those assembled and a mocking bow from Francesco.

'I had not thought we would have the pleasure of a meeting such as this for another month,' said Venier. 'Not till our new doge is elected.'

He turned to Isabella. 'However, the muse has prompted me to thoughts of poetry. *Hah*, you see – I speak in rhymes already. The muse does not wait till the time is right. The time is right when she is ready.'

He bowed to Isabella. 'I offer a poem on the theme of love. Your forgiveness for its part-formed state will flow towards me as naturally as your loves.'

Venier coughed to clear his throat, then spoke.

As a general does, my muse commands me,
'Advance. My love be ground for your glory.'
I, unwilling of danger, yet obey.
Though shot flies, cannons roar, you're all I see.

Marco Venier bowed at the polite applause that followed.

'Delightful, Marco,' Faustina said.

Her neighbour, the Byzantine Iseppo, turned to her.

'Yes, yes,' he said in his thick Latin, 'I agree.'

Iseppo turned back to Venier. 'I thought the conceit well chosen.'

'And you?' Marco Venier looked down at Isabella.

'As always, Marco, you have an ear for rhyme and a heart for metre. It wanted for only one thing,' she answered.

Venier looked hurt. 'What did it lack?'

'More. A quatrain is too little for such a theme,' Isabella said smilingly.

'To offer too little in matters of love was ever your problem, Marco,' said Francesco from the side of the room.

A comment accompanied by an expressive wiggling of his little finger and the laughter of those gathered.

'You speak very shrewishly, Francesco,' said Isabella. 'Marco's pen is mighty enough. Though, 'tis true, it's shorter than it was. No wonder. For it has been worn down with much practice. Whereas yours, I am told, is its original length, never having been used.'

More laughter followed. Andrea applauded. 'A hit, a most wicked hit.'

Isabella bowed her head in acknowledgement.

Iseppo spoke. 'Tell me, Sir William, what did your English ears think of our host's poem?'

It took William a moment to translate the tortured Latin that left his ears full of thoughts.

'I admired it, excellent expression.' William blushed to be asked and to realise the whole gathering waited on his answer.

'But?' asked Venier. 'There's a reservation to your praise.'

William cursed his betraying cheeks.

'I would not presume to judge one far more experienced than I am,' he said.

He looked about. He saw attentive faces.

'Were it me, I should have used a different theme,' he said.

'Show us.' Marco Venier pointed to the centre of the circle.

'No, no –' William waved away the idea. 'I lack that power of invention to speak extempore.'

'No backward fellow now,' admonished Faustina.

She was joined by the urgings of the other guests till William felt driven to stand. His breast prickled with fear and anticipation. So much for cautious modesty, he thought. He reached for part-formed ideas and words to see if they might be fashioned to the theme. His heart was spurring his mind on, to the gallop and the jump.

> If will were all then I, a Will, might speak.
> Simply obey a muse's call to verse?
> Better silence than words devoid of heart,
> Such words are to the ear not sweet but curse.
>
> Lovers hear as owls, taste with Bacchus' tongue,
> Lovers see with far-sighted eagles' eyes.
> So never would I dare to cry a word
> Until my tongue were touched with Lover's sighs.
>
> From woman's eyes this doctrine I derive
> They sparkle with the right Promethean fires.
> No book, no school, no learned men can teach
> That passion which a woman's love inspires.

'Not bad, Sir William,' Marco applauded.

William blushed. His verse seemed to him a schoolboy's dabbling.

'Very good, Sir William. In Latin too.' Faustina patted his knee proprietorially as he sat again.

'We give praise where none is due,' Francesco said. 'For one thing, too many wings flapped through the verse. It was a veritable aviary of poesy.'

Marco Venier turned to him. 'You're in a sour mood, Francesco.'

'Say rather that I lack a flattering tongue,' said Francesco. 'Nor praise a verse as mere seduction of the speaker.'

'You can do better?' said Venier.

'Yes, give us your poem,' said Isabella. 'You can be certain that any praise it earns will not be spoken simply out of love for you.'

Francesco looked around the company. Then shrugging he stepped into the ring.

Venice is at war. Heaven for whores.
Her tongue raises all, rich cost for sweet breath.
Beware England that you have coin enough,
Large is the cost of this, the littlest death.

Some think themselves tall though truly they lie low.
But that her wanton words proclaim her trade,
But that her ill-mannered pride is sign enough,
I'd warn you, have a care, for she's no maid.

A silence had fallen over the room at Francesco's first line. None dared look to Isabella. The poem's wounding intent apparent from the first words that punned in Latin on her name. Save for a slight shift as she recognised herself the target, Isabella had sat steady throughout. When the speaking of the poem was done no applause followed. The guests looked about searching for safe harbour for their gaze; not with Francesco nor with his target Isabella nor with their host Marco Venier, whose guest had so venomously overstepped the bounds of humour. At last the fat little man by Isabella turned to her.

'Did you hear?' Andrea spoke in hushed tones.

'Heard and more than heard,' said Isabella. 'Heard more than I thought to do. For some of the verse had more feet than the verse would bear.'

Her eyes were fixed on Francesco. If looks were claws her gaze would have raked his face from its mounting.

'No matter, for the feet bear the verse,' said Francesco.

'Not these feet, being out of the verse, they went lamely by,' replied Isabella.

'Yet had such strength to kick as they passed,' said Francesco.

'It was cleverly rendered,' whispered Faustina to William.

Then, in response to the shocked look from Iseppo that greeted her remark, she said, 'What? I didn't say I approved, only that the poem was well made.'

'That was neither gentle nor gracious, Francesco,' Marco Venier said.

He was interrupted by Isabella standing. She walked to the centre of the circle.

'Forgive me, Marco,' she said. 'Your gallant defence as much ennobles you as the ignoble attack debases its maker. But what answer would it give if I left my defence to another? And a man at that. In defending me you would give credence to the poem's words.'

She turned to face Francesco. 'Besides, I need no help with one like this,' she said.

Francesco opened his mouth to reply but Isabella spoke over him.

> As graceless as jesting at funerals
> Are words coined at an innocent's expense.
> Ignoble the man who attacks women
> Thinking women to be without defence.

> He who contends with a noble woman
> That lacks for any fault or spear or shield,
> Well 'tis for certain all the hurt is his
> No matter how cunning the sword he wield.

> His wit wins, he wins the crown of cruelty.
> If vanquished, his is the worse condition
> For having threatened undeserving woman
> All he adds is scorn to his perdition.

A general growling of approval greeted the finish of Isabella's verse. She bowed.

'Parried and returned.' Andrea's plump hands fluttered in applause.

'She has pierced you twice over, Francesco,' Faustina pointed at the scowling figure. 'Once for the verse, and once for showing herself the better poet.'

Francesco made to make reply. He was again prevented by another speaking.

'We cannot improve on this last,' Marco Venier said. 'Let us, therefore, refresh ourselves.'

He made to clap his hands to summon the servants, but before he could do so the hot-faced Francesco spoke.

'You will forgive me, Marco. I find I have no appetite and so take my leave.' He gave a curt bow to the company.

Marco Venier shrugged as the door closed behind Francesco Tiepolo. He glanced down at Isabella.

'It's no wonder he's lost his appetite,' he said. 'You left him completely stuffed, darling.'

Isabella said nothing. The sweet sensation of her immediate riposte could not quite take the sour taste of Francesco's vituperative poem from her mouth. Nor disguise the discomfort of knowing she had made another enemy. Nor hide how, when the blows landed, no guest fought on her behalf. Bar a few, their eyes had shied away from her as if fearing contamination. Only when she had shown herself capable of her own defence had she reappeared to them. These were friends only when the skies were clear and the sailing easy.

Marco Venier clapped his hands. Servants appeared to proffer yet more delights to those that remained. The guests rose and gathered in knots of conversation.

For a moment William was left standing alone. He could not take his thoughts from Isabella Lisarro. In all his life he had never seen such speed of wit, such resource of thought, and all so deftly applied. There was a power in that display that William found more seductive than her outward show, for all its glories. At school he had been taught about the gods of Rome. He'd always wondered at the praise of Venus. He understood it. She was the pleasure of the instant. She was the seduction of sweating palms. She was pretty faces and paddling fingers. Venus was nothing next to Minerva, patron of heroes.

'Sir William will know,' Faustina said as she gathered William into her orbit. 'What news is there of the Emperor in England?'

William, brought back from thoughts that had been in ancient Rome, was for a moment at a loss. 'Forgive me? Which emperor?' he said.

Faustina shrieked with laughter. 'Of course, you English would dismiss him thus,' she said and patted his arm. 'I was just telling Marco that there are the most scandalous rumours about the Emperor Rudolf. His – how to put this delicately? His appetites are varied.'

William could think of nothing to say. Not for the first time he cursed his ignorance of this great world.

'I am afraid I know nothing of such things.'

'Such discretion. Admirable in an embassy.' Faustina turned to Marco Venier. 'Dull in a conversation.'

'Hush, Faustina,' Marco said. 'Frontal assault is not the way with the English. You must come at them sideways.'

'Now your personal fantasies are intruding on our conversation, Marco,' admonished Faustina. 'Perhaps I should be asking you for news of the Holy Roman Emperor. Are you not just returned from Bohemia?'

William was glad the attention had turned from him. Until awakened by Faustina's question he had near forgotten that he was here as an impostor. There had been little to remind him. His fellow guests' clothes were finer but their manners little different from the worthies of Stratford. Certainly they did not differ in their love of gossip. William sat quietly and listened to Faustina and Marco Venier talk of the powers in Europe. Whether out of deference to his presence or not, they spoke of England little. William gauged England was for them a strange place, a touch barbarous. It sat on the edge of events seeming too small to count. Yet persistently and unexpectedly England would thrust itself back into the centre of affairs. When Marco spoke of the Siege of Antwerp and how rumour had it that the Dutch were on the verge of surrender to the Spanish army, William was reminded of Sir Henry's fear that when Antwerp fell the Spanish would turn their warlike aim on England. Then all would rest on the few English ships that stood between his home and Philip of Spain, unless England could find an ally.

William's thoughts of England were interrupted.

'How is London?' Iseppo da Nicosia asked.

William was astonished to hear the Byzantine address him in English. It must have showed.

'I have had much commerce with your English merchants on Cyprus and elsewhere. I greet you. Iseppo da Nicosia, merchant.' Iseppo bowed his head before continuing. 'I have also been to London once, many years ago. To trade. I much admired the great Inns of Court in the City.'

'You speak English without flaw,' William said. He was curious. 'Though I wonder if you are mistook, sir. The Inns are not in the City but at its edge. Near to the Temple Bar.'

The swarthy man snapped his fingers. 'You have the right of it. I meant to speak, I think, of the Mercer's Hall on Cheapside, where I had business. It has been some years. I remember chiefly its magnificent edifice.'

'You seek to flatter, sir,' said William. 'We have buildings in London that we think rare, knowing no better. You, I judge, have seen more of this world than I. In praising London, here in Venice, I think you mean to do me more honour than my city.'

Iseppo smiled. 'I am transparent. Let me then be direct in my flattery. I thought your poem brave and good. It pleases me that the Ambassador of England's man is not all counting and scheming.'

'Oh I assure you,' said William, 'there's no scheming in me at all and I only count the feet in a line.'

Iseppo's look turned sad. 'I hope that is not so, Sir William. Or we will not long have the pleasure of your company. One wants a balance. If one is to survive in Venice one needs to scheme, at least a little. Let us take the matter of the names.'

'The names?'

Iseppo reached up to finger the chain about his neck. Hung upon it was a medallion engraved with the winged lion of St Mark, the symbol of Venice.

'Yes. The names of the papal agents in Venice that you propose to exchange with us.'

William said nothing. Their speech had taken a strange turn and he was lost. Iseppo took his silence for caution.

'You prefer not to discuss this now. Perfectly safe I assure you. None here can hear us.'

William's mind was running with hare's feet. He recalled Sir Henry's strange words as he lay dying. Words William had ascribed to pain and the delusions of a man with one foot across death's bourne. Sir Henry had spoken of names, now he heard them spoken of again. That there was a connection was obvious. What reply he should make to Iseppo da Nicosia was far from being so.

Iseppo still took his silence for discretion. 'Very well, we shall arrange to meet in quieter company. You are at the House of the White Lion. I shall send for you there.'

Iseppo turned from his strange remarks to greet Isabella Lisarro as she approached.

'My dear friend, Isabella, we were just praising the institutions of Venice,' Iseppo said in his thick Latin.

'William and I have spoken of this before.' Isabella smiled at William.

He blushed to remember the failure of his promised visit to the Chiesa di San Rocco. It was a day for blushing, he reflected.

'I have not forgotten your advice, lady. Only lacked the time to take advantage of it,' he said.

'I am glad to hear it. I only hope you take advantage soon,' Isabella said to William, whose face turned redder still at her words.

'When you can be spared, Iseppo, come and join Marco and me on the balcony,' she said. 'Marco wishes to discuss preparations for the coronation celebrations of the new doge.'

William started. 'There has been a choice?'

Isabella smiled. 'Not yet, not yet. The Signoria have but begun their deliberations and such things take time. Yet there will be a new doge and it would not do to be unprepared when he is finally chosen.'

She offered him her hand. 'Till later, *Sir* William.'

They watched her walk away. Iseppo saw William's covetous eye.

'Be careful, Sir William,' Iseppo said.

'I would do nothing that might harm the lady,' William protested the Byzantine's warning tone.

'It is not her safety I am worried about,' Iseppo replied.

As if, with Circe, she would change my shape!

Oldcastle was in no better mood on William's return. Worse, in truth, for having been confined to his room all day so as to avoid a succession of visitors calling on the English Ambassador. Salarino expressed his deep concern for the old man's health and proffered a cordial that he swore was a proven Venetian remedy for all ailments. A cordial that Oldcastle, with much ceremony, poured from the balcony into the canal the moment the little man left the room.

William could offer him no cure of his own by way of an imminent departure. The system whereby the Venetians chose their new doge was as layered and intricate as their women's clothing. William's questioning of Marco Venier had revealed that despite the passage of a week they had, thus far, only chosen the membership of the company who would in turn meet to choose the doge.

Oldcastle responded to news of this delay with a lengthy genealogical discussion concerned with whether all Venetians were but the bastard children of the over-cunning Ulysses and one of the witch Circe's pigs. A line of heirs brought forth on a dark night when Ulysses despaired of ever finding home, trapped as he was in the labyrinthine lagoon of Venice. Then incestuously perpetuated and varied only by adulteration of the perfidious Turk. Oldcastle's conclusion to his own argument was then quite shortly summed in language more ribald than rhetorical.

Then William told Oldcastle of Iseppo's strange message at the feast. Such a groaning rose from Oldcastle that William at first feared his friend was having a fit.

'What "names" are these?' said Oldcastle.

'I do not know,' William replied. 'Iseppo spoke of an offer to exchange the names of papal agents. From us the ones in Venice and I presume from them those in England.'

'Do we know these names?'

'Not unless you do.'

'Oh, dead. Dead. We are dead men.'

'Oldcastle, calm yourself.'

'How is it you are calm?' Oldcastle paused in the midst of tugging at his beard to point an accusing finger. 'We might have kept hidden, delivered these three-times damned letters and been gone. Now spies accost us and demand intelligence we do not have.'

'This is no fault of mine.'

'We should have fled Venice the moment we were free of the Count of Genoa's company.'

'We must deliver the letters.'

'Damn the letters,' roared Oldcastle. 'Wait, wait. The letters, they must have the names within.'

'They're sealed, Nick.'

'Slit them open, let us know.'

'And how then to deliver them to the Signoria? Besides, Sir Henry spoke of the letters and the names as separate things.'

Oldcastle sat heavily down in the chair by the balcony and stared out over the canal.

'You patch up excuses, Will. Some witchcraft has caught you and keeps you here.'

'There's no magic to these Venetian islands, Nick,' said William. 'Save that the beauty of a city wreathed in water and light may make.'

'So sure?' said Oldcastle from deep within the chair where he sat slumped. 'Listen to yourself. We sit here in a strange city, far from home and friends. Enemies about us hidden. Our own position false and if discovered so, why, death follows. The course of reason is to fly. Yet you, you ... you stay. Wander the streets, paddle the canals, pen sonnets for strange beauties. As if we did not walk the edge of a knife. Do not be so sure there is no enchantment on you, no charm, no conjuration. Do not be so sure that there is no Circe here among us.'

William said nothing to his unhappy friend in return. He had no argument. Venice had affected them both.

Advantage feeds him fat, while men delay

William enjoyed another comfortless night on the truckle bed and was up and about at dawn the following day. This time his sleep had been troubled by the question of Iseppo da Nicosia and the names of the papal agents. There had been much expectation in Iseppo's speech and in Sir Henry's dying words that told of plans, made long ago. If William and Oldcastle could not match those plans would they not be exposed as the false facers that they were? Yet how to obtain the names of papal agents in Venice? William had not tried to gull Oldcastle, he did not think the names were in the letters. Sir Henry had spoken of them as destined for the Doge of Venice. The names went elsewhere. William feared the names had died with Sir Henry and no earthly power would pull them from him now. Oldcastle was right. They should flee Venice.

Instead, William decided to venture deeper into the city. He dressed quietly, taking a care not to rouse the slumbering Oldcastle for the heaving man had subsided only as hot Etna does, cooled but still spitting forth threatening smoke and rumbles. William was determined that the morning should hold more profit in it than the night before.

'My lord, my lord.'

William paused with one hand on the door to the street. Salarino caught up with him. A certain puckering of his lips left William in no doubt that Salarino found his refusal to use a gondola distasteful. William ignored his judging look.

'My lord, a message for you.'

'The ambassador is still abed. Fetch it to him.'

'No, my lord, the message was for you.'

William took the small fold of paper from Salarino. It was sealed with an imprint of the winged lion of St Mark. William turned it over in his hands, fearing its contents. When he realised that Salarino still hovered nearby on wings of curiosity he tucked the letter into his doublet and took his leave of the little man.

He waited until he had left the House of the White Lion hidden behind him before he reached for the letter.

Let us conclude our private business.
The Basilica dei Frari at noon.
Iseppo da Nicosia

A passing man shied back at William's loud curse and walked hurriedly on, muttering. William had hoped this message would not follow so quickly on.

His first thought was to ignore the message. A foolish notion; the Signoria could not be dismissed as if a pestering child. He and Oldcastle might flee Venice, yet that could not be done before nightfall. More than that, his business in Venice was not ended. There were things he must attend to before he could depart. He would have to find some way to create delay. He racked his brain.

What bargain had been made by Sir Henry? Names for names alone? He had none to give. William did not think that Sir Henry would make so simple an exchange. His talk had been of the importance of Venice as an ally to England. Surely this was part of that grander bargain. If so, might he not put off the exchange until after the doge's election?

He groaned to think of the meeting with Iseppo. His refusal to give the names would surely enrage the man. It was the only way William could see to create delay. His plan made, he set off with speed. Feared things are best done swiftly, his mother was wont to say. Delays allow fears to grow past action.

William took a gondola to the Basilica dei Frari, which stood not far off to the south of the Canal Grande in the *sestiere* of San Polo. It struck him as a strange place in which to arrange a secret meeting. The great brick church whose bell tower soared above the city did not seem very private. William arrived as the bells rang noon.

As he approached the doors of the basilica opened and a crowd came forth as the service within ended. The first flood spilled away and William entered. The basilica was still crowded with people. He walked the edge of it looking for Iseppo. He found him at the front. William came and stood by him and joined him in looking up at the great painting that hung above the altar.

'*The Assumption of Mary*,' said Iseppo.

'A false doctrine we are told,' replied William.

Iseppo turned and smiled at him. 'But a great painting, as you see.'

William nodded. The painting was a wonder of colour and the figures within it had such a quality of movement that William feared they might step forth to join them. His mind was not on such matters at that moment. He thought of the argument to come.

'The work of Titian,' continued Iseppo. 'The greatest artist of Venice, though I dare not say so in Tintoretto's presence. Have you met Tintoretto yet?'

'Good Iseppo, you have called me here to speak of an exchange of names. I have come to tell you that the time is not yet right for such a bargain. We must know who is to be the new doge. We must know the whole bargain.'

William finished his speech. He had composed it on the way to the basilica. It sounded forced to his ear, the crudeness with which it had burst out after Iseppo's question, childish. Iseppo's smile did not waver.

'You are not what I expected, Master Fallow. Your master, Sir Henry, even less so.'

Iseppo took William's arm, an oddly familiar gesture. 'We must discuss these matters further.'

He began to steer him down the aisle towards the doors leading from the basilica to the city beyond.

'You cannot expect Venice to bargain for the purchase of goods when their quality is untried,' Iseppo went on.

William despaired. This Iseppo would not be put off so easily. William fought for any way to buy delay.

'Here and now?' he asked. 'This is a too public a setting for such a private business.'

'It is,' said Iseppo. 'Yet, for me to be at Mass is no cause for remark. Nor is it worthy of comment for a visitor to our city, even one from an heretic nation such as your own that denies the doctrine of the Assumption, to visit the Basilica dei Frari and admire Titian's masterpiece.'

Iseppo waved his free hand in the air. 'And then we two meet and share a discourse on the merits of Venetian art. Caught up in our talk we walk on to see more of the wonders of the city.'

Iseppo weaved them through the gathered remnants of the congregation still present in the basilica.

'What is it that you want from me?'

'Such plain speaking,' said Iseppo nodding in recognition to one of those Venetians still in the basilica as he passed. 'It is the English way. Your letters to us promised three names. We must have one now. To taste the quality of the intelligence.'

'You offer one in return?' said William.

'Of course,' Iseppo's smile stretched wider, revealing glimpses of gold teeth.

William halted. The two men stood in the doorway of the basilica.

'Very well,' he said. 'I must speak first to Sir Henry. Receive his blessing to this bargain. We meet again the day after tomorrow, at noon, the exchange is made.'

He would buy himself two days. No more but it must be enough.

Iseppo shook his head. 'Tonight, Master Fallow, before the chimes of midnight strike. The Campo San Toma, you know it? To the north of the square, opposite the fountain, is an alley. Halfway along, a door. I will await you there.'

William cursed but could do little save nod his own assent.

If Cupid have not spent all his quiver in Venice

As William headed through San Polo he passed from a narrow street into one of the innumerable small squares that patterned the city of Venice and paused to buy a pastry from one of the stalls. He had found a taste for Venetian fare that Oldcastle had not. He wondered if the world divided thus, between those who in a foreign land would eat only as the natives do and those who spent their time in longing for the forsaken fare of home. Before the calamitous ambush the English embassy had been of the second sort. Only he and Hemminges had ventured to try the local delicacies.

William had stood an age after Iseppo departed, thinking. To the problem of midnight he could find no answer in all those minutes. He kicked at the wall of the basilica and then set his path for San Rocco. If disaster was to fall on him, at least let him have seen the wonders of Venice before he died.

William came to the door of San Rocco and stepped inside. The church was cool and light and empty. The high-ceilinged silence of the nave oppressed him. He felt uncertainty come upon him of a sudden, as if the silent magnificence of his surroundings stood in judgment of him. He shuffled in to sit upon a pew. He looked up at the south wall. A vast painting of Christ among a crowd gathered below a low roof hung there. The bustle of figures in the painting seemed to force their way past each other. Their energy a contrast to the silence in the nave. Other paintings, each eager to commend itself with the painter's energetic vision, spanned the other walls. St Roch presented to the Pope, St Roch on his way to prison.

William had come to see the church's interior at Isabella Lisarro's suggestion. That he stayed spoke more of his true interest than did the wonders of the paintings. Why pluck this church from the ten thousand that Venice seemingly possessed? He gazed at a painting of St Roch curing plague victims as if the man could answer him as the other citizens of Venice had done. Answer came there none. St Roch was busy.

The church echoed with its own emptiness. William cursed himself. That she had mentioned the church as invitation had been clear. He should have come the first day after the feast, not waited. He had not wanted to seem the over-hasty boy rushing to greet a new lover, but worldly-wise. Now he regretted his own forbearance. The tide of affairs had passed and he had missed the sailing.

He pulled book, pen and ink from his satchel and, after muttering to himself for a moment and allowing his fingers to count matters out on his leg, bent to writing. After he had been there some minutes more a priest in white surplice walked along the aisle towards the chancel. Casting a doubting eye over William as he passed, subtle as the fox with its prey, the priest disappeared behind the screen. William sensed he had outstayed his welcome. He rose.

'Magnificent isn't it?' Isabella said.

William twisted about in the pew to see the bold smiling face behind him. Only the whisper of her perfume had foreshadowed her arrival. Not enough warning to prevent his startling at her words. She sat in the row behind and looked up at the painting.

'*Christ at the Pool of Bethesda*,' she said.

William stood in a demi-crouch, half risen. His knees bent by the narrow aisle between his pew and the one before him as he twisted to see Isabella. She turned her eyes from the painting to gaze back at him, gently fluttering her fan. Some rows behind sat her maid, head demurely and discreetly bent in prayer. He sat back down.

'What do you write?' she asked.

'Something, nothing,' he said.

'Both at once? There's a skill.'

William blushed. 'Lines, a sonnet.'

Isabella leaned forward in her seat, curiosity writ on her face in a wrinkled cheek and brow.

'Truly? Words for a lover?'

William shook his head. 'Alas, no. A warning to myself.'

'A warning of what?' Isabella asked.

'Not to let the moment pass. To seize opportunities,' he said.

'May I?'

'You could not read it, lady. It is in English.'

She sat back in the pew. The smiling cheek now smoothed by disappointment.

'Can you turn it into Latin?' she said.

'The thought maybe but not the words,' William replied.

'The thought then.'

William obeyed. She listened with eyes closed. When he finished she opened her eyes and said, 'Very pretty, but if you pair "floods" and "shallows" should you not pair "glory" with something?'

William looked down at the page and saw she was right. She did not wait for his reply.

'I thought to see you here before now,' she admonished him with a tap of the fan on his hand where it clutched at the pew.

He tried to think of a reply.

'I do not like to be kept waiting,' she said.

William stared at Isabella.

'Lady, enough,' he said.

She raised an eyebrow. He gestured at his ungainly twisted pose in the pew.

'You see you have already tied me in knots. I don't know what you want of me but I am here, your willing prisoner. Ask of me what you will. Only, I beg you, do not think of me as the ordinary kind of fool. I am the worst kind. The one who sees the toil pitched and knowingly plunges into the trap.'

The fan fluttered on. The priest emerged from the chancel and walked back down the aisle, looking with pointed interest on the tableau of strange young man and courtesan. Isabella waited till he had passed.

'Trap?' she asked.

'Grant me fair?' William said.

'I do.'

'And witty too?' William asked.

'The little I have heard you speak, spake of a wit,' she said.

'All in such measure as might delight a woman of virtue and judgment?'

'I am certain of it,' Isabella answered.

'Baubles before Sheba,' William responded with a dismissive hand. 'I flatter myself many things as this world goes but that I have that which interests a woman such as you? I think not.'

'You do yourself disservice,' Isabella said.

'As do you in thinking still to gull me,' said William. 'There is a web here so fine that I see it not yet know I am trapped within it. I beg of you. Speak honestly.'

'Oh what brave new world is this?' Isabella shook her head. 'That men now think themselves favoured for speaking honestly and expect women to be so too.'

William gave no answer. He had said enough and cast his dice on the tables. Isabella rose and straightened her dress. She turned and walked towards the exit. As she passed her maid rose to join her. Isabella, pausing, turned to look at William.

'Well?' she said.

He hurried to follow.

The lunatic, the lover, and the poet

William emerged into the small square to see Isabella disappearing into the entrance of a grand two-storeyed building with a white marble facing that stood close at hand. He followed.

Inside, there was no sign of Isabella. A clerk went past at the trot, leaving him alone in the entrance. He pushed through the doors ahead and into a vast chamber, the wooden beams of its ceiling supported by columns of white marble and the floor covered in a geometry of red and white marble that stretched to an altar at the far end on which stood a statue of St Roch. The great chamber was empty save that, by the altar, stood an old man staring up at a painting. William crossed to him. The noise of his shoes loud in the open room.

The old man did not look around at his approach.

'Forgive me, sir –' William began.

'Should I? Why? What have you done?' the old man interrupted without glancing round.

William straightened. 'You mistake me, sir,' he said. 'I meant only to beg your pardon for –'

'I understood that.'

The old man turned. William was presented with a bearded face whose fierce brows were pulled tight together.

'I am old but I am not deaf,' said the man. 'Beg my pardon? For what crime?'

He waited for reply.

William did not know how to respond to this unexpected sally.

'No crime. Unless interruption of your thoughts be a crime,' William said.

'It might be,' the old man replied. 'Depends on what I was thinking about.'

The man's mad was William's own thought. Humour him.

'Sir, I wondered only if you had seen a woman.'

'Of course, you codling,' the old man snorted. 'What man has not seen a woman, even if only at the moment of his birth?'

Once, in his cups, William had spoken with an equally drunk merchant who was visiting Stratford. The man's thick northern accent had been impenetrable to William, although he could see that the man was clearly agitated and becoming more so. Apologetic, William had begged him to speak more slowly, more clearly, for William could not understand him. Again he spoke and again William could not penetrate his accent and so asked him to repeat himself. Only after many minutes of this tooing and fro-ing had the drunken man made himself sufficiently clear for William to realise that the slurred words were a threat to beat him. The pair had been so exhausted by this point, and so relieved finally to have reached an understanding, that they had collapsed back to drinking, with both threat and original offence quite forgotten. Compared to his commerce with the old man that conversation in Stratford had been the very model of clarity.

William sighed and looked about the room. Spying two staircases behind him he made to move towards them in search of Isabella. The old man turned back to contemplation of the painting. He spoke to William over his shoulder.

'What is the opinion of Pythagoras concerning plants?' he said.

William cursed but did not wish to provoke the lunatic figure lest it create a greater delay than simple answering.

'That the soul of my grandmother might haply inhabit an onion or a bird or any other thing living,' said William. 'Now, would you excuse me, good father, I must –'

'What do you think of his opinion?' the old man asked.

'I think greatly of his soul and nothing to his opinion,' replied William.

'Think again, lest in the killing of a gamecock you dispossess the soul of your grandmother.' The old man held up his finger in warning.

William nodded for want of better response and turned to escape. The wide staircase ascended in turns to the second floor. When he crested the steps he found another great chamber whose every surface roared colour at him. Isabella stood alone at the far end. She had framed herself in the light thrown by one of the high pairs of windows. That light inhabited her hair turning it to a crown of ruby gold. William approached, aware he had been cast as supplicant to Isabella's monarch.

'You made me wait, again.'

'Forgive me, lady,' William said. 'I was engaged in discourse by a philosopher as I passed.'

Isabella circled him. William stood patient under inspection. He had cast his bait upon the water in the church. Now he must wait to see what fish came swimming to it.

'Who are you, Englishman?' she asked.

'A simple steward. Nothing more,' he answered.

'I think not. There is too much mystery to you.'

'Mystery, lady?' said William.

'Is England so short of men that it sends but two to be its embassy?' Isabella said. 'And of those men it is the steward that speaks like an educated man and the ambassador who stands like a mute dog save for howls at the name of England?'

'We were more,' said William. 'Our party was attacked on the journey. We two are all that remains. We have lost friends, gentle friends since we came from England. It is a wonder Sir Henry does not weep more for England and the safety that we had there. It is a wonder I weep so little.'

William turned to track Isabella's pacing.

'As for Sir Henry's learning,' he said, 'there are other studies than language. It is unwise to judge the quality of a man by the merit of your first encounter. You speak of mysteries when your own are deeper, darker than mine, which are not truly mysteries at all. Just matters that have not yet had explanation.'

Isabella did not acknowledge the implicit question. Instead she stopped. Still saying nothing she turned to look at one of the paintings on the wall of the hall. She had expected something different. Evasion, perhaps, or a clearer bargaining of secret for secret. Not this, this honest, plain speaking. For so she took it. All that he said thus far having been confirmed by report of her own agents.

Her friend Iseppo had tried to tell her so.

'I tested him, Isabella, as you asked. To my every question, the right answer. He is from London as he says. I think him gentle, be gentle with him,' the Byzantine had urged. 'By his look, I think you are more threat to him, than he to you.'

Iseppo had his own mysteries and was not always to be trusted. Yet she did not think he played her false in this. Her friend Faustina had given a similar report.

'For an ambassador's man he is most shockingly ignorant of the world,' Faustina had declared as she left Marco Venier's gathering. 'He is either a master deceiver or a gross innocent. I do hope it is the former. Else it would be too, too dull.'

Isabella heard William and did not think him a deceiver. She began to think that her time was wasted. These Englishmen were not part of Prospero's purpose nor his means to the murder of Vittoria Accoramboni. Most like they were a deliberate distraction by Prospero to lure the unwary from his true intent. She cursed. She had exposed herself to Prospero's watch for no advancement. Decision made, she acted.

'I wish you good day,' she said.

William looked at Isabella Lisarro's back in astonishment.

'You are going?' he said.

She paused and turned to him. 'I am. Please, stay and admire the paintings.'

She gestured expansively and made to turn away again. William took a step forward. His honesty had not disarmed her as he'd hoped. Instead it seemed she took it for an attitude of business.

'There are other sights I would rather admire,' William said.

Again, she halted. This time the smile stayed but was as indulgent as a priest's.

'You flatter me when I am not worthy. Your youthful energy is better spent elsewhere,' she said.

'I do not think so,' he said. 'It was by your invitation that I came. You gave me to think that youthful energy flattered rather than bored.'

William railed at how petulant he sounded. Where was any power of his to read the secret book of people? All gone, if he'd ever had it. In looking at Isabella he'd stared at the sun and blinded himself.

'Then you mistook me,' Isabella said. 'You and your master are the curiosities of the town.'

Isabella waved away her own intentions. Her inward irritation with herself at having led the boy to believe that here might be something more joined hands with her irritation that she had so clumsily dismissed him. She wondered at her own distraction. Since she had cut the boy best make the blow a clean one and sever relations.

'At least let us speak,' William pressed.

'I asked to meet you but to wonder at you,' Isabella answered. 'That curiosity sated I would go.'

'You are too cruel,' William said. 'You may have fed but I am hungry still. Your beauty is as fuel for fire. So fed, so consumed and burning hotter needing feeding more.'

Isabella shook her head at such clumsy wooing.

'That's easily cured,' she said. 'I shall remove that fuel which feeds the insatiable fire.'

Isabella turned and began to descend the stair.

William conscious only that the moment was passing, wondering at his increasing desperation that was leading him to such heavy and lifeless seduction, could not seem to break free of its grip.

'Then will my hearth be cold and black and ashen,' he protested.

'Rake it clear and set it again,' said Isabella.

She disappeared behind the turn of the steps.

William despaired. He'd had no expectation that the seduction of one as beautiful and worldly as Isabella Lisarro would be an easy task. So much the better. Toys snatched from babes win no renown. Victory against odds is fame's foundation. Yet here was ignominious defeat when he'd scarce drawn his sword. He hung his head. The pleasures of Venice were beginning to pall.

Tintoretto watched the boy emerge into the street.

'He's gone,' he said.

Isabella emerged. 'What now?' she asked.

'You are asking me?'

'Who else?' she said. 'I daren't ask myself. I have had proof my own powers of reasoning are not engaged. I've wasted time on this boy and his master while Prospero stands ever closer to his object and I still unknowing how he intends to achieve it.'

She hammered her fist onto the anvil of her palm with frustration.

'The lad could offer no help?' asked Tintoretto.

'His honesty is its own defence against any charge of complicity with Prospero,' said Isabella. 'He's an innocent. Thinks only of lovemaking. I turned him away.'

'Turned away love. Are you so rich in that virtue that you scorn it when it's offered?' said Tintoretto.

'It was such love as lambs offer,' replied Isabella. 'All fresh faces and cold noses pressed where least desired.'

'Yet he had promise.'

'Past doubt,' she said. 'You spoke with him?'

'As you asked me to. I held him long enough?' asked Tintoretto.

'You did. I had time to think,' said Isabella.

Tintoretto peered at her through his brows. She acknowledged the question written in his face.

'Yes, Jacopo,' she said, 'and to arrange myself to suit the light. The effect was, I think, a good one. Now, what did you think of him?'

Tintoretto gave the matter thought. 'Clever enough and a fair face,' he answered.

'Good eyes,' said Isabella.

'I saw,' said Tintoretto. 'And thought him no innocent nor any man with eyes such as those.'

'He writes poetry.'

'These days not to write poetry is the only matter of remark.'

Isabella shrugged and walked over to Tintoretto's painting to look at it.

'What does it matter?' she said. 'I am too old for toys, even pretty ones. He would be the diversion of an idle hour when every minute presses Prospero on me. I must not be distracted.'

' "Too old" is already dead, if you ask me.'

Tintoretto waited but Isabella made no response.

'Even if he is not of Prospero's party can he not assist you in finding out more of Prospero's intent?'

Isabella looked up at the painting Tintoretto had been working on while she was above with the English steward, *The Slaughter of the Innocents*. She thought about the price of redemption for past sins. Then she turned to Tintoretto.

'Jacopo, another favour,' she said.

The old man sighed.

William walked along the narrow street from the church towards Rialto. He had scarce passed some hundred paces when the sound of feet behind him announced the arrival of the mad old man from the Scuola di San Rocco. William cast his eyes about for refuge and found none. The old man pulled to a halt before him and held a ring up pinched between finger and thumb.

'Your ring, sir,' Tintoretto said.

'Forgi— I beg your –' God, let us not begin this again thought William. 'It is not mine, sir.'

'The lady bid me return it to you,' Tintoretto said.

'The lady? You mean Isabella Lisarro?'

'My God, sir. How many women have you given rings to this day? Of course, Isabella Lisarro.'

'You are mistaken, sir, I gave the lady nothing,' William replied.

'Come, sir, you gave it her and she now returns it to you.'

The old man threw it to William, who snatched it from the air and stared at his prize.

'It's none of mine,' he said.

'Then leave it lie here for whosoever chooses to make it his,' Tintoretto said.

'Good father, take back the ring.'

'If you wish it returned do so yourself. I am no servant to fetch and carry at a stranger's command.'

Tintoretto made to leave.

William protested, 'I don't know where the lady lives to make return of it.'

The old man had gathered his coat to him and was pacing away. He made reply over his shoulder. 'Then, if you have no better thought, I can suggest only that you try the place and time again where last you met her.'

Tintoretto rounded the corner and was gone from sight.

Such comings and goings, William thought. It is no wonder that my head spins with it all. I gave her no ring. Why sends she me this? That man was no more mad in speech now than I am. Yet he spoke very strangely to me before.

William looked at the ring, thick gold inset with red cornelian stone and the image of a spear cut in it at the diagonal. Past question, it was Isabella's. He had seen it flash on her hand and thought how heavy it seemed on her delicate finger. He peered closer, the head of the lance resembled the tip of a pen.

With what great state

Oldcastle had a bloody mouth.

He smiled at William. 'Look,' he said. 'Mutton roasted to perfection. Happiness is found again.'

He turned and clapped the back of a grey fellow, thin as a bookmark. 'My good Master Purvis, you shall find that this kindness is not quickly forgot,' he promised through teeth still clacking at the remaining flesh on the little bone.

Oldcastle sat at a table on the *piano nobile* of the House of the White Lion. Before him were seven merchants whose spare appearance put William in mind of Pharaoh's seven lean kine. William crossed to join them.

'This is my steward, Fallow, good gentlemen,' Oldcastle said.

He looked down at the now empty plate before him. A shadow fell across his face at the sight.

'Now, if you will be so kind as to excuse me,' he said. 'Fallow is my man of business and will make sure to record the issues the English merchants would have me press with the Doge. When he is at last elected.'

He rose and the others rose with him. There was clearly some intention to protest his sudden departure, but Oldcastle forestalled it by striding wordlessly through the crowd and disappearing up the stairs. William looked at the seven hungry faces. They began to speak to him all at once.

It took him an hour to rid himself of them for their worries and questions were many. They spoke of the threat to trade with the Netherlands if Antwerp fell to the Spanish, whether the alliance between the Catholic League and Philip of Spain threatened England directly and whether there had been further attempts on Queen Elizabeth's life by the zealous for whom papal edict provided the excuse and Philip of Spain the reward. On these matters William had little comment to make save what he had gleaned from Sir Henry and the earlier overheard gossip of Marco Venier and Faustina. Had William not been already worn from the events of the morning it would have been a tiring hour. As it was, he was broken. When the last of the merchants had been ushered out he made his weary way to the English embassy's room.

Oldcastle watched him slump on the truckle bed.

'Finally, your heavy looks match my mood,' he said.

For answer William merely groaned.

'An audience could not be denied forever,' said Oldcastle. 'When I heard that they had brought with them good mutton, "to aid the English Ambassador's recovery", I knew the moment had come. I do not think I will ever regain Salarino's good regard. He watched me eat as if he saw Cerberus at his dinner.'

Oldcastle gave a little smile at the memory of it, and went on, 'These English merchants will demand an answer when we have seen the Doge. What answer can we give?'

Oldcastle stared out at Venice from the balcony. He turned back to William. 'I wish we had never left England,' he said. 'I am as a tree uprooted from its mother soil. All my strength lay in that grounding and now I am fit for nothing but the axe and the fire.'

'Patience, Nick,' said William. 'The letters delivered, we are gone. We have a duty. To Sir Henry. To England. To our own safety.'

'You say we must make delivery of these letters for our own safety but the delay creates its own danger,' Oldcastle answered. 'This agent of the Signoria, if such he be, who now demands we provide them with the names of papal agents in Venice. We cannot deliver our side of the bargain. We must be gone before he calls again. What if we are exposed? Death comes in so many guises.'

William dared not tell Oldcastle that he must meet Iseppo da Nicosia that night.

Oldcastle snorted. 'You say we must deliver these letters because it is our duty. What's duty but a word? What's a word but breath? What's breath to the dead? Nothing. To the living? They must live to utter it.'

He gestured about him. 'And this is not living. I am dead already, entombed within this room. Fed pasta, black as the soil that buries me. Offered wine thick and cloying as my congealed blood. You fly free like some spirit of the air to view the city, but I do not. I have no more freedom than this window gives.'

William said nothing as Oldcastle argued to the night. He watched the heavy man move to kneel by him with hands clasped in supplication.

'We have waited long enough,' said Oldcastle. 'Let us go.'

William, lying on his back at the end of a day of disappointments and difficulties, stared at the ceiling. He had no answers to the questions Oldcastle posed, to the problem of the names, to the dangers of delay. He heard the long speech from his friend, saw the pitiful gesture, and could do no more. Everyone can master a grief but he that has it. William would have to find another way to fulfil his duty to Sir Henry.

'Very well then. Let us go,' William said.

A dateless bargain to engrossing death!

Behind him William heard the first chime of the bells that signalled midnight. The building was shrouded in shadows. Only the light of a small candle at one of the shrines, the *ancone,* that stood at the corner of the passage revealed its presence. Cursing the darkness that seemed to breed peoples on his imagination, William ventured in.

It was one thing to declare themselves for departure, quite another to achieve it. There was much to attend to, passage to England had to be procured, but not from Venice. William and Oldcastle would have to leave that city as the Ambassador and his man and arrive in their port of departure as plain players again. Some way of passing the letters to the new doge, at least at second hand, had to be considered. And one last matter for William alone to attend to. How then to find the time when Iseppo demanded that he meet that very night?

It had come to him as he lay on his truckle bed, listening to Oldcastle's snores as the minutes till midnight passed, desperate for a way through the thicket. Blame Sir Henry's truculence for the refusal to give the names. Promise Iseppo that he would work at the old man. Give me but two days and I shall deliver to you the names, he would say. It sounded a fragile thing even to his own ear. What other choice had he?

Now, in the darkness of the passage, he wished again for a better answer but still had none. Ahead the darkness of the passage that ran beneath a row of houses was broken by a thin light that came from a candle in the window beside the promised door. William knocked. No answer came. He heard the last chime of midnight and wondered if Iseppo had tired of waiting. He knocked again and tried the handle. It opened.

William entered. The small hall beyond was empty.

'Good Iseppo,' William called. His voice was loud in the silence of midnight.

A door led off to his right and he tried it. The room beyond was as empty as the hall. Another door in the hall proved locked. He called for Iseppo again. Still no answer came. Enough. Iseppo had not waited till the midnight hour but sought his bed thinking William would not come. The thought of bed seemed welcome to William too. If, by this delay, he had bought more time then that was all to the good. He could truly answer that he had come and within the promised time. If Iseppo lacked patience it was not England's fault.

Luca crossed himself as he passed the *ancone*. There was a quality to the darkness of this night that provoked strange fancies. He pushed on into the passage. His fear of ghosts and the forces of Hell was great, as befitted a God-fearing man. His fear of old Antonio, captain of Vittoria Accoramboni's guard, was greater still. The captain had set him to discover what the Englishman was about. The captain was not a man to disappoint.

Among those that the captain had set on the Englishman, Luca had drawn the night's watch. Luca had counted himself lucky it was so, seeing the English in their beds before dusk. Now he counted himself among the less fortunate. Towards midnight the young man had emerged from the House of the White Lion and struck out across Venice with Luca following as close behind him as the quiet of the night allowed.

He had seen the Englishman hesitate by the same *ancone* where he now sought the blessing of the Virgin. Then seen him stride into the darkness. Luca had crept to the edge of the passage and peered along it. He had seen the Englishman knock at the door fifty yards away and, after a moment, enter. He heard a muffled call of greeting from within. Then he waited, not wishing to be caught in the narrow passage should the Englishman suddenly emerge.

After several minutes had passed Luca had summoned the courage to advance when the door opened and the Englishman appeared again. Luca scrambled back to hide himself in a doorway beside the entrance to the passage. He watched as the Englishman made his way back through the Campo San Toma in the direction of the House of the White Lion.

Luca followed him till he was sure the Englishman walked in the direction of his lodging and would not return, then he went back to the passage to view the house the Englishman had entered. The captain would not take kindly to an incomplete report of what had passed and who it was the Englishman had greeted.

Luca's gut twisted as the door swung open at his approach, but no one came forth. After a breath the door swung again. Unlatched, it moved with the slight wind. He crept closer and peered within. The hall beyond seemed empty. He pushed the door open and entered. There was a small room to his right that could be seen to be empty through the open door. Ahead lay another door, also open, from which spilled a dark shadow across the hall. Luca crept closer.

In the deep darkness of the night it took him a minute to understand the shapes and shadows of the room. He saw the line of the body. Then the great rent where the throat should be, and last he understood that it was a head that twisted up to stare with sightless eyes at him.

What tidings, messenger? Be plain and brief

William felt the painful passage of every hour before he and Oldcastle must leave Venice and how few remained. He brooded over breakfast, twisting Isabella's ring in his hand, making it appear and disappear, and left without saying a word to Oldcastle. It was shortly after William had left the House of the White Lion that the messenger arrived for the English Ambassador.

'But, my lord, you cannot refuse the messenger of the Duchess of Bracciano,' pleaded Salarino, whose lower lip quivered at the horror of it.

'Can, will, do,' replied Oldcastle.

Oldcastle had found a new vigour in the prospect of departure. Of one thing he was determined, there should be no delay to his leaving. He should have known that storm-tossed crossing of the Channel for the ill omen it was. Nothing good had come since leaving England. As the demigod Antaeus had been deprived of his strength by being lifted from his grounding on his mother the Earth, so he had been weakened by being taken from England.

'Back to mother,' he sighed in his mother tongue.

'Excuse me, my lord, I did not understand you,' Salarino said.

Salarino's hands were grinding together with such force that, if Oldcastle had wished it, he could have used the little man as a nutcracker.

'I tell you, send him away,' Oldcastle said as he turned again to packing his satchel for departure.

Far from Salarino's dismissal this command resulted in a flight of Latin from the man's lips that rushed at Oldcastle like a flock of birds startled from a bush. Oldcastle sought to wave them down. When the messenger was first announced it had taken him ten minutes to slow Salarino's Latin to the walking pace of Oldcastle's comprehension. Now it ran past his understanding leaving only glimpses. Oldcastle snatched 'grave insult', 'political consequences' and 'ill-omened' from the racing phrases. He held up a hand imperial.

'Very well. I shall tell this messenger myself.'

Oldcastle stared at the velvet-lined box wherein the ruby brooch nestled, then snapped it shut.

'Of course, this is but a token of the Duke's esteem,' the messenger said as he unfolded from his bow.

As with all the servants of the House of Bracciano, he was uncommonly beautiful. Only his slight sneer lent him ugliness.

'The Duchess requests the pleasure of your company that she might properly present England with her goodwill and discuss matters of business,' said the messenger.

'What? Now? It can't be now,' said Oldcastle.

In his confusion he spoke in English. In his breast greed warred with fear of discovery. There was never any doubt of the victor.

'I should be delighted to attend Her Grace,' he said as his hand tucked the box away in his doublet.

The beautiful boy smiled. He gestured to the canal entrance where the gondola lay. Then he looked round with a frown.

'Your steward, my lord?' he asked.

'Out,' Oldcastle answered.

Let's not wait for him, Oldcastle thought. He will only counsel caution, and look where his caution has left us. Let the English Ambassador attend and receive his reward for agreeing whatever the House of Bracciano desires. There was no danger and much profit in such a course. If this English Ambassador caused offence or failed to deliver on his promises, well, thought Oldcastle, this English Ambassador was certain to die and be reborn in a different form a day from now come what may.

When the messenger suggested that they might collect the Ambassador's steward on the way if that suited, he was told firmly that it did not, and that time was pressing. The messenger gave another of the surly looks that seemed to come so easily to his pretty face and, reluctantly, set off with Oldcastle alone to the House of Bracciano. The messenger left but a part of him remained behind, thirty pieces clinking in the palm of Salarino.

Farewell, my masters; to my task will I

Borachio was an unhappy man. Or, since unhappiness was his natural state, say rather that he was that day an especially unhappy man. He knew the Count of Genoa of old. That Prospero he feared; the Prospero who took life as fiercely and inexorably as a winter. Something in Venice had shaken that Prospero from his cold and steady intent. Borachio knew not what.

'Bloody, rash, intemperate fool.'

Borachio quailed before Prospero's anger.

'Do you think,' Prospero said, 'that the Signoria will ignore the murder of one of their own within the confines of the city?'

'The English spy and he would have made exchange of the names of our agents in the city.'

Prospero threw his glass against the wall of his study.

'Kill the Englishman, then,' he roared.

'You ordered me not to do so,' Borachio shouted in turn.

'It could not be left. My man Salerio overheard them in the basilica,' said Borachio. 'The Byzantine had to die that night. I should be praised for my action, not cursed for my rashness.'

Prospero clenched his fist before Borachio's face. The knuckles gleamed white with tension.

'Quiet, Borachio,' Prospero said.

'None saw me,' Borachio protested. 'When the Englishman came I hid in the room, the door locked. I was gone an instant after he had left in the other direction.'

'For God's sake, be quiet.'

Prospero took another glass from the table and poured fresh wine into it. He had been at his breakfast when Borachio had brought him the news of the night's business. He sat again and allowed the process of eating to calm him. He tried to think how this rashness of Borachio's might be turned to his advantage. Time was running out and there was still much to be done in Venice.

'Your intemperate action has cost us time, Borachio,' he said at length. 'You must go at once to urge Francesco Tiepolo to action.'

'What has this business between Tiepolo and this woman Isabella Lisarro to do with our commission from the Pope?' said Borachio.

'Is it your place to question your master?' asked Prospero.

'I tire of this false standing,' Borachio replied. 'You are no more my master than I yours. We have a common employment, that is all.'

'Not so,' said Prospero.

He dabbed a crumb of pastry from his lips with a linen cloth.

'It is by the Pope's command that you are my servant in this. Perhaps you do not recall our orders?'

'Better, I think, than you,' replied Borachio. 'Else we would not spend time on this frolic of your own when all that we were set to do lies undone.'

Prospero poured two glasses of wine from the jug at the table. He held one out to Borachio, who took it with ill grace.

'You are right, Borachio,' Prospero said. 'We must work together on this, to a common understanding. Without it, we shall pull against each other to the ruin of all.'

'On this, at least, we are agreed, Prospero,' said Borachio.

'*My lord*, Borachio,' said Prospero, 'let us remember the parts we play lest we forget them in company and reveal ourselves.'

Prospero sipped at his wine and looked over the rim of the glass at the sullen Borachio.

'I am glad we are agreed. Then you will understand why I must insist you obey me in every particular.'

'*Hah*,' Borachio grunted.

He swilled down the wine and set the glass on the table. 'Enough, Prospero,' he said. 'This business with that peacock, Francesco Tiepolo, and the woman Isabella Lisarro, that is some private grudge of your own. It keeps us from our true business. I'll have no part of it.'

'Very well,' Prospero said.

He rose and went over to a table by the wall. He opened an ornate box and took from it a glass vial. Unstoppering it, he drank its contents in a swallow. He turned and looked back at Borachio.

'You are still here, Borachio?' he asked. 'I thought you went to do the Pope's bidding.'

Borachio was looking at the empty vial still in Prospero's hand. 'What is in that vial?' he asked in a quiet voice.

'This?' Prospero asked. He held the empty vial up to the light. 'This is an antidote to the poison we have both just drunk.'

'Damnable villain,' Borachio hissed.

'Such anger, Borachio,' admonished Prospero. 'I would think you used to the taste by now. I have fed you both poison and antidote this fortnight past.' He laughed. 'You were so ill that first day I feared I had overdone it.'

The chair clattered against the wall as Borachio hurled himself at Prospero. He pulled up. The point of Prospero's blade was before him. Prospero waited till Borachio had recovered himself before he put the dagger away again. He walked over to the chair and righted it.

'You must understand, Borachio,' he said. 'I cannot have this questioning of my commands. I tell you that the business with Francesco Tiepolo and that woman serves us in our commission. It is not your place to question my judgment.'

'The antidote, Prospero.'

'You must earn it, Borachio.'

'I'll kill you,' Borachio growled.

'Then you would kill yourself, since only I know the proper physic for the poison.'

Borachio kicked the chair aside.

'What is this Isabella Lisarro to you?' he said.

'That need not concern you,' answered Prospero. 'Go, track her and lead Francesco Tiepolo to where she is. Then we may speak of antidotes.'

For those thine eyes betray thee unto mine

Isabella was waiting for William when he arrived at the Scuola di San Rocco. He stopped at the top of the stairs. She had not noticed his arrival. She stood captured by the sight of one of the paintings on the far wall. She was dressed simply. Her hair was pulled up to reveal her slender neck, pale in the half-light of the shuttered windows.

It had been in William's mind simply to return to her the ring and depart with what, in the scene as it played out in his imagination was quiet, injured dignity. That imagined scene now appeared to him false, his role dissembling.

What shamed him most in her quick dismissal of him the day before was the sense that he had done nothing to deserve better. He wooed a woman who in learning, wit and spirit was his equal. Equal? Be honest at least in your own thoughts, William, she is no equal but your superior. His own shallow spirit in past affairs now stood revealed. With Alice, with Constanza, even with Anne, he had been drawn by the outward beauty of those he pursued and by the thrill of the pursuit itself. He had not cared enough for the thoughts or wit of those he chased, preferring to display his own. Was it any wonder then that, treating his lovers like ornaments, the affair had proved stiff and lifeless?

When he first set to tilt at Isabella he had thought only to lie where kings and princes had before. A shallow, selfish boast that shamed him. A thing a child might want. Now he understood better. He desired to be with her not because of the kings and princes but because of those virtues that had made kings and princes fall before her. To have one of her mind interested in his? Now there, there was a matter to shout to the echoing hills. Not as a show or trophy but for what he might learn about himself. He would be the better simply for having known her. What a fool he had been. Isabella had stripped that foolishness from him. He had seen the shadows on the cave wall for what they were. He could no longer pretend he knew no better.

She turned and noted him. William approached and held out the ring. 'You gave me this,' he said.

She did not move. He frowned at the ring, which tumbled in his fingers. Then he made it vanish.

'I have puzzled over it. And over you,' said William.

'What is your conjecture?' Isabella asked.

'You called me to you when, at the feast, you talked of the church and the beauty of its interior,' said William. 'Yet, when I came, you sent me from you. Now you call me back with this ring. What washes me to and from your shores? I am driftwood on some tide whose moon is seen in your eyes alone.'

The ring reappeared in his hands. He placed it on the sill.

'What am I to you?' he continued. 'I have wondered at it and my late-night and truckle-bed reasoning follows: You thought to use me and so you called me to you. Discovering that I am useless to your task you sent me hence. It was worry that you were hasty in dismissing my usefulness that makes you call me back.'

He studied her face.

'I see agreement in your eyes though you say nothing. That, I think, unties one knot but leaves another and another and ten times ten more. This most of all: I return to be used. To be a pawn in a game I do not understand. What are you to me that I return? You too are a thought I have pondered late night and in my truckle bed.'

William saw Isabella's face wrinkle with amusement.

'You smile? You think I speak naughtily?' said William. 'Would I did. Such simple problems are solved by simple actions.'

He shook his head. 'No, lady. Only a thoughtless rogue with no more imagination than a post would think, even on one meeting, you were a simple problem or even dare to use that word "simple" within a thousand yards or a thousand minutes of your presence. I have the experience of more than one encounter and I know you for a German clock, seeming perfect in symmetry but in complexity unmatchable, a watch that must be watched.'

Isabella's brow furrowed at the comparison.

'Now you frown at me,' said William. 'I am such a fool as takes your frowns as much for payment as your smiles. Both show me more than just an insensible tool to you.'

Still Isabella said nothing and so William spoke on.

'You think of me as some weapon to be picked up or set aside as opportunity and the fortune of war dictates. That is a poor reward for any man. Though I am certain there are many who would be content to be as little just to be held in your hand, I prize myself at something more.'

William drew himself up.

'Oh, I would be more, much more, to you,' he said. 'For I think, I hope, I love you.'

He took a step towards her. 'Yes, I love you. Not for your beauty, though yours is a beauty radiant, exquisite, unmatchable, for what is beauty but the judgment of the eye and Time's fool? No, not for your beauty but for your wit, which is sharp as a blade and has disarmed me and holds me at the point.'

He had said it. He had dared it.

'I would be more,' he went on. 'I will not be held at less. Therefore, either put up your sword and let me close or strike and put me from my misery.'

Isabella still said nothing.

William did not know what would come of his words but he knew this, he had given his all and no man could do more. He had not feared to try. The rest, the rest was chance and the course of nature.

Isabella picked up the ring and slipped it on her finger. She looked at it in the column of light that fell from the windows.

'A pretty, flattering speech,' she said at last.

'As the poet says, "Whether they give or they refuse, women delight to be asked," ' William said.

'True. Ovid was wise. It makes one wonder at the women he knew.'

'They must have been as fearsome as you, lady. Didn't he also say, "Fortune and Love both favour the brave"?'

She laughed at that. 'No one doubts your bravery, William. I least of all. What stands between us is not lack of appreciation of your qualities.'

'What is lacking then?'

'Trust,' said Isabella.

She twisted the ring on her finger. William took courage from her staying when before she had dismissed him with barely a backward glance.

'As I love you, trust me,' said William.

'No,' said Isabella.

He stepped back at the sudden venom of her voice. She smoothed the fabric of her dress.

'No,' she repeated. 'Love is no basis for trust. No basis at all.'

'There's an injury stands behind that judgment,' said William. He saw it like a scar across her face and thought of Prospero's anger.

'You speak too easily of things you cannot know,' Isabella said. 'You speak too easily of love.'

'Not so,' said William.

'How can love have been born in our brief acquaintance?' Isabella lifted her chin. 'Yours is the love of poets and ballad-mongers. You love the look, not the person.'

'Not so,' William stepped closer. 'Love looks not with the eyes, but with the mind. And it is your mind I love.'

Isabella sighed. 'You might do much.'

She beckoned to him. 'Still. Hasty,' she admonished. 'It is dangerous to move so quickly to talk of love. You may frighten it away by too rapid an advance.'

She took his arm. 'Let us talk of other things.'

She led him from the Scuola di San Rocco.

William and Isabella walked together through Venice and talked as they walked. They spoke of many things and, though neither spoke one word of their true business in Venice, as they spoke they began to understand one another.

At last, they stood in a small piazza. William told her that he thought her mind matchless, astounding, wondrous and she, for the first time, did not respond with wit but with a silent look. William felt such a surging wave of hope in him at the sight that for a minute he was quite oblivious to the low, cruel laugh from behind him.

More than enough am I that vex thee still

Barely had Oldcastle crossed the threshold of the Ca' Bracciano than he was seized by the servants. He was dragged to a dank storeroom of the palazzo and bound to a chair.

'What is this? Why this outrageous dealing?' Oldcastle demanded of the grey-haired man who stood before him.

Antonio said nothing. Oldcastle felt the oppression of his silence, of the room that was empty save for him and the figure of the captain. The door opened and Vittoria Accoramboni entered.

'My lady,' said Oldcastle, 'this is some prank? Some jest of Venice against the English? Very good. Never let it be said that we English do not appreciate good fooling. Now please release me. Your man has been overeager in his part and these ropes chafe horribly.'

Vittoria ignored him.

'My lady –' Antonio began.

Vittoria cut him off with a raised hand. 'I will see to this business myself,' she said. 'Myself, you understand?'

'Your husband –' Antonio said.

'Is not here,' replied Vittoria. 'Nor would he expect me to wait to deal with a threat to us both.'

At her fell tone Oldcastle's terror, which had fluttered in his breast, took flight.

'Your Grace, please,' he said. 'There has been some mistake.'

Vittoria gestured to her captain and he stepped forward. The blow cracked Oldcastle across the crown of his head. He howled with pain and his howl echoed back and forth against the thick walls of the storeroom.

Vittoria's voice was stained with cruel intent. 'Believe me when I tell you, the mistake has been all yours.'

Her voice rose to a sudden shout. 'Did you think I would stand by? Did you think I was some child to lie in my bed or play with my toys while you plotted against me?'

Oldcastle began to cry. Tears fell from him not from the ringing pain of the blow or the rope that cut his wrists. Tears fell from the terror that came on him as he realised he had no understanding of what was happening or why he was there and no thought of how to escape what he knew was to come.

Then the questioning began.

She asked him his business in Venice with shouts and blows. Old-castle, crying and howling and caring not for dignity, had confessed himself ignorant of any plot against her. He begged her to believe him her friend, her most loyal servant. In broken Latin he had urged her to know him desirous only of her long life and happiness.

He was not believed.

There was cruel questioning all that long day.

… rather pluck on laughter than revenge

At the sound of the laughter William turned to see Francesco Tiepolo leaning on a walking stick. His jeering was echoed by a gathering crowd of companions who emerged to stand behind him. Some were dressed in the same gorgeous fashion as Tiepolo himself. Others wore the livery of servants of his House. All were armed with cudgels. William heard Isabella draw breath behind him. Tiepolo stepped forward.

'Step aside, Englishman,' he said. 'This is Venetian business.'

William pulled Isabella behind him. Seeing this, Tiepolo gave another of his laughs.

'How chivalrous,' he said. 'But you should know that chivalry to a whore is wasted.'

'I am no whore,' Isabella blazed behind William.

'Oh tut. You are,' Francesco said. 'I speak it as am shamed by it. For didn't I waste my time on you, whore?'

Tiepolo was enjoying himself. Parading the moment before his companions. William cast his eyes about the square, which had emptied save for the two of them and their enemy. Tiepolo's companions began to spread themselves out.

'Is it the custom of Venice to threaten its guests?' William shouted in hope that someone would hear and someone would come.

Francesco Tiepolo looked pointedly around as if waiting to see if anyone would respond. When silence had reigned for an awful eon he looked back at William and Isabella and smiled.

'Let me tell you of Venetian custom, Englishman. When a whore grows unruly, when a lover is betrayed by a woman, then that woman is punished and put back in her place by the ritual of the *trentuno*.'

As Francesco Tiepolo spoke that word Isabella let loose a harsh cry. She clutched at William's arm to the point of pain. William looked at her fingers, white-knuckled, on his arm and was lost. Seeing this Francesco leaned forward on his stick and spoke slowly for the foreigner to understand.

'The *trentuno* is a rape by thirty-one men,' he said.

He pointed his walking stick at Isabella. 'That judgment is long past due,' he spat. 'My greatest fear is that you will enjoy your punishment.'

Isabella pushed past William to spit back at him. 'Curse you Francesco Tiepolo,' she said. 'No woman would give you willingly what you now take by force. This promised rape is not judgment on me but on you and your –'

Isabella did not finish but turned her back on Francesco. William saw in her face such fear and horror it took his heart in its grip and held it. Francesco spoke to William as he signalled one of his men forward.

'Now leave, Englishman,' he said. 'Or stay and watch. As your humour guides you.'

The servant reached to drag William aside. Unresisting, William was moved as in a dream. As he was pulled past he plucked the man's dagger from his belt. He stepped back, dragging the servant off balance. Then, channelling all the rage and horror roaring in his breast at the vile men before him, he slashed the servant across the arm.

'*Run!*' he screamed at Isabella.

She started like a hare and ran with the wind of terror behind her towards the only remaining escape. William turned and hurled the dagger at Francesco Tiepolo. It tumbled as it flew and struck him by the hilt. For an instant, all were too stunned at the sudden change of tempo to respond. Then Fransceco Tiepolo roared and William ran and the chase began.

When the square was quiet again Borachio stepped from the shadow of a doorway. For a moment he halted, clutched at his stomach, cursed and spat. Then he pulled himself up and headed in the other direction to report to Prospero on the success of the morning's work.

Though the devil lead

Oldcastle recalled a fat priest in London preaching that suffering was part of God's plan; that pain endured, ennobled. Oldcastle thought the priest foolish then; he knew him so now. Pain and suffering do not elevate; they drag you down. Nicholas Oldcastle was chipped away blow by blow. His fear was that even if they ceased there would be nothing left. Least not of the self that he recognised.

To their questions he told all. Oldcastle told how he was not the English Ambassador but a poor player. He told how his party had been set on. How all were killed save him and his companion. He begged for compassion and for understanding.

He was offered only a curious tilt of the head.

The questioning turned to his companion, Fallow. Oldcastle told all that he thought might interest them.

'Why did he kill Iseppo da Nicosia?' demanded Vittoria.

Oldcastle could answer only with a look of incomprehension. He earned a blow for his silence.

'I swear I do not know what you mean,' he pleaded.

Vittoria leaned in close. 'This Iseppo. His throat was cut through. To the bone. Less a murder than a work of butchery. Why? What was Iseppo da Nicosia to you? To England?'

Oldcastle's terror sucked words from him. Vittoria stood back and let her captain work.

Oldcastle answered as best he could, desperate to sate them. 'He is as innocent in this as I, believe me, lady. We are both the victim of circumstance. Circumstance only. Oh, he can be a monster no doubt, and I have known many. I saw Drake in his pomp and Burbage in his rage and they were worse men but lesser.'

Oldcastle gave a little laugh and babbled on. 'He seems to know you so well and know why you do what you do and want what you want. You begin by thinking that a scheme is your idea, an adventure your conception and then, when it is all done, you realise it was his all along. And above all that, he's a poet too. Would you believe it? If I'd known that, I would have known he was not honest. But for all that, he's no murderer. I can't see him killing a fly let alone one such as you.'

Oldcastle gave another little laugh. It was a pitiful thing and came from a bruised face. He gazed up at Vittoria Accoramboni. Her blue eyes were the largest he had ever seen. The rest of her heart-shaped face was perfectly formed, of course. Her skin smooth and lips a delicate coral pink, but the eyes were everything, a murdering child's eyes. Oldcastle looked up at them in hope.

Vittoria struck him hard across the face. She wiped her palm, damp with his sweat and tears, on the sleeve of his doublet.

'I did not ask what your opinion of him was,' she said. 'Tell me where he is. Now. Or I will have your skin cut from you while you still breathe.'

'I don't know … I don't know …'

Oldcastle's voice was shrill in its pleading. Three thin streams of blood ran down his fleshy features from cuts made by her rings. Vittoria watched him for a long minute. She turned from him to her captain of guards.

'He knows nothing, Antonio,' she said in the rapid dialect of Rome. 'Deal with him and return to me at once. We must find his friend. He is the true danger.'

'At once.' Antonio bowed.

Vittoria gave one last look at Oldcastle, who stared back at her. A hopeful and uncomprehending smile crept onto his sweat-slick chops. Surely, he thought, of all things she does not mistake me for a brave man? She sees I have told everything. He gave a little sob at the injustice of his suffering. He would have told them all for half as much a beating. The Duchess, a sigh fluttering through her lips, swept from the room.

Grey-haired Antonio smiled at Oldcastle. The fat fool smiled back.

Both alike in virtue

Isabella hammered at a door.

'Off!' she cried. 'Off the street. We must get behind walls.'

The door remained barred. William looked up beyond the narrow confines of the small street to the spires peering above them. Wordless, he clutched at her arm and pulled her after him. They hurried down the narrow alley beyond. Isabella stumbled from one high shoe. William turned and snatched both off and hurled them away to leave her in stockinged feet in the mud of the alley. Her eyes, wider than a roe, fixed on him, not troubling to challenge his presumption but clutching at his arm.

'For God's sake let us hide. Anywhere.' The thin touch of hysteria was in Isabella's voice. 'Let us be off the street.'

William looked behind them to where the corner had been rounded by the first of the pursuing men. The figure slowed as his companions joined him. A leer spread across the first of their pursuers' cheeks. He advanced with purpose on the two. A moan escaped Isabella's lips. William looked up at the skyline again and pulled her after him.

'Not this one,' he hissed. 'On, on.'

They raced along the streets, turned corners, crossed a bridge and burst into a square marked only by a small well at its centre. Isabella sank to her knees only to be hauled up again by William.

'They are on us. They will have us,' Isabella wept. Her hands shook. Her breast heaved for breath. It is one thing to be brave at a distance, another when dangers are close.

'Hush. Here is the house,' said William.

'House? What house? We are too late.' A sob wracked her. 'Any house would have done had we time. All refuge is alike. If it would only open to us.'

Isabella's head was turned over her shoulder waiting the sight of the preening, swaggering men. She did not see William as he pulled her, stumbling, over to a high gatehouse set in one side of the square. She did not see him beat an urgent rhythm on the door or the little window slide open. She did not see his urgent whisperings. She saw only the men behind her spilling into the square, Fransceco Tiepolo striding at the rear. Faces red from the exertion of the chase and the thrill of the approaching kill.

She did not see but she did hear. A shout came from behind her. William pulled Isabella out of the way as, stepping through the opening and into the square, came three men. At the sight of them Tiepolo's men halted.

'Ho. What have we here?' the forward of the triumvirate demanded in loud voice. 'Francesco Tiepolo, is it? You have strayed far from your cage, my pretty gamecock. Fly home.'

'Stand aside, this is no business of yours.' Francesco Tiepolo elbowed his way to the front of his company.

He pointed with his ebony walking stick at William and Isabella hiding in the lee of the gatehouse door. 'My business is with these here.'

A bell began to toll from within the house. As it rang, more men spilled from the gatehouse door to join the first three till their number matched that of Tiepolo and his companions. Their leader spoke again.

'You know me, Tiepolo?'

'And if I did not, Dandolo,' sneered Francesco, 'I might learn of you by reading what is writ on any wall in Venice.'

Tiepolo's men snorted laughter. Dandolo ignored them.

'Then you know you are not welcome here,' said Dandolo. 'Nor any of your House. If you have business with these two let it be conducted in your own private place. If there be space enough for three in such a "privy" room.'

This punning talk bought appreciative laughter from Dandolo's men this time and angry growls from those behind Tiepolo. William began to pull Isabella with him along the wall towards the edge of the square. Seeing their attempt at escape Tiepolo moved to intercept. An action that prompted Dandolo's men to bare their cudgels.

'Do not move, Tiepolo,' said Dandolo.

Francesco Tiepolo, face hot as the sun, growled back at Lucio Dandolo, 'You command me? *Faugh!* I will move, Dandolo, for I am moved to anger. Stand not in the way of a swooping hawk lest you find yourself the prey.'

'Hawk? *Hah!*' spat Dandolo. 'Pigeon, maybe. Or parrot, all squawk and feathers. You will move, aye, turn to run. Only the valiant stand fast and I see none of that virtue before me.'

With these words the strained peace broke. Roaring, the parties leaped at each other.

William pulled Isabella round the corner of the square as the two sides crashed together like wave on cliff. They fled into the maze of Venice to cries of 'Strike', 'Beat them down' and the resounding clash of arms.

William laughed loudly at a horror escaped. He looked back at Isabella, who ran behind him, breathless, still trying to understand what had passed.

'You see, lady,' he said, 'not all houses are alike in virtue.'

So keen and greedy to confound a man

Devils soonest tempt, resembling spirits of light. So thought Oldcastle as the angelic form of Vittoria Accoramboni left the room in which he sat, tied. A trickle of blood ran down his face, mixing with his tears, to leave him blushing pink before his executioner. Foolish old man am I, Oldcastle thought, that might have sat in comfort in England were I not greedy.

Antonio walked to the nearby table and picked up a length of rope. He tested its strength. Finding it to his satisfaction he began to coil it round his hands as he walked behind his prisoner. Oldcastle found his courage returning as his last moments approached. He thought of his friend Hemminges, whom he would shortly see again. His back straightened against the ache of his bruised flesh. He stared ahead. He did not think of what was to come but of all the good humour that had passed. His only surprise was that somehow, unaccountably, till that moment he had believed William would return and save him from his fate.

The door opened. Prospero stepped into the room. He was followed by Vittoria Accoramboni. Seeing Prospero, Oldcastle thought himself saved. His hopes were in the instant transformed to bitter realisation of betrayal.

The talk in Italian that passed between Prospero and Vittoria, Oldcastle did not understand. Their looks he did, and also the name of Fallow and the questions in Latin that followed. He told again how he was not the English Ambassador but a poor player. He told how his party had been set on and all killed save him and his companion. He begged for compassion and for understanding. He was once again offered only a curious tilt of the head.

Through bloody brows Oldcastle saw the arrival of Borachio. Prospero's servant whispered into his ear. A smile rose on Prospero's face at the news. He announced to Vittoria Accoramboni that the steward Fallow, or whoever he truly was, had been embroiled in a brawl with Francesco Tiepolo. He took care to speak in Latin so that Oldcastle might understand.

'Unless one man can defeat thirty, he is most like now dead,' Prospero said.

At the groan that broke from Oldcastle's lips at this news Prospero's smile grew broader still.

'I shall obtain proof of the steward's death,' Prospero announced.

He took Vittoria's hand and pressed it. Then, with a final contemptuous look in Oldcastle's direction, he took his leave.

'Shall I finish with him?' Antonio asked his mistress.

She looked down at Oldcastle, who boldly held her eye.

'Not yet,' she said. 'Let us be certain the other is dead.'

She waved Oldcastle from her thoughts. 'Keep him safe till the Count returns with news.'

I will live in thy heart, die in thy lap and be buried in thy eyes

Even with the hand of fear to push them on, there came a moment when their flight gave pause to gather breath and then to think. William leaned against the wall of the street and, doubled over, hands on thighs, drew breath against both the chase and laughter. Isabella looked back to where they had come and then at the laughing man. William bent his head up and returned her gaze.

Her hair was in a disarray and tears had turned her woman's artifice to muddy ruin. She stood in stockinged feet, her fine clothes smeared with dust and the mossy green of walls struck close in the haste of their flight. Her eyes were still wide and her chest heaved with the efforts and fears of the moment passed. Then her serious face broke into a smile. It was full and deep with the lips pulled back wide and the dark eyes lit with an inner light. Emerging from her came an open pleasure such as William had seen only in children before, a delight that swept up both the person smiling and the one watching. In that moment William thought he had never seen someone so beautiful.

'I am the fool of Fortune's mood,' he muttered.

He looked past her, listening for sounds of battle ended or pursuit begun.

'A line from one of your poems?' Isabella spoke in gasps.

'Not yet. Perhaps it will be.'

'I pray not. It is a conceit too obvious to mention.'

He frowned at her.

'Oh don't pout,' she said.

'You know something of poetry, I recall,' said William.

'Enough to have had two folios of verse published,' she replied between breaths.

William cocked his head. 'Is there no end to your mysteries?'

'I hope not,' Isabella answered. 'My mysteries are all that I have. All that any woman has.'

'Now it is you descends to common conceits,' William said. 'I have seen many a plain-dealing woman. None that could match you for variety.'

Isabella smiled again, and again the smile appeared most in her eyes. William wondered that any man could resist such a siren call of promised happiness.

'Come.' She took his hand and pulled him after her. 'We must to my house.'

Isabella saw his grin. 'Now it is you that smiles at me as if I spoke naughtily,' she said.

William shook his head. She gave him the kind of look the constable gives when the drunk man slurs denial he is a drunkard.

'Tush,' she said. 'We are not yet safe for you to be at your wooing again. Let us first be far from the threat of imminent death.'

William took the lead and they began to run again, hand in hand.

'Oh you and I,' he panted as she followed, 'you and I are too wise to woo peaceably.'

There was joy bubbling in William's breast as he ran. His memory flew back to another chase, far from here in the cold March of Arden, and the thrill he had felt then. The smell of Venice was strongly in his nostrils, its gold and rose colours in his eyes, its heartbeat of water slapping on walls loud in his ears. Her hand was warm in his.

Later she would question him about his knowledge of the factions of Venice, of how he knew where the Dandolos lived and of their hatred for the Tiepolos. Later she would tell him about the kings and princes she had known, of her poetry and her love of painting. He would ask to hear a verse and she would take a small book of hers and let him read it while she watched his face to see how he reacted. Later she would show him a portrait of her by her friend Tintoretto when she was just William's age. When her beauty was like the power of armies that by their mere show make men crouch down and yield.

Later he would begin to understand that to understand her was as impossible as to understand himself and that it did not matter. That answers did not matter. All this for later, but for now he ran with her hand in his and his heart burned with fierce joy to be alive.

Since night you loved me; yet since night you left me

When William and Isabella had reached the safety of her home that night they found her maid, Maria, waiting for them. Seeing her mistress so late returned and in such a state, Maria had wailed and fussed. Isabella excused herself and left William in the salon of the house. Isabella went with Maria and calmed her with promise of explanation in the morning then sent her to her rest. Isabella changed to fresh clothes and cleaned her face. She returned to William in a simple dress, her face unmade, her hair hanging freely.

'You see me now without artifice,' she said. 'My painted rhetoric removed.'

'I see only that your beauty is ingrained.'

'You're kind,' Isabella said, pouring them both wine. 'Be certain that if the hour were not late and the room dark I would not dare this show.'

'Your maid is calmed?'

'*Calm* is not the word. Maria is content that I am well. She will wait for morning to demand more explanation of me.'

'It is good that she cares for her mistress's safety,' said William.

'As I for hers. She has been with me many years. Her and her boy, Angelo, are all the family I can say I have.'

They sat in the salon of her house. Two candles cast small circles of light but it was the moon that lit the room. She sat across from him.

'You're cold?' William rose to offer her his cloak.

As he reached for it he realised it had been lost in their flight. Isabella held up a hand.

'Not cold,' she said. 'Tremors. The effect of the day.'

She took a long drink from her glass, 'I knew ...'

When she did not say more William gently asked, 'Knew what, lady?'

Isabella leaned back in her chair.

'I knew when I set myself against him that there would be dangers. I knew –' She took a shuddering breath. 'I do not think I understood, not until I saw those dangers this afternoon, how they would fright me.'

'Tiepolo?'

'No,' Isabella said. 'Francesco Tiepolo is a vicious child. An arrogant fool. He would never have thought to take such action without being set onto it.'

She drained her glass.

'Behind his actions is the Count of Genoa, Giovanni Prospero.'

She rose to fetch more wine.

'Before, when you said that there was a hurt that lay behind my words. Do you remember?' she asked.

'I do,' William said. He spoke softly, not wishing to frighten away her explanation by loud noises.

'The Count of Genoa is known to you, I think,' she continued.

'He is,' William replied.

'To me also. Giovanni Prospero came to Venice many years ago, when I was barely more than a girl. He had … has … charms.' Her head lifted. 'We were lovers. I was so foolish. So foolish. So many things I took for accomplishments, for passion, for desire, that I see now were the deceptions of a selfish man.'

She laughed but there was no joy in it.

'I see now there is a hole within him. A hole into which a world of love could be poured and not be filled. We were betrothed. I had such hope that in loving him I had found a kind of freedom. That, together –' Again she broke off. William did not wish to hear more. He could imagine.

'When the time came he left me without a word.' She shook her head as a tremor ran through her. 'Even now. Even now, to think of it.'

'Isabella …' William half rose.

She spoke on without noting it. 'He left me with only two remembrances. This ring,' she fingered the thick gold ring with its symbol of a lance tipped with a pen's nib. 'This ring he left me with and he left me with child.'

She turned to look at William. In the darkness of the room he could not see her eyes in the shadow of her brow.

'It miscarried. And I was glad.'

'He is a monster,' said William.

'No.' The harshness of her reply cut across his words. 'No. He is worse. A monster we know. By his form, his horns, his hooves, his claws. Prospero is a man. The more deadly, dangerous and deceiving for it. I could tell you such stories, things I have learned of him since. I was not the only innocent he destroyed, not the only one to whom he made promises of eternal love and then left to survive by selling their chastity. We, we were the fortunate ones. I have watched for signs of his passing. The children torn from the arms of their parents, murdered at his command. The blameless made to carry charges that should be laid at his door. All the while he smiles and smiles and no stain of blame falls on him.'

She shook her head. 'When I knew the true extent of his evil I vowed that if ever I might spare another what I had endured –'

Isabella stopped. She shrugged away a memory before continuing. 'It has taken me many years to understand him. You know, when he first left me I was broken by it. I thought myself another Dido, abandoned, willing to cast myself on the fires. Then when I healed from that first hurt I thought of him only as you just did. I wrote about him in poems. I thought, let my words stab him, as he has me.'

She laughed. 'That seems to me a naive sentiment now. He never cared for poetry. Though he indulged my writing.'

She twisted the ring on her hand.

William thought back to the journey to Venice in Prospero's company and his dismissive comments about poets. He thought Isabella was right. The Count of Genoa did not seem a man to be troubled by verse. William looked at Isabella's hand twisting the ring and wondered that she kept it, what purpose it held for her to be reminded of Prospero.

Isabella came over and refilled William's glass. She reached and touched his hand with hers.

'Thank you,' she said. 'For saving me, us.' She shivered again in memory of the chase.

'Tell me, truly. How did you know where to lead us?' she asked.

William explained his walks about the city. The things he had learned from them. From this they turned to talk of Venice, of poetry and of art. She showed him the study of her by Tintoretto. William admired it and her in it.

'If there were any doubt of your power this painting dispels it,' he said. 'The wonder is not that kings lay down before you. The wonder is only that you did not receive half their kingdom in reward.'

His praise did not produce the result he sought. She grew sad. She sat. William still standing, tried to understand where her mood had come from. She looked at the painting and he at her. At last she spoke.

'"Reward", say rather "commerce". My flesh has been cut to be sold, piece by piece. Worse, I am my own butcher.'

Isabella looked up at William. 'To be a courtesan, what greater slavery could there be? To eat with another's mouth, to sleep with another's eyes, to move at the whim of another. Always smiling, always attentive, always loving to another's will. What place for me in this?'

She held her face in her hands.

'Yes, I have spoken with princes and kings, worn robes of gold and pearls and been painted by masters of their art.'

She looked up at him again. 'At what price?'

William looked at her. He wanted to speak words of comfort to her sadness. He had none.

'Beauty's a thing will not endure. When it is spent, what will it have bought me?' Isabella said.

'Memories? Is there not the memory of happier times?' William asked. 'To be wanted is to be valued. To be valued is to be worthy.' His words sounded foolish, hollow to his own ears.

'A prize? The object of a hero's quest?' she asked. 'Waiting for some Jason to come and then abandon me? Some Theseus to use what I have and then discard me?'

William heard uncomfortable echoes of his own small understanding in her words and he was ashamed.

Isabella shook her head. 'Of all antiquity I know my role. I am Dido but I see Dido for what she is. Not a queen, but the patron saint of whores.'

Isabella shook herself. It was not her nature to dwell on miseries. 'This is the unsettled nerves of the day speaking. A great many things owe their creation to love,' she said. 'If some of the worst actions have also been borne of it, that doesn't mean we should lose courage. The fault is not love's but love's misuse.'

She looked up at William. He was gazing down at her with such tender care. The thought sealed itself in her mind that she would not let Prospero take hope from her with the rest.

'We should strive, then, to add to the mustering of the good?' William ventured.

'We should,' she said.

Isabella rose. She held out her hand and looked to the door. William felt amazed at what she offered him. Save to take her hand in his, he did not move.

'No,' he said.

He looked into her eyes. He saw she was as astonished at his refusal as he at her offer.

'You will think I have not listened,' William said. 'Or hearing, have not understood. I would not exchange the passing pleasure of moments for an understanding that will inform my whole lifetime.'

He held her hand tight.

'Only this I beg you, do not ask me twice.' He drew a great breath. 'I have only will enough for one no.'

'Alas, and it seems by this I shall have no Will at all,' she answered.

He laughed. She took his other hand and drew him close.

'This simple no moves me more than any fair words, poet,' she whispered.

She took her hands from his. Reaching down she twisted from her finger the gold ring with its dark stone. 'Take this. A token of what has passed between us.'

'I thought this ring had meaning,' said William.

'It did,' she answered. 'It's time to give it a new one.'

Subtle as the fox for prey

It was late when William left Isabella's house. It was later still that he returned to the House of the White Lion. To tell Oldcastle that he could not go, not now. It was, therefore, already too late when William discovered that Oldcastle was not there.

He had at first been glad to find Oldcastle gone. It delayed the moment when he must argue for a stay. As the hours passed his relief turned to worry. Despite the late hour he sought out Salarino, who seemed as nervous as he at Oldcastle's continued absence.

'I could not be certain, my lord, not certain, no, no, but I believe the noble ambassador went to an audience with the Duchess of Bracciano,' Salarino said.

William was incredulous. 'Without me?'

'The Duchess is most generous,' Salarino nodded. 'Perhaps the noble ambassador went in hope of procuring advancement for England's merchants? A messenger from the Duke and Duchess came when you were out, offering to meet that morning. To seize the moment is everything, no?'

William nodded at the echo of his own sentiments from before that first meeting with Isabella Lisarro in the Chiesa di San Rocco. Thought of her set him smiling. Perhaps Oldcastle had stayed late and accepted an offer of a bed at the palazzo rather than brave a gondola at night. Very well then. He would wait till morning.

When morning came and went and still there was no sign of Oldcastle William began to worry again. He set off for the Ca' Bracciano.

The servant at the door looked surprised to see him arrive. He was made to wait thirty fretful minutes before he was escorted into the presence of Vittoria Accoramboni.

She was astonishing in a dress of lace and cloth of gold, more edifice than clothing. She seemed to have grown some foot or so since last William saw her. He judged by that and her stillness that she stood on the chopines, the heightened shoes the women in Venice favoured.

William bowed.

'The golden-tongued emissary of England,' Vittoria said.

Her voice came out thinly, as if she sought to pare a fish with it. William was conscious of its unwelcome tone and of the lowering presence of his escorts behind him. He could not understand it.

'Your Grace, forgive this uninvited intrusion,' he said.

'Forgive?' She gave a short laugh.

William could not fathom her mood. What had seemed before flirtation he now realised was simply her willingness to hold another's eye. Her gaze stayed on him now with cold regard.

William pressed on. 'I was given to understand that my master, the Ambassador, Sir Henry, met with you yesterday. Since which time I have had no news of him.'

The silence that greeted his implicit question added to his unease.

'Do you know his whereabouts?' he asked.

Still Vittoria Accoramboni did not answer. She simply gestured past him to one of the men that stood behind, who bowed and left the room. A silence followed.

The sound of a great weight being dragged across the floor beyond the door broke it. William turned to see two of the Ca' Bracciano's beautiful servants enter. Hung between them was the battered, bloody figure of Oldcastle. William lurched forward to help his friend. He stopped, his arms caught in a grip of iron.

'Assassin,' Vittoria cried. Her voice was now the high-pitched screech of a hawk.

Oldcastle fell to the floor in front of William. He heard with relief the great man's moan. Confirmation that Oldcastle was, despite his bloody, bruised and senseless figure, not yet dead.

'What means this, lady?' William pleaded. 'This is most ungentle treatment of one who never did you harm.'

'No,' Vittoria said.

She advanced on him in tottering steps.

'Nor never will do either,' she promised. 'You are revealed, master assassin, master traitor. You think I have not been watching for the hand of your employer. You think I do not know the Cardinal –'

She broke off to spit on the floor.

'*Hah!* Cardinal,' she said. 'Say rather Pope now. You think I do not know the Pope would seek to avenge his hateful nephew? You think I was not watching?'

Vittoria leaned in as she questioned and, doing so, stumbled on her stilt-like shoes. She reared back to recover.

William was lost. He understood that Vittoria spoke of her murdered first husband's uncle, the Cardinal Montalto, now Pope Sixtus. This much of the story he knew from the common rumour of the city. What the Pope was to William or why it should have resulted in the harm done to Oldcastle was a mystery black as pitch.

'You are mistaken. Lady, I beg you ...' he pleaded.

'Liar!' Vittoria shouted. 'My own men have witnessed you at your butcher's work. They have seen the bloody business you wrought with Iseppo da Nicosia. You are more beast than man.'

'Iseppo da Nicosia is dead?'

'You dare feign ignorance?'

She raised a hand. William felt the hands that held him tense against the shock of her expected blow. Instead a knock came at the door.

'What is it?' Vittoria called. The Duchess's eyes stayed on her prey.

A trembling servant put his head past the door. 'The Count's man, Borachio, is below with two others and says he has urgent news for Your Grace.'

'Bring them up,' Vittoria ordered.

She pointed a finger at William. 'Now you will see,' she said. 'Here comes witness to your villainy.'

Smile and smile and murder while I smile

'Cowardly, foolish, three-inch villains,' spat Prospero.

He had greeted the news that his trap had caught two birds, that the steward Fallow had been there when Francesco Tiepolo had set on Isabella Lisarro and would fall with her, with great pleasure. Borachio had even received a little physic for the poison in him.

The greatness of that pleasure had been matched only by the depth of Prospero's fury when morning brought news of their escape. In vain Borachio had protested that their deliverance was no fault of his. He was just the bearer of the news.

Prospero's displeasure at this first report of the morning was as nothing compared to that which came with the later news that the English steward attended on the Ca' Bracciano.

'We're undone. We'll be revealed,' Borachio said.

'Quiet,' Prospero ordered. 'He'll not be believed.'

'What certainty is there in that? What danger to us if he is?' Borachio flickered between anger and fear. Fear that his master's over-cunning plan had put him in danger. Anger that his master had not struck when he, Borachio, had first urged it. Prospero swung his gaze at him.

'You're right, Borachio,' he said.

The vicious little man had never been so frightened in his life as to hear that devil Prospero, for the first time, agree with him.

'Go swiftly,' the Count said. 'Take your men, Salanio, Silvio, I forget their names ...'

'Salerio and Solanio,' Borachio whispered.

'I care not. Go to the palazzo now. Gain audience with the Duchess. She will be there with the English. Seize the moment. Strike her down. Strike them down. Say they slew her and you them in her defence.'

'Madness,' Borachio protested. 'She'll be guarded and they will be tied. Who'll believe it?'

Prospero leaned in. His eyebrow stood quizzical. 'You'll be a hero, Borachio. Who would believe it of you? Well, we shall find out, won't we? As for her guards, kill them first. There must be no witnesses.'

'I'll not do it. This is no stratagem but suicide.'

'You will, Borachio.' The Count spoke with such certainty that Borachio cowered to hear it.

Prospero held up the little glass vial and waved it.

'Every morning a little poison, Borachio. Every evening a little antidote. Remember? It is now past noon. I suggest you return before the evening falls.'

There was no more to be said. To stay now was a certain death. Borachio knew that much.

When Borachio left Prospero turned to his desk. He drew a sheet of paper forth. In a few short sentences he spelled out his revenge. He sealed the note and rang a bell to call for a messenger. While he waited for the boy to come he wafted the letter in front of him while the wax dried.

When he had told Borachio that he should leave no witnesses it had struck Prospero that there was one whose witness he would welcome. One who, should she see how easily he brought about the Duchess's death, would feel her own helplessness in that instant. That this knowledge would be a crueller blow than any that might befall her after, pleased him. Events had not turned out as he had planned. Yet they might still be moulded to his advantage.

Yes, if the messenger boy hurried and the woman did too, then she might see how little difference she had made to his plans.

Prospero smiled.

So mightily betrayed!

Borachio and his two companions were admitted to the chamber. Seeing Prospero's servant, William understood the source of his betrayal but not the reason. His first thought was that it could not be his love for Isabella; that news was too fresh.

'Whatever this man says he lies,' William railed against the hands that held him. 'This man's master is your true enemy.'

'Silence,' demanded Vittoria Accoramboni.

William knew himself lost. This woman does not look to judge, the judgment's made. She wants only to confirm the sentence. William stared down at Oldcastle. He wished Oldcastle were awake to hear his confessed sorrow for their state and shrive him.

Still looking at William, the Duchess of Bracciano barked an order at Borachio: 'Tell him what your master has told me. Of the plots, of how conveniently these two came into his company. Of the "robbery" that explained their diminished embassy. Ambassador of England? *Hah!* The man can scarcely speak Latin.'

She poked at Oldcastle with her foot, staggering a little to do so.

'As for you,' she turned on William, 'even if my men had not been witness to the murder of Iseppo da Nicosia, you are too cunning to be this fat fool's bastard if you even looked like him. And as for your dress, remarkable assemblage. More player than person of note. The Count knew you, master assassin. Well? Tell him.'

This last was to Borachio. The little man had advanced into the room. His companions had moved too. They stood beside the beautiful servants of the Duchess, just as Borachio now stood beside the grey-haired captain of her guard. That man, Antonio, held William in a grip made hard by long hours at practice of the sword. He was staring at Borachio's scalp and the rivulets of sweat that ran down to his chin.

'Truly, Your Grace,' Borachio said, 'you are betrayed.'

With these words he drew a dagger, long and thin. A dagger that he should never have carried into the Duchess's presence were it not for the hurly-burly haste of the morning's madness. A haste that let him in unchecked; he who should least be trusted. Borachio turned. Antonio was pushing William from him even as Borachio's blade came out. Borachio plunged it into Antonio's chest. As he did so, his two companions fell on the servants of the house. Swift ends achieved with swift cuts.

William stumbled from Antonio's grip to fall across the prostrate figure of Oldcastle. He twisted round and up. Above him he saw the Duchess's eyes grow great and she opened her mouth to scream but no sound emerged.

A loud scraping noise slit the silence. Borachio's blade ran across a breastplate hidden beneath Antonio's finery to plunge into his arm instead of his chest. The captain howled, his own half-drawn dagger dropping to the ground. That same grip that had held William now grasped at Borachio and drew him in. To a sound like splintering logs, Antonio drove his forehead into Borachio's nose even as Borachio plunged his dagger again at the captain. This time it struck Antonio below his armour. The wound opened up his thigh with a great gout of blood. Still Antonio held Borachio. Though Borachio twisted in his grip he could not escape the captain's hand. He gripped Borachio's wrist, turned the blade and brought it up towards his neck. Borachio's companions reached him. Their own stilettos struck. Borachio's blade, whose deadly point had reached so high as his throat, at last lost will and faded with the captain's life.

The three men turned. William stumbled to his feet, seizing the captain's fallen dagger. The Duchess, seemingly released from whatever spell Borachio's betrayal had cast on her, let loose a high and penetrating scream.

'Kill them both. Quickly.' Borachio's hoarse command was uttered from a face masked in blood, a throat from which blood dropped as a curtain.

William hauled the Duchess back and out of the reach of a slashing blade. She, unbalanced from the precarious perch of her shoes, fell into his arms.

He cursed his own stupidity. The Duchess was no shield. Why had he burdened himself with the defence of a woman who had sought his death a moment before? The door burst open. Armed servants of the house flooded in. Borachio brooked no delay.

'The Englishman has her, kill him,' he screeched at the servants. 'Treachery. Murder. Murder.'

Seeing William, dagger held in one hand and the Duchess held in the other, the servants turned toward him. Borachio and his men, ignored, slipped back through the door beyond. William was left with the struggling figure of the Duchess and much explanation to make.

So may the outward shows be least themselves

Isabella had woken past noon. Her maid, Maria, had roused her and brought the terrible news of the murder of Iseppo da Nicosia, a man full of strange loyalties and confidences but ever her dear friend.

'Oh, lady, so wretched,' cried Maria, 'such a bloody thing to be done to such a good, kind man.'

Isabella sat up in her bed speechless with sadness. Her thoughts were full of dread.

Her maid had brought with her a tray that had on it a small bowl of rice with almond milk, watered wine and a letter. She tore open the letter. When she had read it she scrambled from her bed and began to dress.

'Who brought this, Maria?'

'I do not know, lady.' The maid twisted her hands together. 'A young boy delivered it just a few moments ago.'

'Quickly, quickly, Maria. My cloak,' Isabella said.

She pulled her hair up and thrust a comb into it.

'Madonna, lady, you are frightening me.' The maid's distress made her fingers fumble at the ties of the cloak.

'Good,' said Isabella.

Isabella pushed her hands away and tied it herself. She took Maria by the shoulders. 'Good that you are frightened,' she said. 'When I am gone, lock the doors. Admit no one. Do you understand?'

The older woman opened her mouth but said nothing. Isabella shook the woman's shoulders.

'Do you understand, Maria?'

'Yes, lady, yes.'

Isabella left her house to the scraping of bolts. Behind the door the muffled sounds of her maid calling on the Mother of God to protect the house and its mistress.

She was already too late. The letter told her so. She knew the hand that wrote it: Prospero's.

I warned you. For what did you oppose me? For nothing.
Go to Rialto.

Stand on the Campo Erberia.
See and understand how little you matter. How little you
understand of how far my hand reaches.
Then fly if you wish. It cannot save you. It will only grant
you a little more time.

She found herself running again through Venice's streets. The Campo Erberia stood across from the Ca' Bracciano, as she knew. She did not think to stop there. She ran in hope that she might not be too late. She stumbled to a halt. A crowd had gathered ahead of her, blocking her path. She looked about for another route. She saw a bridge and ran to it. She thought to pass around the crowd. As she reached the top of the bridge's span she turned her head. Again she stumbled to a halt, for now she saw what drew the crowd.

The Canal Grande was clogged with boats outside the Ca' Bracciano. On the balcony stood William. He held a blade to Vittoria Accoramboni's throat as she struggled in his arms. Isabella gripped the stone rail of the bridge. She saw and willed her eyes false. She saw the servants of the house gathering about William. She saw the dead figure of the English Ambassador tossed from the balcony to break on a barge below. She saw William's arm draw back across Vittoria's throat. She saw the Duchess fall, suddenly still, from his arms. She saw William vault over the balcony. Isabella fell to her knees and hid her head behind the wall of the bridge. She could see no more.

True! Pow wow

There was no explanation would penetrate the brain of the howling, flapping figure in William's arms. The Duchess strained against him as a falcon seeking to escape its gyves. It was all he could do to hold her still. He looked about him. He dragged Vittoria, stumbling, to the balcony. Escape lay only a leap away but he was held there by the sight of Oldcastle more surely than by any chain about his leg. He peered out over the edge. The screams and cries had drawn a crowd of boats. Among them lay salvation.

'You,' William cried. He pointed with the blade at one of the servants advancing on him, a young man with thick blond hair and the strong jaw of a statue of Apollo. 'Pick up the old man and bring him here. Do it and the woman lives.'

All the men held. William pressed the point to Vittoria's throat, red blood trickled across her white skin. Apollo looked to his left. Their leader, Jove to the younger man's Apollo, nodded to him. Apollo went to Oldcastle and grasped him under the arms. He staggered beneath Oldcastle's weight and his wariness of William's blade.

'Throw him over the side,' William ordered.

The young man looked at him, uncomprehending. The old man was senseless. He would drown if thrown in the canal.

'Do it,' the servants' leader barked, impatient of his mistress's safety.

With a shrug Apollo heaved Oldcastle up to the rail and pushed him over. No splash of water followed, instead the sound of cloth rending, followed by a thump. William drew his arms from around Vittoria's throat, pushed the Duchess away and leaped.

The servants stood astonished, then ran to their mistress, who had fallen without a cry to the floor of the balcony. Seeing her unharmed but faint with fear, their leader ran to the balcony's edge. Beyond it, in the swirl of boats on the canal, now some yards distant, he saw a barge. It was laden high with bales on which an unconscious figure was sprawled. At its rear, demanding obedience at knife's point, was William, who did not risk a glance at what might follow him.

Every gash was an enemy's grave

Isabella was not sure how she came to be back outside her house. Those moments since she'd witnessed all her effort come to naught, herself betrayed, had been as moments from a dream. They passed in scattered instants.

Through it all she was distracted by the question of what followed. What was she to do now? Now that Prospero was triumphant. Now that he had shown how deeply he could deceive her. Deceive her even in the person of the boy Fallow. The whole business with Francesco Tiepolo false? No, but of course, it was Prospero that had told William of the House of Dandolo. All to make her trust him. She shuddered at the memory of what she had revealed of herself to William. How he and Prospero must have laughed at her.

That thought stopped her. Hysterical with anger she turned and beat against the wall. The sharp pain in her hands that came pulled her back to herself. Isabella looked down at her bleeding palms, scraped and chafed against the rough bricks of the alley. Soberly she strode into her house.

To catch woodcocks!

The door burst open. William hauled Oldcastle in and through to the kitchen of the House of the White Lion. Salarino stared at the bloody figure and then at William, who stood, soaked in sweat, his fine clothes torn. Salarino's eyes fixed on the dagger, bare in the young man's hand. William advanced on him. Salarino's hands came out. He grasped at William's outstretched arm but William had the strength that comes from hot-forged fury. He drove Salarino back against the doors of a cupboard. Salarino slammed into it and the plates within shook and rattled in time with his teeth. The dagger hovered before the little man's eye.

'I know,' William's voice was the hiss of fat falling from the spit to the fire. 'I know you betrayed us to the Duchess of Bracciano.'

'I am sorry. I am sorry,' Salarino said.

He stood very still, not daring to deny the maddened William. Fixed by the sight of the dagger's point as surely as if it pinned him.

'You will be,' William said. 'What did she pay you?'

Salarino began to cry. 'Thirty ducats. For information, for information only. Yes, yes. I did not know, I beg you, I did not know that harm would come to him or you.'

'A traitor's price,' William said. 'I will pay you double.'

Salarino was too terrified to understand what William was saying and continued to babble at him. A little maid was cowering in the corner of the kitchen, her head hidden in her hands. William slapped him.

'Shut up and listen,' he said. 'I will pay you double.'

'What, my lord?' Salarino shook his head. His ears rang.

'Men are coming. They are looking for me and for Sir Henry,' said William. He pointed the dagger at Salarino's eye and drew his gaze with it. 'You will hide Sir Henry and tend his wounds.'

Salarino looked at Oldcastle, who had pulled himself from the floor where William had put him to sit slumped against a wall, his head bowed. William reached up and turned Salarino's chin until his eyes were once again on William and the dagger.

'He stays hidden and well,' William said. 'You get sixty ducats. He is found or harmed, I will kill you.'

Salarino said nothing, simply stared. William spoke as slowly as his nerves would allow.

'Do you understand me?'

Salarino gave the smallest of nods.

'Do you believe me?'

Salarino nodded again.

'Quickly now. They are coming.' William turned and ran to the door. At the threshold he turned back to review the kitchen scene.

He pointed the dagger at Salarino, and in the tone of dungeons and the school of night he spoke one last time.

'Life, long life and wealth, Salarino. Or death and no swift death either. Those are your choices. Quickly, quickly.'

William stumbled out into the alley behind the House of the White Lion. He saw Borachio's men at the moment they saw him. He ran to draw them after him and away from Oldcastle. As he ran, he cursed the world that left him with so rich a choice as to gamble his friend in the hands of his betrayer.

The world is still deceived with ornament

Maria did not know what she might do or say to calm Isabella Lisarro. Her mistress was distraught. She had not stood still nor sat in all the hours since her return home. Isabella railed to the uncaring air. Maria longed to send for someone who might speak to her, Tintoretto or Marco Venier perhaps, yet she dared not leave her.

'I have been such a fool.' Isabella's face was smeared with the tracks of her tears. 'Now all is lost.' She beat her fist into her palm. 'Take my defiance then. It's all I have left.'

Isabella sank to a seat in the salon. She put her head in her hands.

'Him, of all people,' she said. 'Is my judgment so put off?'

She spoke to Maria as if the woman would understand about whom she spoke.

'I was so easily deceived in him,' Isabella said. 'I thought I tested him but he just played me. Played. How could I miss his murdering nature?'

She looked up at Maria. 'Am I run mad?' she whispered. 'Oh God, let me not be mad.'

Maria was now crying to match her mistress. Fat tears ran down her cheeks. That she did not understand the cause of her mistress's state made her own fears worse.

There was a hammering at the door. The women looked to the noise. Isabella ran from the salon to the room opposite. She peered through the half-closed shutters to the dark street below. Two figures were huddled by the door. At their feet paced a leashed dog.

'Open up, Madonna,' a rough voice called in the dialect of Venice.

The hand hammered at the door again. A loud sound in the silence of the night. Isabella's hand closed around the sill of the window, knuckles white. So soon, so soon Prospero sought to deal the final blow. Shocked from her self-pity, Isabella breathed deep. She wiped her face and thought.

'Mistress?' Maria whispered from behind her.

Isabella motioned her to silence. If they hurried they might gather the boy Angelo and flee by the canal entrance. No, fool, surely Prospero would not have left that exit unguarded? Think, she urged herself, think.

Below, a figure appeared at the end of the alley. The moonlight caught him: William. A cold flare of fear at sight of him was driven from her by the heat of anger.

'Fetch me the knife from the bedroom, Maria,' Isabella said quietly.

'Mistress. I –' Maria clutched at Isabella's sleeve.

Isabella shook off the hand. 'You know the one, Maria. Go quickly,' she said.

The two men below turned at the arrival of William. He advanced to join them. Isabella could hear the two at her door muttering in Venetian. Fifty yards from them William stopped. Isabella saw him look behind.

'Ho,' he cried and beckoned to the two at her door.

They began to walk to him. William set off at a run. The lead man ran to join him. Isabella saw the other, the one with the dog, pause. He turned back to look up at her house. She held her breath, praying that he could not see her in the darkness of night, concealed behind the shutters. For a whole minute he stood and stared. Then he turned and let the dog pull him after his companion. Isabella drew breath.

Maria returned to the room. She clutched in her hands the stiletto that Isabella kept in her room. She put it into Isabella's outstretched hand. When Isabella tried to take it, for a moment Maria resisted her pull. Then she let go. She looked from the blade to her mistress's face and she was frightened.

You see this chase is hotly followed

William had thought to find refuge at Isabella's house. Instead he found it besieged. Borachio commanded more men than he had anticipated. William had run and hidden and run again until at last he was certain he had slipped loose from the first two. Thinking himself free he had worked his way round to Isabella's house. There he found two more.

In the dark of the night it took him a moment to realise who they were. By that time he was scarce fifty yards from them. At first they did not seem to recognise him. When he finally understood that they were Borachio's men, there for Isabella, he cried out and beckoned to them.

Again, he ran to draw the hunt away from those he loved.

This pursuit was not so easily lost as the first. The man behind him knew Venice as the first two, the ones he'd found outside the House of the White Lion, had not. William turned corners, crossed canals. Still his pursuer gained on him.

He bounded up the steps of a bridge. His chest burned and his throat was raw from heavily drawn breath in the race. At the top of the bridge William saw the marble footprints cut into the floor and knew where he was, the Bridge of Fists. His pursuer threw himself forward.

William was knocked to the ground. He twisted to his back as he fell, the wind driven from him. His pursuer fell across his legs. The man scrabbled forward, trying to clamber up William's body and reach his throat. William wrapped his legs around his attacker's waist. He felt hot breath on him. He tried to hook the man in the head with his fist. His arm tangled in the folds of his cloak. The man blocked the feeble strike with his elbow, then, when William's blow glanced uselessly against his arm, the man cracked his elbow down across William's cheek. William grunted with pain and fear.

The man scraped his forearm down William's face until it fell across his throat. He pressed. William struggled to draw breath. He arched his hips to lift the man up and wrenched the man's shoulder to one side. The man tumbled forward, putting his hands out to steady himself. William twisted his body into the gap made by his own arching hips and pushed his way free from his attacker.

The two men scrabbled to their feet. Prospero's man drew a knife and stabbed at William's gut. William twisted. He let the knife thrust ride along his forearm and divert its course. As he did so, he reached up with his other hand and stuck his fingers in the man's eye. His pursuer howled, reeled back. William moved with him. He kept his forearm riding on the other man's knife hand. In the small part of his mind that was not consumed with dread, he heard Hemminges' voice from weeks ago and a world away saying 'On you is not in you, Will'. With his other hand William reached down, grabbed the man's wrist and bent it so the blade turned inward. Then he let the man's own desperate attempt to pull his hand back and free from William's grip begin the drive. A drive that William, putting all his weight behind his forearm and the hand that bent the knife, finished.

The man gasped as his own blade went into his gut. William drove his head into the man's nose, then let go the hand, the blade now stuck deep in the man's stomach. The man staggered back, blinded by the blow. William dropped his shoulder and charged. The man was knocked from the side of the bridge into the canal. He did not surface.

Across the square the other man appeared with the dog. William turned to run again.

This would not be believed in Venice

The approach of dawn brought with it people. Isabella scanned the crowd, the brisk marching matrons early to market, the yawning gondoliers, a senator and his servants heading to the Procuratie Vecchie.

Isabella stood in the shadow of the portico. The hood of her cloak was pulled low. She watched the Canal Grande. Across the water and to her left was the House of the White Lion. From where she stood she could see the Ca' Bracciano just beyond the bend in the canal. She had stood there an hour or more.

As soon as William and his two men had left her house that night, she and Maria had gathered some things and slipped away. Maria she sent to the safety of Marco Venier's house. Isabella had gone a separate way. To set a watch on the lodging of the English.

She recognised William by his cloak when he appeared. The heavy red velvet cutting through the muted colours of the morning. He looked about him as he walked. His brow was mottled with bruising and the bright eyes she had once admired were sunk in dark circles. He picked up pace toward the Canal Grande. She began to walk towards him.

William was not looking in her direction. She pushed back her hood to see more clearly. Beneath her cloak's swirl she clutched the handle of the dagger. It shifted in her hand; despite the cool of morning her palm was damp. It is one thing to think of murder, another to approach and deal a blow from which there is no return.

She stopped. This was madness. Her grief and rage had betrayed her better judgment. She turned aside.

She saw William look about. She moved left to avoid his glance and was driven by the edge of the canal until she found herself ahead of him. He walked towards her without seeing her, his eyes on everything but what lay in front of him. She moved backwards, still trying to slip away. She saw him raise his hand to hail one of the *traghetto*. It was stained with red. Isabella watched it rise into the air like a banner.

She was pinned by the sight. He moved towards her, still glancing behind him. He turned and looked up at his own hand. As one they looked down from the hand and saw each other. William opened his mouth to speak. Isabella struck at him.

She saw him gasp. She saw him stagger back. Then the crack as the rail split. And he was gone from sight, into the Canal Grande.

Isabella watched William fall and turned away. Behind her she heard a cry go up. The splash of oars in water as people came to see what had fallen into the canal. She did not turn to look.

Oh my prophetic soul, her thoughts whispered to her. The dagger fell from her hand. She reached up to wipe away a tear. She did not weep for William but for herself.

There must be something within her that drew them, that opened her up to them. The dissembling, the cruel, the killers, gathered to her like moths by some foul light within her. First, Prospero. Then this boy.

He had seemed different. Not so. Not in the ways that mattered. Different from Prospero only in outside appearance and age. In dissembling he was Prospero's equal, his master. No more can you distinguish of a man than his outward show, which, God knows, seldom or never jumps with his heart.

What of her own heart? How did she allow herself to be deceived? Was it the thrill of their rashness? Was it her arrogance to think they could be tamed or turned from their path? She dared not believe it. For then the taint would be in her. She would never be free of it.

She had been so sure that William was more than that. Yet how to disbelieve the evidence of her eyes? That hand, that bloody hand, stained red with her failures. Her heart was no sound judge, no judge at all.

Isabella looked back at the crowd gathered around the canal. They pressed and peered at the place where William had fallen. She could see nothing clearly and she was grateful for that. She walked away. At the top of the small bridge she stopped, the same place from which, the previous day, she had seen William drag the Duchess to the balcony and slay her. Murder her and, without a backward glance, leap. Isabella hung her head. She pressed her hand to her breast and walked on.

Amid the swirl of people Borachio's two men had not seen what caused their quarry to fall. One moment he looked to escape in a *traghetto,* the next he was stumbling into the canal. They waited until the crowd dispersed and they were sure the man had not surfaced. Then they went to tell Borachio the man was dead.

A figure crouching in the shadows saw them go. He bent to lift his sodden burden and carry it to safety.

By th' luckiest stars in heaven

'I am in Heaven.'

William looked up at the man above him, whose rough hands were laying him down on a bed and stripping away his soaked clothes.

'I must be if you are here.' William coughed out a laugh. 'I was not sure that would be my lot.'

'Quiet, lad. You're not in Heaven yet. Though God knows you may be close,' Hemminges said.

He pressed him back against the bed as William tried to rise. With quick clean movements he bared William's stomach and pressed at the edges of the cut.

'It's long but it's not deep. If it doesn't fester, you will live,' he said.

Hemminges left the room and William stared at the ceiling trying to make sense of a world turned topsy-turvy in a night. His lover become his murderer; his dead friend reborn. He had new sympathy for Oldcastle's complaints about Venice and its reversals. With that thought he remembered and struggled to rise only to be defeated by his own weakness.

'Oldcastle?' William said to Hemminges when the man returned.

'Recovers below. I'd say between the two of you he's had the worse of it. He was less fitted to endure it.'

Cold water washed across William's bloody stomach making him cry out. It was followed by some kind of paste and then a clean dish clout wrapped tightly about him.

'It'll scar,' said Hemminges.

'No mind,' replied William. 'There never was nor never will be a poem to the beauty of a man's stomach.'

Hemminges sat in a chair by the bed. William turned his head to look at him. The solid rock of his presence seemed undiminished.

'You're alive,' William said.

'Observant as you ever were,' Hemminges said. 'I see you have also kept up your habit of making enemies.'

'How?' William asked. 'How are you alive?'

Hemminges reached up and parted the fall of his hair to show a great puckered scar that ran across the side of his scalp. He tapped it.

'Thick as a ship's keel. I woke, I think, quickly. You and Nick and Sir Henry were already gone. Enough strength in me to hide in the wood and see the robbers come to remove all sign of battle. Then I fell into a mulled sleep again. I judge I was asleep for more than a day.'

'How did you find us?' William said.

'It wasn't easy,' Hemminges answered. 'I found the inn where you and Nick fled and judged by their description that it was you pair that lived rather than the Ambassador of England and his steward. God, that was bold work, William.'

'Thank you.'

'I meant no compliment. Boldness is not judgment.'

Hemminges ran his fingers through his hair and bent forward to let his head hang with tiredness.

'Nor timidity wisdom,' said William.

Hemminges lifted his head.

'The rest is dull to relate,' he said after a minute. 'It took me longer to reach Venice than you, having no barge to travel on and being weak to begin with. Longer still to find where you and Nick were staying. I arrived to find a little chick of a man squawking and clucking over Nick, and Nick scarce better than a corpse. It was not till near morning that I pieced him together enough to judge it safe to leave him. Longer still to piece together enough news to judge it purposeful to search for you.'

'Well that you did,' said William.

'Well that I did and that I swim better than I sail.'

There came a little pause.

'Sir Henry?' Hemminges asked.

'Dead,' William replied. 'He died in the wood not far from where we thought you killed.'

William let out a little sob and turned to look back at the ceiling.

'Jesu mercy. It is good to see you, John,' he said.

Hemminges opened his mouth to speak, then said nothing. Finally he stood and looked down at William.

'You should sleep,' he said. 'It's safe enough for the nonce.'

William nodded without taking his eyes from the ceiling.

'Thank you,' said Hemminges, 'for saving my life.'

'Oldcastle,' said William. 'Oldcastle saved you. Never knew he had such strength in him.'

Again Hemminges opened his mouth to speak but then nodded in his turn and left the room.

No more a rude mechanical

A night of groans and fitful sleep heralded a morning in which to draw breath was pain. William pulled himself from his bed. The dish clout on his side was stained with red. He peeled it from him. The wound wept blood but did not seem hot or angry or wont to fester. The same could not be said of William. He pressed a fresh cloth to his side and shrugged on a shirt.

In the kitchen downstairs, sat at the long table in the middle, was Hemminges. He ate a honeyed pastry with much relish. The figure of Salarino hung about him anxious of his approval. Seeing William, Hemminges rose and helped him to the bench. A glance at Salarino was enough to set the little man scurrying to bring food and drink. They ate in silence.

At last they rose and made their way upstairs to where Oldcastle lay. The great man slept and so was spared the sight of William, who had not wept at the pain of pulling away the bloody bandage of his wound, crying at the sight of him.

Hemminges and William sat beside the old man's bed. They spoke quietly of what had passed in the weeks since the battle at the bridge.

'This Prospero is at the heart of it,' said Hemminges when William was done.

'In some way, yes,' said William. 'What I don't understand is his intent. Or why we came to be caught up in matters when it seems now that the Duchess of Bracciano was his target. Or why the Duchess blamed me for the murder of Iseppo da Nicosia. Or if he is truly dead. Nor do I understand why Isabella Lisarro should want to kill me. That least of all. I thought there was more –'

William broke off. He turned his head away lest Hemminges see him cry a second time. Hemminges held his arm till he recovered.

'Of all the strange parts to this story that is the strangest,' Hemminges nodded.

William wiped his face and said, 'Exhaustion and loss of blood had made me weak. I am recovered.'

'What now?' Hemminges asked.

William looked up. His expectation had been for Hemminges to take command, to chart the course. Now Hemminges looked at him with that same expectation.

'Home, I suppose,' said William.

Hemminges nodded and looked over at Oldcastle. 'It is the sensible course.'

After some minutes had passed William spoke again.

'It is what Oldcastle would want,' he said. 'He has begged for us to return home from the moment we arrived in Venice, from before, from when you were killed.'

'But?' said Hemminges.

William drew a deep breath. 'I must still deliver Sir Henry's letters. Duty to an old man's wishes. That and Sir Henry managed to persuade me that their safe conveyance was for England's good. No greater persuasion could there be than that he was murdered to prevent it. Were it not so, their delivery is still the guarantee of welcome on our return to England. Essential now that we have so committed ourselves as to spend Sir Henry's money and use his name. And ...'

'And?'

'And, I cannot leave this mystery,' said William. 'I cannot leave Venice without speaking to her. I must understand what happened. Why she thinks ... We –' He broke off again. 'And I will not leave without vengeance for what has been done to Nick, to you, to me,' he finished.

'The pleasure of vengeance is short lived. The price, high,' Hemminges said.

'I have been moved about the board by others' hands too long,' said William.

Hemminges looked from William to the sleeping Oldcastle. William softened his voice from its sudden rise.

'I will not be a player in another man's drama any more,' he continued. 'I will write the part I play. From where I sit now that part looks bloody, black and vengeful.'

'What is going on?' said Oldcastle. Without wishing it, the venom in William's voice had roused Oldcastle.

Hemminges leaned towards him. He took his friend's hand and spoke softly. 'William wants us to stay in Venice a while longer, wants to deliver Sir Henry's letters, wants revenge for the insults paid to him and to you.'

Oldcastle looked up at Hemminges and smiled, teeth red-rimmed with dried blood.

'Good. I'm in a vengeful humour.'

Full of decay and failing?

Prospero stood by the window looking out at the canal below, willing the gentle stillness of its waters to impart to him their calm. When he felt in control once more he spoke to the miserable figure in the chair behind him.

'How have you failed so completely?' said Prospero.

'The failure is not mine,' said Borachio, 'but yours.'

Prospero strode to where Borachio sat, his arms wrapped about his stomach, a silvery sheen of sweat across his broken face.

'Say that again,' Prospero demanded. 'Say it again, little man.'

'If you had not delayed,' muttered Borachio. 'If you had not allowed obsession with that woman to blind you ...'

'Tell me, Borachio,' said Prospero, 'how it is my fault that you and your two men failed to kill Vittoria Accoramboni when she stood before you unguarded save by a senseless old man and a stripling boy?'

'It was not the boy that broke my nose,' replied Borachio.

'I'm sorry. You speak true,' Prospero said in mocking tones, 'there was also that old and antique captain. His service an ornament for a vain woman. How you must have quaked at his threat. When he moved did dust fall from him to blind you to his blows?'

Prospero strode back to the window and pointed to the city beyond.

'The streets are littered with your failures, Borachio. To the rashly murdered intelligencer, Iseppo da Nicosia, we add the bodies of two of your men. The Signoria cannot fail to notice so many dead.'

'None of this was necessary in the first place,' shouted Borachio, 'if you had done as I advised and killed the English before we reached Venice!'

'Now, in this last night, at the house of that whore, your men, Borachio, rogues whom you vouchsafed sufficient for the labour, were sent to kill two women and a child,' Prospero said. 'Two women, a thin-wristed whore, a broken-backed servant and a little boy.'

'The Englishman must have intervened,' said Borachio.

'So we come back to your failure, do we not?' Prospero said. 'For that murderous Englishman lay within your hands, Borachio, and you let him go. You and no other. The one achievement of the day, the steward Fallow's death, was not your doing but an accident.'

Prospero gripped the shutters of the window. 'Get out,' he said.

'All your fine argument cannot disguise whose the failure truly is,' said Borachio. 'The Pope shall hear of it.'

'Get out, Borachio,' repeated Prospero. 'Go and try and do something of value to me.'

'I have already achieved more than you,' said Borachio rising from the chair. 'I have the English packet of letters.'

Prospero turned. 'Give them to me,' he demanded.

'The antidote,' said Borachio.

'You think the letters worth your life?' asked Prospero.

'I know them worth yours,' replied Borachio.

He reached out and plucked up a cushion. He wiped at his nose, which still leaked blood, and cast it aside. Prospero watched the ugly man with distaste written plainly on his face.

'At least with the letters, you may say to our master that you have succeeded in some small part,' said Borachio. 'Without even that, why, I would not look for your welcome return to Rome.'

Prospero said nothing. Instead, he walked round to his desk and opened a draw. He took out a small glass vial and threw it to Borachio. Prospero held out his hand.

'The letters, Borachio,' he said.

Borachio was incapable of answering for a moment as he threw back his head and swallowed the contents of the vial. When he had tipped the last drops down his throat he threw the vial at the wall. It shattered with a loud report.

'In good time, Count,' Borachio said, 'in good time. When I am certain that this antidote is sound physic for the poison you have fed me. Meanwhile, I shall go. I shall see if I might make good the harm your perverse delays have wrought.'

When Borachio had left, Prospero sat behind his desk. He drew a sheet of paper from it. On it he wrote four names and then leaned back in his chair to think about how he might kill them all.

You spend your passion on a misprised mood

William stood in the shadow of evening by the church and watched Isabella. She had not seen him. He had not been sure it was her at first for she wore a veil. It was only as she lifted it to enter the Scuola di San Rocco that he had known it was her. He waited. When she left, he followed.

He took his moment as she approached Campo San Toma.

'Lady, a word,' he said.

Isabella turned at his voice.

'Devil.'

William strode towards her. Isabella backed away. Campo San Toma was quiet, empty, save for Isabella and him. William stopped and stood where he was.

'Why? Why call me so?' he asked.

'How do you live?' was all her answer.

'Why did you try to kill me?' he demanded.

Their voices rose against each other's questions. There is no passion like the convert's; there is no anger like love turned to hate.

'Are you the Count's creature still?' William said.

'You ask that of me? You whom I saw carry out his commands?'

'Saw me?' William thrust out his arms and looked himself up and down. 'Saw me?'

'Saw you kill the Duchess of Bracciano,' said Isabella.

'She lives,' protested William.

'I saw you, knife at her throat, strike her. I saw her fall lifeless,' Isabella insisted.

'Fainted,' William said. 'She lives, God's sake, lady, she lives.'

'I know,' said Isabella. 'I did not say you were competent, only that you were an assassin.'

Isabella thought back to the moment she heard the Duchess lived. So many questions had filled her mind. She had tried to see her but Vittoria Accoramboni would admit no one to her presence. The Duchess was caged by her own fear.

'Now fled from Venice in fear of her life,' said Isabella.

'Wisely,' replied William. 'For there are killers on every corner, as well I know.'

'Fled, in fear of her murderer's return,' Isabella said. She searched William's face.

'Murderer?' He flung the title back at her. 'How dare you? You. You who stabbed me?'

'And missed. Small wonder, I aimed for your heart when you have none,' Isabella said.

The anger ran out of William.

'Of all the wounds you have given me, that is the cruellest,' he said. 'You have seen my heart laid bare.'

'A serpent heart, hid with flowering words,' she said.

William looked at the woman whom he had loved for her wit and her exquisite liveliness. She looked back with hate and fear of his hurt and the anger trembling in his hands, fear of her own misjudgment.

As he looked at her, he realised she was looking past him. Something glittered in her eyes.

He stepped aside only a moment before the sword thrust. It missed him by the intake of a breath. The old man, meeting air where he had thought to meet flesh, stumbled forward. William looked in astonishment at the mad old man from the Scuola. The one who had peevishly thrown the ring to him now angrily threw a sword at his back. William hammered his fist into the old man's ribs as he staggered past. The air went out of Tintoretto and he collapsed to the ground, the sword clattering to the cobbles.

'What are you doing?' William shouted.

He strode towards Tintoretto. The old man, winded, made no reply save to scramble back from the advance of the angry youth. William turned back.

He stood still. Isabella held the old man's sword before her. It was a flimsy thing, more ornament than use, yet its point was sharp. That point was levelled at his throat. William waited for the thrust.

That man that hath a tongue, I say, is no man, if with his tongue he cannot win a woman

William stared at the point of the blade.

'I am a fool and a liar, lady,' he said, 'but I am no murderer. I swear it. If words nor oaths move you, then think, what does my standing here before you mean if not my innocence?'

William spoke slowly and carefully. He didn't wish to startle Isabella or give her cause to ram her fears home.

'I see anger and doubt and fear in you that mirrors my own,' he said. 'I think we two have been most grievously abused. The villains are known to you: that Count of Genoa, Prospero, and his man, Borachio.'

'I saw you strike the Duchess,' said Isabella. 'I saw you order the old man thrown from the balcony.'

'I held the Duchess but as a shield against her servants' anger. I saw no other way to safety. Oh Isabella, I am a liar,' said William again. 'A liar and a fool but no assassin.'

'What do you mean?' Isabella demanded. 'How have you lied? How are you a fool?'

'The old man and I are not the Ambassador of England and his man,' confessed William. 'We were of the ambassador's party but what I told you in the Scuola was true, the embassy was set upon and all murdered. All save us two, poor players in his entourage. As I think now, that piteous massacre was at the order of Prospero and at the hand of his man Borachio. In fear of our lives we took on the mantles of Sir Henry and his steward. The which guise we have not been able to shake off since being taken into Prospero's care. A wicked care. He smooths, deceives and cogs that he may murder. You, I think, know this better than most.'

Her sword still did not strike, still did not waver. William spoke on, recounting what had passed until he came to the moment Oldcastle had been dragged into the room in the Ca' Bracciano and his voice caught at the memory of his beaten friend.

When he had recovered he said, 'I think the Duchess would have killed us both. Except that at the deadly instant Borachio and his men took the opportunity to strike at her. I think they thought to kill us all and blame us for her death and that of her servants.'

'I saw none of this,' said Isabella.

'What you saw was no more than my desperate escape from Borachio,' William pleaded. 'Saw her servants' misguided attempt to rescue her from me when, in doing so, they allowed the true killers to escape. It was to you I fled.'

William's voice, already quiet, died to a whisper. 'It was to you I fled. But I found Borachio's men already there. I tried to draw them from you. I did –' Again his voice caught at the memory. 'I did grave things. I am not the same man that left your house. I do not think I am worse.'

He faltered.

'You struck at me in error,' he said at last. 'I should be angry that you did not first question me before you struck.'

William's voice rose. 'I am angry. That is why I am a fool. Not only for being blind to how great the danger, for failing to unpick the knots of the trap sooner. I am a fool to be angry that in your passion you struck at me when it is that passion that I admire, adore, love. When the passion that led you to strike can only be a reflection of the passion I had aroused in you.'

William touched his side. 'I should be grateful for this cut.'

He drew a great breath. 'Your love to me is a religion. All else is error,' he said. 'I want only two things in this world. To return to that state of grace with you we had for one brief night.'

The point of her blade did not falter. 'The other?' she asked.

'Revenge against the author of my fall from that state of grace, of my companions' murder and my friends' hurt, Prospero.'

Isabella's eyes, that had not flickered from William's during his confession, closed.

'Is this the truth?' she said.

'This is the truth, Isabella Lisarro,' William replied. 'I swear it. If it is not believed, then strike. "It is annoying to be honest to no purpose."'

Isabella, eyes still shut, smiled. 'Catullus?'

'Ovid,' said William. 'He also said, "I can neither live with you nor without you," and finally, finally, with you I begin to understand what he meant.'

She opened her eyes and William saw they were melting with tears.

'Maybe my judgment is not all wrong,' she said.

So quiet were her words that William almost did not hear her.

'You should not have lied to me,' she said.

William stayed silent. What denial could he make?

'All that you say, I believe,' Isabella said. 'That Giovanni deceived me in you, as he deceived me in other things, is all too easily believed. I see his hand in all you speak of.'

She let the sword's point drop.

'The love of wicked men converts to fear. The fear to hate. The hate to thoughts of deception and of death. True for him –' She drew a great shuddering breath. 'True for me.'

Her voice trembled when she spoke again. 'I saw you, as I thought, strike at Vittoria. The Lord knows she is no friend of mine, or any man's friend. Yet I feared that history turned in its wheel and threw up another Prospero. I thought I saw her struck down and I-I feared for myself. I feared my own judgment was – wrong, stained. My fear blinded me. I should have thought. I should have thought. Instead I acted.'

She looked at William through tearful eyes. 'I am sorry. Forgive me.'

'There is nothing to forgive,' William replied. 'Your own forgiveness cancels all grudges.'

'I doubted you because I doubted myself. Never again,' Isabella said.

'What is your true name, liar?' she asked.

'It is William. But Shakespeare, not Fallow.'

'Oh William,' Isabella said, 'we shall have such vengeance, you and I, that they will write plays about it till the end of time.'

Interlude

Venice, August 1585

Trust not to rotten planks

Prospero stood on the balcony overlooking the canal. The bells of Venice's thousand churches pealed welcome for the new doge. His election finally made. Flags fluttered from every balcony. The boats on the canal were decked with flowers and ribbons. Below Prospero streamed people heading towards San Marco. Firecrackers spat and music filled the air in competition with the bells. Venice in celebration did not scant and scorned to speak of surfeit. For the coronation festivities no expense had been spared in the Count of Genoa's clothing. The fine velvet of his doublet was studded with rare black pearls.

'You still have the letters?'

Prospero spoke over his shoulder to Borachio.

Borachio, whose form had been ugly to begin with, had been made more hideous still by the great crusting scab across his nose. His voice was tortured by breath sent through a face still swollen, black and bruised.

'And with me they will stay until our business is completed,' he said.

'Borachio,' Prospero said and turned to face the man.

'Can it be you still fear poison?' the Count asked. 'Did I not give you the antidote as I promised? Even though you failed me?'

'I failed? I?' Borachio shook his head. 'The failure is yours. Yours alone.'

He counted the failings on his fingers as he listed them. 'The Duchess of Bracciano escaped. The reason for her flight and our part in it surely known to the Signoria. Yet you, unheedful of the danger, prepare to attend the Doge's coronation. The English Ambassador fled too; whereto the Lord alone knows. Disaster and danger all about us when instead there might have been triumph and reward. Only the letters have we obtained. You gave me the antidote for their sake. For their sake alone and well I know it. All this because you must play your games.

'Be assured,' Borachio continued, 'our master, the Pope, shall have full account of what has passed.'

He finished with a long breath that crackled in his broken nose.

'So many times have you promised to do so,' Prospero said as he brushed past Borachio, 'that I am only surprised it is not already done.'

He walked towards the stairs to the lower levels of the palazzo. Borachio fell in behind him.

'Oh I would have done,' Borachio replied, 'but that my men and I have, these three days past, been out looking for the Ambassador. All the while you sit here preening yourself in black velvet. When I come to make explanation I, at least, shall be able to say I did all I might.'

'You cannot find him?' Prospero asked.

'Not for want of searching. Nor the woman, her maid or anyone else,' Borachio said. 'The task is made impossible. The city is set to merry-making. Men go masked for mischief. We search for the English Ambassador in vain where once we had him in our hands. We might have done all that was needed weeks past, but you must have your pleasures.'

Prospero raised a finger but did not look back nor slow his pace.

'You overreach yourself, Borachio. Such plain speaking in a servant is not admirable frankness but rank presumption.'

'I am no servant of yours but of the Pope's.'

'And yet, you say, your master is still ignorant of your efforts,' Prospero said over his shoulder as he turned the corner of the stairs.

'Have you not been listening?' Borachio said. 'I tell you I have searched without rest for those whom you let escape.' He grumbled on, 'The Pope shall know of your failure.'

In his anger he did not note how his words worked on Prospero, how the Count heard that Borachio had not yet betrayed him to the Pope, nor offered him valuable service in the matter of the English. Borachio thought himself safe because he held the letters. Such safety has the con-demned man who waits behind thick walls and stout bars for the day of his execution.

On the ground floor stood Borachio's two men. Prospero nodded to them and walked to the end of the corridor. Borachio and his men followed. Prospero paused at the door to the storeroom.

'I think all that poison has unsettled you, Borachio,' he said. 'What is it the Bible tells us, "A little wine for thy stomach's sake"?'

He pushed through the door.

Behind him Borachio protested, 'Our time is too short, Count, for wine.' He did his best to feed as much contempt into the title as would fit.

'My men and I will try the House of the White Lion again to see if the English Ambassador is returned. What effort will you make?' he demanded.

Within the storeroom Prospero had approached a barrel. He signalled to one of Borachio's men, who levered it open. Prospero took a stone cup that sat nearby and dipped it in the open barrel. He offered the cup to Borachio. Borachio shook his head in bemusement that Prospero should think him so foolish as to accept a drink from the man who had so recently poisoned him.

Prospero shrugged at Borachio and drank deeply from the cup.

The Count of Genoa sighed with satisfaction. 'Sweet Rhenish wine, with not a drop of allaying water in it. Of all pleasures, those that come in purest form are the best.'

He set the cup down.

'I cannot have you speak in such ungenerous terms about me to the Pope,' he said. 'While I had you by the stomach, so to speak, I was not worried. Now?'

Again Prospero gave a little shrug. Borachio began to feel the chill of the storeroom.

'So selfish, Borachio, to deny me my little leash over you,' the Count continued. 'Fortunately, your self-regard is also your undoing. For while you watched your own food and drink you failed to watch your friends.''

The two men at Borachio's side seized him. He looked in terror and astonishment at them. One looked ashamed. The other spoke in anger. 'Fool. You let him snare us in his web.'

Prospero took a step forward. 'Poor Borachio,' he said. 'Always one step behind.'

He held up the small glass vial of antidote in one hand.

'No man can be the servant of two masters. This the Bible also tells us.' He reached out his other hand.

'He'd hidden them where you thought he would, my lord,' said one of the men as he placed into Prospero's outstretched hand the sealed packet of letters stolen from the House of the White Lion.

Prospero stuffed it away inside his doublet and patted the fabric behind which they now lay. 'To enjoy later.'

Borachio's eyes stayed pinned on where his one defence now sat snug in Prospero's bosom.

Prospero placed the glass vial into the man's hand and gestured again. 'Now put him in the barrel.'

'No!' Borachio screamed. His voice echoed against the thick walls. 'I can still be of use to you, my lord. Please, please.'

His begging took on a fevered intensity as he was dragged towards the barrel. His feet scrabbled for purchase on the storeroom floor.

'Why yes, Borachio, yes you can,' said the Count. 'You can be an entertainment.'

The two men lifted the madly struggling man and tipped him head first into the barrel. Briefly, he got one hand free and pushed against the barrel's edge. The butt of a knife smashed against his fingers and he was shoved in up to the waist. Wine sloshed out to make space for his body. More fountained out as his legs kicked and fluttered above the rim, but his arms could find no purchase against the barrel's confining sides. After a minute more the movement stopped.

With shoving and pushing the squat legs were forced into the barrel to join the rest of the little man. The lid was hammered shut.

'Drowned in Venice. How common a fate,' said Prospero over the rim of his cup of wine.

One deed done, Prospero thought, as he drained his cup. The dangerous turn of events with the Duchess of Bracciano would be put back on its proper course that very night. Then, there was only the question of the English Ambassador, or whoever he truly was. Disasters are opportunities, he thought, if only one thinks them so. Prospero turned to the two men, once Borachio's, now his, for the moment. They too would have to be wiped up in their turn.

'I go to a feast,' he said. 'When I return we will address the question of the Ambassador. Be ready.'

'My lord?' The other man held out his hand.

Prospero looked at it.

'You gave only one dose of antidote, my lord,' Borachio's man spoke in a tone that said he should not need to make explanation.

Prospero made a show of patting his clothing.

'Alas, I have only the one vial on me,' he smiled. 'I suggest you share. That should stay the poison's march till the morning when I can speak to the apothecary about more.'

His eyes glittered beneath the enquiring eyebrow.

'Or, fight it out, let the stronger man claim his freedom now,' he said.

He closed the door on the storeroom to the sound of argument.

Prospero, his appetite sharpened by the first events of the evening, made his way to the gondola that would pole him to the feast. As he stepped into the boat he noted his shoe was stained red at the toe with spilled wine. Irritation flashed across his face, to be replaced with a smile. One of the few that had crossed his face since he came to Venice.

Never before had he met such obstruction to his schemes. Not all the failures could be laid at the feet of that fool, Borachio. The hand of Isabella could be seen in Vittoria's guarded state. With her too must lie the explanation for the English Ambassador's disappearance. Was her regard for him so scanting that she opposed him? Did she hold his warning at so little that she opposed him from the start, flaunted the boy Fallow in his face?

'Ho, there, gentle,' cried Prospero's gondolier as Prospero struck the side of the boat in sudden anger.

He closed his mind to thoughts of Isabella. Before that pleasure he would deal with Vittoria Accoramboni and her husband. They thought themselves safe. Fled to their estates in Salo. How innocent they are, thought Prospero, they think the murderer must stand in the same room as the one murdered. I will kill them both, though I never see them.

The gondola took Prospero to the Ca' Venier and the means to their destruction.

Act Five

Venice, August 1585

The strict court of Venice

The three days since Hemminges pulled William from the Canal Grande had passed in a roar. William's rebirth had come at the same moment that the electors, after their nineteenth day of deliberation and fifty-two inconclusive votes, had united on a name for the new doge, Pasquale Cicogna.

As a dam bursting, news of the election of the next doge had flooded Venice with festival. All ordinary traffic ceased. The days became filled instead with processions of decorated barges along the canals, parades of the guilds in their finery by land and water, contests in the squares, jousting by boat in the lagoon and the general halloo of a citizenry easily inclined to celebration.

William thanked Heaven for it. Amid the feasting he and his companions had been able to slip about unhindered. Twice Borachio and his men had passed within the breath of grace of William as he left Tintoretto's studio. They would have had him but that he was disguised in the fantastical masks and visors all Venice now seemed to wear. Such risk had been a necessity if all was to be in readiness.

A council of war had been held the very hour that William and Isabella had been reconciled. Isabella, William and Tintoretto had gone straight to join Hemminges and Oldcastle. They were hidden in a building that Salarino owned, near to the House of the White Lion. Once the value of good relations with Hemminges was made clear, Salarino had shown them how it could be reached through the cellars that connected several of the houses. They were not comfortable lodgings but they were secret and had the benefit, to Oldcastle's mind, of being the storehouse for Salarino's wine. He took from that store in liberal measure in fine for Salarino's betrayal.

'They're gone,' Hemminges explained once all had been introduced to all.

'The letters from England to the Doge,' William clarified for Isabella and Tintoretto's benefit. 'We must assume Borachio's men found them and took them when they searched the House of the White Lion for Nick.'

Tintoretto simply nodded and drained his glass. Oldcastle, full of fellow feeling for another old man battered by fortune, had pressed some of Salarino's good wine into Tintoretto's hand the moment he had arrived. Isabella paced the room with Tintoretto's sword still scabbarded in her skirts. Tintoretto had protested when she took it from him, but she reminded him that he had made no good use of the weapon and informed him she had plans of her own for it.

'They are the least of our concerns while Prospero lives.' Isabella was in no mood to be distracted. 'He will have the letters still if he has them at all. Most likely on him. He is not so foolish as to leave things of such value where anyone might find them.'

She raised an eyebrow at William, who acknowledged her criticism with a good grace. He knew the charge well founded and thought it, of all her cuts, the kindest. And, of all his foolishness in Venice, he felt the shame of this failing least.

'Then there is the question of the names of the papal agents in Venice,' William added.

With haste he unfolded the story of his meeting with Iseppo da Nicosia.

'The Signoria will not let that matter rest. They will look to see England's bargain met along with the delivery of the letters.'

'Another charge to lay at Prospero's door,' Isabella said. 'Surely he or his men overheard your commerce and struck poor Iseppo down before the Pope's creatures in Venice could be exposed.'

She slapped her hand to the hilt of Tintoretto's sword.

'Find him. Kill him. That is all to achieve all.'

'To find him is easy enough.' Hemminges scratched at his scarred head. 'To kill him is not. He'll stay hidden behind the walls of his palazzo with his guards about him. All the while Borachio will search us out and dispatch us all as he finds us. Let none of us be fooled we are a match in strength for men whose seasoned meat is murder.'

'Not to mention that Prospero need but whisper the word to the Signoria and we are exposed as false embassy,' Oldcastle added. 'Without the letters and the seal of England on them our standing is as nothing. We have nothing to set against these threats.'

Isabella turned to face them. 'You are right and you are wrong,' she said.

Hemminges' brow furrowed. 'My Latin has a little rust on it, lady,' he said. 'Did you just speak of paradoxes?'

Isabella stepped back, the better to address the gathered men. 'You speak of absolutes when perspective is all. Where there is strength there's also weakness. Pit yourself against another's point of strength and you go a sure way to swift defeat. It's only men engage in such foolish bouts.'

Isabella saw puzzled faces. She fought her frustration. She tried again. 'A feat of strength goes always to the young, the swift and the strong.' She beat her argument home by pointing to the elderly Tintoretto, the lumbering Oldcastle and the wounded William in turn.

'We are not of that mettle,' she said. 'We should not match their points of strength. We women know better, than to do so, of necessity. We should use what we have to our best advantage.'

'Think. Think.' She knocked at her head. 'It is a question of seeing the matter aright. He has the letters, but what else? The Duchess of Bracciano is not dead but fled. The English are lost to him and he must fear that they will reveal his part in matters. Behind Prospero lies the Pope. These blows are at his command. Whatever else, Prospero must fear to fail such a man. If the Pope wants Vittoria Accoramboni dead then Prospero stands on a spear point until he knows it done and no finger of suspicion to fall on him. He must fear that you possess the means to expose all the Pope's agents in Venice. He cannot let that happen.'

Hemminges finished off his glass of wine. 'This reasoning brings us back full circle,' he said. 'We want the man dead. He in turn desires our end. He has all the means. We none.'

William smiled and looked up. 'I have an idea,' he said.

Oldcastle refilled Hemminges' glass and his own. He smiled up at William in turn.

'Of course you do.'

'You hesitate, Nick?' William asked.

'You are not known for your plots, William,' said Oldcastle. 'As I recall it, each one of them has done little but gather enemies to you. Hunt, Greene, this Prospero ...'

Oldcastle drained his glass and filled it again, prompting Hemminges to move the jug out of his reach.

'Well I know it, Nick,' said William. 'Rest assured, this plan's to the ending of an enemy, not the making of a new.'

He turned to address the company. 'Why trouble with invention when we may use another's plot? Prospero's. Isabella has the right of it: in drama it's not the scenes' events that matter but their meaning. We'll play the parts we've been given but the lines will be our own and we shall write, for Prospero, a tragedy.'

Isabella spoke. 'What's my role?'

'A man's part,' answered William.

Oldcastle snorted. The little sword flashed out to sit beneath his nose. His scoffing smile vanished.

'It's a piece I know how to play well,' she said.

Isabella let the point of the sword droop as she tilted her head mournfully at Oldcastle. 'When I can find it,' she said.

Isabella sheathed her sword again to the sound of William's and Hemminges' laughter and Oldcastle's bluster that he meant no offence and she'd no cause to give any.

'I shall need something from all of you,' William said. 'Yet only one piece of cleverness is needed, and for that we have all the tools we require.'

He nodded at Tintoretto, who looked back at him bereft of understanding. William proceeded to lay out his plan. Then he turned to meet the objections of Hemminges and Isabella as best he could.

'It's admirably simple,' was Hemminges' conclusion.

'Yet more complex than the orbit of the spheres,' was Isabella's comment, given with a shaking head.

'I would object but have found my objections only worsen my eventual suffering,' said Oldcastle, reaching for the wine.

The final word was left to Tintoretto.

'It's madness and will most likely end with us all hanged between the columns in San Marco.'

On that, at least, all had been agreed.

Who chooseth me must give and hazard all he hath

Now, as night fell after three days of action, William was poled on a gondola through the canals. Tomorrow the Doge would be crowned. His new status blessed at a ceremony at the Basilica di San Marco. Tomorrow William would see his vengeance come. So he hoped.

Tonight he went to a feast.

So many things are left in Fortune's hands, William reflected. A minute here, an inch there, and all is changed. Fortune plays her part in every game, yet not all is chance in the result. There remains the imprint of our effort in the pattern of events.

William's plan turned on many things. He went to be certain of one of them.

The Ca' Bracciano was dark. It alone of the palaces on the Canal Grande was not lit with revelry. As he was rowed past it William looked up at the fateful balcony.

The gondola passed the bend of the Canal Grande and drew to its destination. Ca' Venier was a riot of light and colour. As he approached a roar of fireworks came from the roof. They burst and lit the air. The gondola pulled in to the water entrance. William stepped out. There was scarcely space for him to stand, so crowded was the palace with guests. He pushed in and began to hunt for his quarry.

The walls of the palace surrounded a courtyard. On the first floor a colonnaded walkway looked down on the courtyard. It was there William found Prospero. He was visored as many of the guests were; as William was. A plain black mask hid the Count's face. What drew William's eye to him out of all those at the feast was his manner.

Prospero was talking with another man. That man turned to leave; Prospero reached out and held his arm. He pulled him back. He whispered words urgently to him and pressed something into his hand. The man pulled his arm back. He strode away. The Count was left alone among the revellers. He turned to look on the throng in the courtyard below. William approached.

'I thought you dead,' Prospero said without looking up.

'If thinking were enough, Count, I were killed some twenty times by now. And you, I guess, some twenty times twenty more,' said William.

The Count's visored face turned from the crowd below. 'You're bold. Had you stayed dead I might have overlooked you. As it is, you live again only to be killed again.'

'So swiftly reduced to threats,' William admonished. 'I thought your manners better.'

'I need no lesson in manners from you, boy.'

'I shall school you nonetheless,' said William.

The Count straightened and turned to face him. 'Against my better judgment,' he said, 'I find I like you, Master Fallow.'

'The admiration is not mutual,' said William.

'Humours so rarely are,' the Count replied.

He gestured to the feast. 'Why are you here? Not to exchange protestations of affection.'

'Give me the letters you have taken,' said William. 'Do that and I will leave you alone. Lay no report against you with the Signoria. Seek no vengeance.'

The Count looked out again at the feast.

'Do you play chess?' he said.

'The letters, Count,' insisted William.

'Come,' said Prospero. 'I believe I saw a quiet room where we might play.'

He set off. Seeing William did not move he turned back.

'Play and talk, Master Fallow. Play and talk.'

Thus foolishly lost at a game of tick-tack

The two men sat alone on the balcony. Two floors below in the courtyard the feast carried on. The sound of music and laughter rose up to them like smoke from a fire. Between them lay a chess set, the game half played.

'Concede, Count,' said William.

'Why? I am ahead in material and position,' said Prospero. He looked over the board as if William spoke about their game.

'You are played out, Count,' William said.

'Early losses do not portend defeat,' the Count replied.

'I would spare more lives, if I might.'

'Your wishes will have little to do with it.'

The Count's smile was wicked as a sinning priest. It angered William.

'I do not doubt that you could do more harm. It would be a valueless thing,' William urged. 'The squalling rage of an unhappy child. Nothing to your purpose. All to your vanity.'

The Count's smile did not alter. 'You are mistaken, Master Fallow, if you think that I ever acted to any purpose but my own vanity.'

William, looking at that smiling face, came to an understanding. As a boy he had fought with another child at his school. The other child had struck the first blow. William had been so amazed by the sudden turn from argument to violence that he had been struck three more times before it came to him that he ought to defend himself. So it was here. William had come to parlay thinking Prospero was a man as he was, amenable to reason. Now he saw into the man's soul. William spoke in wonder at what he saw.

'Your lusts pollute you, Prospero.'

'*Shush*, Master Fallow,' the Count tutted. 'You are not a child to think in such terms.'

'No,' said William. 'No, I am not.'

He took from his doublet a small packet. He pushed it across the table to Prospero. The Count did not touch it.

'There are three names writ there,' said William nodding at the packet. 'Those of the Pope's agents in Venice.'

'A brave pretence.'

'Each name is proved.'

'By magic or prayer?'

'By your own hand,' said William, 'for which I thank you.'

'Tell on.'

'At first I struggled to the answer but then I recalled that most men are not villains without reason. For most the reason is simple greed. In your special villainy you are unique, Prospero,' said William.

'Now you seek to flatter.'

'Not so. I simply observe. You are sick of self-love, Count. That sin of pride is writ across your clothing in little pearls. Such sins are costly. So my first question: who pays you? Answer: the Pope, the Cardinal Montalto as was. Little difficulty then to discover who was his banker here in Venice. You led us to him. Your tailor must be paid. You must send for funds and so, so often. Far greater difficulty to see the books of that banker. For that I must thank others. You frown at me, Count. Do you think I have made no friends in Venice in all the days I have been here?'

William enjoyed Prospero's sudden doubting look. Truly it had been no easy matter to persuade Marco Venier to help them gain access to the bank through his friend, the fat Andrea. Nor to have Isabella distract the clerk long enough for William, all unnoticed, to look through the ledgers and find the information needed. Harder still to repeat the process the following day so that he might have the time to copy out the entries that he needed from the ledger while others set their watch over the names he had discovered.

'The greatest challenge of all – to trace out the accounts and ascribe to the Cardinal Montalto certain payments and all to certain persons. Then to set a watch upon them. One by one your man Borachio has visited them these three days past at hours ungodly and dark. Tell me,' asked William, 'what had so unnerved him that he should make so bold a show?'

Prospero glanced down at the packet. 'Throw your guesses in the Devil's teeth.'

'Guesses? No, Count, no. I know a book of accounts. In that packet, each name, each time, each payment, a record of treachery to sate the strictest court in Venice.'

'I thought you too much a poet for such auditor's labour.'

'May I not be both?' answered William. 'I offer, Prospero. I shall not do so again. Leave off your vile intent, return to me the letters you have taken, flee Venice and no word of these names shall reach the Signoria.'

'What do these names matter to me? I shall not hang for them. If you seek extorted treasure there lie three names will make for more profitable labour.'

'If I cannot buy them, still I will have the letters,' said William. He held out his palm. 'Give them to me.'

Prospero looked at the open hand. He did not hide his scorn. 'I do not know which amazes me more, Master Fallow,' he said, 'that you think I should keep such valuables on my person at a feast. Or that you think I would hand them to you if I had.'

'I think you do. I think also I shall take them.' William stood quickly.

Before he had fully risen Prospero's knife was out. William's own appeared in mirror to it.

'Sit down, Master Fallow,' Prospero said. He pointed with the knife. 'This is too public a place for me to murder in.'

As William slowly sat back the Count slipped his knife away.

'Besides, you would brawl with me for nothing. I do not have the letters. They're safely sent from Venice. You're too late. Trust me on this.'

'Trust, my lord, is something I have in short supply,' William said.

Prospero shrugged. 'The game is not yet over.'

William gathered up the packet from the table.

Prospero gestured to the board. 'Your move I believe.'

William cast a glance at his pieces. 'I see that there is to be no reasoned peace,' he said.

'That was always and ever the most likely way of things,' said Prospero. 'However, I will make you an offer as you have me.'

'Well then,' said William.

'Leave Venice now, tonight, and live,' said Prospero.

'What of Isabella Lisarro?' asked William.

'What of her?'

'What do you offer in exchange for her?'

'There is no price will save her,' said Prospero. 'There is no place where she will be safe. Though you hide her in your heart, there will I rake for her.'

William heard the anger in Prospero's voice as he spoke. He understood Isabella's anger at Prospero. Prospero's at Isabella was a mystery still.

William took his eyes from Prospero to the board. He moved.

The Count of Genoa looked at William's move. His brow furrowed. He shrugged and moved his piece in turn.

'It does not concern you that after your next move I shall take your queen?' Prospero asked.

William reached out his left hand and moved his knight. The gold ring Isabella had given him, with its sigil deep cut in the red stone, gleamed in the light of the candles. He leaned back and looked at Prospero, whose eyes were on William's hand.

'Why should it?' William asked. 'When I have already taken yours.'

When, after a minute or more of silence, Prospero's eyes lifted to William's they were grey with rage.

'You think yourself very clever, Master Fallow.'

'I tell you truly I do not.' William shook his head. 'I have learned many things since I left England. About others, about myself. Chief among them, that I am clever only in knowing that I am indifferent clever and that I have much more to learn. I hope to learn from her. She is wondrous, is she not?'

Prospero made no answer to William's question.

William watched the Count carefully. His right hand, hid below the table, was on his dagger. He had taunted the Count to a purpose, to test his will, to see the discipline of his intent and what might shake it. He did not know if he had tried him to the point of action. The Count, however, seemed to return to calm with each word he spoke.

'If you are in a learning mood, let me teach you one more thing, Master Fallow.'

Prospero leaned forward. 'Have you ever killed a man?'

'Thanks to you I have now killed more than one,' William said.

'Then you have the advantage of me,' Prospero said. He waved a hand at William's look of incredulity. 'Oh, do not misunderstand me. Many men, more than I can count, have died at my behest. Only one has died by my hand. A Spaniard.'

Prospero took his glass and held it to the light.

'We fought over a dog, of all things,' he said.

He looked at William.

'A very fine one, I grant you. But when account is made, only a dog. Mine by virtue of a wager won. The Spaniard disagreed. I stabbed him for it, in the heart.'

'Your lesson is that I should not wager with you, Count?' William asked. 'Or that you are overfond of dogs?'

The Count ignored him. His eyes saw to another time. 'My blade went into him in an instant. It struck him in his most vital part.' He shook his head at the memory. 'Still, he lived a whole minute.'

Prospero pointed to his scarred brow. 'Gave me this and more in that minute. That long minute between the fatal blow and his death.'

'Your point, Count?' said William.

The Count of Genoa beckoned William close and hissed, 'My point, little man, is that even the dead may wound. Think then what I, who am but discomforted, shall do to you.'

William only smiled, for he saw the Count's calm was a player's thing. The crack was opened. Now William need only strike at the wedge.

Your jest is earnest

The two men stood at the water gate of the Ca' Venier. The press of guests brought them close.

'Farewell, Master Fallow,' said the Count. 'I do not look to see you again in this life.'

'Nor I you in the next,' replied William.

The Count's gondola approached. He turned and walked to the water's edge. A woman's loud cry broke over the laughter and the music.

'Thief. Thief. I am robbed. My purse picked.'

All turned at the shout save one. William stayed watching Prospero. At the cry of pick-purse Prospero's hand had risen to his breast. It returned beneath his cloak in an instant. It was enough. He stepped to his gondola and was gone.

A tall woman came up behind William.

'Well, Sir William,' said Faustina, 'did your jest fall as you planned?'

'No jest but earnest, lady,' William smiled. 'I shall be eternally thankful to you for your part in it. Without you I fear the evening would have been quite wasted. All my attempts at the object of the jest had failed till then. Instead I have learned two things of great importance.'

'Think nothing of it. I am one who loves a prank,' Faustina said. She put a proprietorial hand on William's shoulder. 'There is, of course, a price for my service.'

William took her hand from his shoulder and kissed it. 'I give you this kiss for it.'

Faustina sighed. ''Twill have to do. Now come, drink.'

'Just the one glass, lady,' said William as Faustina poured wine.

'Oh, I only ever have the one glass,' said Faustina. 'I need my other hand free for ... other things.'

'True,' said fat Andrea, joining them and relieving Faustina of the bottle. 'It's not the number of glasses that matters, but the number of bottles one pours into them.'

'Your visor is quite grotesque, Andrea,' said Faustina. 'Oh, forgive me. I see you are no longer wearing one.'

'Whereas you have put yours back on, I see,' replied Andrea. 'Oh, forgive me, I see I am as mistaken as you are.'

William left them to their banter. He had business of more serious intent. Now that he was certain of all.

Much more monstrous matter of feast

The preparations made, the day had come; the readiness was all.

The morning of the coronation ceremony, William, Hemminges, Oldcastle and Isabella stood among the crowd in the Piazza San Marco. They swayed in the tide of people pushing to find a vantage from which to view events. They looked across the square to the great facade of the Basilica di San Marco. In a moment William and Oldcastle would make their way there to see the Doge enthroned. From there to the Ducal Palace for the coronation feast. William looked down. His hand trembled at the excitement of the day and the risks of the night to come.

They watched the dignities making their way into the basilica. After anxious moments they saw Prospero enter. Hemminges turned, nodded to the other three and slipped away into the crowd towards Rialto.

'Jesu, we shall all be hanged,' Oldcastle muttered as he too pushed out into the crowd.

Oldcastle's vigour had been reborn with his friend Hemminges, though from the beating he'd received he walked limpingly still.

Behind him William turned to Isabella. The eddy of the mob pushed him and they were pressed close, body to body.

Isabella pressed his hand, fingers twining for an instant.

'You need not do this, William,' Isabella said.

'I know,' he answered.

'Then go. Go now, with your friends,' Isabella urged. 'Flee Venice. This scheme of ours, the dangers are too great. Prospero has but to draw the attention of the Signoria to you and all is done.'

'You'll come with me?' William asked.

Isabella shook her head.

'Together, then,' he said. 'Besides, I can no more leave Prospero free than I can leave you.'

The crowd surged about them. He held her hand tightly.

After a moment she nodded.

He whispered to her, 'You are ready?'

She leaned in to his ear. 'All things are ready if our minds be so.'

Then they pushed apart, William to his place of battle and Isabella to hers.

The hope and expectation of thy time

The doors of the Basilica di San Marco were flung open. A silence rippled out across the square in anticipation. A cry rang out from the darkness of the doorway.

'Your Doge.'

A great answering shout came from the gathered crowd as the golden figure of the new doge emerged.

The coronation Mass was complete. William and Oldcastle, present as Ambassador of England and his man, were among the last to leave the church. The ducal train and the nobility of Venice stretched in a column in front of them. White- and red-robed priests mingled with the black-garbed senators. The gold- and ermine-robed figure of the new doge, now stamped with the authority of the Church, was at the front. Held aloft in a great chair, the Doge travelled the circumference of the piazza. As he passed his hand dipped into a basket of coins and flung them high and wide. Hands snatched and bodies leaped for the largesse like gulls snapping after bread.

'Well, that's one way to ensure one's elevation is well received,' Oldcastle commented as he walked stiffly down the steps of the basilica.

William was not so sure. It was an observation of his mother's that expected reward received no thanks. Yet, if the reward fell one whit below the expectation, no matter its size and generosity, only resentment came in return. It was now a tradition of long-standing that the new doge would throw coins to the people at his coronation. William had already heard mutterings that this Pasquale Cicogna's failed rival, Vicenzo Morosini, would have thrown gold where now flashed only silver.

The expectations of the world. William counted on them. That England should send embassy to see the new doge throned was expected. Thus, their presence went unquestioned. That he and Oldcastle should cower and hide before Prospero was expected. Thus, to stand boldly forth would buy them opportunity.

The Doge completed his orbit of the piazza. Men in the livery of the guild of the Arsenale, where Venice built its great fleet and whose men served the Doge as his guard, held back the crowd with barge poles as the great ones passed through the square. William and Oldcastle fell in behind as the entire train moved towards the Ducal Palace.

William had spotted Prospero only briefly in the church. His clothes were so dark that he had seemed at times more shadow than man. There was no mistaking the arched eyebrow. His head was bent low in whispered conversation with a nobleman of Venice. The same that William had seen Prospero speak to at the Ca' Venier. Prospero scarcely looked up throughout the ceremony. Only once and then it seemed his eyes fell straight on William's.

Now William searched for him in the procession ahead. He felt a hand at his elbow and turned.

'Well played, Master Fallow,' Prospero said. 'I did not think you would so dare as continue your play-acting at the coronation of the Doge himself. Of course, I see now, you must make a show lest the absence of the English Ambassador be cause for greater remark than his quiet presence.'

Prospero walked beside him, matching pace. He raised his hands and gave a little clap.

'Sir Henry,' Prospero bowed to Oldcastle. 'If that is your name.'

Oldcastle mustered all his dignity in a sneered reply, only to see Prospero laugh.

Prospero gestured to the procession. 'I feared I would have to bring the Signoria to your door and, look, you have brought yourselves to theirs. Truly, there is much to be seen in Venice that defies reason and imagination.'

'I am surprised to hear you say so, Count,' said William. 'You seemed to spend little of your attention on the ceremony and much on your companion.'

Prospero tilted his head. 'Ever observant, Master Fallow. You saw me speak to Lodovico Orsini? You know him? Cousin to the Duke of Bracciano? We whiled away the idle hour with speculations on matters philosophical. Possible worlds wherein much might occur if only the opportunity presented itself.'

Prospero smiled. 'He tells me his cousin the Duke is not well. Some sickness of the stomach. He and his beauteous wife are gone to Salo in hope the air there will present itself more pleasant to his disposition.'

'I am certain that the air smells sweeter where you are not,' said William.

'Now, now,' admonished the Count. 'We play a game, you and I. It is not becoming to lose with ill grace.'

'You call this a game?' said William.

'I do,' replied Prospero. 'With men for pieces. The best kind. One where the stakes are at their highest.'

A smile briefly flashed across his face before turning to a look of sadness.

'This sudden sickness of the Duke,' Prospero went on, 'so unexpected. Lodovico had been to see the Duke only the day before, he tells me. The Duke had seemed in good health. Well enough to receive a gift, a dish of preserved figs, for which he has a fondness. Lodovico assures me that he consumed them with relish and great appetite.'

'You poisoned him?' asked William.

'Of course,' said Prospero, smiling again. 'I expect him dead by now. As you will shortly be.'

Prospero patted William on the arm and looked at him and Oldcastle both. 'Though your deaths, I promise, will not be one half so merciful.'

He bowed to them both again and walked ahead.

'Truly, he's the Devil incarnate,' Oldcastle said.

William heard his name shouted. He turned and saw beyond the fence of liveried guildsmen the face of Hemminges. William walked quickly over to where the crowd was held back. Hemminges leaned in.

'My part is played,' he said. 'I searched Prospero's house well.'

'The letters?' asked William.

'As you thought, not there. The house is empty. Well, save for three bodies in the storeroom.'

'Three?' said William.

'Two men I did not recognise and a third, who by your description is Borachio. The two are dead by each other's hand. Borachio was drowned in a butt of wine.'

'Prospero's work,' said William.

'As I read it,' said Hemminges.

'He saves us so much labour.'

'Such work is no labour but a pleasure.'

Even William, who knew him well, blanched to see the anger writ on Hemminges' face.

'See to him, William,' Hemminges said. 'Such a man should not walk this clean earth. He makes sweet things foul.'

'It is done. I swear it,' said William.

Hemminges vanished into the crowd. William turned and hurried to catch up with Oldcastle. If the Count wished to game, then William meant to play such a set as would bring his head from his shoulders.

With Ate by his side

William and Oldcastle passed through the Porta della Carta that led into the courtyard of the Ducal Palace. William looked up at the statue of blind Justice under which they passed and hoped it an omen.

Many of the guests were gathered in the great hall that was the Sala del Maggior Consiglio. The Doge was not there. He waited on the floor above to greet the select.

'There you are, Sir Henry.'

William turned at the sound of Prospero's voice. He was accompanied by two of the liveried guildsmen of the Arsenale. Prospero gestured to them.

'I feared you had become lost amidst the crowd. I told these men that the new doge would certainly wish to see the English Ambassador. Allow us to be your escort to his presence.'

He pointed the way to the stairs leading up to the Doge's apartments. William glanced at Oldcastle and from him to the doors leading out of the Ducal Palace. Prospero saw his look and stepped between the Englishmen and any thought of escape.

'Come, Sir Henry, we must not keep the Serene Lord waiting.'

He strode ahead. William and Oldcastle fell in behind, the guildsman following after.

Above, they found the Sala Scudo, the smaller hall in the Doge's apartments beyond which lay his private offices. The hall was crowded. At the far end two gilded doors were guarded by the same liveried guildsmen of the Arsenale that had marked the procession's path. At their command small groups were breathed in and out the doors to the chamber beyond. Each time the doors opened a glimpse of the room's extravagant decoration was revealed. Each time some new guests were drawn in to this Scarlet Chamber, where the new doge sat enthroned. There, in the quiet of the smaller room, they approached to offer their congratulations and make their first petitions. Each time the doors opened the previous company, their obesiance made, were blown out to rejoin the crowd and the revels below. To encourage their return, servants passed among those in the Sala del Maggior Consiglio proffering wine to men and women desperate from long hours of dry ceremony.

Their passage through the press of the Sala Scudo stretched an eternity. William found the steadiness with which Oldcastle marched a contrast with his own trembling gait. Oldcastle, who had seemed most aware of all the dangers that drew like black clouds over them, now seemed least heedful of that danger.

Ahead, William saw Prospero waited by the doors to the Scarlet Chamber. The moment for action draws near, William thought. Unbidden, the lines he'd penned in San Rocco that week past sprang to his mind:

> There is a tide in the affairs of men, that taken at the flood leads on to glory. Omitted all the course of our lives is dwelt in shallows and in miseries.

Needs work, he thought and wondered if he'd live to see it done.

William and Oldcastle arrived at the gilded doors. The Count of Genoa turned.

'The moment of truth approaches, Master Fallow,' Prospero whispered.

It does, thought William.

Then came that honey breath of perfume that was her herald and Isabella Lisarro appeared among them, smiling.

Prospero's face turned to cloudy thunder.

Your beauty was the cause

William saw how Isabella's arrival shook Prospero. There was some magic to her presence that worked on the Count. William had seen it clearly the night before, at the feast. He saw it again now. Prospero's mind was full of scorpions.

The Count recovered himself. He stepped to the liveried guardsmen.

'The Ambassador of England is here to greet the Doge.'

William looked on in unwilling admiration. Here was the Prospero who was deadly as the poisonous spider. Who cared not if his web was broke but calmly spun it new and snared you still. Whose unseemly pride was born from his ability to control himself and all. Such an ability, thought William, was often crafted from necessity. Only those who wrestle with a wild temper craft such strong chains to check it. Break those bonds and they would rage in self-destroying madness. One needed only to bring forth the key.

Isabella Lisarro spoke. 'Still going where you are not wanted, Giovanni?'

'It is not my presence that is unwanted here,' said Prospero.

'So sure of the feelings of others, Giovanni?' she asked.

'Sure of my own,' he said and leaned a little toward her. 'You were warned.'

He spoke more softly still; William scarcely heard it.

'For that love we had for each other I forbore to strike at you. It did not need to be this way. It never did.'

'Oh Giovanni, what love?' Isabella's reply came just as quiet. 'Can you be so blind? You, who claim to see so clearly? How little there was of love. All that time you were making mooncalf eyes at me and dabbling palms under a gondola's awning? All that time, I made report to the Signoria. I was paid twice for that work, by you and by those I betrayed you to.'

She leaned back to gauge his face. Prospero's eyes swelled.

'I was little better than a child then,' Isabella said. 'I have learned what it truly means to have a lover since. Our affair is not to be compared with that, save as a shadow is to the thing itself.'

Prospero stumbled to make reply but a great gout of emotions was knotting in his throat. Isabella laughed and spoke clearly for all to hear.

'It is as well, then, that I was paid, for work it was. I know now your company was not to be endured except at twice the usual price.'

With a speed faster than thought, Prospero's hand swept out and lashed Isabella across the face. She cried out and faltered back. William snarled at Prospero and grappled him close till one of the guildsmen pulled him back while the other hauled off Prospero. Like leashed dogs they strained to be at each other. The gilded doors opened. A scarlet-robed secretary ushered out a group of nobles, then stood with them in amazement at the violent scene.

Is there no man here?

'What is this disturbance?' the Doge's Secretary hissed at the guildsmen by the door.

'We were about to admit the Ambassador of England when this man and this woman, my lord, fell to argument. He struck her. Then this man,' he gestured at William, 'grappled with the first. The men wrestled and we parted them.'

'Admit the Ambassador of England at once,' the Secretary ordered to the guards.

'These rest should leave,' he spoke in a hissed whisper to Prospero and Isabella.

Prospero's fire, that had been tamped by force of will, blazed hot again. 'Rascal, do not dismiss me at the shriek of a whore.'

'Oh, your corrupted blood!' cried Isabella.

She turned to address the liveried guildsmen. 'You hear him speak in such ungracious and ungentle terms of me,' she cried. 'One who has done nothing but be the butt for his show of arms. Why do you stand there mute witness to my shame?'

The liveried guildsmen grew red as their tabards.

'Is there no man among you that will defend me?' demanded Isabella.

One of the guildsmen went to speak in defence of his honour. The Secretary, desperate to end this unseemly brawl at the very door of the Doge, cut him off.

'This is neither the place nor the time for such accusations or for such riots,' he said. 'Take yourselves from here at once.'

Isabella ignored him. Such was the press of people that, as yet, only those that stood closest to the gilded doors perceived the drama. To these, who stood amazed, Isabella turned.

'Will no one act?' she demanded. 'Prefer you your lives to honour? Not I. I would rather fall on the swords of these soldiers than turn my cheek at the provocation of this knave. Is there no man here will defend my honour?'

She looked about. 'Then will this woman do the duty of a man,' she said.

With these words she lunged at one of the guildsmen and made to draw his sword. The two struggled for the weapon.

'For God's sake, what mars the peace of my coronation day?' The Doge himself had stepped from his throne to view the matter.

'What brawl is this?' the Doge demanded.

His Secretary made to reply but Isabella cut him off with a cry. 'Justice, Serene Lord. This man wrongs me.'

A quivering finger pointed at Prospero. The Doge looked about him. Beyond the scene before him stood an attendant crowd, watching. They saw a Venetian woman, face still crimson from the blow, call to her ruler for justice against this Genoan count who struck at her. They saw England watch to see the mettle of Venice's new doge in dealing with this dispute. He saw all this and made his first judgment as Doge. It fell as William had hoped.

'Bring them all in here,' he said, 'and let us deal with this beyond the common view.'

Now follow – if thou darest – to try whose right of thine or mine is most in Helena

William and the others were ushered into the smaller room. William felt the press of the armed guildsmen behind him. Sweat prickled at his neck. Angry Venetian faces gazed on William, Oldcastle, Isabella and Prospero. William looked to his right. Through the window he saw the tops of the two statue-capped pillars that stood in the Piazzetta di San Marco, between which they hanged the enemies of Venice. William fought for calm. He needed it. The scene was not yet finished, the play not over and the game not won.

The Doge resumed his seat on the throne of State. He picked up his cup and drank from it as he eyed the four before him.

Prospero broke the silence. 'Serene Lord, there has been –'

'Quiet,' the Doge ordered.

He pointed to one of the guildsman. 'What passed out there?'

The liveried figure spoke hastily, anxious for his part in matters to be short. When he finished the Doge turned to Prospero.

'Why did you strike this woman?'

'I am most grievously abused,' said Prospero. 'I came to warn you, Serene Lord, of a great danger to your person and to the State. I fear it was to distract me from that charge that this woman spoke to me in such scurvy and provoking terms that I was forced, on my honour, to strike her. It was intemperate.'

Prospero cursed himself for his own hot-headedness. Yet he saw how he might turn events to his advantage.

He went on: 'I apologise from my deepest heart for the discourtesy to you and your office that I should have upset the harmony of this day. Yet if you heard her speak, no man might do less with honour.'

'Honour?' Isabella looked sadly at Prospero. 'What do you know of honour?'

She turned to the Doge. 'Serene Lord, look on the Count of Genoa and see a man whom envy has made mad. It is no insult of mine but the green-eyed monster of his jealousy has turned my face to crimson. Calumnious envy, that I prefer this witty youth to his choleric age.'

The Doge was amused. He cast an admiring look over Isabella. He raised a hand and spoke behind it to the Secretary, who stood beside him, in a voice that carried clear enough. 'There's honey guarded by a sting? Eh?'

The Secretary, fast adapting to his new lord's ways, gave a polite laugh.

'Serene Lord,' Prospero said, 'this is a distraction from a matter of far greater pith and moment.'

'The danger to our person and State of which you spoke,' replied the Doge.

'The same. These men who claim to be the Ambassador of England and his man are no such thing,' pronounced the Count.

'Come, man, there's a charge that's scarce to be believed,' said the Doge. 'Far more credent ear I give the lady's talk of envy. To be envious of this youth for having supplanted you with this rare pearl is a thing entirely understandable, forgiveable.'

'Beware, Serene Lord, for this Isabella Lisarro is in league with your enemy, the enemy of Venice,' insisted Prospero. 'Serene Lord, these are no more the English Ambassador and his man than I am the Doge. They are English agents, spies, assassins. You have heard, Serene Lord, of the attempted murder of the Duchess of Bracciano? The blame lies with them.'

'Another heavy charge,' said the Doge.

'I dare more, Serene Lord,' Prospero replied. 'The Duke of Bracciano is lately taken ill.'

The Doge's Secretary started at this news. He signalled to a clerk, who approached and whispered in his ear.

Prospero continued: 'A sickness that followed swiftly on a gift sent by the English embassy.'

A clerk was sent scurrying to the door by the Doge's Secretary.

Meanwhile Prospero spoke on and in such terms that William began to doubt his own innocence.

'It is true that this whore and I have known each other,' said Prospero with a glance at Isabella. 'What man has not?'

'You are vile, Prospero,' Isabella said.

Prospero ignored her. 'True also that our angry words were over this Englishman. Yet jealousy was not the cause of our argument. Her anger is because I had discovered their foul plots and would not spare them Venetian justice for all her pleading.'

'Lies,' Isabella said. 'I have ever been loyal to Venice.'

'They are not lies,' said Prospero. He spoke as if sadly, but William could see the excitement in his eyes.

'This is a scandal to my State and office,' said Oldcastle. 'Serene Lord, am I to stand and listen to these insults?'

The Doge looked between Prospero and Oldcastle.

'He says you are a spy and an assassin. You say that you are not. How am I to resolve this?' the Doge asked.

Prospero looked at William as he spoke. 'No simpler matter, Serene Lord. If these be the English embassy, where are their papers, their letters of recommendation? They have none. For they are dissembling players both.'

Prospero turned to face the Doge. 'Serene Lord, let the English Ambassador produce his letters of recommendation or stand proved an enemy to Venice.'

All eyes turned to Oldcastle save Prospero's alone. His gaze was fixed on William.

'Well?' said the Doge to Oldcastle.

'I do not have them,' said Oldcastle.

Prospero leaned close to William's ear.

'Checkmate,' he whispered.

The whirligig of time

William looked into the face of Prospero and saw in it a vicious triumph. He witnessed that triumph change and fade when Prospero, in turn, did not find in William's face any tremor of fear. Beyond them Oldcastle spoke.

'I do not carry such things,' he said. 'My steward deals with such matters. Fallow?'

'Yes, Sir Henry?' said William.

'The letters, and quickly,' said Oldcastle.

William shook off the restraining hand of the guildsman behind him and reached into his doublet. He took from it a packet of letters. He stepped forward past Prospero and placed it in the hand of the Doge's Secretary. Prospero looked at the packet, uncomprehending. He could feel the weight of the letters in his own doublet still.

'Forgeries,' Prospero pronounced.

'The seal is correct in every detail,' replied the Secretary.

'Must we endure this dishonour longer?' demanded Oldcastle of the Doge. 'I do not know this fellow but, sure, he is some kind of madman.'

'I tell you this is no knight but an English spy, a player,' insisted Prospero.

William spoke, 'Serene Lord, break open the seal, question us on the content. It speaks of an alliance between England and Venice to the benefit of both our merchants. It discusses our mutual support for Henry of Navarre against the Guise in the French succession. Would we know this if we were not the English embassy?'

At the Doge's nod the Secretary slit the seal and read. William prayed that he had understood Sir Henry's lessons in France. There had been no moment between when he had taken the packet from Prospero's doublet in the struggle and now to read the letters for himself. Nor would he have dared disturb the seal. He saw sweat beading on Oldcastle's brow as they both waited for the Secretary to finish reading.

'It is as he says, Serene Lord,' the Secretary pronounced.

All eyes were now on Prospero. The clockwork of his thoughts turned furiously but its balance was out and the gears no longer bit with each other.

'I would say this talk of jealous madness has some truth in it,' said the Doge. 'It were best if you withdrew, Count, before your fancies cause you to repeat your slanders.'

Isabella spoke, 'There's more than madness here, Serene Lord. Of all that this man has said only one part was true. There is a threat to your person and to Venice. This man is an agent of the Pope. The same crimes he accused the English of were all his working.'

'Ridiculous,' scoffed Prospero.

He looked at Isabella Lisarro and saw the hatred in her eyes. Prospero seethed. He still could not fathom what had passed. He reached into his doublet to check that the packet was still there. That, truly, he was not run mad.

'A blade,' cried Isabella, 'he reaches for a blade!'

The guildsmen threw themselves on Prospero and held him.

'Get off me, fools!' cried Prospero.

'What do you reach for?' demanded the Doge.

'Nothing, Serene Lord,' said Prospero.

'Search him,' commanded the Secretary.

One of the guildsmen reached into Prospero's doublet. 'No dagger, Serene Lord, only this letter.' He passed it to the Secretary.

'That is not for you!' cried Prospero.

The Doge looked up at him, his brows raised at the intemperate tone. Prospero struggled for calm, understanding flooding him. He saw now how William had wrestled with him. Felt again those quick, thin fingers grapple at his clothing. Knew then that substitution had been made.

The Doge held out his hand. The Secretary placed the packet in it. The Doge examined it.

Prospero felt the danger gathering about him. He saw it in the cold faces of William and Oldcastle, in the sorrowful anger of Isabella. He began to see that it was not he who had brought the English before the Doge to be exposed. It was they who had lured him to this place. He had put himself beyond escape. With all his might he raged against the arms that held him.

'I am the Pope's servant,' he snarled. 'You lay your hands on me at peril of his anger.'

The Doge passed the letter to the Secretary. 'It is the Pope that writes,' he said.

At Prospero's look of confusion the Doge signalled to his Secretary, who approached and held the paper open before Prospero's eyes.

In the matter of Sir Henry Carr, Ambassador, and of the Duke and Duchess of Bracciano I charge you, Marcantonio Bon and Francesco Tiepolo, by the debt you owe me, to render Giovanni Prospero all assistance that he shall require and absolve you of all sin that may fall upon you in the course of his service, which is the service of the Holy See.

At its base the seal bore the crossed keys of St Peter and the name of the Pope.

'Forgery. This letter is forged,' Prospero said.

'The seal is the Pope's. I know its look,' said the Secretary.

William gave a silent prayer of thanks to Tintoretto's skill.

'Besides, it was in your doublet,' added the Doge.

'Some sleight of hand,' said Prospero, 'some trick of the English.'

'Really?' said the Doge and shook his head. 'The English Ambassador does not seem one for swift hands.'

Then, again in an audible whisper that held little subtlety in it, he said to his Secretary, 'Unless it was at the table. There I would say the man was a very tempest of activity.'

The Doge looked about pleased with his own wit. His Secretary leaned in and muttered into his ear. The Doge heard and nodded. He held up the note with the Pope's seal.

'There are five names writ here in addition to the Count's.'

He read them aloud.

'The purpose of the first three names is clear,' said Isabella. 'They are the murderous task to which this man was set.'

'Those last two names I know too,' continued William. 'Like this man they are the Pope's agents. I was to have met a servant of the Signoria some eight nights ago, Iseppo da Nicosia. He and I would have made exchange of names.'

'The "names"?' echoed the Doge.

'There is mention made here of them,' his Secretary answered, pointing to the ambassador's letters. 'An exchange of the names of papal agents in our lands for our knowledge of those in England.'

'Just so,' said William. 'Before our bargain could be made Iseppo da Nicosia was murdered.'

'Murdered?' muttered the Doge.

'Most foully and by this man's servant, Borachio,' said William, 'before the names of the spies of their master, the Pope, could be given over.'

'What has this to do with Marcantonio Bon and Francesco Tiepolo?' asked the Doge's Secretary.

'They are two of the names I would have exchanged with Iseppo da Nicosia,' William said.

'Rank lies,' shouted Prospero. 'Why, this Francesco Tiepolo is no agent of the Pope but another rival for the love of the whore, Isabella Lisarro.'

'No word of a lie,' replied William to Prospero's raging. 'I have here the list of names together with details of the traitors' payments and the name of the Pope's banker in Venice. Once our bargain is complete you may speak with him, ask of payments made to the people named here. See too that this man, Prospero, is paid by the same hand.'

To the three names he had discovered William had added that of Francesco Tiepolo. If any man should face Venetian justice it was him. No payments would be found with his name upon them. William hoped the taint of association would suffice. Even if he escaped hanging, Francesco Tiepolo's days of glory in Venice would be done with.

'A forged letter? Some names, no more than that? Is it with such paltry testimony that you accuse me?' cried Prospero.

'Far more than that,' declared William, his eyes on Prospero. 'Where is your servant, Borachio, Count? Search this man's lodging in the city, Serene Lord. I fear you will find all the proof of this man's villainy that you desire.'

Prospero grew still.

'So many accusations I scarce know how to proceed,' said the Doge staring at Prospero. 'They have the ring of truth to them. Still, it is not for me to decide such matters.'

He signalled to his Secretary. 'It will be put in the hands of the Signoria. They will, I think, wish to discuss with you many things, the unfortunate matter of the Duchess of Bracciano among them.'

'You fool,' hissed Prospero. 'You defy the Pope and Venice will suffer.'

The Doge looked at him. The ribald glimmer that had sat in the Doge's eye was extinguished. Without taking his eyes from Prospero he spoke to his Secretary, 'Talk of murder should not go unexamined.'

The Doge's Secretary began to feel he had an understanding for the moods of his new master. 'Serene Lord, you wish the matter fully tried?'

'I do,' replied the Doge.

'Then, Serene Lord,' said his Secretary, 'I shall inform the gaoler he should use all measures in search of the truth.'

'All measures,' repeated the Doge, eyes still on the man who'd called him fool.

Prospero turned pale and hung limp in the hands that held him. The liveried guildsmen pulled him towards the door that led to the rack and the cudgels and the questioning to come.

As Prospero was dragged past William he changed from resignation to furious action. He pulled his arms free of those that held him and snatched his dagger from his belt. He lunged at William, who caught his hand and turned the blade aside. For an instant the two wrestled before Prospero, with mad strength, wrenched his hand free and lifted it to drive the blade down at William's neck.

Prospero howled. The point of a rapier pinned his wrist to the wall. Isabella leaned with all her weight on the blade. The guildsmen recovered and grappled Prospero to the ground. When they dragged him to his feet again he spat at Isabella.

'You should have killed me, whore, for I will be revenged.'

'A swift death, Prospero?' whispered Isabella. 'No, first you must be questioned.'

She held out the sword to the shame-faced guildsman from whom she'd snatched it.

William watched as a previously unseen door at the side of the room opened. As Prospero was dragged through he looked back at William and Isabella. They heard his cry as the door closed behind him.

'I'll be revenged on the whole pack of you.'

Why, here it is. Welcome these pleasant days!

'A most unpleasant scene,' the Doge said. He turned to Oldcastle. 'I hope you will forgive it, Sir Henry. The Count of Genoa has made most grievous slander of you. We give his words no ear and, for ourselves, ask only that you lay the blame at Genoa's door, where it belongs.'

'Of course,' said Oldcastle with a bow.

'Chimes with their policy, of course,' the Doge said to his Secretary, 'the Genoese were ever our rivals and our enemies. Yes, I think we should thank England for its timely exposure of this Genoese danger. Wouldn't you say?'

The Doge's Secretary rushed to agree. It seemed there was to be no more talk of Rome or the Pope. Such are the ways of States. The Doge smiled broadly at his Secretary's agreement. His jolly look gave no sign of what had passed. The door had shut on Prospero and with it the Doge's interest in the man.

'Now, what to me from England?' the Doge said.

His Secretary placed the packet of letters in the Doge's hand. The Doge cast his eye over the first letter. He hummed an air as he read. He looked up.

'I see, I see. Well, there is much here to be considered,' he said. 'This too must be placed before the Signoria. Certainly in the matter of this bargaining over names. So much the better. A feast is no place for such dry discourse as this. Let us leave this till later.'

With no more discussion he placed the packet of letters into the hand of his waiting Secretary and nodded to Oldcastle, William and Isabella. Then he glanced away to take up his cup again and await the next group of supplicants.

The Secretary stepped forward and, with arm's spread wide to gather them in, ushered the trio towards the door. They took their cue to depart and swept to the gilded doors, which opened to reveal the thronging guests; they who had scant moment ago seemed to balance on the precipice's edge, plunged in to enjoy the coronation feast.

Made for kissing

The guests whirled about them, all oblivious of the drama that had passed or the significance of the three actors that now stood in their midst.

'What did Prospero's letter say?' Oldcastle asked.

William told him.

'So little?' Oldcastle's eyebrow arched in mimicry of the condemned Count.

'Little and yet enough,' said William. 'The more said, the more to be questioned. With Tintoretto's skill set to the forging of the hand and seal it had enough semblance of authority to carry all before it. All is done, Prospero is damned, the Pope's hand revealed and we are freed to flee Venice.'

William felt his hand caught by Isabella's.

'Flee? Not tonight I hope,' she said.

William turned to her. 'Never. If I had my wish.'

Oldcastle saw his cue to depart. He seized Isabella's hand from William and with much ceremony kissed it.

'Goodnight, lady,' he said. 'I thought you Helen for your beauty but I see that in our wars you are Hippolyte, Queen of the Amazons.'

When Oldcastle had disappeared into the crowd William turned to Isabella again.

'Truly Oldcastle has it,' he said. 'Who can touch you for daring? I feared all would come for nothing when that steward intervened and sought to banish you and Prospero both. That was quick-thinking to seize the soldier's sword.'

'All fell out as you had written it,' she replied.

She took his hand again. 'There is a rare understanding in you.'

There was so very much to be said. Neither William nor Isabella knew where to begin. Music struck up and the crowd parted to allow room for those who wished to dance.

'Shall we?' William gestured to the gathering couples.

'Again you sense my mood,' Isabella said.

She looked him up and down. 'Do you dance well?'

'I hope that it will not savour too much of my youth to say that there's none can match me for the backstep.' William struck a pose.

Isabella made a show of judgment. 'Indeed, I did think by the excellent constitution of your leg that it was formed under the star of a galliard.'

'Let us test our partnership at a dance then,' said William.

'Very well. We shall see if your feet are as nimble as your fingers,' Isabella said. She leaned her head in to his. 'But do not spend all your all in capering.'

'At last I see you do speak naughtily,' William said.

Isabella made no reply other than to draw him into the whirl.

Epilogue

Venice, August 1585

To the latter end of a fray, and the beginning of a feast

Oldcastle consumed the final pastry with the relish of a man who had not been certain he would see out the night and now wished to savour every sensation. Hemminges thought Oldcastle's greatness lay in his always having lived so. They sat by candlelight in the House of the White Lion. Outside the sound of revels could be heard carrying on into the early hours of the morning.

Salarino looked on, pleased. He had been sure that given time and the right ingredients even this barbarian Englishman could be brought to savour Venetian cuisine. So it had proved. He disappeared into the kitchen to produce more proofs of Venice's superiority in this, as in all things. There would, of course, be no charge. Hemminges had made it quite clear that he considered Salarino well paid in keeping his life. To be frightened of Hemminges, that Salarino considered simply wisdom.

Hemminges and Oldcastle were left alone. Oldcastle finished the tale of the night. Hemminges shook his head; in admiration or disbelief Oldcastle could not tell.

'I can scarce believe it myself,' said Hemminges.

'It was all in the performance. I flatter myself that I gave good account in my own role,' replied Oldcastle.

'I do not doubt it,' Hemminges paused. 'Still.'

'Still,' Oldcastle acknowledged.

'What if Prospero had not reached for the letter of his own accord?'

'Aah,' said Oldcastle, 'do you doubt William had some further prompt to it?'

'No.'

'Nor I.'

'I would rather we had run the man through,' said Hemminges.

Within Hemminges' eyes there was a distant flash, as when lightning is seen in a thundercloud some miles away.

'It does not seem enough for such a man,' he said.

'If you had seen them talk of the questioning to follow, you would not say so,' said Oldcastle.

'What if the Signoria let him go?' asked Hemminges. 'As well they may. The man is no more mad than you or I.'

He stopped. 'Why are you laughing?' he asked.

Oldcastle wiped his eyes. 'Jesu, Hemminges. If the man is no more mad than you and I then he is well locked up. What is it but madness for us to be here on this adventure instead of safe at home in England?'

Oldcastle sobered, ''Sides, I do not think they will let his crimes go unconfessed. The men that dragged him away looked to have some skill with the poker and the press. Even if the Count leaves those walls I doubt he will so much walk as crawl.'

Hemminges tipped his head in acknowledgement of the truth of his friend's words.

'Still, I do not think we have put that danger past us,' Hemminges said. 'There is also his master, the Pope, to be thought on. If he discover our role in his servant's fall?' He shrugged. 'And to rely on Venetian justice, for all they boast of it, would be a rash thing. For certain, the English Ambassador must make discreet and hasty departure.'

'Tell that to William,' said Oldcastle. 'As easily prize him apart from his new passion without hurting yourself as prize apart an oyster's shell. We shall have to be patient.'

'We wait to travel with him?' asked Hemminges.

Oldcastle looked up from refilling his cup in surprise. 'Of course.'

Hemminges spoke, 'He's clever but he reckons without the consequences of his cleverness. We have been swept up in his schemes once already. Look what it cost us.'

Oldcastle reached out and gripped his friend's arm. 'It is good to have you with me again, my friend,' he said. 'I have missed the wisdom of your counsel. When I thought you dead –'

He broke off and finished his cup to hide the swell of emotion.

'But ...' he said.

Hemminges, knowing his part, prompted Oldcastle, 'But?'

Oldcastle raised his glass in toast.

'Let life be short, before boredom be too long.'

Historical Note

On 2 February 1585, William Shakespeare's twin children Judith and Hamnet were baptised in Holy Trinity Church, Stratford-upon-Avon. That is the last we hear of him until he emerges on the record of the London theatre scene in 1592. The intervening period has come to be known as 'the Lost Years', and into the gap we pour endless speculation: how does the son of a glover and wool merchant from the middle of England become an actor and playwright in London?

Various theories have presented themselves, usually on very thin evidence. One of the least speculative – that he went to Lancashire to become a tutor, based on the dubious similarity of the name 'Shakeshafte' with 'Shakespeare' – struggles to reconcile its dates with William's need to be in Stratford with Anne if Judith and Hamnet's arrival is to be accounted for.

He must have made it to London before 1592. That is the year that Robert Greene, a figure every bit as scandalous as he is presented in the novel, had published his *Groat's Worth of Wit,* in which he damned Shakespeare as 'an upstart crow' for trying to write plays the equal of his own. Even allowing for time in which to have written the things that drew Greene's contempt and allowing further that Shakespeare is the figure mentioned in certain court documents in late 1588, at least three years are left unaccounted for.

With the historical record left blank we turn to the plays for clues: thirteen of Shakespeare's surviving plays are set in Italy, more than any other country bar England. The plot of *Othello* is taken from a collection of Italian stories – Giraldi Cinthio's *Gli Hecatommithi* – available only in Italian until the 18th century, which suggests William spoke the language. In more than one place in his works Shakespeare mentions artwork found in Italy, report of which seems to bear the hallmarks of first-hand knowledge. *The Taming of the Shrew,* for example, mentions a painting that first went on display in Milan between 1585 and 1600. Might he have gone to Italy?

To travel to Italy and to Venice, despite its dangers and expense, was not unheard of. John Fletcher, who succeeded William as the playwright for the King's Men, had a brother, Nathaniel, who went to Venice in the entourage of Sir Henry Wotton, the English Ambassador. Actors in the Chamberlain's Men, such as William Kemp, were also known to have travelled to Italy. It is the report of one such Englishman's visit to Venice, that of Thomas Coryat, published in 1611, which I have drawn on for contemporary colour. Coryat's claims to fame include the introduction of the fork to the English dining table, an instrument till then unknown – a spoon or the hands being preferred.

So maybe William went to Venice.

It is hard to overstate the turbulence of the times that William lived in, or their wonders. In 1585 England sat surrounded by powerful enemies. None was more powerful than Philip of Spain, whose Habsburg Empire stretched from Spain, through Italy into the Netherlands. Philip's armies were unrivalled, his fleets vast, his fanaticism for the destruction of England unmatched. In a few short years he would rip every tree from his lands to build ships for an Armada against England.

Religious division tore through the whole Continent. Dutch Protestants had rebelled against Philip's rule, and by 1585 had been fighting for nearly twenty years against his forces. The year 1584 had been terrible for the Dutch rebels. Their leader, William the Silent, had been assassinated by one of Philip's agents. Meanwhile, the Duke of Parma with forty thousand men had laid siege to Antwerp, supported by a long supply chain that ran through Spain, Italy and on to the Low Countries, the famed 'Spanish Road'. France was also divided between the faction of the staunchly Catholic Duke of Guise and that of the Huguenots' Henry of Navarre. The war for control of France between these two factions was marked by assassination and massacre and still raged.

Into this turmoil England was repeatedly thrust. Elizabeth I had been offered sovereignty of the Dutch rebel provinces but declined. Yet in August 1585 she had felt obliged to sign the Treaty of Nonsuch and dispatch the Earl of Leicester with a force to assist the Dutch rebels. It is the prospect of this expedition that Hunsdon bemoans to Sir Henry Carr at the Paris Garden, a popular venue for plots; it could not be avoided. The fear of

Catholic France and Spain joining forces loomed over Protestant England. Meanwhile, encouraged by a papal edict against Elizabeth's reign, Jesuit agents came to England intent on preserving Roman Catholicism against the heresy of England and seeking to place Mary, Queen of Scots, on the throne in Elizabeth's place.

Amid all this turmoil sat Venice. A city of wonders, it was an object of fascination in England. Venice was rich beyond the dreams of Croesus but, perhaps unbeknown even to its citizens, in decline. The terrifying Ottoman Empire had begun to snatch its Mediterranean possessions from it one by one, cutting it off from its unique position at the heart of trade between Christendom and the East. The great naval victory over the Ottomans at Lepanto in 1571 had been preceded by the loss of the last Venetian outpost on Cyprus. At the same time, Spanish and Portuguese ships had opened up new routes to the East around the coast of Africa. The edifice of Venetian mercantile power was crumbling.

Venice was proud of its unique republican political system, to which it attributed much of its success and which caused it to look with disdain on other, less fortunate, nations. Venice revered the law and would, in 1605, choose to defy papal excommunication rather than compromise the principle that all, even priests, were subject to it. It was also a city of license and remained a place where all religions met in relative freedom.

Prized among Venice's wonders were the *cortigiana onesta*, the honest courtesans, women of great beauty and refinement. Of all of them the most famous is Veronica Franco – Isabella's inspiration. In any time she would have been remarkable; in a world and an era when every die was loaded against women, she was astonishing. That she was beautiful is clear from the portraits that Tintoretto painted of her. That she had a matchless mind and a generous heart emerges from her poetry and from the record of her charity to others. The battle of poems at the Ca' Venier in my story steals from the historical battle between Veronica Franco and one Maffio Venier, in which Maffio had punned off Veronica's name and she responded defending herself and all women in words similar, but better, than those I have given Isabella. Some of Isabella's words when she speaks of the horror of being a courtesan are also Veronica's, taken shamelessly from her letters, which speak to us movingly from across five hundred years. I do not find it difficult to believe that William met her in Venice, or that it was her inspiration that led him to write characters like Hermione or Volumnia or Isabella.

Veronica is not the only remarkable figure to have been in Venice in 1585. Vittoria Accoramboni is as my story has her. The vengeance of the monstrous Pope Sixtus V was as terrible. It was, indeed, said of this Pope that he had as many spies as others had soldiers. The tragic tale would become a play by John Webster in 1612 called *The White Devil*. I like the idea that he was inspired by William's recollection of events.

The history of Europe in 1585 contains more adventure, tragedy and romance than any novel. I recommend *A History of Venice* by John Julius Norwich to those wishing to know more of that amazing city. Better yet, visit; February is a good month – the carnival is over and the city is relatively quiet. For those wanting to know about England at the time, they would do well to read *The English and Their History* by Robert Tombs, a book that contains many pleasurable discoveries. More specific to the period is *A Brief History of Britain 1485–1660* by Ronald Hutton. Mention of Sir Francis Walsingham and the spy network of Elizabethan England is very hard to avoid in any novel set in this time, but I suggest that you come at him through his role in Christopher Marlowe's life in *Christopher Marlowe: Poet & Spy* by Park Honan. As for Veronica Franco, her own *Poems and Selected Letters* edited by Jones and Rosenthal are worth reading for their insight and beauty.

Meanwhile, what of William and his companions? They are still in Venice and far from home. Dangers gather, for this Pope is not one to let his white robes stay his hand, and meanwhile the Signoria will not welcome the attention that England has brought on their city. Above all else, William must find his way home. It is not in Italy that he makes his name…

Acknowledgements

Thanks, Rosencrantz and gentle Guildenstern.
Thanks, Guildenstern and gentle Rosencrantz

This is a book of long gestation.

It begins with the support and encouragement of Robert Hudson, a fine writer and wonderful friend. It travels through various versions during which other good friends and great minds like Claire Broughton, Edward Docx, Mark Booth and Bash Doran steer me towards some kind of sense.

Then my sister Saethryd Brandreth provided invaluable editorial assistance. I have always been envious of her writing skill and judgment but I am nothing but grateful that she lent those talents to me to turn a tyro's effort into something worth reading. (Without her there would have been five times as many bird metaphors. All that remain are my fault entirely.)

Thanks are due to the readers of early and much worse versions of this book: my sister Aphra Brandreth, Nick Falk, Susannah Pearse and Sally Watson. I am also hugely grateful to the artist Sally Spector, who has forgotten more about the history, places and people of Venice than I will ever know. Sally read the book and corrected many errors, and guided me around Venice and taught me almost all I know about that wondrous city.

Finally, I was extraordinarily lucky to catch the tide of affairs that is Bonnier, Twenty7 Books and Joel Richardson and his colleagues. Everything they touched made the book better.

Throughout the process several people made it all possible. My clerks and in particular my senior clerk, Ashley Carr, found the time for me to have a secret life as a writer even as they propelled me to greater heights as a barrister. I am grateful. I stole the names – but nothing more – for many characters from people in my chambers. I would have used Ashley's name too but, it turns out, that wasn't a very common name in Elizabethan times. At least, not for a man.

My parents, Gyles and Michele, read early drafts, encouraged further work and offered advice drawn from their own experience. All of which was invaluable, and yet as nothing compared to the contribution they have made over many years to my love of language and writing. To them thanks and love are owed for many things, this book but one of them.

Special thanks are due to my agent, Ivan Mulcahy. It is no exaggeration to say that this book would not have come to be without his encouragement and faith in me, nor had one fraction of that merit to which it aspires. I count myself very lucky to have said something bumptious in his presence and caught his eye.

Finally, my children, Cornelius and Atticus, and my wife, Kosha. My sons endured a father who tried to have two full-time jobs when all his focus should have been on them. I'm sorry. I'll try to make it up to you; meanwhile think of the royalties. My wife endured the same and did so uncomplainingly, reading early versions of the book, giving invaluable advice on all aspects, on plotting, writing and marketing. Why a woman so talented, so beautiful and so busy puts up with me I shall never know but I shall always be grateful. I love you.

Printed in Great Britain
by Amazon